ALSO BY CHRISTOPHER SCOTT BROOKS

PLAYS
O'Donnell's Pub
A Flutter of Butterflies, A Murder of Crows
Deadline

This is the first novel by Mr. Brooks

THE FIVE-YEAR PLAN

A Novel

CHRISTOPHER SCOTT BROOKS

Crossfade Publishing
NEW YORK

For more information, write to:
Crossfade Publishing
517 w. 46th Street,
New York, NY. 10036

Crossfade Publishing is a division of
Crossfade Music, Inc.

Printed in the United States of America.

FIRST EDITION

ISBN 978-1-7352415-1-7

*For all of my friends from Zanesville who left,
who stayed, and especially those who returned.*

*In loving memory of
Francis Jacqueline Brooks*

1

Jim drove the same route as usual that morning, passing Tufts—full of memories of med school—continuing past Harvard, where he and Madeline met in his last year of pre-med. With the exception of two bone-chilling years of residency at Cook County in Chicago, he had lived every day of his professional life in Boston.

He was lost in thought when Madeline vomited on the floor of the BMW. She was too weak to insist on pulling over. He brushed her hair from her forehead, cracked the window and pulled into the Boston General doctors' parking structure. Her internist met them in the parking lot with a wheel chair.

Madeline's illness was nothing out of the ordinary. She had contracted some stomach virus and had become dehydrated. She was given a normal course of fluids and instructed to rest.

Three days later she was only getting worse. Jim was breathing down every last stethoscope, insisting that his wife be made better, "now!" The results of a battery of tests turned up nothing. The breakthrough came at one end of the finest medical center in New England, while Madeline slipped into cardiac arrest at the other end. The verdict was thought to have been a rare infection, but it was too late for a simple course of antibiotics. Madeline's body had shut down, her kidneys first then, directly behind them, her heart. She was gone and no amount of screaming or brow beating was going to bring her back. Jim went coldly silent and stayed that way until the funeral.

Every window twinkled in the house at the far end of Alcott Road. A steady stream of visitors descended the steep, darkened driveway to the street below. The men wore suits with overcoats, the women muted fall colors, some with scarves wrapping their shoulders and heads. Everyone seemed to know one another. There was no revelry in their leaving.

The house was finally quiet. "I thought they'd never leave." Jim fell back against the kitchen door, feigning exhaustion.

Doctor James Langley was tall and elegant, with close-cropped salt and pepper hair and a single dimple in his left cheek. He wore a fancy suit with a grey and white silk tie, picked with great care by his now deceased wife.

"How about a pizza, Frank?"

Frank Monahan stared blankly in disbelief. "You're ordering a pizza with all of this food here?" Frank did his best to conceal 62 years of working class Boston as he motioned to the island heaving with food in front of him.

Frank betrayed many of his Irish roots, a victim of prosperity. He was a plumber with a plumber's build. His hands were indelicate, but his smile showed a soft, curious side. He lived in a fancy neighborhood because he married well. He enjoyed his life in spite of its trappings.

"No, of course not. Don't be silly." Jim produced a frozen pizza skin from the industrial freezer that Madeline detested. She could not understand how anyone could install industrial refrigeration in such a demur French colonial masterpiece of a kitchen.

From a picked over cheese plate, Jim extracted a beautiful piece of Roquefort, dusted off the cracker crumbs and held it up like a small trophy. "Here, I'll use this lovely piece of Roquefort, for some reason neglected by our hungry mourners." Turning somber, "Frank? Can I ask you something serious?"

Frank's first thought was that finally, after all of this week, Madeline's sudden death, the friends, the family, the funeral arrangements, that Jim was ready to let go. All of this preparation and entertaining and now, at midnight, over pizza, Jim had chosen his neighbor, the plumber, his best friend, as his confessor. Frank felt pride and a sense of duty. They had been neighbors for 12 years and had spent many nights right here in this kitchen. Frank, the student, learning from a master about the finer things in life: Foie gras, prosciutto, white truffles. He could now taste, even smell the difference between a Pinot Noir and a Cabernet. So, it was not really a huge surprise that his great friend Jim was about to pour his heart out to him. He braced for the worst, "Jim, you can ask me anything. I am here for ya buddy. Go ahead, lay it on me."

"Okay, I think you can handle this. I mean, after all, how long have we known each other, eleven, twelve years, right? And you've been right here by my side, eating some tasty food and drinking some, well, lots of really great wine. Seriously Frank, I feel a deep sense of pride in being chiefly responsible for your wine education. You've been a model student, but I digress. So here's what I want to ask you: Would you please do me the favor, no, the honor, of going down to the wine cellar and choosing the proper wine for this pear-prosciutto pizza that I'm about to create?" A rye smile failed to disarm his friend.

"Jesus K Christ, man!" Frank, no longer bothering to hold back the accent, "I thought you were gonna pour your heart out. I mean, you've been through a hellava time here and well, Jesus Christ, man."

"Oh Frank, please, I just needed a little levity. Get us something really nice would you, then we can talk. I really do have a few things that I need to discuss. Please?"

As Jim saw Frank close the cellar door behind him, he gently exhaled, momentarily frozen in grief and guilt. Should he be laughing and joking after just burying his wife? He didn't have an immediate answer to this or any of the other questions racing through his mind. He loved Madeline truly, but he didn't often like her. For all of her irascibility, she had always been his light, his center. Her tacit approval kept him going. From his first days in medical school he knew that if he saw a twinkle in her eye, a hint of a smile, or a tiny nod, he was on the right path. Any positive acknowledgement bolstered his confidence more than any grade, or word of encouragement from a professor. Hers was always the most important and final word. And her derision was equally as strong. When a blunder or false move landed him in her doghouse, her retribution was relentless. In the early days she simply withheld sex, which was stinging punishment for Jim. As their years wore on, she was more verbal, attacking his dignity, knowing his every weakness. Jim grew tired of her manipulation, but it didn't ever stop him loving her. And now she was gone and he was lost.

Frank felt his way down the basement steps and immediately entered the hidden door to the right of the cellar, so carefully disguised as just another panel in the octagonal shaped entrance hall. He had installed the refrigeration system and always snuck away to check on its health. All of the equipment was in the real basement behind the hidden door. The basement was not much more than a utility sink, some empty wine cases and a discarded chopping block that Jim had optimistically purchased at a garage sale, but deemed too disgusting by Madeline to be in the kitchen. He quickly glanced at a few custom gauges and rested his hand on the compressor for a moment. And now for the wine, he thought.

Frank crept back into the wine cellar entrance hall and stepped across the threshold into a wine lover's paradise. The dimly lit room was large enough for the table of twelve in the center and a separate tasting table. The picture was right out of Wine Spectator. Several cases of newly acquired wine were piled somewhat haphazardly in front of the floor-to-ceiling shelves. Unlike the new boxes, the organization of the racks was clear and thoughtful: verticals together from youngest to oldest, regions, and varietals all stacked and grouped in such a way that one could anticipate what was coming next. It was like the perfect world tour of wine, effortlessly striding from France to Italy, New Zealand, Australia, South America and ending on the west coast of America. Jim cared for his wine with passion and love, like fathers cared for their children.

Frank was mesmerized as always. He could easily find what he was looking for, if only he knew what that was. The coolness of the travertine under his stocking feet prompted him to look down. Madeline always made him take off his work boots at the back door. A sudden tear was not what he expected. Maybe it was the must of the cellar.

Upstairs, Jim stared at the blank pizza skin, thinking how much Madeline actually liked his pizza. He did not do many things that pleased her, but his pizza could soften her stoic New England character. If he added oysters to the culinary seduction, there was a chance that they would end up in her bed, a rarity in recent years. The only pleasure left in their relationship; the only real joy that Jim derived from her, was sex. He knew that even in bed she was selfish, but he enjoyed pleasing her. That was the one thing they had in common. He loved bringing her to orgasm and she enjoyed that too.

Frank reappeared, finding Jim exactly where he had left him, standing and staring at an empty pizza. "Lynch Bages, 1974. What do you think? Delicious yes, but maybe not quite (searching for one of Jim's words) impetuous enough for a pizza?"

"Well, well Frank, ah," Jim wiped a stray tear from his cheek, recovering, "Spare no expense for the humble pizza, I say. Oh shit, I better get the oven on. I nearly forgot."

Jim worked effortlessly on the pizza. He stoked the gas assisted, wood fire pizza oven. He loved this pizza oven, even though he could only fire it when the temperature dipped below freezing outside; even then the heat for the rest of the house had to be turned off. He retrieved the long, slender pizza peel he had acquired, actually stolen, in his college days from "Slice" on Boylston Street—a bold move induced by cheap, Father's Five pitchers of beer and one too many shots of Jack Daniels.

Frank knew the wine procedure. He placed the Lynch-

Bages on the space of counter reserved for the ritual and carefully removed the wax with the knife designated for this task. He screwed in the slender, single thread cork screw, knowing by Jim's often repeated lecture that the "only" cork screw was one that had a continuous piece of finely sharpened steel that followed itself into the potentially moist cork and did not boar a hole like so many of the devices resembling the flying nun and sold at Stop and Shop.

All red wine needed to be decanted, and Jim's selection of decanters filled two complete overhead cabinets. Frank selected the one that looked delicate enough to hold such an impressive wine. He held it just as he had seen Jim do so many times before and watched carefully as the ruby liquid flowed from vessel to vessel. At the first sign of sediment he stopped.

"So, are you really retiring?" Jim asked Frank, out of the blue.

"Yep. I'm done. No more diggin' ditches; no more backed up septic tanks."

Jim, "Have you looked into the kind of plumbing they have in Tuscany?"

"Umbria, actually." Frank corrected. "Not very far from Tuscany though."

"It sounds great, Frank. I never thought to ask you this before, but why Italy?"

"I'm Italian!" he says in his best Boston-Irish accent.

"I thought you were Irish?"

"My father's Irish, my mother's 100 percent Italian. She actually grew up in Umbria until she was 12. Besides, I wasn't about to go to Ireland. It's too much like Boston: cold, damp and full of Irish people. Oh, and the food sucks."

They both laughed honest laughs. Jim selected two Bordeaux glasses and poured a taste in one. He swirled it, sniffed it and stared blankly at it for a little too long. With eyes closed, he tasted it with as much tenderness and care as he would caress the face of a lover. "Frank, for a plumber you sure do know your wine. Nice choice."

"I had a great teacher and a great cellar. Besides, sweating pipe is way harder than choosing a nice wine."

"And nice wine it is. Cheers." Jim offered a slightly more filled glass to Frank and toasted. "Here's to your new adventure in (his best Italian accent) Um-bri-a. Oh shit, the pizza."

Jim ran to the oven and rescued the pizza in the nick of time. It slid right onto the peel and looked delicious. The stinky cheese was melted perfectly, covered with the thin slices of pear. Jim carefully draped several pieces of paper-thin prosciutto over it. He added a handful of baby arugula and a last drizzling of very young olive oil.

They sat on high stools at the center island and ate directly from the peel.

"Madeline said that no one would ever sit on these stools. Of course, once they were delivered, she sat there every breakfast and often for dinner. She was so full of shit."

Frank stopped mid bite, "Do you really think …"

"She was. She complicated the easiest procedures and thrived on chaos, all the time not doing anything that made a difference. She was so full of shit. Had this … thing not happened, we would have divorced."

Frank looked shocked.

"There, I poured. See, I poured. I told you I might."

"I thought, well, I thought that you two loved each other and were … I mean, I knew sometimes there were problems. But not problems like Betty and me. I mean, I wanted to kill that woman, and when she ran away with another woman, man, that was a blessing in the form of the biggest slap in the face ever." Frank caught his breath. "But you two. I knew there might have been a transgression or something, but you seemed meant for one another."

Insulted, "Oh, thanks! I was nothing like that woman. Yes, I did love her, but I just couldn't stand her. She did NOTHING! Nothing worthwhile that is." Jim calmed down a little. "She was a city council woman because she wanted the annual parade rerouted. She wasn't doing her civic duty. There was always a personal motive. She was selfish."

Frank was stunned. He didn't really know what to say. This was the dearly departed of which he was speaking so harshly. Not something that would have ever been done in his household. Even his ex would not receive this sort of lip lashing, God forbid she would ever die. But then again, Frank thought, Jim must have been holding this all in for who knows how long. Frank managed sheepishly, "Were you really going to get divorced?"

Jim took a long, wistful drink of his wine. "I thought about it a hundred times. I would even leave, sit in the car and try to figure out where I was going. Sure, I could check into the Ritz and piss away a few grand on champagne and 'friends' but it wasn't the answer, it wasn't right. I was searching for what was right, and it just never came to me. I knew that there was something missing, a hole in my life, a hole in our life together. I sensed that without the answer I couldn't leave. That answer never came. Even in death Madeline upstaged me, proving once again how much smarter she was. She beat me to it. She just died, taking the answer with her."

Frank looked a little perplexed, "What answer?"

Jim took a bite of pizza. "That's the point, Frank ol' boy. I don't know the answer. There is a hole in my life that is completely empty and no matter how much money I make or how much wine I pour into it, there's still a hole. Maybe it's that we didn't have kids, but we were both too busy saving the world to bother. I'm not sure how corporate mergers and knee replacements really saved anyone except us."

With a plumber's sensibility, Frank asked just the right question, "So, you don't like your job, either?"

"I hate my job. I stand on my feet 8 hours a day, up to my elbows in blue blood, so some rich basketball player or heir to the Polaroid fortune can walk without a hitch in his getteup. Having to pay outrageous mal practice, huge overhead, and fucking Medicare. Oh, don't get me started on Medicare. Try replacing a knee for what Medicare pays. You couldn't replace an elbow joint, and I mean the one under the sink! Fuck all of them."

"Wow. Jeez Jim, I had no idea. Did you ever think about quitting?"

"Quitting? What? Are you kidding? Doctor's don't quit. We work our whole life just to get to this point. I'm at the very top of my game, top of my field, at the goal. I can't just quit." Jim stared Frank down, trying his best to be superior.

Not having it, Frank, "Why not? You hate it AND you've reached your goal, you just said it yourself. I quit. I'm not a rich guy like you, but I quit and I'm moving to Italy. Everyone said I couldn't do it. What was I going to do in Italy? What's the difference? It's just a plane ride and a warm, beautiful country with really nice people and fantastic food and wine. I didn't give a shit about plumbing, and I am sick and tired of the job, the weather and, quite honestly, the people around here get to me a little, too. So I quit. I'm no big fancy doctor, but I seriously fail to see the difference between you and me when it comes to reaching the end of your rope."

Jim went mute. He was perplexed, suddenly exhausted, and maybe a little drunk. Oddly though, he could see his way forward. He knew that he didn't have all the answers, or any answers really, but he had an idea.

Frank realized that he had said too much. "Look, Jim, I'm sorry. I'm talking shit, I mean ..."

Jim held up his hand, stopping Frank's rambling. He raised the decanter, poured a few more fingers in Frank's and his own glass and finished the wine. He held up the empty decanter, "That will never do. You're not going anywhere, are you Frank? Of course not. I'll be right back."

Jim skipped down the basement stairs, carelessly careening around the curved banister. He punched in the code and flung open the dark, heavy, tinted glass door. Regardless of the force, it glided to rest at its programmed stop. Jim went straight back to Bordeaux, stopped and re-aimed his desires. He took two steps to the right and concentrated on the few Barolos that he had acquired. He stood directly in front of them, but could not read the labels. He had spontaneously burst into tears without any warning. He was steaming through really treacherous territory without any glimpse back. He knew that he must be lost, but he didn't feel lost. He felt fine. He actually felt finer than he had felt in years: liberated. Could Madeline's death have been the catalyst for the change that he needed in his life? Did he wish her dead? He quickly shook that thought off and immediately resumed his wine search, tears wiped dry and focus returned. Sassicaia, 1979. Not quite as good as a first growth Bordeaux, but you could never tell an Italian that. He shouted, "Perfect!" which echoed up the staircase and bounced around the kitchen, stunning Frank out of his glowing enjoyment.

"Another Bordeaux?" Frank asked as Jim reappeared, grinning widely.

"Something even better for this occasion." Jim began a rushed bottle opening and decanting ritual.

"Occasion?"

"This, my friend, is a 1979 Sassicaia, grown near your new home. It's as close as the Italians come to a Bordeaux style wine. It's 85% Cabernet Sauvignon and 15% Cabernet Franc. Sound familiar? And this may be one of the best examples of the breed in existence and my last bottle."

"We shouldn't, I mean don't you want to save it?"

"You can't take it with you, Frankie. And, as I said, it couldn't be more appropriate for the occasion." Jim produced two extremely large, fine crystal glasses from the very top shelf, hidden behind decanters.

They must have not been Madeline approved, thought Frank. "So what is this occasion? I mean, I understand what occasion it is, but how is this appropriate again?"

Jim quickly decanted and poured small amounts, or so it appeared, in each of the extra large glasses. "You make much sense, my friend."

Frank touched the new glass to his lips. Jim stopped the sip, "Give it a moment. It's been in that little bottle for quite a while. It needs some time to breathe some life back into itself."

Jim continued, "Your quite clever analysis of my professional situation is both astute and timely."

Frank, "What the ..."

Jim, "What I mean is, you're right. I hate my job, I have reached many of my goals, I have a ton of money, now more because Madeline was so fastidious about life insurance for both of us AND..." Jim took a breath, annoyed that he has to, "I want out of this place. I've known that part for a while. Every morning I wonder why am I still in Boston? Nearly everyone I went to school with moved when they graduated. I stayed behind with the students."

Frank tried to contribute, "But you don't live like a student, and you've travelled and enjoyed your life."

"I have. You're right, and all the more reason to start a new chapter. This one has come to a logical conclusion." Jim picked up the oversized glass and took a long sniff.

Frank, "So what now?"

Jim indicated to him with his new glass, "We toast: To a new life in Italy."

Frank, "To a new life in Italy. But wait, what about your new chapter?"

Jim, "To a new life in Italy."

Frank smiled, confused, but spellbound by the magnificence of the new wine. "Oh, now that is what I am talking about. Yeehahhhh!!!!

Jim, "So what do you think? Think I can find something sufficient in Umbria?"

"Wait, what? You want to move to Italy too?" Frank was shocked, pleased, pissed and a little drunk.

"I love Italy. I always have. Madeline and I planned to one day have a place in Tuscany. But that isn't going to happen now, and it would be great to have a neighbor that I can talk to about the Red Sox and the Bruins. I mean, what do Italians know about hockey?"

"I never thought about that." Frank was warming to the idea. "Good point."

"And I don't have to give up medicine. Medecins Sans Frontieres is based in Europe and I can continue to volunteer. And then I can return to the beauty that is Italy. Maybe I'll even meet una bella donna."

The sound of a distant phone interrupted their banter.

They looked at each other as if to say "the phone?"

Frank, "I'll get it. It can't be anyone you know. You saw everyone today except for your sister. Where was Jackie anyway?"

Frank disappeared down the hallway and under the stairs into the phone booth. This must have been the only house in Lexington with an old fashioned phone booth, thought Frank.

Jim raised his voice to travel down the hall, "She had to stay in Ohio to take care of my mother. She's not been well, or so Jackie says."

Frank returned, "It's Jackie."

Jim, "Oh Christ, what now?" He hurried down the hall; stopping to admire Madeline's phone booth that he secretly thought was a clever idea. Into the phone, "Hi Jackie. How's Mom?" He listened and listened and listened. Finally he got a word in, "Which hospital? Oh I forgot. There is only one now." He continued to listen to the all too familiar strains of his sister. He eventually capitulated, "I'll come tomorrow."

2

Frank pulled his Maroon Mercedes S300 sedan to the curb
in front of the Delta terminal. He preferred his Ford F-150
pickup truck, but his wife bought the Mercedes and he kept
it for driving people to the airport. It had the added benefit
of giving the neighbors something to talk about, "Look at
the plumber with the fancy car."

Frank, "There you are. Travel safely. Tell Jackie I said,
'Hi.'"

"Will do, thanks again. I'll bring you something special
from Zanesville. Maybe a bottle of that famous Ohio wine!"

"Bon Voyage!"

Jim waved, "Arrivederci!" He paused for a second, staring at the concrete and steel that shaped Boston's international airport.

Jim pushed past a long line waiting to check in and
headed straight for security. He'd been traveling too long to

check bags. Considering the length of the serpentine line at the curb, Jim was delightfully surprised to see only a dozen or so people in the security area. The post 9/11 revamping had spread the rows of identical x-rays, blue seas of TSA employees and conveyer belts out into a manageable arrangement. He quickened his pace across the newly tiled departures area, anticipating at any moment the tide would change and all of those curb waiters would inexplicably be cut in front of him. No matter where he traveled or what he had experienced, he could never shake his father's voice, "Whatever is too good to be true usually is!" It still didn't make sense to him, but it stuck with him like his father's other quips. "There are no free lunches." "You get what you pay for and sometimes less." And his favorite, still jammed between his ears, tuned and played back in exactly the same rhythm and lilt for which his father was famous, "Nothing is ever easy, nothing is ever simple." It didn't even rhyme. But, nevertheless, it haunted Jim and he knew exactly what it meant. So when the line was short, or the upgrade to first class was offered, he always thought that some mistake had been made; some dishonest perpetration of the truth must have occurred. "There must be a catch."

Jim's routine was always the same. He took his shoes and belt off and put them in the first bin, then his bag, computer and computer bag followed. He knew that if there was any hitch with the rest of his stuff he had time to put his shoes and belt back on while waiting. Fortunately, there was no hitch, so he quickly got re-dressed and slipped his Mac Book back into the safety of its black foam sleeve, inside his weathered computer bag. As he set his wheelies back to the floor and headed for the gate he heard a familiar bellow.

"Doctor?"

"Doctor?" Jim returned the well-worn routine.

When he saw Mark, Jim immediately dropped his bags and grabbed his old friend, hugging without any embarrassment or hesitation.

"How the hell are you, Mark?"

"Great, Jim. You?"

Mark Fitzsimmons was an old colleague from Medecins Sans Frontieres (aka Doctors without Borders) and a fellow foodie. He was a towering man with grey temples and a collegiate smile. Jim added a spring to his step as they walked away from security.

"What on earth are you doing here, Mark?"

"Headed home. For some reason, the new MSF travel coordinator figured that Boston was near Ohio. She's Swiss and I get the distinct impression that she's never left the shores of Lake Geneva."

Jim and Mark walked step in step toward the far gates, "I was in Haiti again. Wow, what a mess. And you? Where you headed?"

"Actually I'm going to see my mother in Ohio. I assume we're on the same plane. Mansfield right?"

"Great memory for an old guy."

Jim retaliated, "I'm the young one, remember: August 17th 11:15 p.m., weren't you born a little earlier that day?"

Mark cracked a familiar smile, "You haven't changed a bit. Still remember every tiny detail. That always impressed me. No wonder you did so well in med school when the rest of us were struggling to remember the difference between a tibia and a fibula."

"Yeah right, false modesty was never your strong suit. How long you been out?"

"The usual three months. Fortunately, my partner has kept all my patients alive. God knows what he's been doing with my wife. Speaking of which, how is your crazy wife?"

"Madeline died last week. She came down with some pervasive infection and it just took her. We buried her yesterday."

Mark stopped in the middle of the concourse. His shoulders slumped and his head hung low, "Oh Jim, I am so sorry. I really didn't mean ..."

"Don't be silly. She WAS crazy, among other things. I think I'm still in shock, but as usual, Madeline knew exactly what to do and when to do it."

Mark stared blankly.

"Sorry, Mark, I don't mean to sound ... well maybe I do. I don't know how I want to sound right now. I loved Madeline and I will miss her for the rest of my life. She gave me a gift. I think that's what I guess I am trying to say. She gave me an unexpected gift of freedom. I just don't know from what. Well ..." Jim nearly didn't say it, "from her, I guess."

"You're talking crazy. You had all the freedom you could possibly have wanted. We traveled the world together. The only time we ever saw Madeline was when there was a Four Seasons nearby. I think that was a grand total of twice in all of the years that we were on the road. Didn't you and I actually fly in the back of the plane once while she sat in first class?"

As they continued toward the gate, Jim looked down at his boarding pass and laughed, "So, I take it that, once again, we're in the back of the plane together?"

They both burst out in laughter. They laughed themselves to tears.

As they squished into the last row of the faded, mauve seats, "Great to see you, Mark. I flash on Marbella often. How did we manage that? A beachfront cottage, a private chef and where did that wine come from? Richard Branson? How the hell did that happen?"

"It's amazing that either of us IS married after that week. At least we did some good work."

"And we were justly rewarded."

"Thank goodness for ... what was her name?"

"Valerie."

"Valerie, right. Thank goodness for Valerie. And thank goodness for your restraint. Her whole reason for inviting "us" to her hacienda was you."

Jim employed his best coy, "I don't remember, exactly."

"Bullshit. You would have fucked her on the kitchen table had I not been hanging around. And I still assume that was the reason I was hanging around, so you wouldn't fuck her on the kitchen table."

"I could have fucked her in the bedroom."

"And what would have been the fun in that? You could have fucked MADELINE in the bedroom."

Jim winced.

"Sorry. Jim I ..."

"I certainly would never have fucked Madeline on the kitchen table!"

They both burst into plane filling laughter, turning many heads but no one cared.

"Why don't you come back? Seems like this might be a good time for you to give a little of yourself. We sure could use a few more deft hands and hearts in this crazy, fucked up world. I'll send you the 'new posts' number that I just got from the Geneva office. Check in with them if you're ready to go."

"Thanks, Mark. I'm too out of the loop. I've been reading about these new drugs for tapeworms. That was a huge problem in Zimbabwe the last time I was there."

"There's a new NGO supplying them. They're making huge headway and saving thousands of lives and nobody knows it. Sometimes I think that we need a PR person more than a doctor running this thing. Bill Gates sells software for a living and more people know about he and his wife giving shots in Africa than all of the work that we've ever done. Thank God for them, though. You and I have been in those trenches too long to give a shit if the fella handing you a suture has a turban on his head or a goat ..."

Mark glanced over to Jim who was fast asleep. All of the stress had caught up with him. Good thing, Mark thought, as he had nowhere to go with the goat metaphor.

Jim woke on touchdown. Mark smiled cautiously at him. Doctors have a built in sleep-to-stress barometer. It's instilled in them during all of those sleepless nights of residency. If someone didn't get enough sleep to suppress the ever-present stress, then the others knew better than to confront them, even with a cup of coffee.

As they crawled up the jet-way, Jim, "You were saying about Bill Gates?"

"No idea. I had two drinks and wrote my summary report while you snored right through the friendly skies."

"Oh, right. Guess I might have been missing a bit of sleep over the last few weeks."

"Understandable."

The airport corridor was a vast tunnel of fast food, and plaid covered obesity. They stopped at a crossroads.

Jim, "There's the sign for rental cars. Where do you go?"

"My wife actually drove down here to get me. I assume that she's at the curb. I'm going this way."

They embraced. Jim held on for an extra second or two. He knew that his next steps were inevitable, and painful. He was weak, tenuous, but circumspect. He had a solid overview for someone so utterly lost. He looked Mark in the eyes and waited.

"Call that number. They know you. They love you and they need you. You need that. OK?"

Jim stood and said nothing. His resolve needed no affirmation.

Driving toward Zanesville, Jim was on familiar ground. Every exit, every rest stop and every county road visible from I-70 brought back floods of memories, peculiarly unrelated sketches of his childhood. High on one hill was an overbuilt brick house, only slightly visible through the woods grown up in front of it since the house was first built. Others may have not noticed it, but Jim knew it was there; he knew two doctors built it (a husband and wife) and that they had outfitted the basement with a bomb shelter. He laughed to himself, thinking it sounded exactly like something Madeline would have done.

As he came closer to his exit, he thought he saw his junior high school sitting on top of the barren hill to the north. Fall had come early and most of the trees had already shed their color. There were only a few times of the year that you could actually see the monument to the pain of adolescence that sat upon the hill. He looked again and remembered that it had been torn down; a sure sign that he was not going to like everything in the new and improved Zanesville. Even when he came home during college and found the cleaners on the Terrace Point was no longer there–not exactly an emotional loss–he knew the old adage was true, You can never come home again.

Jim continued north through neighborhoods of small, well-kept houses, single story apartment buildings and the occasional park. There were empty lots between some of the houses that had been there as long as Jim could remember. It occurred to him (possibly for the first time) that an empty lot was such a commodity in most towns; to have one just sitting there was rare. Zanesville was rare in many ways, and annoyingly ordinary in many others.

The hospital was still approximately where he remembered, except all of the entrances and surrounding buildings had changed. Since the two hospitals in town had been bought and combined into one large regional health center, the once quaint hospital was now an enormous complex and the largest employer in the area, far surpassing the steel mill or other manufacturing that were the mainstays of Zanesville during his youth.

Jim always had mixed feelings about visiting his mother. She spent 40 years as an elementary school teacher and often treated Jim like one of her students. Her students, on the other hand, were prized and lauded by her and she them–often stopping by to check in on her or making pronouncements about her everlasting influence on their lives. She was also an artist with a hard-edged view of the world, educated, informed and extremely opinionated. That was the Ruth that Jim enjoyed. She had always been wise, and now as a shrinking, grey haired 91 year old, had grown into the role. He just never knew which Ruth he would get, hence his trepidation.

Ruth was in a private room on the third floor. He didn't have a bearing on whether the private room was an insurance upgrade, a perquisite of the Zanesville social order or just Ruth's charm. She had been known to clear a room with one off color comment. His instinct told him that her reputation preceded her and the hospital administration, regardless of its ridiculous growth, had enough common sense to keep her separate and treat her well. This was still a small town in many ways, and if you lived here you knew that some people were not to be crossed. Many were related and most of the north end had cliques of friends, so one never knew who was speaking to whom (and who was not speaking to whom) and that included families as well as friends. Existing in a small town was a lot harder than it looked on television.

Jim could hear her bellowing voice echoing down the tunnel of tile as he stepped out of the elevator. He was all smiles. He knew by her rancorous tone that she was fine. He quickened his pace instinctively, knowing that she was causing some consternation that maybe he could quell. As he approached the distinctive sound of a bedpan bouncing off tile, his sister Jackie came dodging out of the room.

"Oh, thank God you're here, Jim. She's being impossible. Maybe you can deal with the situation." Jackie, who was two years older than Jim but looked much older, shook her frustration off and gave Jim a hug, "Sorry, baby. How are you?"

"I'm fine, Jackie. How's Mom?"

"Oh, I don't know" she whined. "You can't tell. You know if you ask her she's fine, but the doctors say that there are all kinds of things wrong with her."

"She is 91 years old. Of course there are all kinds of things wrong with her. What exactly is wrong with her right now, Jackie?"

"She fell and bruised her hip."

"Did she break her hip? Is that why she's in the hospital?"

"No, it's just a bruise, but it's a really bad bruise."

Jim gently moved past Jackie and triggered the automatic

door opener.

Ruth Langley was a slight woman with wisps of nearly white hair and piercing blue eyes. Her small form was not the least bit frail. She looked physically and mentally strong, even in the compromised state of a hospital bed. As Jim approached she was tugging on her I.V.

Nonchalantly, Jim, "Here, let me give you a hand with that."

Ruth immediately heard his voice. Relieved, "Oh, Jim I am so glad you're home. Oh baby, I am so sick about Madeline. How are you? Come here and give me a hug."

They hugged. Jim carefully uncurled her hand from the I.V. "How ya feelin', Mom?" Jim subconsciously slipped into his Southeastern Ohio drawl like an old pair of jeans.

"I'm fine. Get me out of this Godforsaken place, will you, Son?"

"Sure, Mom. Don't worry." Jim clasped the nurse call button with one hand as he held Ruth's hand with the other. "What happened that got you in this joint to begin with?"

"Oh, nothing. I fell. It was no big deal. I got a big thing on my hip but it's fine. I can walk; nothing broke. I hate hospitals. You only get sick in these places. Get me out of here, would you?" Ruth started to get agitated again and tried to rip out the I.V. Jim tried to stop her from hurting herself. He also took a quick glance at her hip.

The nurse came through the door and looked directly at Ruth, "Ruth, what have I told you about the I.V.? It's a pain in the ass for me to have to put that thing back in, especially in your old veins. And who are you?"

"I'm Doctor James Langley ... and Ruth's son." He realized immediately that he had nowhere to go with the big doctor routine.

"Nice to meet you, Doctor Langley. Do you have privileges at this hospital?"

"Well, no, I ..."

"Thank you, but I'll take it from here." She pushed past him and took control of Ruth's arm. Ruth struggled, but gave up quickly in defeat. Obviously, they had a routine.

Jim turned his complete attention to the nurse. She was in her late 40's, short bobbed and overly highlighted brown hair and, if it weren't for her brusque manner, Jim would have considered her attractive.

In an attempt to retake his ego, "And you are?"

"Carla Jenkins. I work here and your mother does not seem to like our hospitality very much."

"Maybe it's your bedside manner that doesn't appeal to her."

"Maybe it's a genetic predisposition to look down one's nose."

"It's more likely the hiring policy of this institution not requiring compassion as a pre-requisite for patient inter-action."

Ruth butts in, "Children, could you please behave your-selves."

Jim, "I will not stand here and participate in a battle of wits with an unarmed ..." he searched briefly for just the right condescension. He spit, "nurse."

Carla's glare left no more room for retorts. She turned on her heals and smacked the door open.

Ruth, "She is actually very nice, Jim. You shouldn't be so rude. Get me out of here will you, please?"

Jim walked out into the hallway and directly to the nurse's station, "Nurse, Carly is it?"

She did not look up from the chart in front of her, "Carla."

"Carla. I'm sorry about my little outburst. I've had a bad

last few days, but I realize that's no reason to be rude to you. I would like to speak to the attending about my mother's condition. Could you please help?"

Still without looking up, Carla handed Jim his mother's chart, "It's all there."

"Thank you." Jim thumbed quickly through the chart, seeing exactly what he thought he would see. He removed his cell phone from his jacket pocket and dialed the number next to the doctor's name on the chart.

Doctor Jeffrey Miller answered his cell phone while he walked down an identical hospital hallway to the one in which Jim was currently standing. He, "Langley, how the hell are you? Are you in Zanesville?"

"Jeff, why is my mother in the hospital?"

"I was just walking to her room to see how she was doing. Where are you?"

"At the nurse's station on the third ..."

Interrupting, Jeff appeared from around the corner. "Langley, how the hell are you?"

They shook hands then hugged. Jeff looked remarkably like Jim. They were the same height and same build. Jeff had a little more grey hair and a little less hair in general. They had the same perfect posture and yellowing teeth—the result of the lack of fluoride in the Zanesville water.

It's obvious to Carla that this was not a professional relationship. Jeff and Jim went to grade school together and had a great deal more in common than was obvious to Nurse Carla at that moment.

Jim, "How's the family?"

"Great. Growing like weeds. Pam is in college now. Jack is at West Muskingum High School and Jeffrey Junior is finishing his residency at Grant. How's that wife of yours?"

Jim knew this was coming, but still was not prepared.

He stared for a long beat before gently guiding Jeff by the elbow down the hall. As he reached a safe distance from the ears of Nurse Carla, he, "She died last week, Jeff. Sudden massive infection, lost her in a week."

"Holy Shit!" Jeff practically yelled, then immediately lowered his voice to a whisper, "Holy Shit. Oh, Jim, I am so sorry. How are you doing? I mean, oh, Christ. I'm sorry. I don't know what to say."

"It's okay, Jeff. I don't know what to say either."

Carla glanced too many times in their direction. Jim caught her looking and turned his back toward the nurse's station.

"What's up with my mom? She seems to have a hematoma on her hip. Not exactly worthy of the private room treatment."

"Yes, I know. She came to me and couldn't walk. Jackie was afraid that she would try to do too much and fall again, so we held her here for a few days."

"That's an expensive rehabilitation, Jeff."

"It's still Zanesville, Jim. The Medicare payment will cover it. Anyway, she should be able to go home now that you're here."

"Great. Sign her out, will you?"

"No problem, Jim. How long are you here? You should come over for some dinner or a drink."

"I don't know how long I'll be here yet; maybe a week or so. I'll be in touch. I better go get Jackie."

Jim found Jackie in the cafeteria. She was sitting alone in a sea of plastic and tile, the colors of which do not exist in nature or anywhere else outside of medical center cafeterias. It was one of the aspects of Jim's job that he hated.

Why was there such a comfortless aesthetic in hospitals; the one place where the senses should be relieved of as much of the external stress as possible? Jim found his sister sitting on a plastic chair, staring at a bank of fast food vending machines. What could be more stressful?

As they began the ten-minute walk back to Ruth's room, Jim thought that their mother should be ready by the time they find their way back to her.

Jackie, "Thanks for coming now, Jim. I know it was bad timing. I am just sick about Madeline. How are you doing?"

They walked by brightly lit labs and cobalt colored hallways leading to radiology, physical therapy and dietary services. Jim marveled as all of the development in the little hospital that he once admired. When he was a child, his father used to bring him on the occasional Saturday to the obstetrics ward. He would hang out at the nurse's station or wander around into the labs. Everyone knew him and shared with him their daily tasks–an experience impossible in today's locked down world. Jim's father was a hero there, delivering more babies than any other doctor. Jim often thought, "He must be really good at his job." And he was, but the reason he was chosen by the majority of the pregnant mothers in Zanesville was because of his kindness and charm, traits that slowly rubbed off on his son.

Jackie nudged him, "Jim! How are you doing?"

Jim, "I'm doing fine. This hospital sure has expanded."

As they entered the room, Carla was trying to get Ruth into a wheelchair.

Ruth was arguing with her, "I don't need that damn thing now! Just carry my bag and let's go."

Carla struggled to get Ruth in the wheelchair, "It's hospital policy, Mrs. Langley."

Jim knew that it was this and every other hospital's policy that patients leave in a wheelchair, and he also knew that his mother would never stand for it. He quickly hatched a plan, "Oh, Carla, could I speak to you outside for a minute? Jackie will wheel mom to the car." He winked slyly toward his mom.

Carla slipped into the hallway, happy to leave the confrontation. Jim let the door shut behind her. He whispered, "Jackie, help mom to the elevator while I distract Nurse Ratchet."

Jim came out of the room and quickened his pace to catch Carla. He gently urged her down the hall, careful to position her back to his mom's door. Jackie peeked out to check that Carla could not see them. She scurried her mom toward the elevator. Ruth giddily pranced across the hall, with only a slight limp. She betrayed her 91 years with her child-like spring. Jim's eyes widened as he heard her giggle. Carla turned, but luckily saw nothing.

"So, what did you want?" Carla was growing impatient with the stalling.

In a measured, if not slow cadence, Jim, "I want to apologize to you for being so rude earlier and I wanted to thank you for taking such good care of my mother."

"You already apologized; apology accepted."

"I know my mom can be difficult."

"I was only doing my job, Doctor Langley. But thanks again."

The elevator bell rang, which cued Jim's quickened tempo. "Great. Thanks. See you later."

Carla stopped him rushing, "Doctor Langley?"

Jim stopped, as he detected an unexpected twinkle in her voice, "Yes?"

"I overheard the news about your wife. I am so sorry for your loss. My husband was killed in a car accident last year. I know what you must be going through. Please let me know if there's anything I can do." Carla extended her hand with her card, mixing professional behavior and a personal compassion previously kept well concealed.

Jim was charmed, "Thank you. I don't know what to say. I am sorry about your husband. You are so young to be doing this ..."

Suddenly gruff again, "Doing what, exactly? Living, working, raising my kids? Don't patronize me because I was being nice. And I am not that young."

"Excuse me. I'm truly sorry for your loss. I'd better go."

"Oh, shit. I always do that. I'm sorry Doctor Langley, I get a little too defensive."

He found her vulnerability endearing. Jim, "Please call me Jim." He waved her card, "And I will call. I will. See you later."

Jim caught up with Jackie and his mom as they crossed the threshold of the automatic front doors. He hurried past them, "The car is right over there. I'll pull up. You stand here, Mom."

Ruth stepped into the driveway on her own, not a blink of hesitation in her gate, "Don't be silly. I'll walk. Which car is it?

Jackie and Jim leaped forward and took her by either elbow at precisely the same time, not obvious, just reassuring to them more than Ruth. They walked at her clip the rest of the way to the car.

Ruth's house was perched on a knoll, far enough back from the road to be a showplace, but close enough to feel like part of the world around her. Everything in Ruth's world was carefully orchestrated. She was surrounded by exactly what she wanted. Even the trees in her front yard seemed to be artfully trimmed to frame her Cape Cod cottage like a Grandma Moses painting–primitive, but full of stories.

Jim pulled up the driveway and hustled to the passenger's side. Ruth was already trying to gingerly escape the wet and leafy driveway, "Mom, for goodness sakes, let me help you. These leaves are slippery."

"That neighbor boy was supposed to have them cleared off by now. I even called his mother to remind him."

Jackie followed behind, nodding and shaking her head as she had most of her life. "These kids are not reliable anymore. Will you take care of this, Jim?"

"Yes, of course. I'll clear it off in the morning. I need to go get some groceries and things right now. Do you want anything, Mom?"

"There's plenty of food in the house, Son. You don't need to go."

"Mom, you've been gone for a few days and even when you were here I can guarantee that there was only a bottle of pop, some waffles and a few black bananas."

"Oh, Jim! I am perfectly capable of buying and fixing my own food. I've been doing so for ninety years."

Jackie interjects, "Ninety-one, Mom. You've been gone for a while. Get some wine will you, Jim? I like that Falling Leaf or whatever it's called."

That made Jim wince. "I'll find something drinkable. Is the Kroger still on Maple?"

Ruth, "Don't go to that Kroger. They are a rip-off. Go out to Wallmart."

Jim argued, "I will not go to ..." He stopped short as he realized the argument was fruitless and not essentially his reason for leaving, so he retracted, "Where is that Wallmart?"

Jackie, "It's out where the beach used to be. I don't go there because they paved over our beach."

Ruth, "Who ever heard of a beach in Ohio anyway? Wallmart is much more useful."

Having had this exact same conversation as many times as visits to Zanesville, Jim bowed out, "See you in a while. Love you, Mom."

Jim headed north, traversing the streets of his childhood. He found a new short cut that led him to the backside of the Kroger's. He would never admit it to his sister, but he wouldn't go to Wallmart for the very same reason.

Jim stocked up as quickly as possible. He was in no mood to run into anyone he knew. He couldn't take explaining his unannounced arrival in Zanesville or his recent catastrophic loss. Anonymity was his goal.

After a perfunctory shop, Jim drove straight down Maple Avenue, curious about all of the changes. There were more fast food drive-ins and big box stores than ever. On two miles of commercial frontage he only recognized two landmarks, the Brown Cow restaurant–home of the blue hair, blue plate special–and Donald's Donuts, his childhood favorite.

The town was starting to twinkle in the early evening crispness and despite rows of McDonalds and Burger Kings, his hometown still shined through. He was alternately infuriated and misty eyed at the changes. Although he did this on every visit, it had been a few years since his last tour and things seemed to have changed radically.

Jim crossed the freeway and took the Fifth Street exit.

It might have been the shortest trip on any freeway in the United States. The route was quite literally an on ramp connected to an off ramp, but it was the easiest way to get to downtown from Maple Avenue. He drove up and down the one-way streets slowly; looking at each of the now abandoned or converted buildings. Except for banks and law offices, none of the buildings served the same function that they did when Jim was young. There were no local department stores; there were no more Sears or Penney's or Kresge's. All the family owned shops and businesses were long gone. There used to be a guy that sold nuts and candies on Main Street. His venue was called the Nut Shoppe and was nothing more than a hole in the wall. There was room enough for him to sit and dole out nuts and candies through a sliding glass window onto the sidewalk. Jim had never seen such a place anywhere else on earth and he longed to see it again. What a shame, he thought.

Jim found himself at the end of the downtown area, on the river. For a moment he was lost. He knew the street, but all of the old buildings—including the federal building where his grandfather once worked—were gone. He came to the bridge and stopped at the light. The light was green but no one was behind him, or anywhere around him for that matter. He sat and stared for a long time at a building that he had never before noticed. He knew it was there, but had never been inside it and never thought of its location or architecture. Given the proclivity for destruction in the downtown area, he was surprised to see it still standing.

Jim pulled over and got out. He braced himself against a cold breeze off of the Muskingum River. He crossed the street, walked down a steep driveway and up a slippery grass embankment overlooking the locks. There was no river traffic this late in the fall and the little house where the locks keeper would wait to raise or lower the water level was long abandoned. Jim stood on the perch next to the little shack and looked back. The two-story brick building with impressive river frontage, multiple garage doors and massive paned windows, had once housed the Triangle Motor Company. The downtown dealer for Jeep and Chrysler had moved north, following the money. The building must have been sitting empty for more than forty years.

There was something special about a place with such a beautiful location that had been forgotten by the town's people, Jim thought. Was the location too difficult? There seemed to be plenty of parking. Maybe the building was unsafe. But wouldn't they have torn it down? Jim could not figure out why this building was still there. It made him happy and he didn't know why.

There were only shards of sunlight left, but Jim was curious. He found an unlocked door cut into the lower garage door. He carefully eked it inward and stepped over the jagged metal threshold into the pitch black. In the corner was a set of steel steps illuminated by just enough of the upstairs sunlight to see its outline. He hesitantly shuffled toward the steps. Halfway there he gained confidence that the place had been totally cleared of any leftover Jeep parts or other paraphernalia. At that very moment he kicked what sounded like an empty gas can, which sent him sprinting the remaining distance to the stairs, up them two at a time and into the magic of the second floor, where he froze in instant awe.

Once the showroom, the expanse of the entire second floor was before him and it was breathtaking. There were windows everywhere, with the most astonishing views of the river and just a little peek up Sixth Street. The locks in the foreground framed the view to the south; the bridge cut across the river to the right and the steep bank of the distant shore masked the development on the other side. The picture was timeless. Jim was thrilled to have discovered something so unique, so beautiful and untouched that he spewed an uncharacteristic, "Holy fucking shit!" which echoed throughout the empty building.

He stared for minutes before he moved. He slowly approached the windows' edge to discover that the view did not diminish. He was giddy with excitement. He poked around a few of the other rooms but returned to the main marvel. He felt something emotional about the place. It felt like he was in love. He had been charmed by her beauty and perpetual youth and had been seduced by her unique view of the world. He let that absurd feeling pass and shook it off like a sudden winter's chill. There must be more to her than her beauty.

3

Glen McKinney sat in his corner office surveying the views of the Charles River below. He noticed a faint reflection in the glass, but did not react.

Jim, "Am I interrupting?"

Glen was a tough old doctor. He grew up just below the hospital in South Boston, the sixth son of a hard drinking Irish longshoreman and a mother who died giving birth to his youngest brother. He was extremely bright, but still working-class Irish. He worked as a bouncer all the way though his residency and still had the reputation of being a fierce fighter, even though it was unlikely that he had landed a punch since his childhood. He was the perfect Chief of Surgery.

Glen looked up at Jim's reflection but did not turn. "What the hell do you think you're doing?"

Jim, "I thought I better come ..."

Glen interrupted, "What the hell do you think you're doing leaving here? I never said you could leave. You do not just quit Boston General, and you certainly do not do so without my blessing."

Humbly, "That is exactly why I am here ..."

He interrupted again, "And I have to find this out from that little pipsqueak Barnes? Is the lease on your goddamn office more important than your job? What is wrong with you Langley? Have I taught you nothing?"

Jim sat down and braced for more abuse.

Glen spun around in his black leather, high backed, executive desk chair and stared at Jim. His tone changed to that of a father forgiving a son. "What's going on with you, Jim?"

Jim, "I have thought long and hard and made up my mind. I have to be honest: I will not miss this place. I will miss you, and a few of the good people in Boston and the Bruins and maybe the Celtics."

"Well, why the hell wouldn't you miss the Celtics? Where are you going, Africa? Oh, hell, you probably are going to Africa. What am I saying?" Glen sat back, resolved, "So where ARE you going?"

Jim was relieved by Glen's change in posture. He responded in the most positive and confident voice he could muster, "I am moving to Italy. Umbria to be exact."

"I suppose you are going to go make pro-shoot-o or something." Glen gently poked fun at Jim's foodie ways.

Jim smiled, "I might, or I might open a restaurant. You never know."

Glen sat up and glowered at Jim, "You are a really fine doctor, Jim. This is not just some job that you can walk away from. I hope you have seriously considered what you are doing. It seems selfish to me, but you have to make that decision. I just hope you aren't going on some wild goose chase that you will regret after a few months. You are welcome to come back if you wish, but it won't be as easy as quitting, I can tell you that. And you're going to piss off a lot of people. You know that?" This was obviously rhetorical. "Yes, you know that. Wherever you are going and whatever you do, you will always be a doctor. You were born to be a doctor, you went to school to be a doctor, and you live your entire life as a doctor. You don't just fucking quit. I've said enough."

Jim was not daunted. He expected more of a lecture. Gently, "Thanks, Glen."

Glen barked, "For what?"

Jim, "Everything. Everything that you've ever done for me, for always having my back, for teaching me to never give up and for being the grouchy son of a bitch that you are."

Glen, not moved, "One last thing, Jim. Do not give up medicine. I don't give a shit if you do another ACL. God knows you've done enough of those. But do not give up. Open a little clinic and give out band-aids or go on those Doctors without Brains things, but just don't give up. You understand me?"

Jim smiled and shook his head, holding back the tears fostered by the wealth of emotion packed into the ruddy face of his old friend.

"I'm sure you have plenty to do. Get the hell out of here." Glen turned back toward his view, but Jim could detect a microscopic ding in his veneer. Uncharacteristically, Glen growled, "Arrivederci."

Rosemary Parsons stood in front of a medical filing system

so well organized, precise and perfectly aligned that it looked more like an Agam painting than a working wall of information. If it was possible for a sixty-five year old, tall and handsome woman to look like a drill sergeant, Rosemary did. She wore a business suit, her auburn hair up in a bun and feathered a scarf over her aging cleavage. Her desk was brightly polished black hardwood, barren of any clutter except two perfectly formed piles of folders, at right angles opposing one another, obvious from their position that they were "work in progress," and "to be filed," although such trays would never blemish her desk.

Jim did not have a secretary; he had Rosemary. Rosemary kept Jim's professional life in order. She did all of the books, negotiated with all of the vendors, coordinated all of the nurses, lab and operating room schedules, and navigated the complications of insurance filing with the grace of a dancer and the forcefulness of a truck driver. All calls went directly to a computerized voice mail system, so there were no phones to answer. There was one direct line to Jim's office that only rang when there was a medical emergency that he needed to respond to—which rarely happened—or a call from Madeline, which never happened.

Rosemary's office was right next to Jim's and connected by an inner door as well as a door to the hallway. Because of the records, files and supply cabinets in her office, it appeared to be quite small, although architecturally it was identical to Jim's. They must have originally been designed as partner's offices.

Jim opened the inner door and, without turning, Rosemary spoke first. "I've taken care of the lease."

By this time Jim was getting pretty fed up with people addressing him with their backs to him. He cleared his throat and waited. Rosemary finally turned. "Rosemary, we need to discuss my plans."

"This is not a big deal. I've already compiled the outstanding cases and follow-ups. The schedule should be in place by the end of the day, tomorrow at the latest. I've already rerouted all new patients to Dr. Brenner or Kaigel, depending upon the initial referral. You may need to work past five a few days but we can do it. I will probably have insurance issues dwindling in for the next few months and some stragglers to chase up, but I can do that from home."

Jim shouldn't have been startled at her efficiency, even in the face of something as emotional as losing her job, but he was. "I was thinking that you could work from my home office."

"What for? You aren't seeing any patients and have nothing to do with collections or idiot insurance auditors. Why would I schlep all the way out to Lexington when I have other things to do with my life?"

Jim was surprised at this candor. Rosemary had always been frank—if not downright blunt—but he expected more empathy and maybe even a little comfort. The unbridled truth was that he was essentially firing her, so maybe he should have a little more empathy. "Well, I guess that is true. Okay, fine. I could pay you some extra for using your home office. Rent."

Rosemary thought that maybe she was a little harsh: "If you really wanted me to I could come to you, but there won't be much to do once we are out of here. And you don't need to pay me rent. I've got other projects I'll be working on most of the time and would feel guilty taking rent for what is mostly my office with my work in it."

Jim stood and stared at Rosemary for a long minute. He then shrunk into the straight wooden chair in the corner of her office, the one reserved for pharmaceutical salesmen and specifically chosen for its discomfort. "What sort of projects?" He asked, like an ex-lover inquiring about the new boyfriend.

Rosemary felt like the awkward ex-lover too. "I don't think you would be interested in it."

Jim, "In it? What? Of course I would be interested. Try me."

She shed her professional manner and got as comfortable as she gets in her office chair. "If you insist." She gained the pose of pitchman and continued: "Okay, so I've been working on a composting system that speeds up the process and works very efficiently. It's all organic, locally produced and dead simple to manufacture and distribute. I have some investors interested and the patent attorneys are about to start on their due diligence."

"Composting, as in gardening?"

"I've been gardening since I was a kid. I even had a roof garden in college, long before the 'green' roofs movement. I'm also going to expand my 'meals on wheels' work and maybe volunteer for the board again. I had to resign a few years ago because this job took too much of my time, but now I can re-commit myself. I'm thrilled."

Jim stared off into space. He appeared to not hear a word she said.

"Doctor Langley?"

"Meals on wheels. That's great. Really good work." Rosemary and Jim stood up at the same time. Jim half waved, "See you tomorrow," and disappeared through his office door. Rosemary looked worried and relieved. She had seen the many moods of a competent doctor, but never had she seen him so distracted and dismayed.

Jim popped his head back in Rosemary's office: "Oh, and could you do me a huge favor and help me organize a going away party next Saturday night?"

All semblance of pity immediately drained from her body. She searched for a pad and paper: "Where, when, which guest list, food, drinks? Catered or party in the kitchen?"

"What do you mean, 'which guest list?'"

"Your wife organized all of your contacts into guest lists. There is the strictly professional list, the friends and family list, the local but not too friendly list and the friends only list."

"I see. Invite everyone. I miss her so, but she really was nuts."

"And the food and all the rest?"

"At the house, catered with a bartender. Wine from the cellar and I will cook pizzas too."

"Done." Rosemary was relieved that they had transformed back to their former shorthanded, familiar, but professional relationship. She was back in her comfort zone.

Jim took no time to list the house. The real estate market was depressed in the greater Boston area, but the beautifully manicured estates of Lexington remained immune from such cyclical behavior. The shear number of tenured professors and other professionals in the area upsizing and downsizing regularly created a micro economy of their own. Jim's custom home on the hill fit perfectly into this insular market and even had some advantages lacking in the other houses for sale in the neighborhood. The wine cellar, the double-wide property and the great care taken in every detail of the construction would not be lost on the eminent buyers.

The realtor had a broker's open on Tuesday and was already fielding sight unseen offers by Thursday. By Friday evening, three couples had toured the house and all made cash offers over the asking price. The house sold on Saturday. He invited the new owners to the party.

On Saturday night the house was once again full of people; not lost on Jim how many of the same people were there that filled the house a few weeks ago for a distinctly different occasion. He thought, or was it that different?

Jim didn't care for large gatherings. He was comfortable with a few people in a room. He once spoke to a medical conference in front of 2500 doctors and he was quite comfortable. It was the numbers in-between that freaked him out. He felt closed in and completely self-conscience. His antidote was to ensconce himself in the kitchen and hold court with a manageable number of people while staying busy making pizzas.

Frank barged in the room with all of the grace of a plumber. "What's cookin', Jim?" He didn't really need to ask. He had been sous chef on many of these occasions. He knew the drill and the rich, smoky aroma coupled with the pungency of burning corn meal spelled Jim's pizza. Frank was just playing his role.

"Pear prosciutto, Frank. Did you get the prosciutto?"

"Of course. Took a while in the North End. The traffic in and out of there is worser than ever. Oh sorry, far worse than ever. And I had to stop at the 7's and have a drink with John and the boys."

"How was the Plumbers local and the local plumbers?"

"Very clever turn of phrase, Jimmy boy. They were fabulous as usual. John was tanked, Jimmy was even more tanked and his brother Jimmy was tanked because his wife had left him."

"Jimmy has a brother named Jimmy?"

"He does actually. Adopted. But I was referring to John's brother Jimmy. His second wife left him for another woman."

"Really? Is that common amongst your types?"

"Which? Plumbers or Italians?"

"Yes."

"Very funny." Frank changed the subject. "How goes the party?"

"I'm cooking pizza, Frank. How bad could that be?"

"Good point. How can I help?"

Jim turned and removed the first of his pizza creations from the oven with his long, familiar pizza peel. He paused to admire the pizza oven that he built by hand with two Italian craftsmen. It took more emotional energy to talk Madeline into the installation than it did to pass his boards. So many of his memories were intertwined with conflict and confrontation with Madeline. He snapped out of this tangent and yelled, "Pizza's up!" He turned back to Frank: "Do me a favor, pal. Go down to the cellar and get a little something for you and me. I got a few cases of California's finest for the masses, but I would really enjoy something special with my best neighbor."

Frank understood and completely concurred. "Anything in particular?"

"You know what to do."

That presented a real problem for Frank, but he was not going to let on. "No problem. I'll be right back."

Jim turned over the pizza making reins to the catering person and went off to the phone booth to call his mother.

Frank was once again lost in the wine cellar. He made a quick detour to make sure that the refrigeration system was still healthy. He knew that it was nearly a moot point, but the work ethic was so ingrained in his marrow that he couldn't help himself. Besides, he thought, if this thing stopped working before the wine got moved out of here he would be killed, dead, done. No point in risking it.

Once in the cellar, Frank stood, transfixed as usual. He knew exactly what was there and what would please Jim, but he still felt the weight of responsibility of this choice. He heard Jim's voice in his head: "It's just a bottle of wine, Frank. Pick one that looks good." He grabbed a 1993 Chateau Latour and leapt up the stairs, three at a time, stopping on the top step to catch his breath.

Frank and Jim bumped into one another as Frank came out of the basement stairwell. "What did you get us, Frankie?" He instantly recognized the distinctive label. "A modest choice, but drinkable. Well done. But first let's have a little bubbly."

Jim grabbed two glasses off a passing tray and handed one to Frank. "Let's venture into the great abyss, shall we?" Frank followed Jim into the hallway and eventually in the living room. Jim gently pushed his way through the gathering crowd and leapt up the steps to the landing. Frank couldn't figure his friend out. He knew that this was a trying time and Jim always had a manic streak, but all of the sudden activity to get out and start anew had Frank perplexed. It took him two years to arrange his retirement, and he was still three months or more from actually getting on a plane. Jim may actually beat him to Italy. This fear was about to be dispelled.

Jim clanked on the crystal champagne flute with his wedding ring. "Excuse me everyone, excuse me. May I have your attention? Does everyone have a glass of something delicious?"

A neighbor shouted, "Impossible not to in your house, Jim."

"Thanks, Michael, I hope so. Anyway, I would like to make a toast. Thank you all for coming on such short notice. Life is on short notice after all. We must all get as much in as we can and try not to miss anything along the way. Conveniently, this is the topic of my toast. As you are all well aware, I...we lost Madeline prematurely. Thank you all for your support, thoughts and prayers through this tough time. I really, really appreciate it. As some of you may also know, I am leaving my practice at Boston General; I have sold the house—speaking of which, I would like for all of you to meet your new neighbors: Pete and Jane Sampson."

There was a smattering of applause as Pete and Jane waved politely, and Jim took a long pull on his champagne and continued, "I think you will all get along famously. Now back to the toast. I would like to raise a glass to all of my friends, neighbors and colleagues who I have admired, enjoyed and have often been envious. To you." Jim raised his glass to a chorus of "to you's."

Michael toasted back: "To you, Jim. We're all dying to know, what now? What's your next move? Frank here claims that you're joining him in Umbria."

Jim finished the glass of champagne and stared down into it. "I love Italy. It would be a great place to live and a perfect place from which to base my continued efforts with MSF. I do plan to continue my work with MSF and plan to spend more time trying to rid the world of poverty and starvation. However..." Jim paused for both dramatic effect and to catch his emotional breath. "I have no intention of stealing Frank's thunder. I will still drop by for the occasional bowl of pasta, if that's all right with you, Frank?"

Frank smiled and nodded his approval and relief.

Jim continued, "I have made up my mind and have just

confirmed the next chapter of my life. I am moving back to my old hometown, Zanesville, Ohio."

There were gasps, whispers and moans throughout the house. Jim was not surprised by the reaction.

Jim tried to hold down the murmurs. "Hang on. I have good reasons. I can live anywhere in the world and still travel." Receiving no sympathy, he stuttered, "My mother is 91 years old, and, unless you believe her, she will not live forever. She is never moving, so I must." Resolute, "Frankly, I can't wait."

4

Jim drove all day to arrive in Bucks County for dinner. The drive from Boston to Zanesville took 14 hours and the towns of New Hope and Lambertville, on the border of New Jersey and Pennsylvania, were a little past halfway. He checked into a beautiful little inn perched on the riverbank near the Lambertville Bridge. It was out of the way, but ever since he was a kid he wanted to stay in the quaint little art colony. It was a chilly night when he arrived. There were few guests in the hotel, but fortunately, the dining room was open. He sat next to a gigantic roaring fire and enjoyed a perfectly cooked roasted chicken, potatoes and vegetables with a heart-warming bottle of Burgundy selected from an impressive list. He was happy to be on his own and felt like the next chapter was beginning.

The second day's drive was quite manageable. From Bucks County, the drive took about six hours, a little slow because of intermittent rain. When he arrived at his mother's house, it was dusk and the little Cape Cod on the crest of the hill was lit up like the Currier and Ives paintings that he remembered from the books his mother always drug home from the library. His knowledge of art was purely from osmosis. His mother was a self-taught artist. She consumed as many materials as she could find in her little town. Jim remembered being impressed at how much his mom knew about art history. When "College Bowl" came on the television on Sunday night and there would be an art question, she would casually look up from her fashion magazine and identify the most obscure painting or architectural detail, spanning the Dutch Masters to Post Modernism. "Modigliani," she would mutter, or, "Corinthian column." She never got an art question wrong.

When Jim opened the kitchen door, Ruth greeted him. "Rosemary called and told me you were coming, so don't think you are surprising anyone." She didn't turn in her swivel chair behind the easel as she continued painting. Jim stood in the kitchen doorway frozen by her frankness.

"Can't you at least say hello to your son?"

Ruth turned toward Jim, "What on earth are you doing, Doctor Langley? Your wife dies and you think that's an excuse to abandon all hope, your practice, your patients, your life?"

"Nice to see you too, Mom."

"You're not staying here. I have my life all organized and don't need you lazing around here trying to tell me what to do and when to do it. I have a schedule and a to-do list that I am sure will outlive me as it is."

"Can I stay here for a few days?" Jim felt like he was five years old and running away to his grandmother's again.

"Certainly you're welcome to stay here." Ruth turned back to her painting, "For a few days." At least she had a smile in her voice.

Jim looked around the kitchen. Ruth's kitchen never smelled like anything other than paint thinner. She was not a good cook and often forgot to eat altogether. She ate bananas and cookies. He opened the refrigerator in vein.

"What are you looking for?" Ruth brayed.

"I was going to go out to the store and pick up a few things and wanted to see if you needed anything."

"I'm fine. If you want something special for yourself please be my guest."

Although he had been driving all day, Jim felt exhilarated. He didn't need anything other than a bottle of wine and a little more time to prepare himself for his mother's casual cruelty. He loved her dearly, but knew that he needed to limit his exposure to her or she would drive him away. She had a special talent for clearing a room, even when full of her closest friends and family.

The only dedicated wine store in Zanesville was on Maple Avenue. It opened after Jim had moved away so he still considered it "The new wine store." He was constantly corrected on historical references such as that. It was like the people of Zanesville were on a mission to keep the legacy as pure and accurate as possible. Once he had mentioned to a childhood friend that he used to get his hair cut in a barbershop on Third Street in the Zane Hotel. He was immediately corrected, "The Zane Hotel was on Fourth Street next to the courthouse where the sheriff's building is now." He learned to keep his observations to himself.

After a cursory glance around the store, Jim headed to the California section. California wine seemed to be the largest selection in the store and much more likely to have something interesting than the perfunctory Italian or French selections peddled by the local beer distributor. He stood in front of the pinot noir choices trying in vein to find something from the Sonoma Coast or the Santa Rita Hills.

"Well, if it isn't Doctor Fancy pants!" Jim turned to see

his mother's nurse from the hospital.

As if picking up on their last conversation, "Good evening, Nurse Ratchet. What brings you out of your ward? Some of the inmates in need of an oaky chardonnay?"

"You never called. I guess you were too busy reconstructing O.J."

Jim was beginning to enjoy the banter, but was a little too exhausted to continue at this pace. "O.J.? Oh right, athlete. Right, funny. I am sorry I didn't phone. I've been preoccupied with moving."

Carla lightened her tone, "Moving? Where are you moving to?"

"I'm sorry." Jim squinted, trying not to make the same mistake twice, "It's Car-la, right? Right, Carla Jenkins. I'm moving here ... to Zanesville."

Carla was confused and intrigued. "To Zanesville? I'll be damned."

"Or maybe I'll be damned. The jury is still out on that." Changing the subject, "Listen Carla, I know this sounds a little weird but, do you happen to know of any houses for rent? I can't really stay with my mother. She's, well, let's just say she is set in her ways."

"Yes, I remember. No, don't know of any houses."

Jim, "Well, thanks anyway. Nice to see you."

Carla turned to leave, stopped and turned back. "Oh wait, as a matter of fact there is a house near me that is really cute and I think is for rent. Would you like me to check?"

"That would be fantastic. How about if I call you tomorrow?"

"Do you still have my number?"

"Of course. Maybe we could go have a drink or something one of these days."

"Are you asking me out?"

"Well, I guess I am, yes. Do you mind?"

"So you think you can just move back here and take over the place, date the most eligible widow in town?"

Jim looked very confused and tongue-tied.

"I'm just kidding, Doctor Langley. I would like that very much."

"Oh, phew, I thought I had stuck my foot in my mouth again. Great. Oh, and it's Jim. Please call me Jim."

"No Jim, you call me. Tomorrow."

"Right. Will do."

Carla turned on her heels and walked away. Jim studied her walk with a little more than casual interest. Carla glanced over her shoulder, knowing she had gotten his attention with a little extra swagger. Jim blushed and turned his attention back to the pinot noirs.

Jim was in no hurry to get back to his mother's house. He drove around his usual route, but this time with renewed interest. The possibility of staying in Zanesville was nothing he had ever before considered. Now he was committed. He was excited, amused and terrified. He needed to come up with a plan. Driving around in circles he searched for that plan, as if it were going to appear out of the toasty warm little houses on Taylor Street.

He headed downtown, straight to the river on the other side of Fifth Street, hung a left and came up to the little dip in the road. Sitting in front of him was the building that captured his imagination on his last visit. He crept along South Street, stopped at the light and stared at the corner. He had no idea why this place fascinated him. It had been there for as long as he had lived in Zanesville and he never paid it any attention whatsoever. Now, he couldn't stop fixating on this intriguing, old brick skeleton.

He turned down the little alley next to the building and onto the access road. He stared out onto the river and saw something that not one Zanesvillian could have imagined. He painted a beautiful sunset in his mind, on the terrace of an historic building that celebrated delicious food, fine wine and human nature—a far cry from McDonalds and the other drive-thru's where most of Southeastern Ohio dined.

Tears rolled down Jim's cheeks. What was he doing with his life? He thought he had already come to grips with the tragedy of losing his wife, and he had even resigned himself to moving to Zanesville (at least temporarily) to spend time with his mother. But he didn't know exactly what he was actually going to do. He couldn't spend all day every day sitting around watching his mother get on with her life. He knew there was something missing in his life, but was he really going to find it here? What the hell was he doing?

Jim got out of the car and walked around the perimeter of the building. He could see through the broken windows and boarded up doors that there was a solid and majestic structure that was perfectly perched on this knoll above a waterway, once a lifeline to this little city. His skin swelled with goose bumps. He had forgotten his jacket and the wind was whipping off of the river. The light twinkled, reflecting off of the churning water as he descended the driveway back toward his car. He stopped and looked over past the bridge and could see through an upper window what looked like a balcony. Most buildings along the rivers of the Midwest had some sort of vantage point overlooking the river. Originally, it wasn't because the waterway was picturesque. The businesses located in those buildings were directly tied to the commerce along the river and the comings and goings were important to their everyday functions. Supplies arriving, or a shipment being loaded meant business as usual. To Jim, the balcony meant that his vision was beginning to come into focus.

David Weinstein was one of Jim's oldest friends. They were bowling partners in the fourth grade. David never really left Zanesville. He studied at the local branch of Ohio University and transferred to Muskingum College in his junior year to major in accounting. He commuted the 15 minutes from his parents' house for those two years. It wasn't until he got married to his high school sweetheart that he moved out of his parents' house. His office was located in the "Legal Arts Building," which sat on its own along lower Main Street. David's father owned the building.

Jim fidgeted in the spacious, empty waiting room of David's office. Patient he was, but waiting was just wasting time. He was preparing his rant for his old friend when David walked in from the outside door.

"I'm so sorry for making you wait, Jim. I had a goddamn flat tire." David was wiping his hands and sweating through his winter cap and trench coat.

"You changed your own flat?" Jim forgot for a moment where he was. David didn't answer, barely broke a rueful smile and gestured for Jim to follow him back to his office. They entered a beautiful, wood paneled office overlooking the courthouse. David sat in one of the two guest chairs facing the desk and waved Jim into the other.

"So, what the hell are you doing here, Jim?"

"I need some advice, David. I'm thinking ..."

"No man, what are you doing in Zanesville? You did it. You left. You made it. You did what the rest of us only dreamt of. What the fuck are you doing back here?"

"Things change, David."

They sat there staring at each other for an uncomfortable moment. David, nearly yelling, "That's it? Things change?"

"Yep. My wife died, my mom's old, I needed a change. How's the family?"

David stared at his hero. It took him a while to process. He knew that Jim was a brilliant man, so he must have some reason for doing something so completely crazy as moving back to Ohio. David got up and walked over to a blank counter that easily transformed into a bar. "Drink?"

Jim raised an eyebrow. "Drink?"

"I had a fucking flat tire that I had to change myself, my wife was yelling at me about the kids and my oldest friend in the world who I have been jealous of my entire life walks into my office and tells me that he "needs a change," and I am NOT supposed to want a drink. Fuck that. I have scotch, vodka and gin. I'm having a bloody fucking mary."

"Make it two."

David got busy behind the bar. "So what did you want to see me about?"

"I need something to do while I'm here. I was thinking of opening a restaurant."

David spit an olive across the room. "In Zanesville? What, have you lost your mind?"

"Why?"

"Why? Seriously? This is the place that God had in mind when he invented fast food. Poor, stupid people do not want a fine dining experience."

"First of all, not everyone here is poor and stupid."

"They are certainly poor."

"I don't agree with you. I think people will come to my restaurant. I have this place in mind..."

"Nobody will come to your restaurant, unless you are serving two dollar burgers and can wing them through a window as they drive by."

"Okay, okay. Let's just say, for the sake of argument, that I open a restaurant and nobody shows up."

David handed him his drink and sat behind his desk. "What would be the point of that?"

"It doesn't matter, just bear with me for a second. If I wanted to open a restaurant and I had ..." Jim hesitated. He took a piece of paper and pen from David's desk, scribbled the amount of Madeline's life insurance payout and slid it across the desk.

David raised his eyebrows. "That would be quite a restaurant."

"How long could I keep the doors open?"

"Depends."

"On what?"

David got serious, pulled out his pen and readied his calculator. "First of all, where is this restaurant going to be? How much is it going to cost to build out and furnish? How many seats? How many people will you have a day and how much will you charge? What kind of food? Will you have a liquor license? That's 30 grand right there."

"Fine. I want to buy the Nicholson Motors building on South Street and renovate it."

"Jesus, Jim."

"How much?"

"That building is falling down."

"No it's not. It's in good structural shape. How much?"

"To bring it to code, install a kitchen, fixtures, the works ..." David punched in hypothetical numbers in his calculator. "The building is for sale for 65. We could probably get it for 45 or 50. It really depends on how much business you can do."

"Forget about that. Just tell me exactly how long I can keep the doors open if I don't have any customers. Figure out how much to have food on hand, a full staff and a beautiful restaurant and not one person walking through the door."

"That would be ridiculous. Why would anyone open a restaurant ..."

"David, can you do this? I want to know?"

"Of course I can do it. One second." He continued punching in numbers and wrote a few items on his note pad. "What kind of food and drink?"

"Top notch, sustainable, organic, local with full bar and great wine list."

He shook his head, turned his back to Jim and searched a few web pages for additional information. "With no customers at all?"

Proudly, Jim sat back and sipped his cocktail. "Not one."

"Give or take a few days, weeks or months, I'd say about five years! But you'd be nuts..."

Jim stood up and placed his drink on David's desk. "Thanks, David. Five years it is."

"Wait, what do you mean? You're not actually going through with this are you?"

"Why not?"

Jim was out the door and through the lobby when he realized he'd forgotten something. He popped his head back in David's office, "Make an offer on that building, will you please?"

Jim drove by the building again in the frozen daylight. It still looked as beautiful through his frost-covered windshield as it did in his mind; he made the right decision.

"Carla, it's Jim. Did you find out about the house?" Jim sat staring at the building from across Sixth Street and held his cell phone precariously with his leather-gloved hand.

"Hi, Doctor Jim. Yes, it's available. When you pick me up for our date you can see it. The house is empty and the owner told me where the key is hidden."

"Oh, fantastic. Well, in that case, how about if I pick you up now?"

"That's a little pushy don't you think? Besides, I work the afternoon shift today. Tomorrow is Saturday and I'm off. How about tomorrow?"

"Great. I have an idea. I'll pick you up at one o'clock?"

"I think I can manage that. See you then. Oh, 1430 Sunset."

"I know exactly where that is. Looking forward to it." Jim pressed 'end' and stared at the phone. He had just made his first date in 37 years. He felt like a teenager.

He drove by Carla's address, ostensibly to see if he could find the rental, but he was also curious to see her house. As he slowed, a tingle cursed through his body–the sweet smell of testosterone, long dormant until now; or maybe it was the bloody mary. He was excited and couldn't wait until tomorrow. The ring of his phone startled him out of his adolescent fantasy. He looked down at it. "Hi, David. What's up?"

David sat in his office, sipping his second drink of the day with his feet up on the desk, "I talked to Troy and he says he'll take 45 cash. You can do cash, right?"

"Yes, I can. That was fast."

"Jim, this is Zanesville. People can do whatever they want and usually don't."

"What's the next step?"

"Troy says to call an inspector, which I've already done, and meet them there at 2."

"Today?" Jim was astonished at this efficiency. "That's in a half an hour."

"Is that a problem? Are you busy?" David said somewhat sarcastically.

"I'm on my way." Jim continued down Sunset and turned left toward downtown. He drove slowly, looking in vein for a cute little house for rent. There were no signs in the yards and no signs of life. It was the middle of Friday afternoon and everyone was at work, at school, or at a bar. That off handed little thought planted the first doubt about his fancy new plans.

Jim pulled up and parked behind his future restaurant. Troy, David and the inspector were all parked and waiting for him. The inspector turned out to be Nick Jennings, a high school pal of Jim and David. Troy Nicholson was several years older than Jim and was never a friend. But, like most people that grew up on the north side of Zanesville, you were known. Troy also now lived in a house around the corner from Ruth, and his wife worked at the hospital. She must be close with Carla

Troy, "Hey, buddy, I hear you have a date with Carla." Just another sign that maybe this wasn't the best idea that Jim had ever had.

Changing the subject to the building, Jim, "I had no idea that this building was still in your family, Troy. You guys moved out north when I was still in high school."

"Yeah, my father thought it was a good rental property and he was right for a while. Then everyone else left downtown except the banks, the lawyers and David." Troy glanced at David with a look that could have only been cultivated by traveling in the same microcosmic circles for all of their lives.

High school for life, thought Jim.

"Shall we have a look?" Nick broke the awkward silence.

They entered through the same hole in the garage door that Jim had clandestinely snuck through a month before. "Great to see you, Nick. How are Sue and the family?"

"All good, thanks. Hard to believe you're back here, Jim. Welcome home." Nick didn't waste any time. "There's a pretty nasty crack in that foundation there and all of these columns need to be reinforced. Not bad though, considering how old this place is." Nick got right to work, taking digital photos and scribbling in a notebook.

They continued through the building. The romantic shadows from Jim's first visit were revealed in the cold light to be discarded remnants of past tenants - broken stools and ladders, empty display racks and piles of trash. Paint was peeling from partial walls and most of the small pane windows on the river's side were broken. Jim was encouraged when he saw several bare brick walls that had not been painted and could easily be sandblasted back to the original architectural detail.

Nick was up on a ladder peering into the attic. "I don't like that." He said to no one in particular. He came down with a flashlight in one hand. He handed it to Jim and, "Here, have a look. There's some wiring up there going to the outside floodlights that's probably original. It isn't to code, strictly speaking, but would be grandfathered in. I recommend replacing it."

Jim climbed the ladder and looked into the abyss. Not only did he not see any wiring, he didn't see anything. Faking it, he came down the ladder, "Yeah, I'm sure it'll be fine."

"That's about it, Jim. I'll write up my report, but I would

say that considering the age of this building and its location here on the river, it's in good shape. Probably about five grand in structural and the rest you would do in renovations anyway. I'm going to take a few more pictures of the exterior and get out of here. Great to see you guys." Nick shook their hands and traversed the creaky stairwell.

Jim looked Troy straight in the eye. "Five grand in structural, Troy. How 'bout we just split that and take off another two grand for the rest of it. I'll write you a check right now for 40 grand."

Troy grimaced, "Well, I ..."

Quickly, Jim, "Any other offers on the table, buddy?"

"Well, no, but ..."

"So, forty grand it is, then? I can have it wired, if you prefer." Jim reached for his checkbook in his breast pocket.

"Yes, fine. No, a check is fine. Please make it out to The Nicholson Family Trust."

Jim's doubts were now sealed in the ink that he applied to his Bank of Boston check. With his signature he just became a Zanesvillian again.

Ruth was napping on the couch when he burst through the back door, excited to deliver the news of his newly hatched plan. She stirred and grabbed the golf club that she always kept by her side. Jim popped his head into the living room; fortunately, far enough away from the radius of a 7 iron that he was spared the blow.

"Why on earth are you making so much noise?" Ruth squawked from her daze.

"I'm so sorry, Mother. I was just excited to share with you my new plan."

"What hair-brained scheme have you come up with now?"

Jim was somewhat confused by this attitude since he had been an extremely successful surgeon and all of his "schemes" had been incredibly lucrative. He used to come up with crazy ideas when he was a kid and that was obviously what Ruth was referring to, but, in this case, he couldn't help but think she might be accurate.

"I bought the old Nicholson Building on South Street, and I'm going to turn it into a restaurant."

"You have lost your mind. I'll call Dr. Hendrickson first thing Monday and see if I can get you in. For now, you should rest and stay inside. For God's sake do not go out again."

Dr. Hendrickson was the only psychiatrist in Zanesville and was himself fairly mad. Jim knew there was no explaining any further at this point. Ruth had been napping and didn't want to comprehend anything past Sunday morning.

"Don't worry, Mom. Everything will be fine and I'll call Ben myself on Monday. I haven't seen him in a long time." After Big Jim died, Ben played an important role in Jim's life. He was Jim's mentor until Mrs. Hendrickson died. After that, he took to prescribing his own meds, slowly stopped seeing patients and ceased to be much of a role model.

Fortunately, Ruth had fallen back asleep and would probably forget the whole incident. Jim thought about Carla and slipped out the back door without waking Ruth.

He returned to the wine store. They had a serviceable deli section where he loaded up on anything that looked vaguely exotic. The salami was from South Zanesville and the cheese from Wisconsin, but it would all have to do. They baked their own bread, which permeated the store and reminded Jim of the streets of the left bank of Paris. He bought a loaf that resembled a French baguette and found other yummy items in the aisles. A jar of black olives, cornichon and some roasted red peppers were perfect. He knew he had to impress, especially considering his ridiculous plan. When he returned home he even found the perfect carrier, buried deep in Ruth's basement.

He arrived early to the dilapidated mansion on Sunset. Anxious to see Carla, but he also wanted to secure housing as soon as possible. Living with Ruth was already taking its toll. She snored all night and kept him from his beauty sleep. And, if her 7 iron ever connected with its intended target, she could do some real damage. He loved his mother but knew the best way to help her was from a safe distance. He would see her regularly but would also lead an adult life, something that he had never before attempted in his old hometown.

Carla answered the door in a flurry of activity. Her two boys were yelling from different parts of the house, and she was yelling back. Jim stepped into an unexpected whirlwind. She waved him in, talked on the phone, made what looked like a sack lunch and yelled past the receiver, covering the mouthpiece after the fact. She whispered, "So sorry. Have a seat and I'll be ready in a few minutes."

He sat quietly for twenty minutes as mayhem continued in the adjacent rooms. At one point he thought of leaving, but realized that he would have ended his first date in 37 years without even a peck on the cheek or a slap in the face.

Carla appeared with both boys and pushed them out of the door. She turned back to Jim and let out an intentional sigh. "Sorry for all of that. They are going to their aunt's for the weekend and that's sometimes easier said than done. I would have introduced you, but, we'll save that pleasure for another time." She wiped her brow in a grand gesture.

"Now, where were we?"

"We were about to go on a date. Are you ready?"

"Don't I look ready?" Carla posed, modeling a mess. "I'll be right back." She disappeared for nearly an hour.

"Okay, ready?" woke Jim from his awkward napping. He looked out the window and realized that the winter sun was setting fast.

"Let's go now!" He jumped up and grabbed her hand, realizing immediately that he had overacted. "Sorry. I mean: Are you ready to go, Carla? Your chariot awaits."

"Indeed, Dr. Jim." She took his arm and they walked out onto the porch. Jim took one more look at the sun and realized that the rental house would have to wait.

"So what are we doing? What is this plan?"

"You'll see, my dear. You will see." They drove in silence the short distance over the bridge and to the other side of downtown. Jim turned into the alley next to the Nicholson building.

"What the hell are we doing here?" Carla was not amused.

"Don't worry. I have a plan."

"It better be a good one." Carla was now clenching her coat and clearly not comfortable with this date.

They parked and Jim hopped out, hurried to the passenger's side and opened her door. "Wait right here" he said as he went around to the rear of the car. He opened the trunk and removed an old-fashioned picnic basket and a couple of blankets. "Shall we?" He offered her his arm and she reluctantly took it. They walked to the embankment in front of the river, between the building and the water. He laid out the blanket and wrapped her in another blanket. He spread out the rest of the picnic before her. He produced two glasses and a bottle of fine champagne. She took all of this in without saying a word. She thought it was romantic in a completely crazy way.

Finally, "What is all of this?"

"It's a picnic."

"I can see that. Do you know that it's about 30 degrees, and we are sitting on the bank of the river? You are nuts, aren't you? Maybe we should go."

"No, no, no. We are here for a reason." He sat down next to her and very slyly maneuvered his arm around her to point her toward the building. "We must toast." He looks her in the eye, "To the five-year plan!"

Carla jerked away. "What crazy nonsense are you talking about? Take me home right now." She started to stand as Jim gently guided her back into his arms. She really didn't want to leave, but he was talking nonsense.

"The Five-Year Plan is my restaurant and you are looking at it. Shall we? To the Five-Year Plan." He held his glass and she stared at him. "Shall we toast?" Still nothing. "Okay listen, you see that building right there? That is going to be a restaurant, my restaurant, and it's going to be open for exactly five years. You are the first to see it. Now can we toast?" She begrudgingly clicked glasses.

"You are nuts. First of all you can't open a restaurant in Zanesville, nobody will come. Second, wait, what ... What do you mean it will only be open for five years?"

"That's right. I'm investing just enough money to keep it open for five years, even if nobody comes. I figure if I plan to close it in five years from now, nobody, including me, will be upset when it closes." Jim stared at Carla. He expected her to continue berating him for such a stupid idea, but she just looked at him longingly (he hoped). He poured her another glass of champagne.

"You are an interesting man, Doctor Langley." She drank her drink and looked hard at the building. Her imagination was doing its best to see what he saw, but was failing. "This place is a dump, Jim. What do you see in it?'

Jim seized the opportunity to point over her shoulder toward the upper floor. He wrapped himself around her and explained, "See those windows? Imagine a balcony over-looking the river and you sitting with a close friend under a beautiful, white umbrella as the sun sets over the river and you and your friend eat fresh oysters and sip cham-pagne. The sun goes down and the outdoor fireplace is blaz-ing. You have a second course under the moonlight–maybe a poached salmon—a strolling violinist walks by playing Vivaldi and your waiter pours a velvety pinot noir. Your friends are inside and you finish the evening around the indoor fireplace with them, eating homemade ice cream treats and sipping Armagnac from warmed snifters, laugh-ing and having the time of your life."

She stared hard at the derelict building and then at him. She knew she was going to kiss him, but not yet. "You are indeed an interesting man."

They ate their picnic in silence. She couldn't figure out who he really was and if this whole thing was real. Jim didn't want to act too quickly and wasn't sure if he hadn't already played too many cards. He was quietly embarrassed at all that he said, but knew that saying it out loud meant that he was now truly committed. If Carla was as big of a mouthpiece about this as she had been about their date, he was sure to read it in the morning's Times Recorder.

The champagne was gone and they watched the sunset–not quite as he had expected. "I hope this works, Jim. Our segregated, bitter, insular little community could use some-thing classy like this. Something with character, not cynical and cheap like the rest of Zanesville."

At last what Jim was looking for: An honest assessment and a look inside Carla's real soul. They were both a challenge that he felt he was ready to tackle.

As they approached Carla's house, she, "Want to see your new house?"

Jim had almost completely forgotten about it. "Sure. If it's not too late."

"Of course not. The keys are on the front porch and the tenants have moved out."

She directed him to turn the corner and park in front of a cute little two story colonial. It was painted a pleasant green and had a well-manicured garden on one side. The other side of the house faced Findley Avenue and the front faced Culbertson Avenue. Carla reached under the petunia plant and produced the key to the front door. The dead of winter didn't prevent the faint perfume of honeysuckle from washing over them. She opened the door and flipped the light switch to no avail. The power had been turned off, but fortunately the heat was still on. A full moon lit the hallway and most of the rooms just enough to see. "Do you think we should be in here without light?" Jim was more nervous about being alone with Carla than in the house.

"Don't be silly. Just don't fall over any furniture." The house was cute and completely empty. It had a perfect floor plan and, even in the dark, it was obvious that every attention to detail had been paid. The kitchen had modern appliances and a fireplace and an adjacent screened in porch. The dining room had swinging doors to the kitchen and a big bay window. And the living room was cozy and organized around another fireplace. Carla creaked up the stairs,

"Let's look up here."

Jim followed closely behind. He was filled with every emotion that had been with him since childhood and was enjoying every jolt of the endorphins that rushed through him. They reached the master bedroom, which was (thankfully) void of a bed, and stared at each other. Jim had blown many opportunities with women in the past and was doing his best not to repeat himself. He gently, slowly and accurately caressed Carla's cheek, brushed her hair away and then followed with the other hand, held her other cheek and deftly kissed her. He smelled the tangy aroma of citrus mixed with fresh shampoo lingering in her hair. She felt secure in his firm arms. She returned the embrace and they kissed passionately. Neither were teenagers, but they enjoyed the moment as if they were. Once broken, they returned to being grown up and descended to the first floor.

"So what do you think?" Carla asked, trying her best to hide any irony.

"I think I'm in love ... with it. This is a great house. Where do I sign? You do mean the house, right?"

"Yes, of course I mean the house. What did you think I meant, Doctor Jim? I'll give you Ginny's number and you can call her on Monday and work out the lease. It's reasonable, I think. Unless you want to look around some more?" The double entendre was not lost on Jim.

"No, I like this. I want to stay here and enjoy the neighborhood and all that it has to offer."

"Okay, Doctor Jim. That's enough for tonight. I'm happy you'll be a neighbor, I think."

Jim walked Carla to her doorstep around the corner and kissed her goodnight. He knew better than to ruin the night by trying to take it any further. He returned to his new house and stood against the car, staring at the house for a long time. Everything was old and new and a little more than he could handle. He was committed and enticed, but he was also scared to death. It wasn't the money or even the work that scared him. It was the fear of the unknown. His entire life had been planned (including his wife) but now, for the first time, he was on his own.

5

The Cracker Barrel restaurant sat high above the freeway, near the original site of the hospital where Jim was born. He was not a fan of chain restaurants. He knew that the food arrived by truck in frozen packages and that the only cooking going on in the kitchen involved microwaves and box cutters.

David was on his way to a meeting in Columbus and The Cracker Barrel was the most convenient spot open that early. 6 a.m. was tough for Jim's accountant and old friend. Consequently, he was late. Jim was used to scrubbing up early for surgery, so this was normal. He arrived a little early and took a seat at the counter.

"Jim? Doctor Langley?" That was not David's voice coming from behind him. He spun to see who on earth would know him in the Cracker Barrel at 6 in the morning?

"It's me, Terek, from Sarajevo." Terek, a good looking Bosnian with a tightly trimmed beard and a trucker's cap sitting awkwardly on his chestnut hair, stood at the cash register waiting to pay his bill.

"Terek? Is that really you? I can't believe it. Really? Oh my God!" Jim jumped to his feet and hugged his old friend. Zanesville's early birds and all nighters squinted at the sight. "What on earth are you doing in Zanesville? Come on, sit down. How's your brother and your little sister? What's going on with you?"

"It's so strange to see you here. Is it really you, Doctor Langley?"

"It's really me and of course, call me Jim. Sit down. Tell me what's going on. When did we last see each other?"

Terek sat down next to Jim at the brightly lit counter. "The last time I saw you I was up to my elbows in plaster, making a cast for a 12 year old kid. You had just set his leg. I looked down to finish the wrap and by the time I looked up you were hanging on the back of a bus with a cevapi wrap in your hand, waving up at the hospital window." Terek looked away, "You didn't even say goodbye."

"That sure was good cevapi." Jim was lost in the delicious memory. "So what are you doing in the States?" Jim signaled for a couple of coffees to the waitress and waved off the laminated menus.

"NATO was evacuating children and I went along with a few of the injured kids. Somehow I got lucky enough to get lost in the shuffle and landed in Baltimore. I got a green card and stayed with a Bosnian family in the suburbs. He was a truck driver and took me along for some of his hauls. I liked it and got my license. I've been driving ever since."

Incredulous, "You were a second year medical student before the war. What the hell happened?"

"There was no school after the war. The university was shut down and most of the buildings were destroyed. There were plenty of doctors, but no hospitals and no money.

There was nothing to go back to so I saw an opportunity and took it." The waitress plopped coffees in front of both of them. "Thank you, ma-am."

Jim took a sip and stared through the pies. He knew that most of the world was unjust, but hadn't been reminded of it for a while. He muttered, "I'm sorry."

Terek smiled sheepishly and tried to change the subject. "How is that crazy wife of yours?" Terek had never met Madeline, but Jim never stopped complaining about his "Type A" overachieving wife. Terek figured that it was Jim's way of coping with missing her and "crazy wife" was a term of endearment.

"She died." Jim said bluntly without a shred of emotion in his voice. He saw Terek immediately shrink in embarrassment. He laughed sardonically. "Sorry, Terek. Life just isn't fair and is often painful, but at least we can still laugh."

There was an awkward moment then they both burst into laughter. Jim remembered how much they laughed in the face of such adversity before. It was dark humor, but it kept them both going. Jim made friends from different lands easily. He offered just two things: medical help and a healthy appetite for whatever the locals ate. This made people love him, no matter where he was or what the horrific circumstance.

"So she really did die? How did she die, I mean when, I mean ... oh fuck, I don't know what I mean. I mean, I'm sorry for your loss." Terek stared helplessly into his coffee.

Jim placed a reassuring hand on his shoulder. "Don't worry about it, Terek. It was a fluke. She died of a rare infection. She went fast. I'm sorry I sprung it on you like that. I'm the one that should be embarrassed. You had no idea."

"Well, I'm so sorry for you and your family."

Jim took a sip of coffee and looked around for David. He still wasn't there. He changed the subject, "So you drive a truck? What's that like?"

"I love it. This country of yours is really big and there are lots of opportunities. It's just like they say on the television, except I am "being all I can be" as a truck driver, not an army soldier."

Jim laughed at his unique view of U.S. propaganda. "Do you come through Zanesville often?"

Terek looked puzzled. "Why are you here Jim? I thought you lived in Boston."

"Oh right, sorry, I skipped something, didn't I? After Madeline died I kind of freaked out. It's a long story, but suffice it to say, I'm originally from here and I've moved back. I'm about to open a restaurant."

Terek may have been Bosnian, but he had been travelling through this part of the country for along enough to know what was and wasn't here. "A restaurant ... here?"

At that moment, David walked in and boldly interrupted, "Hi, Jim. Sorry I'm late. This is fucking early." David finally noticed that Jim was not alone. "Oh hi, sorry. I'm David Weinstein." David offered Terek his hand.

"This is Terek. An old friend from Sarajevo." Jim knew that would shut him up. David wasn't exactly a world traveler. He wasn't stupid, but suffered from a very common malady among small town dwellers. He had a fear of anyone that didn't graduate from the same school that he did.

Terek turned to Jim, "I really better hit the road." He smiled at David, suspecting his discomfort, "Nice to meet you, David. Have a good morning." He reached for his wallet and pulled out two business cards and grabbed a pen from his jacket pocket. "Jim, here's how to reach me. My phone works just about continuously all the way along 70 from New Jersey to Utah. Write down your number will you. I'm usually through here about once every week or two."

Jim scribbled his number on the card and handed it to Terek. He stood and they hugged. Jim buttressed his shoulders and looked him straight in the eye. "It was truly great to see you, Terek. We'll figure out how to get together and catch up in the next couple of weeks. What a treat. Great to see you."

Terek waved from the door and was gone. Jim and David sat back down at the counter and signaled for more coffee. David ordered some eggs and bacon. "Okay, so your building closes tomorrow. Paying cash sure does make escrow go smoothly." He slid a manila envelope across the counter. "Here, sign these and get them back to my office today. The deed should be ready tomorrow."

"What did you find out about your pal in restaurant supply?"

David winced, "He can get you everything that you need. That's not a problem. He did have to look up a few things. He didn't know some of the French words that you used, but he was able to get some translations."

"That's great. When can we expect delivery?"

"There in lies the rub. It seems that this time of year is very difficult to get some of these larger pieces from the manufacturers. He says that 10-12 weeks at the earliest and that there is no way anything ships before the New Year."

Jim's eyes bugged out. "I need this stuff in half that. We're going to open on New Year's Eve. Shit!"

"I understand, but he said there was nobody in the Midwest that could do any better. Most factories shut down for Christmas and right now they're filling orders placed earlier this year. He did say that he has a lot of the small stuff in stock: glasses, plates, flatware, stuff like that. You can have that in a week."

"Great. We can set the tables but won't have any food to serve our guests, if we even have guests. What about the contractor?"

David looked crest fallen even though the situation was beyond his control. He squinted one eye and tried to sound positive. "Sam Donley is really the only guy with this sort of experience and he just had a triple bypass."

"Damn, these people eat way too much red meat. Wait! What about Nick?"

"Nick Jennings? He's an inspector."

"Yes, but he was a builder at one time."

"Oh, really? I didn't know. You want me to call him?"

"Do you have his number? I'll call him."

David took out a little spiral notebook and scribbled Nick's number. As Jim got up he threw down a 20-dollar bill and, with the same gesture, grabbed the number.

"Take care of the bill, will ya? I gotta move on this."

David sat there stunned, barely nodding his head. Jim ran out the door, leaving a cold wind in his wake. He got to the parking lot just as he saw what he imagined to be Terek's truck pulling away. He grabbed his cell phone from his lined corduroy coat and retrieved the card from the other pocket. He stood in the middle of the dark, gravel lot and punched in the numbers.

Terek answered right away. He was on the speakerphone. "That didn't take long. What's up, Jim?"

"Terek, where are you headed?"

"Unfortunately, I'm going north. 70 over to Dayton, then up 75, then 80 out to Nebraska. Why? You want a ride?"

"No, no. So, just those three freeways, 70, 75 and 80?"

"Yep. Should be there in three days and back in two since I will be light on the way back."

"Your truck will be empty?"

"That's right. You got a load for me?"

"Well, I might, I might. Keep your phone on. I'll get back to you." Jim hung up and walked toward his car. The sun was rising over the hill directly behind him and the Cracker Barrel was filling up. He reached for Nick's scribbled number in his pocket, hesitated and looked at his watch. He dialed anyway. "Nick, can you meet me at the building in 20 minutes? I know it's early but we have no time to waste." Jim hung up before Nick had a chance to argue.

Jim sat in the empty parking lot across from the building on South Street. He hadn't seen a car since he left the Cracker Barrel. Downtown Zanesville was always light on traffic—which sometimes gave Jim pause, considering that he was about to open a retail business downtown—but at 6:30 in the morning there were no signs of life.

He was busy flipping though web pages on his iPad. When Madeline gave him this toy for his birthday he thought he would never use it—just like all of the other gadgets that she so wanted him to adopt. Jim was not into toys. He treasured books and writing longhand; he often thought that he was born in the wrong century. It wasn't that he didn't have any aptitude in the high tech arena. He used all of the latest technology in his practice and even was a pioneer in some of the early arthroscopic procedures, working with MIT students while still in medical school. He was also adept at all of the Internet applications. He understood all of the concepts and the importance that it played in society. He just preferred a good book to Facebook. He continued flipping.

He found a site for used restaurant equipment and book-marked two restaurants selling all of their gear, one in Iowa and another in Chicago. The Iowa place was intriguing. The ad said that the restaurant had only been in business for two years and listed among the kitchen items a pasta maker. Most Midwest restaurants bought dried pasta in bulk. Someone must have been a little too ambitious for the neighborhood, Jim thought. He stared for a moment at the equipment list when Nick tapped on his window and made him jump.

"Oh, for God's sake, Nick, you scared the shit out of me."

Nick smiled amiably, "Sorry about that, Jim. So what did you need? Is there a problem with my inspection?"

"Oh, heavens no. I want to show you what I want to do with the building." Jim slid his iPad under the seat and climbed out of the car. They walked across the street and around the back of the building, stepping over trash that had already been removed from the building. Jim spun the numbers on a newly installed padlock and forced the corrugated door open. As they passed over the six-inch high threshold cut in the garage door, Nick looked at the opening and wondered why he bothered with the lock. A good tug from any kid and that door would pop right open.

Jim bounded up the steps and Nick lumbered behind. When he reached the main floor Jim was standing by a row of broken windows. Jim put his arm around Nick's shoulder and pointed out the windows, "Imagine a beautiful summer evening, the outdoor tables all set with white tablecloths and crystal, and all of these windows slid to the sides. The smell of a wood fired grill wafting through the restaurant and people laughing and talking and enjoying this beautiful view, as waiters effortlessly deliver the most delicious meals ever tasted on this river." Slowly rotating Nick inside, he motioned over the dark, musty room, "The restaurant itself will be elegant and subdued with not one fork out of place. The lighting will be dramatic and all of the mechanisms of the restaurant tucked out of view of the patrons. It will be beautiful. You with me?"

Nick stumbled back, tripping over an empty paint can. As he caught his balance and looked around, in the most optimistic tone he could muster, "Looks like a lot of work to me. Who you going to get to do it?"

Jim smiled, pondered various approaches and chose the straight-ahead one, "You."

"Yeah, right. What are you talking about? I don't do this kind of work."

"You used to, if I remember correctly."

"That was a long time ago ..."

Jim interrupted, "Look, Nick, I've known you all of my life. You were the most trustworthy person I've ever known. You built houses and commercial buildings and you know everyone in town."

Shaking his head, he looked down, "Even if I said yes, which I am not, I don't have a crew. I haven't been a contractor in ten years."

"You still have your license, I checked online. Sam Donley's crew is available. He just had a triple bypass. You must know all of those guys anyway. You don't have any other inspections for the rest of the year–I also checked that–and you need the money."

Nick just stared at him, knowing that he really did need the money. "I suppose you checked that too." Changing his tone, "Do you have plans?"

"I know exactly how I want it."

Nick interrupted, "I need drawings. Do you have any

working drawings?"

"No, but I can get some right away. Will you do it?"

"Keep talking."

"I want you to start today. Name your price. Will you do it?"

Nick walked around the room and looked out around the corner, stalling. "I call all of the shots."

"Alright."

"You can put your ideas out there, but I make all of the decisions on how things get done. I don't need some big city doctor telling me how to hang drywall."

Jim stared at him. That was uncalled for.

"I'm sorry, Jim. You know what I mean. You aren't some big city doctor, but if you want me to do this, it has to be my way. It's the reason that I got out of contracting to begin with. I couldn't take fussy rich bitches from Willow Lakes telling me that the tile didn't look straight or that one of my men peed in her azalea bush."

Jim reached out his hand and they shook, "Fantastic. So the plan is to open New Year's Eve. You better get busy." He headed down the stairs. Over his shoulder, he, "I'll get you those plans right away."

Nick chased after him, "Wait, what? What the hell did you just say? This New Year's Eve?"

Jim turned as he climbed out the door, "You might consider hiring two crews, but I agreed not to tell you how to do your work." With that he was gone.

Warming in his car, Jim called Ginny Gibbs about securing the lease to his new home. As he dialed he wondered why he bothered. He knew the kitchen, bar and dining room of the restaurant would be where he would spend his waking hours for the foreseeable future. What did it matter where he laid his head? Ginny answered on the fifth ring, a single landline in a large house, Jim thought.

The lease was as simple and seemingly pre-arranged as the rest of his dealings in Zanesville. The price was lower than he expected and a year was the perfect "getting to know you" length for both lessor and lessee. In a few more calls Jim arranged for the furniture and his other belongings from the Boston house to be shipped. He also called about the power, cable, and Internet. He would only have days left to endure his mother at close range.

The rest of the morning was spent in the only coffee shop left in downtown. DRIP was fairly new and had delicious coffee, both of which intrigued Jim. Maybe he wasn't alone in the gentrification of his old hometown. Maybe there was hope.

Ruth was in the kitchen making coffee when Jim returned home. Hesitantly, "I rented a house today."

"Why on earth would you do that? Why don't you go back to Boston where you belong?"

For her age, Ruth was sharp as a tack and often tactless, but sometimes she would forget what had happened yesterday. "I'm moving here, Mother. Remember?"

"So you say," sarcastically covering her temporary slip. She took her coffee and headed into the den.

He chased after her, "Don't you want to know where? And when I'm moving and about the restaurant? I've hired a contractor and we open on New Year's Eve."

Somehow she mimicked Nick, "This New Year's' Eve!?"

"Yes, Mother. This New Year's Eve!"

"Well, good luck to you. A restaurant in this town is

about as much use as an ashtray on a lawn chair."

Ruth had a habit of mixing her metaphors, and this one baffled Jim more than most. "I've got some calls to make. And, by the way, the house is on Findley and I move in next week, if my furniture shows up."

Jim called the number listed for the restaurant sale in Iowa. He got them to email him some additional pictures of the appliances, then called back and made a deal for the entire kitchen contents. He passed on the dishes, glasses and icemaker. He needed to create a more upscale look for his restaurant and a used icemaker was just gross. Even if no one dined there, for his sake, he wanted it to be as nice and clean as possible.

He reached Terek just outside of Toledo. His route would take him near the restaurant in Fort Dodge, only about an hour and a half out of his way, and he would be light. Terek took the details from Jim and promised to be back in Zanesville with the kitchen gear by the following Tuesday, fortunately the same day Jim would take possession of his new house. There was certainly no way to store a room full of kitchen appliances and associated gear on the building site, so his new living room and dining room would have to do. Ironically, he only had bedroom and kitchen stuff coming from Boston. He could furnish the living room after the restaurant was open.

The week crawled by, filled with pulling permits and fine-tuning plans. Other than hauling a few dumpster loads of trash, nothing progressed at the restaurant. By Friday, he was bored, apprehensive and more than a little curious about his newly found nurse friend.

"Would Saturday night be available?" he rehearsed. "If you're not doing anything Saturday ...?" Why was this so hard, he browbeat himself? "Are you free ...?" he murmured, interrupted by the ring of his phone. It was Nurse Carla.

"Where have you been?"

"How serendipitous that you would call now. I was just this minute rehearsing our conversation where I ask you out for Saturday night." Jim always resorted to honesty when he didn't know what to say. He found that the stark truth disarmed people. Not so with Nurse Carla.

"Wow, you really are full of shit, aren't you?"

"No really, I was. Whatever. Do you want to go out Saturday night? No picnic, I promise. Just a nice dinner at the Coach House." The Coach House Inn was the only remaining restaurant with tablecloths left within a 60-mile radius of Zanesville. More than a little disconcerting, but such was his lot and he was beginning to accept it.

"Sounds great. Let me see if I can get a sitter. I'll call you back in a few."

"Or we could take them. I'm sure they would love to have a nice dinner out."

"Ha, these boys. Not a chance. No, I'll be able to find a sitter. How about 8 o'clock?"

"Fantastic. I'll make a reservation."

"A what? Oh, I don't think you'll need one of those. See you then." As Carla hung up Jim swore that he heard her laughing to herself.

Saturday night came too slowly for Jim's current tempo. He spent hours laying out sport coats and ties, rejecting one after another. He found all of his shirts too dressy and even considered a turtleneck for a minute. Finally, a blue blazer, pink shirt, contrasting tie and burgundy sweater would have to do—a classic but with a dash of whimsy. He paced in his mother's kitchen for a full hour before he drove the mile or so to Carla's vintage red brick home.

"Am I early? Maybe you could introduce me?" Jim peaked around in search of her two sons.

"To whom?" She was totally deadpan, or serious. Jim couldn't work out which.

"To your sons, silly. I have yet to meet your progeny."

"They're across the street at their friend's house for a sleepover. Shall we go?"

Jim didn't completely read between the lines, but suspected a sudden shift in Carla's mood, something that inexplicably made him uneasy. He held the door in silence and drove over the bridge and a few blocks to the restaurant, chilly quiet along the way.

"Sure is amazing that this place is still open. Saturday night and there are only three cars in the whole parking lot. What a shame." Carla's empathic statement broke the silence and relieved Jim from his first taste of something possibly darker lurking under the effervescent, quick witted Nurse Carla.

The restaurant was a little busier than the empty parking lot suggested, but by no means what any restaurateur would consider a successful Saturday night. They were seated right away, near the fire as requested. The menu was thorough and more enticing than Jim remembered. The prices were what surprised him. The most expensive main course was surf and turf at $18, which came with salad and dessert. Most would appreciate the bargain. Jim's heart sank with fear and trepidation.

Nancy, a very bubbly waitress, relieved his apprehension with the specials for the evening, presented in mock Shakespearian couplets—including the cutlets. Jim was more than mildly amused and began to banter, riffing with Nancy on her theatrical presentation. Carla was not impressed, and smiled through gritted teeth. Nancy finally took their drink orders–a bottle of 2008 Burgundy that Jim thought might be risky but worth a shot–and scurried off to the wine cellar.

"Flirting with the waitress on our second date? Well, Doctor Jim, that sure was impressive."

Jim didn't know how exactly to take this. Was she serious, or still caustic? Regardless, he had the answer to stop her jealous tone, "Flirting? My dear, that was not flirting, that was a job interview."

"A what?"

"Young Nancy, if she plays her cards right this evening, will be auditioning for the role of head waitress at "The Five-Year Plan.""

"So that's why we are here? I thought this was a date."

"It is a date, a date that I have looked forward to all week. I fretted about what I was going to wear, and paced up and down for an hour before I came to pick you up." Jim thought a little more brutal honesty might ease the discomfort and jealous nature that was seeping through her attractive veneer.

"You look very nice, Jim. I'm sorry. Thank you for asking me out. This IS very nice."

Lightening the tone, "But don't you think she would make a great head waitress?"

"You are something else, Doctor Jim. Yes, I think Fancy Nancy would make a spectacular head waitress at, wait, what? The Five-Year Plan?"

Tuesday was unseasonably warm and sunny. If Jim were a religious man he might have seen it as a minor miracle. Thankful nonetheless, he arrived bright and early to his new home. Camping out on the front porch, sitting on a lawn chair—oddly equipped with a small, bolted on, brass colored ashtray—borrowed from his mother. He waited patiently for all of his appointments for the day. He had them neatly spaced and anticipated clockwork precision, just as he was accustomed to in his operating room.

The first appointment was with Ginny Gibbs to sign the lease and turn over the keys. She was late. The next appointment was Terek, who called from the truck stop outside of Newark, Ohio. A tire had to be replaced and he would be several hours late, probably not until the end of the day.

The cable guy was on time. The one contingency that Jim had built in was for the cable guy. How dare HE be on time? Unfortunately, Ginny hadn't yet arrived with the lease and the keys. He checked under the flowerpot but the key was no longer there. Joey the cable guy didn't seem bothered. After a few minutes of fiddling in his truck, he joined Jim on the porch, making himself comfortable on the top step. He was talkative and seemed genuinely interested in Jim's return to Zanesville. Joey didn't know Jim, but had heard the small town scoop picked up at one of the Linden Avenue watering holes.

Since his entire schedule had gone to crap, Jim relaxed and enjoyed the pleasant conversation. "Did you grow up here?"

"No sir, Canton. I followed this job down here a few years ago. My brother lived here then and so I stayed here with him."

"Is your brother no longer here?" Jim was being careful how he phrased his question. Proper grammar did not come naturally to people around here, but this young guy had a better chance of saying what he meant than the locals. Jim thought it was rude to ever correct anyone, but he knew that what someone said wasn't always what one meant. Rephrasing the question to get a clear answer was tricky, but he was starting to get the hang of it again.

"No, sir. He moved up to Columbus for work. He's a cook. Well, he says "chef" but that seems pretentious to me. Anyway, I think he's moving back down here because he lost his last job when the funny little French place closed."

Jim was intrigued. He knew finding a chef in this small town with little culinary history was going to be a challenge. And now one just appeared from nowhere. He thought to himself that maybe he should reconsider that faith thing. He had just received two beautiful blessings in one day, and it wasn't even lunch yet.

"How much longer do you think before we can get into the house, Mr. ..."

"Doctor, but just call me Jim."

"How much longer Mister, Doctor, Jim?"

"Oh shouldn't be more than a few minutes. So, your brother is a chef and he's out of work?"

"Yeah, I never understood why he went over to that fancy New York school and even to Paris, France, just to come back to this hillbilly town."

"I thought you were from Canton."

"Yeah, but Buddy, he grew up down here with his mom. My dad remarried and had me in Canton." His phone vibrated and he answered quickly and stepped a few steps away. It was obviously his office. He only said two words, "Hello. Right."

Approaching Jim, "That was dispatch. I need to go over to this other job right now. I can be back in about an hour. Sorry about that." Joey headed back to the truck just as Ginny pulled up to the curb in her pink Cadillac.

Ginny Gibbs wore an aging but timeless purple tweed

Chanel suit and walked like a realtor. As she confidently approached the porch Jim had no doubt who she was. He offered his best business grip, "You must be Ginny. So nice to meet you. Excuse me one sec." Jim darted toward Joey as he reached the truck. "Joey, I was wondering if you might give me your brother's number? I might have a job for him."

6

Monday morning came quickly. The sun was shining but the wind off of the river held the winter's first breath. Nick pulled up in his truck parallel to Jim. They were not the first on the site. The construction crew had been there since dawn, working feverishly on what exterior work needed to be done. Winter halted any outside work and the race was on. Consequently, there were only a few workers inside when Jim and Nick stepped through the makeshift plywood door.

Jim bounded up the stairs and stopped quietly on the top step. He was taken aback by the expanse. All of the debris had been cleared and the wall of windows completely removed and cleared away. The tracks were not yet installed for the disappearing walls of windows that were so critical to the design of the indoor/outdoor feel. The great room looked like it floated above the river.

Jim made room for Nick. Staring out over the river, Jim, "Nick, this is exactly the feel of the restaurant."

"Empty?" Nick joked.

"Very funny. No, this feel of the indoors meeting the outdoors, floating high above the river, on a cloud of deliciousness."

"I see." Nick responded, somewhat annoyed at the poetics. "Where do you want the wall for the kitchen? The working drawings don't show a wall."

"There is no wall. I want the flow to be casual, natural, organic, like you were at the home of your best friend."

"So just this fireplace is going to separate the kitchen from the dining room and sitting area?"

"Exactly."

"Okay. I hope the health inspector doesn't have an issue with that. But, whatever you want, Doc. Oh, by the way, I saved a whole bunch of the bricks from the front wall. I've got one of the boys cleaning them. We should have enough for at least the front of the fireplace. Should look real nice."

This gesture of good taste and self-motivation gave Jim renewed hope in his contractor. "Great idea, Nick. And please, call me Jim."

Jim set up a table in the opposite corner from the front door and positioned a few folding chairs right inside the door. He had taken an ad out in the paper and on Craigslist for kitchen and wait staff. Today was interview day. He had also reached Buddy Sanders—Joey the cable guy's brother–and was to be the first to be interviewed.

Fortunately, Buddy was punctual, a talent that Jim treasured nearly as much as the five essential sauces, or the perfect omelet. It didn't take long to determine Buddy's aptitude or attitude. Along from being a qualified chef, he appeared to be the only qualified chef in Zanesville. In addition, Buddy had an amiable presence with an easy smile and spoke passable French, albeit with a Southeastern Ohio accent. Not that the French would be of much use, but at least he would know how to translate the more pretentious ideas that Jim knew he would probably invent. Jim was smart enough to know that he was a snob and went to great and sometimes preposterous lengths to overcompensate.

He hired Buddy on the spot and asked him to stay for the other interviews. Jim thought it would be best to start building a family. If these people were going to stand around all night every night without anything to do, they better like one another. And if, as Jim had secretly hoped, they were busy with packed houses every night, they better love one another like a family.

The turnout for the advertised jobs was overwhelming. The area was far more economically depressed than Jim had imagined. Busboy spots were filled ten fold and lower level kitchen staff the same. There were far less applicants with wait or real kitchen experience and no one stood out as a potential manager. Those who did have experience seemed to all express the same apprehension when told that there were going to be no tips. That abated when Jim announced that everyone was going to make a straight salary, including the wait staff, and it would amount to about double what any of them had ever made in a restaurant before.

As dusk fell and Jim and Buddy folded up chairs and cleared away the room, the door opened. Jim turned and, without hesitation, "I thought you might come."

Nancy, the waitress from the Coach House Inn appeared in the doorway, hardly recognizable without her kitschy colonial costume.

Jim, "I have to tell you that I have a firm policy on poaching. I will not consider hiring anyone who already has a position elsewhere." He knew he was just making that up, but if some of the lingering staff heard it, it might get back to the owner of the Coach House and peace would remain in their little hamlet.

Nancy, "I quit this morning. I gave them a month. You will be open in a month won't you?"

"Presumptuous to think I would hire you, don't you think?"

"I've got 14 years experience there, eight of which as manager. Before that I worked in Columbus for three years, and before that four years in New York while I went to NYU."

"I must admit, if I were you I would've also presumed. You graduated from NYU?"

"I said while going to NYU. Does this position require higher education?"

Jim gestured to Buddy. "Buddy, I would like you to meet our new head of wait staff, Nancy ..."

"Andrews, just Andrews, not Andrews-Bolton. That was a long time ago and I changed it back."

Confused with all of the sudden information, Buddy, "Well, nice to meet you ... too. I look forward to working with you."

Jim hoped that Nancy's over sharing was not part of her normal tableside manner.

Construction continued feverishly. Nick had taken Jim's advice and hired another crew from Cambridge to work nights. They worked almost completely indoors, concentrating on the kitchen. Fortunately, there was an experienced bricklayer on the crew and he focused on the fireplaces and the wall repairs that the weathered building so desperately needed.

Inside, the workers were only slightly more protected from the elements than outside. The large wall of windows was nothing more than a thin layer of plastic awaiting the overdue custom movable glass doors. They were going to be beautiful and quite appropriate, copying the original pattern of the small panes originally on that wall. They would be, however, modern in their functionality. The double panes would seal the winter out and float open in warmer months, all but disappearing off to the sides, leaving the outdoors and the indoors as one.

Jim was most proud of this concept and called nearly every day to check on their progress. The only other time in his life he ever waited in such anticipation was when his older brother was to return from the army, but never did. He hated waiting. He hated remembering waiting. He needed to be assured that his waiting was going to be worth it.

He called again.

The week had evaporated. Construction was moving ahead, but Jim had little else to do, and was no good with a hammer, so most of the work happened as he watched. Fortunately, he had plans with Carla and was promised, at long last, to meet her kids.

As dusk set in over the McIntyre Terrace, Jim selected a bottle of white from the makeshift wine storage in his basement and headed out the front door. Carla did not like red wine, much to Jim's chagrin. She said it gave her a headache. Jim walked around the corner to her rambling old brick house and knocked on the rickety screen door.

Carla yelled from the back of the house, "Come in. It's open."

Jim let himself into the front hallway. There were no signs of life. He hesitated to go any further. "Hello. It's me."

Carla yelled, "I'm in the kitchen. Come on back."

Jim followed his nose. He found her at the oven, door open, the fragrance of rosemary, garlic and roasted chicken wafting forth.

"Should be done in about twenty more minutes." She took the wine from Jim and kissed him on the cheek.

She deftly slid a corkscrew into the uncut foil of a 2014 Meursault. "I've got some chardonnay if we get though this."

As she glugged a couple of glasses full of the golden white Burgundy, Jim, "That might need to be chilled a ..."

She offered him the glass, "Chin, chin." And clinked glasses as Jim stared incredulously at his full glass of wine.

He changed the subject, "Where are these kiddos?"

"They should be back any minute."

The back door burst open at that moment and the room filled with youthful exuberance and the unmistakable putrid smell of dirty athletic socks and sweat.

"Hey, boys, this is Jim. Jim, this is Kyle and Sam."

Kyle and Sam looked like twins but were actually 18 months apart, Sam being the older. They had stringy brown locks falling over their faces and mild acne with the occasional premature whisker showing through.

"Hi boys. Let me guess, 14 and 16."

Sam challenged, "Yeah but who's who."

Jim studied them closely. Pointing to Sam, "You're Kyle and just turned 16 and you're Sam."

Kyle, "Wrong!" and they both bolted up the stairs,

taking them two at a time.

Carla shouted after them, "Wash your hands. Dinner in 20."

Jim, "They sure are energetic." He looked for approval of his interaction, not something he was adept at. His patients were all adults and the closest he came to adolescence was the annual visit from Madeline's niece, with whom he had barely ever spoken.

"You did good. At least one of them spoke. That's better than most people get. Usually it's a grunt and an eye roll. They're in that dark period. I hear that they do eventually come out of it. They're good kids, though. Their father is a dipshit, but they came out all right."

"I thought you said your husband died?"

"He did. But dipshit is very much alive."

"Oh, I see. So there is an ex as well. Got it. Do you get along with him?"

Carla growled, "You really don't want to go down that path. We would be up all night and there would be a lot of yelling and crying."

Jim tried to make nice, "I'm so sorry. Please forget I ever mentioned dipshit."

Carla laughed and returned to the stove. "I hope you like garlic bread. It's the boys' favorite and since I made them stay home tonight I thought it was the least I could do."

#

The dinner was silent. Jim attempted small talk with both boys and Carla. He could see where their demeanor came from. All were quiet and concentrated on the garlic bread, chicken and salad. The only words spoken at dinner were Jim's, "This is delicious. Could I please have some more garlic bread?"

Kyle hesitated, took two pieces for himself and passed

the breadbasket.

With bread still dangling from their mouths, the boys stood and bounded up the stairs again, not to be seen for the rest of the night.

Carla noticed the empty bottle, "I'll get another bottle. Would you like to retire to the living room?"

Jim was relieved that the dinner ordeal was over and there might still be a chance for a civilized evening. "That sounds great. Can I help you clear?"

"Nah. I'll make the boys do it in the morning before basketball."

In the living room, Jim chose the couch and was swallowed by the under stuffed pillows. He was reminded of couches from college days. Maybe dipshit got the furniture in the divorce.

Carla entered with the opened chardonnay in one hand and their wineglasses in the other. She poured both full again.

Jim very, very slightly flinched, but not without notice.

Carla, "Is everything all right?"

Jim, "Fine, lovely. Thank you again for that delicious dinner. And your boys are so charming."

Carla, "Okay, cut the crap. They were obnoxious. I bet you were even worse when you were their age. And that's the dinner they will eat. At least they ate the salad. I blame you for that. They saw you eat it and didn't want to be rude."

"They didn't want to be what?" Jim caught himself. "No, no. That's great that I had an ever so subtle influence. We must eat our veg." This was not going well and Jim was perplexed as to why.

Carla took a sip of her wine and stared off into the ceiling.

Jim changed the subject. "Hey, if you have the day off tomorrow, I'm going over to my mother's and, since you two are so close, I thought you might want to come along."

Carla, "You've got to be kidding me. I got paid good money to be nice to that woman. If you want to match my Sunday pay ..." She stopped herself. "I'm sorry, that was rude. But, I don't think tomorrow will work."

"Do you have something better to do? I really think you will like her when she is in her natural habitat. In control."

She snapped, "NO, I don't want to go." She paused, and then under her breath, "Why don't you take that waitress."

Jim, not sure that he heard her, "What did you say?"

"You heard me. Why don't you take that waitress? I drove by the building the other day and I saw you walking her to her car."

Jim was surprised at another ugly sign of jealousy. "You did what? I should do what? You are what? Jealous? What?" He couldn't believe that an adult could behave in such a manner and had no idea what to say, so he stammered, and searched for his trademark honesty. "You are jealous of the wait staff?"

Carla, "Don't be ridiculous. Of course I am not jealous. Why would I be jealous? She's not even attractive and I'm, I mean we, NO! I'm not jealous."

Jim carefully placed his glass on the table and eased himself out of the discomfort of the couch. "Maybe I should go."

Carla leaped to her feet. Jim flinched. She stepped back, then slowly touched his arm. "I'm sorry. I did it again. I do it every single time. Every time I meet a man I chase him away. I'm self-destructive."

Jim turned toward her and rested his hands gently on her shoulders. "We will go as slow as you want. I understand that you have a full and complicated life. We'll go slow, okay?"

Carla kissed him on the cheek and then the lips, with just enough promise to temporarily keep his interest.

Sunday lunch as Ruth's was always an event. Ruth detested cooking, but she could make a handful of dishes, most of which were suited for her Sunday lunch. She would invite a small cadre of friends, enticed by copious quantities of cocktails and wine served with a passable roast. David Weinstein and his wife were invited—Jim assumed for his benefit—his sister Jackie and Father Brown (the Episcopal priest from her church), and Dr. Hendrickson.

The afternoon melded into evening and the party moved to the living room. Dr. Hendrickson was asleep in the armchair, snoring occasionally, and the rest of the group gathered around the couch in front of the fire.

Jackie, "So how is your restaurant coming, Jim? When do you open?"

Jim, "We seem to be on schedule, thanks to Nick and most of the carpenters local." Proudly, "We open on New Year's Eve!"

The room laughed in unison. David, "Will it really be ready?"

Ruth, chimed in, "Another one of your hair brained schemes."

Jim looked at her, still not exactly knowing why she kept saying that. "Yes, we will be ready. I just hope people show up."

David, sarcastically, "I thought that wasn't necessary."

Jim, "Well, I would like to think that people would at least try it out before staying away." Jim was clearly going against what he had always been taught. 'Saying so often made it so.' He tried to backpedal, "People will love it and will come often. I'm sure of it."

David, "How you going to get anyone to come on New Year's Eve? All of the north side of Zanesville will be at the Country Club. The Coach House even closes early on New Year's."

Jim hadn't even considered who would be at his opening night. "What do you suggest?"

David, "A miracle."

The roar of a diesel engine echoing down the street woke Jim. The distinctive air brake release signaled that the truck was right out front. By the time he got to the front door Terek was standing on his porch.

Terek, "I thought I'd stop by before my run out west and say hi. See how it's going."

Jim wiped the sleep from his eyes, "What a surprise. Come on in and I'll make us some coffee."

Terek followed him through the living room, dodging the fryers, cooler, prep tables and other kitchen gear piled throughout the downstairs and into the less chaotic kitchen. Jim made coffee and room at the kitchen table. "What an unexpected pleasure. I still can't thank you enough for bringing me all of this stuff."

"Don't mention it. How are you going to get it down to the restaurant? Do you want me to help? I can swing back by in a few days if you'll be ready for it then."

"That's so kind of you, but no, Nick and the boys plan to come get it piece by piece as they need to install it. Seems like a logical plan to me. Plus, I promised to stay out of those sorts of details. This project is just barely going to make the deadline as it is, without me jeopardizing it by putting my oar in the wrong river."

"If you change your mind, you've got my number. How's the little lady next door?"

"Terek, women are crazy. I mean, obviously I know from women being crazy. I was married to the craziest of the crazy in Madeline. I just didn't realize that it was built into the chromosomes. I may have to gracefully bow out of this one."

"Doc, you live next to her. How are you going to get away with that?"

"Technically, around the corner. But yes, it's going to be a little tricky. I won't do anything rash. After all, the holidays are coming and the restaurant opening ..."

"Still New Year's Eve?"

"You bet. Are you going to be here? You are going to be here, right?"

"Of course. Staying at the Holiday Inn, where I can park the rig."

"You'll be in the truck?"

"Yeah, I got a post Christmas run. They always pay double. I need the money and it brings me right through here. So what if some car parts sit in a parking lot for a couple of days? It's the holidays. I might be in your country, but still Bosnian."

Jim knew exactly what he meant. He saw Terek to the door and dialed his cell phone. "Lina, Jim Langley. Please put me on the available list. Anything after the first of the year."

On Monday morning the custom made disappearing glass wall finally arrived. Nick was calling to let him know just as Jim pulled up. "Hey, Nick. This is exciting, the pièce de résistance."

Nick stared at him blankly.

Jim translated, "The best part!"

Nick smiled and shook his head in agreement.

The restaurant interior was starting to take shape. The wall was carefully being assembled. The rail alone took until the middle of the afternoon to get up and get right. There were many failed attempts; laser lines cut the air, and many levels, shims and other gizmos that Jim had never seen before were flailing and flying everywhere. Finally, as the sun was setting, the first door went in. It was a thing of beauty. It looked surprisingly like the original windows. That was the idea, but Jim was skeptical that anything brand new could have the same charm and design details as something built by hand in another century. He was happy to be proven wrong.

There were several more hitches as the doors went up, one by one, tested, removed, adjusted and mounted again. One end of the opening had to be rebuilt completely to receive the accordion stacked doors, which took several hours. Jim gave up seeing the completed wall just after the night crew showed up. He knew that the wall of doors' real drama would be in the light of day. He had waited a long time for this spectacle. He could wait until morning.

The next several days were filled with deliveries of fixtures, dishes, glasses, flatware, and installation of each of the pieces of kitchen gear, making Jim's living room more and more navigable. Jim spent most of his days approving, rejecting, signing for and unpacking deliveries. He kept to his promise to Nick and only weighed in on the construction when asked. As the building came down to the little details, Nick consulted Jim more often and so the days were filled and went by quickly. On Christmas Eve the construction was complete and Jim was lucky enough to schedule the health inspector the day after Christmas for the final signoff. Nick assured him that this was usually just a routine visit and next to never a problem with new restaurants.

Christmas Day Jim spent unpacking his personal boxes. All of the kitchen gear had finally been removed, revealing tons of items shipped from the Lexington house. He was wiped out by the evening, but had promised Ruth he would come for dinner. Surprisingly, Carla had agreed to accompany him. The boys were having their second Christmas at dipshit's, she explained.

For some reason, she insisted on driving. This made Jim nervous, given Carla's proclivity to drink more wine than she should. It was Christmas, after all, and he had a restaurant opening in a week's time. He could always drive home if need be. No need to make a scene.

Ruth's house looked like a Currier and Ives Christmas card, sitting high on the hill, lit with twinkling white lights; the perfectly trimmed tree in the front window, visible from the street. When he arrived, the party was in full swing. Jim somehow imagined an intimate family gathering, maybe a store bought turkey and Cutty Sark in Ruth's tumbler. Instead, there was a houseful, most of whom Jim didn't, at first, recognize. Instead of hiding in a corner, as would have been his previous M.O., he decided to make the most of it. He relentlessly made his way through the party, introducing himself and shamelessly plugging the restaurant, inviting one after another to the opening New Year's Eve party. And one by one, he was thrown over by the big bash at the Country Club.

The Five-Year Plan

The evening died down faster than Jim had imagined. The only ones sitting around the fire were he and Carla, David and his wife Barb, Jackie and Ruth. Dr. Hendrickson was again asleep in the armchair, occasionally snoring.

Jackie was the first to approach the Christmas tree and produce perfectly wrapped gifts for everyone; sweet gestures and all returnable to local merchants. Ruth also surprised everyone by directing Jackie to a few gifts hidden deep under the tree, beautifully wrapped and well considered from Amazon. Carla excused herself and went outside. Jim followed, not to closely, to see where she was going. He was still a little unsure about Carla's stability and wanted to make sure she wasn't doing anything that she might regret tomorrow. When he saw her removing a large package from her trunk he stole back inside, avoiding her glance.

Seated next to the fire, as if he had never moved, Jim acted surprised as Carla carried an extremely large, gift-wrapped box toward him. She, "I'm sorry I only have a present for Jim. I didn't realize we would be exchanging gifts. No one told me." She shot a look and a smile simultaneously to Jim.

Jim held the awkward box on his lap. "I don't know what to say. This is huge. What on earth could it be?"

The guests speculated, oohed and aahed as Jim carefully unwrapped his mystery present. Once unwrapped, he sat the box, still unopened on the floor. With some force, he popped the staples off, one by one, holding the top flaps of the box. Finally inside, there still packing peanuts and bubble wrap to get through. The prolonged procedure produced an electronic device of some sort, box like with what appeared to be seven segment displays strung together. He found the electric cord and plug and moved toward the wall outlet.

Carla shouted, "NO, don't plug it in. Yet!"

Jim looked perplexed.

Ruth joked, "Is it a bomb?"

Carla, "No. It's sort of a clock. It's programmed to count backwards as soon as it's plugged in. It will count down from five years!"

With that sudden realization everyone broke into spontaneous applause, Jim jumped to his feet and hugged and kissed Carla. He held her at arms length and proclaimed, "This is the single most thoughtful gift that anyone has ever given me. Thank you."

They hugged and everyone applauded again.

8 a.m. the day after Christmas, Nick had agreed to meet the health inspector. He told Jim there was no need for him to be there. It was just a technicality.

At 9 a.m. Jim's phone rang. As he sat in his bathrobe next to Carla, he listened intently to Nick's report.

Nick, "She wouldn't pass us. She said that there were clearance issues with the fireplace, the flat top and the fryer. We needed to have additional clearance for the burners, even though the manufacturer says they need zero clearance. She also says that the hoods need to be six inches lower, even though the manufacturer...you get the idea."

Jim, deflated, "What do we do?"

Nick, "We fix it."

"When?"

"Now. We've got five days."

Jim counted on his fingers as Carla caressed his back, "Wait, we have six days."

"Nope. New Year's Eve is considered a holiday. The inspectors don't work. I've already scheduled her for 8 a.m.

December 30th, just in case there's any last minute tweak."

"Can we do it?"

"We have to." With that they hung up and Jim tried to return to the amorous arms of his new love. Within thirty seconds of disrobing, he was up and dressing. He could not stand by and let some functionary ruin his restaurant.

Both crews worked day and night for those five days. Walls were torn out and rebuilt, chimney lowered, stove moved, fryer relocated. Every item on the punch list checked off one by one. Jim bounced back and forth between the construction and his makeshift office in the basement, calling everyone he knew, sending emails, writing press releases, trying anything to attract people to opening night. The RSVPs were few, and fewer were positive. He was beside himself.

At 8 a.m. on December 30th Jim was waiting in the parking lot for Nick. He decided that there was no way some part time health policewoman was going to ruin his restaurant without having a say in it. Jill Peterson pulled up next to him. No sign of Nick. They got out together and she introduced herself. Jill was a middle-aged woman, probably younger than Jim, with beautiful brown eyes and hair, smartly dressed and all business. Jim understood that right away, but her beauty somehow put him at ease.

They entered the building and she went right to work. Jim's phone rang in his pocket but he ignored it. Jill spent 30 minutes going item by item on her list, nodding and occasionally clicking her tongue. Jim had no idea what any of her gesticulations or sound effects meant. He sat at a far table admiring the windowed wall and the river he was so cozily insolated from, and awaited the result.

"Where is your contractor Nick?" She bellowed from behind the broiler.

"He was supposed to be here. I don't have any idea. Is there an issue?" Jim was on his feet and approached the kitchen.

"No, I just wanted to express my appreciation for all of the excellent, hard work that he and his crew have done." She ripped off a signed form from her clipboard. "Congratulations. You are officially open for business!"

Jim stared for a moment at the form. He couldn't actually believe that he owned a restaurant, a legal, fully functioning, beautiful restaurant. Jill was half way out the door when Jim, "Thank you, Ms. Peterson. I hope you will join us for our grand opening tomorrow night."

"I'm in Cincinnati, but thank you. And good luck with a restaurant in Zanesville."

Nick showed up out of breath. He ran up the stairs, just after Jill walked out the front door. "Did I miss her? What did she say? Did we pass?"

Jim, calmly, "Where have you been? Yes, we passed. Where were you?"

"I got called on an emergency. It might actually be good news."

"What are you talking about?"

"I got a call from the Country Club. They had a sewer back up. Their septic tank must have ruptured or something. I couldn't tell. The ground was frozen. Anyway, the whole place smells like, well, like human waste. They wanted to see if it could be fixed by tomorrow. I had to tell them no. So ..."

"So that means that they have to cancel the New Year's Eve festivities and the whole of the north end of Zanesville has nowhere to be tomorrow night!"

"Something like that."

Jim grabbed Nick and twirled him around the restaurant. "We're in business!"

After spending the rest of the day negotiating with the Country Club to email their members and guests about "The Five-Year Plan" grand opening, plus calling everyone else he knew, Jim collapsed into bed.

The next afternoon he dressed in his tuxedo and stopped at Carla's to pick her up. They walked into the restaurant, greeted the staff and snuck off to the basement. Jim grabbed a bottle of bubbly and two glasses from the wine cellar. They went out the new, secure door and walked hand in hand to the perch above the locks where the hair-brained scheme was first introduced. They stood, looking back at the beautiful, sparkling new restaurant and toasted, "To the Five-Year Plan!"

The party was packed. The Country Club detour definitely worked. Ruth made a grand entrance with Dr. Hendrickson, David Weinstein and his wife Barb. Terek was there and Joey the cable guy. Nick came in a suit and Jim didn't recognize him. Nancy and her team floated through the crowd with plates of finger food as Buddy and the kitchen kids built a scrumptious buffet.

Nearing the stroke of midnight Jim stood on a table next to the countdown clock and clinked his glass several times before he got everyone's attention. "I would like to thank everyone who came tonight to celebrate the grand opening of our restaurant. I know many here didn't think it was possible to build a beautiful restaurant with fancy food and great wine here in Zanesville, but here you all are. Enjoy it tonight and tell all of your friends. Please come back often, but, next time you'll have to pay." The crowd laughed and applauded. "Oh, and one last thing." Jim checked his watch and grabbed the plug. Jim raised his glass, plugged in the countdown clock and said, "Happy New Year!"

7

The call came in the middle of the night. Could he be on a plane later that morning? He called Ruth on his drive to Columbus. The first flight to Houston was a little before noon. He spent the entire day flying to Michoacán, a part of Mexico he had never been.

It was late by the time he landed at the Lazaro Cardenas Airport, but there was an MSF volunteer waiting for several doctors, nurses and staff that were on his small plane. He had kept to himself on the plane, studying the early damage reports and the initial plan of action. MSF had been called early to many disasters and knew how to organize an efficient operation. He hadn't noticed any of the fellow MSFers on the plane.

Jim felt a hand on his shoulder as he waited to get on the faded yellow, old school bus. Mark Fitzsimmons whispered in his ear, "Fancy meeting you here. I wondered if you might not kick in on this one."

Jim spun around. "Mark. Wow. Happy New Year! Were you on the flight from Columbus? I didn't see you."

As they loaded into the rickety bus, Mark, "No, I had a flight out of Cleveland. It's about the same distance as Columbus. Went through Miami and just got here a few minutes before you."

They found a couple of seats near the front. Jim had been on these third world buses before and knew it was better to see what was coming and brace for it than to be thrashed about in the back of the bus.

Mark changed the subject, "Have you had a look at the brief?"

Jim, "Yeah, tons of un-reinforced concrete, adobe, wood shacks. The two and three story structures are probably a burial ground."

Mark shook his head, "Did you hear that there was a mudslide on the edge of town? Nobody thinks anyone was in it, but they're digging anyway."

They both sat silent as the bus ascended a hard packed dirt road, up the side of a mountain. As the road got steeper, pavement kicked in and a series of harrowing curves lay before them. The bus skidded to a stop twice to let motorcycles pass, and then an old Volkswagen beetle passed on the wrong side of the road. As they reached the summit and took a sudden curve, the bus jerked hard right, narrowly averting a broken down big rig in the middle of the road. Jim and Mark looked at each other. That was close, but they had been on these sorts of roads before and knew the descent was the most hair-raising part.

The driver sped up as he crested the hill. There were more tight curves ahead, and, after taking the first one a little too fast and sliding the tail end out over the dense vegetation below, he slowed down. Even at a crawl, the road narrowed, and dropped off with little warning. There were rockslides barely averted and an extremely large rodent made the bus swerve wildly and regain control just before the next hairpin turn.

Jim and Mark cracked up. Like most missions, the darker the situation, the easier it was to laugh. Mark, "So, how's the restaurant going?"

"We nearly didn't open, then we did. The opening night party was a huge success, thanks to bad plumbing at the local country club. And now I'm here. I probably won't know anything else until we get out of here."

The bus ride was a harrowing four hours. Every few minutes they would have to pull to the side of the road to allow emergency vehicles to pass. The brief reported that there was only one ambulance and a small community hospital in Arteaga. All of the power in the valley was out and the broken and splintered tarmac as they approached Arteaga made navigating the only road into the village treacherous. As daylight peaked over the mountains to the east, the signs of devastation were everywhere. The downtown area was now rubble. Most of the buildings were two or three stories and had all collapsed. The street was navigable through a single lane path cleared by first responders with a bulldozer.

The road toward the hospital went through a residential neighborhood. Jim noticed a park with several soccer fields. He made a mental note of the large space away from any structures or power lines.

The hospital was a low-slung wood and concrete structure. Little damage was first apparent. There were a few lights glowing from within the small, frosted windows of the block glass entrance. The auxiliary power must have been functioning. Thank God for small miracles, thought Jim.

The bus pulled along side the Emergency Room doors as aid workers were helping unload the injured from every imaginable vehicle. Victims were being carried on flatbed trucks, a tractor pulled trailer, an old Honda Civic and two of the ambulances that had passed them on the road. Bus passengers piled out and went immediately to work. Hospital workers appeared with boxes of gloves and protective masks for the newly arrived MSF, with reassurances that fresh coffee and churros were waiting, once this new batch of patients was safely inside.

Jim and Mark skipped the heavy lifting and found the head of hospital waiting for them in a small office just off of the waiting room. Dr. Ramirez greeted them at the door and offered two chairs. He waved for an orderly to bring coffee and they discussed the situation. This was going to be the last time either sat for a very long time and they knew it. Jim slouched and crossed his ankles. Mark dangled his boots over one arm. They looked like they had just come in from a round of golf, not about to kick into 15 hours of action.

Dr. Ramirez was fluent in English, "Welcome, Doctors. I read your bios—quite impressive. I did time in Bosnia during the war there. Dr. Langley, we probably crossed paths. I won't have this chance for small talk again, I fear, so thank you both in advance for coming."

Jim, "Call us Jim and Mark. And, I suppose you are right about the time. Can you get us up to speed on the numbers?"

Dr. Ramirez, "170 dead so far, approximately 1800 injured, most not life threatening. We have a couple of triage centers set up on the edges of town. Most people are just in shock. The big problem is that there are very few safe structures left. There's no place for anyone to sleep. The housing area to the south seems the least damaged, but the rest of the town has basically crumbled. Some have already loaded up and left the area. That's also a problem because we're having a hard time figuring out who is missing and who have fled. Most of the injured that need help are here or in the school gym on the south side of town. We got one doctor that did an ortho residency but switched to gyno, so he's doing the best he can but he's really only good at catching babies. He really needs your help, Jim."

Jim and Mark were the two highest-ranking MSF workers during the first two days on the ground. It was therefore their responsibility to organize the workers and set up camps for both the displaced and the volunteers flooding into town. Fortunately, the National Defense Army showed up the next morning with much of what was needed to construct camps. Jim guided them to the soccer fields that he spotted on the way in. The camp was up and running by nightfall. Jim and Mark didn't find themselves in one of those tents for another 30 hours. Jim set record numbers of broken arms and legs, by far the most common injury. Mark managed the internal injuries and cardiac events in the ER. The nurses took care of the contusions and stitching.

By the end of the first day all of the hospital beds were full and Jim assigned a nurse practitioner to evaluate the admissions and clear as many beds as possible, prioritizing children, the elderly and severely ill. All cell and Internet service was out in the valley. There was one landline in the hospital that still functioned and was reserved for the nearest helicopter service, who, when called, could transfer critical patients that could not be treated in the compromised and overburdened community hospital.

Jim met a volunteer from the valley, a tall, dark skinned young man with a friendly smile called Luis. He was 18, very good with the patients and with his hands, and spoke passable English. Jim enlisted Luis as his cast assistant, like he had done so many times in these dire situations. Four hands were better than two when it came to creating a plaster cast, and the work was more basic shop than medical procedure.

The days melted into weeks and the rains came. Power was partially restored to the valley. As the aftershocks died down the rebuilding began and the injuries, especially broken bones, spiked again. Luis became one of the team and Jim saw potential. He noticed that Luis rapidly grasped the techniques of evaluating the patients and often noticed small signs that others missed. Jim asked Luis if he could meet his parents.

Communications to the valley was still challenging. The cell phone and Internet service was never very good and with the few towers downed in the earthquake, there was no hope for restoration for a long while. The mail came twice weekly. Jim wrote to his mother and Carla. He only received one letter from Ruth, who relayed that the restaurant didn't seem to be doing well. This didn't surprise him since he left without any warning, let alone spelling out any clear chain of command. He would be lucky if the doors were still open upon his return. It bothered him more that he had written to Carla twice with clear instructions on how to write back, but received nothing in return.

Luis invited Jim to dinner one evening just before Jim was scheduled to go home. Jim looked forward to meeting his family in order to assess the situation and see how possible it might be for young Luis to go away to college, and eventually medical school. He also realized that this was his only opportunity to taste real, Michoacán cuisine. He salivated at the thought.

Jim rode with Luis in his 1968 dirt colored jeep fifteen minutes south to his grandfather's farm. Luis told Jim his story on the bumpy ride. His parents had both been killed when he was a toddler. They died in a car accident on the same road that brought Jim to this valley several weeks before. His grandparents raised him.

As they approached a dirt patch along the road, Luis pulled in. His grandparents' farm sat right on the road. There was a short, chain link fence between the small parking area and the front of a single story, brightly painted green house. A chicken coop peeked out of one side and a vegetable garden ran down the other. It was dusk and hard to see very far, but Jim imagined some sort of fields for animals and crops beyond the simple little home.

Both of his grandparents were slight, at least a foot shorter than Luis, but stood very tall and proud, especially when they were talking about their grandson. They knew he was special and they were very happy that he had been so much help to Doctor Jim. They spoke very little English, but could communicate clearly how thankful they were and how welcome Jim was in their home. He resigned himself to forgo the conversation about college and speak to Luis later.

The spiced aroma of chili filled Jim's nose and flushed his

cheeks. Luis gestured for them to sit down. They gathered at a perfectly set, round oak table at one end of the living room. The placemats were doilies, and fresh sunflowers bounced in a brightly colored vase in the middle of the table. Luis' grandmother replaced the flowers with a large platter of what looked like chicken smothered in the richest dark red sauce. Jim sat silent and stared at the most delicious looking sauce he had ever seen. He couldn't believe a sauce could elicit such excitement and promise by it's look alone.

Everyone served themselves and ate silently, Luis checking on Jim occasionally, smiling. He knew this was what Jim was after—a culinary memory—and knew this was going to be it. His grandmother's molé was famous. The poblano chilies were grown in her garden and dried on the back porch. The local restaurant cooks came often for her recipe, which she would never divulge, but she would sell them a few chilies and sometimes feed them lunch.

Jim helped himself to seconds, but only after Luis did, and contemplated how he could ask for the recipe. He carefully tasted every bite, mentally cataloging individual flavors, all but ignoring the chicken, which was also the most amazing chicken he had ever tasted. It was small and skinny, but somehow tasted meaty and sweet. He worked out what he imagined were the few ingredients she probably used, or at least what he thought they might be, and was satisfied enough not to embarrass himself or Luis by asking.

They left with a small paper bag filled with chilies that Jim would later conceal in his luggage, and warm, full bellies, and two very proud grandparents smiling and waving goodbye.

8

Jim burst into the restaurant ready to seize the day. It was a little early for lunch; he had come straight from the airport after flying all night. The door was open but nobody was in sight. "Yoo-hoo, anyone home?"

Buddy plodded up the stairs, carrying a tray of various foods from the downstairs walk-in. "Hey, Doctor Jim. We didn't expect you."

"I guess not. Where is everyone?"

"Well, I'm here. Nancy should be here soon. We don't open until noon. That's what we decided anyway. And we both decided to take turns managing since, well, since you really didn't say…"

"Buddy, I'm really sorry to leave you all like that. I had to go to Mexico all of the sudden."

Buddy looked at Jim with great apprehension, as if to say, "You had to go on vacation for three months?"

Jim realized that Buddy, and probably all of the staff, had no idea where he went or why. "Oh shit, Buddy. You had no idea where I was. Is that right?"

Slowly, not to be too much of a smart ass, "Well, I guess you were in Mexico."

"But do you know why I was in Mexico?"

"To get a tan?"

"That's what I thought. No, not to get a tan!" Jim had to think quickly. He had a feeling he was about to have a mutiny on his hands if he didn't explain. He was surprised that it hadn't already happened. He also had a new plan for the restaurant. "When does everyone get here?"

"Everyone is just Nancy and me. We decided since we rarely have more than one or two customers in the daytime that we didn't need any help. The rest of the staff comes in for dinner service at 4:30. We close at 9 if there aren't any customers, which there usually isn't except on Friday and sometimes Saturday."

Of all of the bad news Jim just got, this last bit was the most surprising. He, "Sometimes Saturday?"

"Yeah, we think that we have a few customers on Friday because it's the weekend and they are still downtown at work. I guess on Saturday they don't want to come down here."

Jim scratched his head and walked toward the windows. He stood for a second, admiring the river view and fantasizing that the balcony was full, the windows had been slid from view and the restaurant was jumping. He was lost in what could be.

"You okay, Doctor Jim?"

"Buddy, when Nancy gets in, get her to help you call the staff for a meeting at four o'clock this afternoon. I want to explain where I've been and sketch out a new plan."

Jim bounced toward the door with new commitment in his step.

Buddy, "Okay, Doctor Jim, will do."

Jim poked his head back in the door and shouted toward the kitchen, "And once and for all, please, just call me Jim!"

Jim drove by Carla's but no car was in the driveway. He dropped his bags off at his house, glanced at the mail and watered the dead plants on the front porch. Jim didn't have a green thumb; he didn't really have any thumb at all with plants. He never planted anything in his life. He passed biology with straight A's, but the care and feeding of plants, flowers and vegetables was never in his sights. He wished that weren't so, but he wasn't about to learn something so utterly foreign. He might as well learn Greek, he thought.

Ruth was standing on her front porch as he pulled up, ironically, watering her spring flowers. She didn't bother to look up, "Well, the prodigal son has returned."

Jim kissed his mom on the cheek, "Hello, Mother. Your flowers look like they have a good chance this year. How beautiful."

"How was Mexico? Eat any burritos?"

"It was a mess. It took far longer to stabilize that little village than it did Sarajevo after the war. But I did have some yummy molé."

"What on earth is molé?"

"Well, it's kind of hard to describe. It's a spicy choco-late sauce, but not really chocolate. I mean, it has a small amount of chocolate, but it's not for ice cream or anything. It's a sauce that can be served over anything: fish, chicken, turkey, steak, well maybe not steak. Although it might be good on some beef."

"Disgusting. Have you been to the restaurant? I went by there and it was as dead as a door nail."

Jim, "Yes, I stopped by on my way into town. I've got some catching up to do. But I have a great idea. You should come to dinner Saturday night. My treat. I'll even have someone come pick you up."

"I can drive myself. I'm old, not senile."

"Clearly, you are not senile. I want you to try a new drink and you probably shouldn't drive after it. I will send you a nice car and driver."

"What on earth are you talking about, James? There is no such service in Zanesville. Don't be silly. What time?"

"You will be picked up at 7:30. See you then."

The staff gathered in the unfinished part of the basement. The restrooms, storage and walk-in had all been finished for the inspection and opening, but there was still a fairly substantial area with a view of the lower parking lot and the river beyond. Jim had a makeshift office in one corner and there was an improvised dining table made of a 4x8 sheet of plywood balanced on a large, wooden, industrial wire spool that had been the only interesting item left behind when Jim purchased the building. The table was covered with overlapping tablecloths and was used for staff meals and, Jim imagined, late night drinking sessions when he wasn't around.

Jim leapt down the stairs, making a visual attempt at showing his enthusiasm. He went around the table, greeting everyone by name, then stood at the empty head of the table, staring out the window toward the river and the spring wildflowers just coming into bloom on the riverbank.

After a pregnant pause, "Look how fertile that ground is. Look at those wildflowers blooming without any help from anyone."

Buddy, gently tried to move him along, "Jim, service starts in 20."

"Oh, sure. Thanks Buddy. So, everyone, I owe you some sort of explanation. You all know that I am a doctor. I'm also not always a very good communicator. When I left, I never thought that you all wouldn't know where I was going, or at least why I was going. You had no idea that I was actually going to Mexico."

Grumblings started to grow around the table.

"Not on vacation! No, no, oh God no. You see, I am affiliated with an organization called Médecins Sans Frontiéres. You might know it as Doctors Without Borders. We volunteer to go to remote parts of the world when we're needed. There are full time doctors, nurses and staff and there are per project volunteers such as myself. That means that, from time to time, when we are needed, we get a call to go to these places and help out. There was a large earthquake in a remote village in Mexico while we were all here having a wonderful New Year's Eve. I left the next day as soon as I got the call. I know that it's not a really good excuse for leaving you all in a lurch."

Nancy chimes in, "I've heard flimsier excuses."

Buddy, "Me too."

Others around the table concur.

Jim, "Well thank you all. It was rather sudden though. For that, I extend my most heartfelt apologies."

Nancy, "Yeah, yeah, okay we said you were forgiven. So

what's this big idea?"

Jim, "Oh right, the big idea. Well, when I was in Arteaga I met a wonderful family and I found the most amazingly delicious food. On the plane back I had an idea. What if we have International Night every Saturday night? Buddy tells me Saturday is slow."

Interrupting, Nancy, "Every damn night is slow."

"Okay, yes, every night is slow, but Saturday night is a night that should not be slow. It's the weekend and people go out. So, I want to try it. Buddy and I will get together and figure out how to make molé and we will feature it this Saturday. Tell all of your friends."

Jim called the local paper, radio and television station. He didn't expect to get any free advertising, but always remembered what he dad used to tell him, "You'll never know if you don't ask." It turned out that the local television station invited him on their Saturday afternoon show to talk about International night and to cook molé.

The show went well, but Jim was skeptical that local origination television would reach many people. When the doors opened at five, there was a line waiting to get in. The restaurant was packed for the first time since New Year's Eve. The day was warm and dry, so the balcony was opened for the first time. It was everything that Jim had dreamed. The indoors flowed seamlessly into the outdoors. The evening cooled down enough to have the outdoor and indoor fires set ablaze.

At 8 o'clock he panicked. He had completely forgotten about Ruth. Buddy's brother Joey walked in and was talking to a friend about his new car. Jim spun around and quickly pushed Joey out the door, scribbled Ruth's address on the palm of Joey's hand and stuffed a twenty-dollar bill in the other. "Please, please run up and grab my mother, will you please Joey? And if you stay sober tonight, I'll give you another 20 to get her home, plus I'll comp your dinner."

Joey, "You got it Doc. I don't drink anyway, but thanks for the cash. And, by the way, I love molé. My mom used to make it. She's from Arizona and had Mexican neighbors ..."

Jim pushed Joey toward the parking lot. "The matriarch awaits!"

As Jim turned and walked inside, he could hear raised voices on the balcony. He walked over to see if he could help. Nancy was standing over a man with a cell phone in his hand. "May I assist with something here, Nancy?"

"No Doc, this gentleman doesn't seem to grasp the concept of no cellular telephone usage in the restaurant."

The customer argued, "But I need to call and check on the sitter. What am I supposed to do? Go out on the street? I'm already sitting outside."

Jim, "I'm sorry for the inconvenience, Sir, but we do have a no phone policy so the other guests are not bothered. I'm sure you appreciate others not talking on their phones while you are trying to enjoy your night out. If you go downstairs I believe you can find some privacy. When you return I'll see to it that you have a fresh ..." Jim glanced at the table, "Budweiser waiting for you."

The man excused himself and the restaurant returned to the new Saturday night bustle, Jim's dream coming true.

Ruth insisted on sitting inside by the fire. She sat in a chair that presented her to the customers like the thrown of a queen greeting her subjects. Jim tried to coax her to a table for dinner but she insisted on eating by the fire. She had found her spot.

As the night wound down and Joey drove Ruth home, Jim basked in the empty, well-used restaurant. He sipped on a margarita of his own concoction; no mix, just fresh lime, Meyer lemon juice, a splash of Grand Marnier and the best reposado tequila he could buy from his importer.

Nancy appeared in her street clothes and was walking out the door when Jim caught up with her. "Let me walk you to your car, Nancy."

"Sure, Doc, you never know who is lurking on the deserted streets of Zanesville."

"I wanted to talk to you about the little altercation on the balcony this evening."

"That guy was a jerk. I was trying to be as nice as possible."

"Yes, I know you were and I really appreciate your professional attitude. I think I have an idea about how to make this sort of confrontation easier in the future."

As they reached Nancy's car, Carla's car appeared at the lower end of the street and slowed to a stop, just out of view and hearing range of Nancy and Jim.

Nancy leaned against the car, "I'm all ears."

Jim leaned in to her, not wanting to speak too loudly. "In my home in Lexington, my crazy wife built a detail under the stairs that I rather liked. She built a phone booth. I think that's a fantastic idea here. I'll try to find a bank of phone booths for the basement. They won't have phones in them, but they will be old fashioned booths where customers can enjoy their cell phone calls in privacy, and the novelty should attract them, without a scene like we had to experience this evening. What do you think?"

Nancy wrapped her arms around his neck with joy and kissed him on the cheek, "You're a genius, Doctor Jim."

Jim registered a slight tinge of affection, but ignored it. "Well, Madeline was the actual genius. I just happen to have a good memory."

Nancy got into her car and, with a tap on the door from Jim, drove away. And down the street, so did Carla.

The Columbus Dispatch slammed against the screen door and startled Jim awake. He recognized that sound of the Sunday newspaper landing on the porch, giving him some impetus to get up and seize the day. It was his first Sunday off in months and he was determined to enjoy it.

The coffee was dripping and the cushions were cleaned and situated just so on his screened-in porch, ready for a leisurely morning. He was even considering a bloody mary. He opened the front door to retrieve the morning paper and, instead of the paper stood a disheveled Carla with a scowl on her face and his paper in her hand. Jim jumped at the surprise. "Carla! There you are. I've tried to call and stopped by several times."

As Jim leaned in for a hug, she pushed past. "Where have I been? Where have you been?"

Jim followed her into the living room. "Um, Mexico? Didn't you get my letters?"

"Yeah, I got your letters. Where have you been since you've been back? With that waitress?"

"Wait, what? I was at the restaurant. I don't know if you heard, but it didn't fare well while I was away."

"And you just expect me to wait around while you go off for months? What sort of woman do you think I am? I have responsibilities. I have KIDS!"

Gently, Jim, "Carla, please. Sit down. I think we need to talk."

"Talk about what? The waitress."

"Look, I don't know what you are talking about."

"I saw you with her."

Jim raised his voice, possibly for the first time in twenty years. "I don't give a damn ..."

Carla stood up, threatened.

"I'm sorry. I don't really know what you are talking about regarding Ms. Andrews, but that is NOT what I want to talk to you about, exactly. You were showing signs of jealousy before the holidays and I let it go. But, I just moved back here and I have a failing restaurant and an old, dramatic mother and an even more dramatic sister, who I never see for some reason, and I really, really do not need any more drama in my life right now. I hope you understand. Now, if you don't mind, I'm going to enjoy this beautiful Sunday morning on my porch, with my paper and my coffee and not you."

Carla began to cry, "You're dumping me? I can't believe this. I do it every time."

"Carla, stop. I know you have an issue with this, but right now, it's going to have to remain your issue. I'm sorry. I enjoyed your company, but ..."

"But what? But what?"

Jim opened the door for her, "But nothing. Goodbye, Carla."

Jim spent Sunday afternoon driving around the countryside looking for antique and junk shops. The sun was bright and warm. The wafts of fresh rain fallen on concrete reminded him of his childhood. The scent always made him nostalgic, and reinvigorated his dreams. He visited many of the old haunts that his mother used to drag him to when he was young. Surprisingly, most of them were still there. He found several interesting bits and pieces of pottery and decorative junk. But the hunt for phone booths was a cold trail.

On his way home he drove down the old creamery road and nearly missed it. He skidded to a stop and reversed. A rusty sign nailed to a telephone pole:

CPR RECLAMATION
YOU THROW IT OUT WE BRING IT BACK TO LIFE
WE SPECIALIZE IN ARCHEKSURE PIECES FROM
OLD BUILDINGS

He didn't know that such a place existed in Zanesville. He always wondered what happened to all of the architectural artifacts that gave so much character to the old buildings in the downtown area, long since torn down to make room for parking lots and banks. As he drove down the long, gravel road—following the misspelled signs—he was captivated by the large objects that popped out of the woods: defunct gas pumps, a Texaco sign, single letters the size of his car. The twisting road led to a clearing so crowded with giant antiques, cars, signs and buildings that he was lost in the immensity. The only other time Jim had seen such a plethora of architectural objects was in the west of England at a reclaim yard that stretched the length of a football field.

Carl Priestly appeared from behind a truck just as Jim climbed out of his car. He wore a MAC truck hat and overalls, barely covering his bulging belly. His boots were covered in mud and the stench of cheap cigar and dog shit preceded him.

"May I help you, sir?"

Jim was startled out of his junkyard trance. "Hello there. Is this your place?"

"Yes sir, been here since '82."

"I'm Jim ..."

"Langley, I know ya. Carl Priestly. We were in third grade together. I sat behind you."

"Wow. Hi, Carl, I didn't recognize ..."

"Yeah, that's alright." He raised his cap and rubbed his hairless head. "Went bald in the army, then married a good cook. Hell, I don't recognize me half the time."

They shook hands, "Great to see you. If you didn't know, I opened a restaurant in the old Nicholson building downtown. I don't know if you can help me, but I'm looking for something pretty specific."

"Well, Jim, I got a shit ton of pretty specific. I've been hauling crap out of buildings all around Ohio for thirty some odd years. What, specifically, are you looking for?"

"A phone booth, actually, phone booths. I'd love something ..."

Carl turned and walked away without a word. He took giant strides, nearly running. Jim struggled to keep up through the mud. Carl stopped suddenly, turned and smiled a shit-eating grin. He reached up and grasped the top corner of an army surplus tarp. With one swoop, he uncovered a bank of phone booths, circa 1935. "Something like this?"

Jim stood in front of his prize; stunned at their perfection.

Carl, "Recognize these?"

"Umm, no. Should I?"

"They're out of the lobby of the Zane Hotel. You probably got your hair cut at the barber shop right next to 'em."

"I'll be damned, I did indeed. I don't think I ever noticed them. They look like they are in perfect shape."

"Well, the phones got taken out by the telephone company. They owned all the phones back then. This was actually the first thing I ever hauled out here. The hotel got torn down the year I set up shop and I bought truckloads. This is the only thing I couldn't sell. Who the hell wants a bunch of phone booths?"

"I do. And I don't care about the phones. People have their own these days. What do you want for them?"

"Four-hundred. That's a hundred a piece."

"Will you deliver them?"

"Sure. I'll even clean them up a bit for ya."

With an enthusiastic shake, "Deal!"

Spring was beautiful in the restaurant. The balcony doors were open nearly every night. On evenings with rain, the awnings kept the tables dry and the faint scent of the river was just enough to give an ambience, without reeking like a fish boat. Unfortunately, the patrons were few and shrinking.

On the first day of summer, Ruth showed up unannounced. Daughter Jackie accompanied her and they sat in Ruth's favorite seat, next to the fireplace. At 92, the night on the balcony was too cool, and the comfort and view from the chair near the fire was her catbird seat.

Not long after Ruth's arrival, the restaurant experienced a noticeable uptick in attendees. Each seemed to greet Ruth when they came in. Some lingered over a cocktail or glass of wine with her, and none missed a final goodbye. Ruth never hesitated to mention the nightly special or make a gentle reminder about the no cell phone policy and point out the charming bank of phone booths in the basement. Jim didn't question the surge in customers—nothing he was doing could coax them in the door—so if Ruth was a secret weapon, why did she wait until summer to deliver such a pleasant invasion?

Ruth continued her regular visits, sometimes with Jackie, and often driven by Joey, her new part-time chauffeur. Each evening that Ruth appeared so did a few new customers. Jim was pleased for the business but perplexed by her attraction. Her roots must run much deeper than Jim had ever imagined.

Unfortunately, the Ruth magnet was short lived. By the end of summer she still attended regularly, enjoying the free food and wine, but the entourage seemed to dwindle. She would nod and wave to the occasional customer—she had become accustomed to her new roll, not unlike a Walmart greeter—but was no longer the influential force in filling the restaurant.

By the end of August the restaurant was dead. Some nights Ruth was the only customer. No matter how Jim had prepared for such poor business, it was still disappointing. By fall he had reinstituted "International Night" on Saturdays. The first night featured the Vietnamese noodle dish Pho. Twenty people came to the Pho night and, every single person ordered and hated the Pho. Jim spent the first part of the evening explaining how to pronounce 'fu' as in fudge, and the second part of the evening having the meal returned, always with the witty retort, "What the Pho is this?"

Ruth stayed that whole night, most likely amused by the disastrous Vietnamese dish. Jim volunteered to drive her home at the end of the evening.

On their drive home, Ruth, "You should have just asked me. I could have told you that these people wouldn't eat anything from Vietnam. Jim, they may not be worldly, but they remember Vietnam and they really remember Kent State. They don't want to be reminded. They may have made fun of the food, but the reason that they didn't like it was that it reminded them of unpleasant times around here. Don't underestimate these folks, Jim."

He drove her home in silence. It had been a long time since his mother gave him a dressing down and was right. He just took it.

After he dropped Ruth off, his phone rang. The caller ID said "Nurse Carla." He had broken up with her, but was both curious and a little worried, given the lateness of the hour.

"Hello. Carla? What's wrong?"

"Doctor Jim, I'm sorry to call you so late but you were the only person I know that would still be up and not on a shift."

"I am. I just dropped Ruth off at her house. What do you need?"

"My car broke down on Military Road and I can't get a tow truck. Could you come pick me up?"

"I'll be right there. Hang tight."

Jim drove the two miles out a pitch black and hilly Military Road, past the Country Club and the cemetery where his brother and father were buried. He came across Carla's car at the crest of the hill, pulled off the side of the road into a field, emergency lights flashing.

She jumped into his car and hugged him. "Thank you so much for coming to my rescue."

"You are quite welcome. Do you just want to leave it here?"

"Yeah, I'll get Dale to come get it tomorrow. It's far enough off the road that nobody will care."

They drove to the bottom of Military and stopped on the right side of the road.

Carla, "You should go left."

"Too late."

Jim had been gone for a long time but still knew his way around most of the town. This particular area was where he spent a lot of time when he was young and in love. He had a special reason to take the slightly more scenic route. The first time he made love to a girl was in the parking lot of the bar just across from the next intersection. Along with his brother and father's graves, this was a regular spot for him to drive by to spark those fond memories.

The road sloped down and around into a dip, before coming to the stop sign at Newark Road. As they turned the corner, bright spinning lights and a horrendous crash hit right in front of them. They pulled cautiously to a stop as two cars splayed out across the intersection, one upside down and spinning on it's roof like a child's top and the other wedged in the muddy ditch, radio blasting and blinker incessantly flashing.

They both jumped from the car. Jim grabbed his phone, and succinctly gave instructions to 911 as he waved Carla across to the upside down car. He held his hand over the receiver and, "Be careful, watch out for cars."

Carla rolled her eyes. She had been an ER nurse for many years before transferring upstairs. She had done her share of EMT ride-alongs. She did look both ways as she was assessing the damage. The windshield was shattered and it looked like the passenger was protruding through the broken glass. She went to her first. She felt and found no pulse. She quickly moved to the other side where she heard moaning from the driver. As she got to him, he slumped over the wheel.

Jim leaped into the muddy ditch. He ran into the light, and then around the car into the dark ditch. He felt his way around the car until his eyes adjusted. As far as he could tell there were no passengers in the car. He climbed up the hill and found the driver sitting behind the wheel, conscious but in shock. Jim reached in and the driver flailed about, surprised by the sudden hand. The driver managed to turn the radio off.

Jim, "Are you alright? Can you hear me? I'm here to help."

The driver was staring straight ahead, hands by his side. He slurred his words, "I can hear ya. I'm okay. Is there anybody hurt?"

"I don't know yet. Sit right there. The ambulance will be here soon. Are you sure you aren't hurt?"

"I'm not hurt. I better go."

Jim reached in without thinking and turned the car off and retained the keys. "You are not going anywhere. You may be hurt and don't know it."

Jim suspected that he wasn't hurt, but he sure was drunk. "I'll be right back."

Jim crossed the road. Carla had pulled the driver from the car and was administering mouth to mouth alternating with chest compressions. As Jim knelt down, she found a pulse. The driver's eyes opened.

Carla, "You're going to be all right. There is an ambulance on its way."

As if on cue, flashing lights appeared, cresting the hill in the distance. There was a fire station out near Dillon Lake, less than five minutes away. Jim stood up and crossed the road to check on his drunken patient. He looked back at Carla, holding the driver's hand. He stopped for a moment, perplexed at his arousal.

He reached the drunken driver as he was trying to open his door. Jim opened the door and slammed it shut. "You are staying put, pal." Jim looked at him in the eyes. "Hey, weren't you at the restaurant tonight?"

The driver smiled sheepishly and, "What the pho."

Jim and Carla sat in silence as he drove them home. Both had been in many harrowing emergencies, but rarely did they happen so unexpectedly. Both were so well-trained that their responses were automatic. What just happened? Jim thought. And what just happened with her?

He turned onto Sunset headed to Carla's house. She, "I can't go home yet. Too much adrenaline."

"I agree. Would you like to come over for a drink?"

"Yes, please."

Just inside the door, Jim pinned Carla against the wall leading upstairs. He kissed her passionately and she didn't resist. With each step up the stairs they kissed, tossed a coat, unbuttoned a blouse. They fell onto the bed and finished the disrobing. Jim buried his head deep into her loins. She held on to his hair with one hand and squeezed a handful of sheet with the other. She pulled him up and into her with one lustful move. They made love with more passion than either could remember. They were so committed to this fleeting moment that any playful position changing or teasing was out of the question. The sex was slow, hard and constant. Jim had never lasted so long. He only paused for her orgasms, whose number he lost count. He finally, forcefully came inside her. It was as if he had let go of everything in his life, had admitted to himself that this was what he needed–a self satisfying romp in the hay with someone who he had just witnessed save a life. This was the ultimate, after all. He shuttered when he dared to think that it was like having sex with himself.

They lay motionless for an hour. Carla eventually slid off the rumpled bed and gathered her clothes. Jim did not move. She dressed and kissed him on the cheek.

"That was fun," Carla whispered. With that she slid down the stairs and out the front door.

The following weeks were worse than the end of summer. Jim attempted another International Night with Indian curry. A few people showed up but no one trusted the curry.

The gross receipts for the year were looking really bleak. The total did not make expenses, let alone payroll. He had expected to be out of pocket, but there were a few glimmers of hope along the way, just enough to tease him into thinking that he might actually have a real restaurant. He consoled himself in the thought that most restaurants operate at a deficit the first year, or so he had been told. He knew that he really didn't know the slightest thing about making a success of a restaurant, and he began to wonder if he knew the slightest thing about making a success of a life.

He saw Carla in passing, but, other than a friendly wave and a yell out her car window, "Thanks for rescuing me the other night," there was no rekindling any relationship. Jim began to wonder if it wasn't all a dream.

As Jim and staff prepared the restaurant for the holidays, a young man with a flat top and trimmed sideburns walked into the entry. He wore a sheriff's uniform and clasped his hat in both hands in front of him. "I'm here to see Dr. James Langley," he said with newfound authority.

"I'm Doctor Langley. How can I help you?"

"I'm here to serve you with this subpoena." The young sheriff handed Jim an envelope and replaced his hat, tipping it slightly, "Good day."

Jim looked at the envelope then looked at Buddy and

Nancy, who stared back.

Buddy, "What is that?"

Jim slowly pried open the envelope. "No idea. I can't imagine that it's good news."

Jim unfolded the paperwork and read slowly, not believing his eyes. "We're being sued!"

The lawsuit seemed to set the tone for the holidays. The drunk driver of the car in the accident claimed that he had been drinking at The Five-Year Plan before the accident, and the driver of the other car was suing Jim and the restaurant for negligence and wrongful death of his wife, who was the passenger in the upside down car. The same guy who's life had been saved by Carla.

The Christmas reservations were just about as bleak. They had a small office party booked in on the Monday before Christmas where, instead of bonuses, the boss handed out pink slips and, one by one, the guests filed out the door without even drowning their sorrows.

Christmas was on a Sunday and Jim decided to stay open. Five people made reservations and only two came.

He was getting nervous about New Year's Eve. There were no reservations and he heard that the Country Club had booked a live band for this year's celebration. He hastily took out ads on the radio, television and the newspaper. Calling friends and friends of friends to no avail, he went through his reservation book and called the numbers taken with reservations—a big no-no in restaurant etiquette. Nobody was coming.

New Year's Eve was a bitter cold night with a star filled sky and a raging fire. The restaurant was decorated, warm, delightful and empty. Jim incessantly poked his head out the door until the constant draft from the frigid wind penetrated the kitchen staff. Buddy finally insisted that Jim relax and leave the damn door shut.

The evening wore on. Ruth didn't even show up. Jim sat staring at the river, trying to figure out what to do next. There must be something he could do to fill this place.

After midnight had come and gone Jim gathered the staff, most of which were twitching to leave. "Buddy, go down and grab that magnum of Crystal from the cellar, will you please?"

The staff all sat around the fireplace as Jim poured each a glass of grand cru from the large bottle. A year of training had most excited to taste the incomparable champagne. Jim had shared many a bottle from the cellar, so they would be familiar with the extensive wine list (most of which had not moved) but never had they had Crystal. They had only heard tales from rap videos about the fine bubbly.

Jim raised his glass, "To a fine year and a finer year two."

Everyone looked discouraged, but enjoyed the dancing effervescence on their noses. Buddy, "I'll drink to a better new year. Couldn't be worse than this one!"

Jim's eyes twinkled and he smiled, "Don't worry, folks, I've got an idea."

As the staff joked and laughed about another one of Jim's ideas, he slipped downstairs and shut himself in the last phone booth. He called Terek.

"Terek, Happy New Year. I have a question for you. A favor, actually."

9

Jim slept and fretted all New Year's Day. It was hard to believe that having no customers was as exhausting as having a full house. The appointment with Bob Brewer, his attorney, was coming up on Tuesday and he was fretting about that. Usually lawsuits didn't faze him. As a doctor of high-profile patients he routinely faced threats from lawyers. Plus, he was married to a powerful lawyer and heard frivolous lawsuit stories all of the time. This was uncharted territory though and, with no such thing as restaurant malpractice insurance and not knowing the ins and outs of Ohio law, he was adrift. Bob had been a friend since they were young kids and Jim knew he could trust him. He better be able to trust him, because Jim felt completely out of his depth.

On Tuesday morning Jim drove downtown. He got a call from Nancy at the restaurant with some good news.

Nancy, "Jim, you will never believe this. We just got a call for a reservation for 42 for lunch on Friday. Forty-fuck-ing-two!"

Jim smiled, "A busload?"

"How did you know? Yes, it's a tour bus passing through from Philadelphia."

A call clicked in to Jim's phone. "Nancy, I'll call you back. Hello?"

A frantic Jackie was on the phone, "Jim, mom had a stroke. Meet me at the hospital."

"Jackie? Jackie? Shit!"

Jim did a u-turn on Maple and headed out toward the hospital.

Jackie was in the ER waiting room when Jim arrived. He walked straight toward the ER double doors, ignoring Jackie.

She yelled across the waiting room, "She's having a CAT scan."

Jim stopped and walked to her, slowing his gait. "What the hell happened?"

"She said she didn't feel well on New Year's Eve and yesterday said she had a headache. I stopped to check on her this morning and she was lying on the couch. She didn't know who I was at first and was disoriented. I called 911. The paramedics thought she had a stroke."

"Oh Christ, a kid driving an ambulance made a diagnosis that you relayed. For fuck sake, Jackie."

Jackie started to cry. "It's just what he said. I was scared. I'm sorry."

Jim sat next to her and put his arm around her shoulder. "No, no, I'm sorry. I was being harsh. Where is Miller? Is he here?"

"Doctor Miller is with her. He called the radiologist

to make sure he was standing by to read the results right away."

Jim pulled his phone out and called Jeff Miller. "Miller, how is she?"

"Hi Jim. Where are you?"

"In the ER."

"I'll be right there."

Doctor Jeffrey Miller walked through the double doors at the far end of the pink waiting room. "Ah, there you are."

They embraced. "How is she, Jeff?"

"She's fine. We saw three very small lesions at the base of her skull. Don't know how long they have been there or if they caused her little episode. She said she never lost consciousness but complained about the back of her head. I'd like to check her in to just keep an eye on her for a few days. I would hate for one of these to rupture. It could be minutes..."

Jim knew the vulnerability of brain aneurisms and did not want to subject Jackie to the mortal details. "Yes, of course. I'll talk her into it. She hates hospitals but I'll get her to stay."

Jackie piped in, "No, I'll get her to stay. I'll get the water-works goin' and she won't say no."

Later that night Jim went to visit Ruth in her room. Surprisingly, she was calm and requesting dinner from an orderly. She got a little surly when they wouldn't bring her a glass of wine, but that was the only hiccup.

"Hi, Mom. How do you feel?"

"What on earth did you do to that nice nurse? She was in here earlier and was nice as can be until I mentioned you. Then she was the ice queen."

"We broke up. How are you?

"I'm fine. When can I get the hell out of this god-forsaken place? You know I hate it here."

"I'm aware of your distain for the institution that has been my professional world for most of my life, and quite frankly, I don't blame you."

"Yeah, whatever. So when?"

Jim knew that he couldn't bullshit Ruth. He fell back on his brutally honest approach. "The CAT scan revealed three small lesions at the base of your skull. They may be scaring from some mini-strokes. It's hard to tell how long they've been there, so Miller wants for you to stay for a few days just in case one decides to go north and try and take you out."

"Jesus, Jim. Good thing you got out of this business. Your bedside manner is atrocious."

Jim laughed. He knew that she understood exactly what he said and was doing what all Langleys do when they worry: make jokes. "Get some rest."

He walked out of the room toward the nurse's station where Carla sat, eating a salad and staring at a computer screen. She sensed his presence. Jim, "Nurse Ratchet."

"Doctor Feelgood."

"I see we are on speaking terms. Take care of the good witch, will you please."

"Anything you say, Doctor Jim."

"And thanks."

"For what."

"You know. For taking care of her." He smiled wryly and walked away.

Bob Brewer's office was on the top floor of the same building as David Weinstein's office. These professional types don't have much imagination, thought Jim. He sat in the waiting room, in a row of the same boring tweed chairs and table full of the same sports and fashion magazines as in David's office.

Bob Brewer came in the front door with brief case in hand, wearing a tan trench coat, a dark brown, wide brimmed hat and a smirk that Jim remembered since they were in grade school. With faux formality, "Doctor Langley. Kind of you to bless us with your presence."

Jim stood, offered his hand then awkwardly embraced his old friend. "Sorry about the other day. Ruth had a mild stroke and you got upstaged. How the hell are you, Bob?"

Bob lead Jim through the inner doors and back a non-descript hallway, past the open door of a paneled law library (right out of a television show set) and back to his "corner" office. The corner of Fourth and Main Street was not exactly midtown Manhattan. The view was of the beautiful and well-maintained turn of the century courthouse and not much else. Bob sat behind his giant mahogany desk in a tall, ostentatious desk chair, all chosen for the drama and expensive feel. Jim was certain that Bob wanted his poor and uneducated clients to think they were getting the royal treatment, and the several hundred dollar an hour invoice would seem somehow worth it.

Jim wasted no time, "Did you look at this suit, Bob?"

"Coffee?"

"Sure. Black, please."

Bob pressed an old-fashioned intercom button on his multi-line phone and ordered two coffees from an unseen secretary. "Yep. I had a gander at it. Pretty standard stuff around here. A whiff of deep pockets and lawyers get involved."

"You have to help me here, Bob. I was married to a lawyer but have no experience with this sort of thing. Do they have a case?"

"That depends."

"On what?"

"On whether they can prove that your establishment was negligent in this man's intoxication. It's pretty hard to prove and we will dig up stuff to discredit this character."

"But could they win?"

"Possible. But I'll take care of you. Even if they win, your liability insurance should take care of most of it."

Jim was getting a little worried and screeched, "Most of it?"

"Calm down, Jim. If the jury decides to add punitive numbers then it could get a little pricey, but I wouldn't worry about that."

"Of course you wouldn't worry about that. It's not your money."

"Look, I've had several of these over the years. We will figure this out. It's like a puzzle. Remember when I played the detective in our high school show. It'll be just like that. It'll be fun."

"For fuck sake, Bob. Fun?"

"Yeah, fun. Let me see what's what. Give me a call in a couple of weeks. It might take some time. Our first court date isn't until April. These civil things move really slow around here."

"Okay, great. Thanks, Bob. Sorry for snapping."

"Don't worry, Buddy. It'll be fun. Let me ask you a couple of questions then you can go. Do you remember seeing …" Bob thumbed through the file on his desk, "James Blue, the driver?"

"Yes. And I saw him in the wreck."

"Was he at your restaurant that night?"

"Yes, with a young woman. I didn't really notice him. She was drinking milk."

"Milk? Why do you say that?"

"Not too many people order milk. I saw it going to their table and remembered it. I probably wouldn't have even noticed them otherwise. Well, and she didn't send the Pho back. I remember that too. She was the only one the whole night."

"Pho?"

"We were having International Night, and I thought Pho would be good. It was a disaster."

"Isn't that Vietnamese?"

"Yes. I know. Ruth already lectured me."

"So, did you see them leave?"

"Yes."

"Were they together?"

"Yes. I think so. Yes, they were. She was sort of helping him."

"What do you mean, helping him?"

"He walked with a limp and she held his arm as they walked out."

"I see. Thanks. I think that's all I need for now."

Jim got up to leave without having his coffee. "Could you please stop saying that it's going to be fun? Please?"

"Yep. No worries. It's going to be … fine. How's that?"

"Better. Talk to you soon."

Ruth stayed in the hospital for three days and showed no signs of deterioration. Her memory was tested and retested, only to her annoyance, with no sign of damage. Her vitals were rock steady and an additional CAT scan revealed nothing new.

On his way to the hospital, Jim swerved into a used car lot on Maple Avenue when a rare sight caught his eye. A 1975 Cadillac stretch limo in immaculate shape was parked next to the office. It must have just arrived. The paint was spotless, the interior looked brand-new. Somebody must have restored it. After walking around the car several times, not believing his eyes, a sales person appeared from behind the office. He wore a plaid sport coat like Jim sold when he worked in a men's clothing store in the 70's. He smelled of English Leather and Marlboros. The car, the jacket and the salesman were frozen in time. Only in Zanesville, Jim thought.

"It's a beauty, idn't it? Name's Dick Brady but my friends call me Rusty. In the market for a limo?"

"Nice to meet you. This is an interesting car. It looks brand new. How is that possible? Is it a restoration?"

"Nah, I just came across it last week. The story goes this rich old lady up in Coshocton bought it brand new when her husband died. She never drove and wanted to be chauffeured around. She lived out on a farm and got a local kid to drive her. She kept it in the barn all covered up. People said they remember seeing her riding around in this thing. Then, about three months after her husband kicked she did too. I guess her kids rented the house out and never bothered to clear out the barn. They lived down in Florida and just came up for the funeral. A family lived in that house until a few months ago. Then last week the kids came up to sell the house and found this beauty in the barn. They called me and I took it off their hands. Dusty, but perfect other than a few gaskets, belts and rubber parts. I had them all replaced. It runs like a top. Want to give it a spin?"

"That's quite a tale, Rusty. What do you want for it?"

"Seein' that it's next to brand new, I'm gonna have to ask 52 for it."

"Fifty-two hundred?"

Rusty chuckled, "Thousand. Fifty-two thousand."

Jim chuckled, "I may not know much about cars but I suspect you're a little high. I tell you what, I'm going to have a friend come have a look then we can talk about price. Deal?"

"You can have your friend come look at it, but I can't guarantee that somebody else won't buy it. It's going up on E-bay tomorrow."

"Okay, Rusty. I'll get my friend out here this afternoon."

On his way to the hospital Jim called David Weinstein. Troy Nicholson was the best person in town to evaluate this car, but Jim didn't know him well enough to ask this favor. If he could get David to take the car to him, he was sure that Troy could have a look and know a fair market value for this odd vehicle.

Carla was waiting in the pickup area with Ruth in a wheel chair when Jim pulled up. This was such a stark contrast from her last visit to, and escape from, the hospital. As easy as it made his life, he worried that his mother was starting to lose her biting edge.

Ruth growled, "It's about damn time. We've been sitting here for an hour. Where the hell have you been?"

Maybe she wasn't losing her edge after all, Jim thought. Standing behind Ruth, Carla held up five fingers. Jim smiled, "Thank you, Nurse Carla for taking such good care of my mother. Say thank you, Mother."

Ruth pushed herself out of the wheelchair and turned toward Carla, "Don't listen to that bullshit. Thank you, my dear. We will see you soon, I hope. Even if it isn't with Mr. Charm here."

"That's Doctor Charm to you, Mother." He smiled at Carla. "Thanks again."

David Weinstein drove out to Rusty's Used Cars as requested and feigned interest in the limo. He took it for a test drive straight to Troy's dealership. A mechanic put it through a few diagnostics, and Troy showed David several similar vehicles on the Internet. David thanked Troy and drove off. He called Jim. "Yes, Troy says that it is in original, really great shape. He also showed me some comparative prices and it is worth quite a lot of money, but he also knows that Rusty paid $7,500 for it. He left the receipt in the glove compartment. He bought it from an auction in Canton. The story may or may not be true, but it has never been wrecked and, as far as Troy's mechanic can tell, those are original miles. The thing is practically brand new."

Jim was pleased. "Offer him $10,000 for it."

"He'll never go for it."

"Yes, I know. But when I come back and offer him 15 after I show him the receipt in the glove compartment, the well will have been primed."

"That's pretty sly for a doctor. I'm on it."

The Five-Year Plan was empty, but bustling. The tour bus had just come and gone and the staff was cleaning up. The restaurant is rarely that full, and when they come all at once, it's hard to keep up with all of the bussing and cleaning. Jim stood in the kitchen talking to Buddy. "I think I'm going to buy a limo."

Buddy was used to Jim saying things that nobody in Zanesville had ever heard. But this was even more peculiar than usual. "A lim-what?"

"A 1975 Cadillac stretch limousine."

"That seems a little ostentatious for driving around here."

"It's not for me to drive. It's for the restaurant. I want to offer free limo service to our customers. No more drunk drivers leaving here, and it'll be a special extra to attract patrons. What do you think?"

"As usual, I think you're nuts. But I also think that's well established, so it sounds great. Who's going to limo it?"

"Chauffer. That's what I wanted to talk to you about. What about Joey?"

"Joey has a job. And he's not a chauffer, whatever that means."

"I looked into it. There's a class in Columbus that he takes before he can take a test for a commercial livery license. That's what it's called. I'll pay for it. And it won't interfere with his work. It will only be for a few nights a week and I can't imagine that he wouldn't like the extra money."

"I suppose the money would be nice. You're gonna have to ask him yourself."

Nancy bounced up the stairs and into the kitchen. "Hey Doctor Jim, there's a fancy car in the downstairs parking lot."

Jim grabbed Nancy by the hand and led her back down the stairs and out the back door. David was standing by the limo with a smug smile on his face, dangling the keys in front of his face.

"How long have you had it out? Isn't Rusty wondering where you are?"

"Nope. I offered him 10, like you said. He countered with 12 -5 and I bought it. You owe me 12,500 and you better write me a check today. I'm not sure the one I wrote to Rusty will go through."

"You're not sure? You're a goddamned accountant."

"Yes, but I'm not a wealthy goddamned accountant."

"Wow, he took 12-5. I guess he must have had an alimony payment coming up. I bet he did a little Googling after I left and knew he was never going to get a big payday, especially around here. Hang on, let me get you a check."

Jim came back a few minutes later with a check and his coat. "Nancy, want to go for a ride in our new limo?"

Nancy grinned a double entendre. "Sounds like fun. Let me get my coat."

Jim and Nancy dropped David off at Rusty's to pick up his car and drove down Linden Avenue toward the Y-Bridge. Jim turned into a little street that dead-ended into a park. He jumped out and knocked on the door of a small, white house with a tidy yard and a dog barking at the window. Joey answered the door.

"Hi Doctor Jim. What's up?"

"I thought you might want to take it for a spin." Jim backed up with a grand gesture, revealing the limo parked in front of the house.

"Holy cow. Sure!"

Jim tossed him the keys and skipped back to the car. He waved Nancy to the back seat. "Shall we?"

Nancy and Jim sat in the way back as Joey carefully adjusted the seat and mirrors and gingerly turned around. "Where to, boss?"

"Just drive around and get used to the feel. I'd avoid the freeway for now, but anywhere else is fine."

Nancy was playing with the buttons on the ceiling. She shut the privacy window and raised her eyebrows, indicating to Jim that they were alone and she was definitely interested. Jim smiled and stretched out, casually placing his arm around her. "I could get used to this."

Nancy rested her hand on his thigh and Jim immediately stiffened, everywhere.

"Do you think you should be doing that?"

"What?" She slid her hand up his leg, cupping his erect penis. "I probably shouldn't do this either." Like a magician, she made his penis appear, then disappear as she slid her head over it.

Jim pressed the intercom button, "Drive on out Linden Avenue, Joey. You probably shouldn't drive in traffic yet. I'll let you know when to turn around."

Jim dated Nancy a few times after the limo incident. When she wasn't satisfying him sexually, which she did quite often and quite well, she was either talking about work, people at work or other people that Jim didn't know. Any attempt at conversation about literature, politics or travel would be met with crying, rage or baffling statements. She was not interested in reading and thought Jim was insulting her anytime he brought it up, hence the crying. Maybe a blowjob wasn't the best way to start a relationship, Jim thought.

She was very good at her job, and that was more important to Jim than a relationship or the great sex. When he told her that they should stop seeing one another because they worked together and he didn't want anything to spoil that, he meant it. Fortunately, an important call came just as he was breaking it off.

Jim answered it, "Yes, this is Doctor Langley. Oh, I see. It must be mango season."

10

After 22 hours of flying, Jim stepped off a Lear commercial jet at the airport in Juba, South Sudan. It was a steaming hot afternoon and the tarmac was sticky. The runways were all concrete in this part of the world, so landing and taxiing were safe, but the planes stopped just short of the tarmac that connected the stretch between the landing strip and the gates. The midday heat made it too risky to drive heavy aircraft onto the softened blacktop.

Jim was accompanied by a dozen other MSF doctors and nurses, coming to bolster the staff at Aweil Community Hospital. These yearly reinforcements were timed to coincide with the mango season. Every year, young boys would climb high in the mango trees to pick the ripest mangos, a lucrative cash crop in this most destitute part of Africa.

Inevitably, many of the agile boys would lose their footing and come plummeting to the ground, nearly always fracturing an appendage. Rarely were the injuries more serious than contusions and breaks. The falls didn't seem to lessen the effort, as there were many repeat visitors to the ER, evidently adept at climbing and tumbling out of these dense fruit trees.

There were two helicopter airlifts scheduled for early the next morning. The hospital was about an hour north by air, and given the political instability and the condition of the roads, MSF deemed airlift the only safe way for staff to travel. Jim detested helicopters, but preferred an hour of white-knuckle fear to ten hours of rough roads and the possibility of a rebel execution.

This was Jim's second visit to the region so he was familiar with the territory and the cuisine. The area was often food insecure, depending on the military stability. It varied widely from month to month and sometimes from day to day and was dependent on what supplies could get through. Much of the staples had to be imported, although these were a resourceful people and would always find a way to feed a stranger. The people that ran the restaurants were friendly, clean and loved to cook and create delicious food out of whatever they had available. Their cuisine was similar to Ethiopia, ironically also known for both starvation and superb food.

Jim and his cohorts checked in to the airport hotel; took naps and showers, and waited for the temperature to drop. The hotel had few amenities, but, as Jim liked to point out, it had the two most important ones: showers and beer. The local beer tasted like licking the bottom of an ashtray when warm, but ice cold it was the most delicious and thirst-quenching beverage ever. The MSF group gathered one by one around plastic tables at the bar; watched the sunset over the town, which glowed orange in the steamy last rays of daylight; and shared stories of past adventures, while downing beer after beer.

Jim sat with Raul, a doctor from Barcelona whom he had met in passing in far-flung airports and hospital corridors. The waiter delivered a tray full of cold beer as a beautiful woman approached their table.

She, "Puis-je prendre ce siege?"

Jim pulled a cheap plastic chair back and gestured, "S'il vous plait asseyez vous."

"Do you speak eng-lish?"

Jim smiled sheepishly, "Etes-vous de Paris? Only Parisians spot the accent."

"Your French is no, quite good."

"I'm Jim and this is Raul."

"Nice to meet you. May I have a beer? Oh, I am Sophie. Doctor Sophie Miller."

Sophie was a slender, immaculately dressed five foot nine brunette with sky blue eyes and an aura of Chanel No 5. Somehow her Hermes scarf didn't seem suffocating in the 90-degree evening. The whole bar was smitten.

Jim slid her a cold beer from the tray in the center of the table. "Is this your first MSF outing?"

"No, my father was one of the men who started it. I did staff work while still in medical school and my first mission the summer after my residency."

"Your father was a doctor?"

"No, he was a journalist. He covered Biafra war and they started MSF with some doctors just after. He was a good man."

Raul, "I'll drink to that." He held up his beer to the table of MSF volunteers and toasted. "Are you hungry? They're bringing in some food in a few minutes."

Jim answered while looking directly at Sophie, "I'm going out. I know of a little place across the street that is going to be way better than Sudan take away or hotel food."

Sophie, "May I join you?"

"By all means." Jim stood and offered her his arm.

Raul, "Be careful out there and don't go too far. It's pretty dangerous these days."

Sophie looked at Jim.

"Don't worry, we're just going down the block."

They excused themselves and flapped across the lino-leum-floored lobby. Once outside, they noticed that there were no streetlights and the only illumination came from inside a few of the houses and shops. Jim led Sophie around the corner and spotted soldiers walking toward them in the distance. He gently pushed her into a doorway, turning his back to the street.

He whispered, "Don't say anything and play along," and began kissing her. He continued until the soldiers passed.

"What was that?" Sophie asked, not the least bit put off by the sudden gesture.

"I'm so sorry about that. I've heard that soldiers will ignore white people if they are engaged in amorous entan-glement. I guess it must be what so many NGOs seem to get up to in these parts. Whatever it is, they leave you alone."

She smiled, "I'll have to remember that."

Jim offered her his arm and they walked down the street. They stopped in front of a hole in the ground between two single story shacks. "This is it, or was it. I'm sure this was the spot. Where did it go? Damn." He spotted a light near the end of the street. "Let's try that."

Jim quickened his pace down the sandy road. Sophie tried to keep up, "Try what?"

They stopped in front of an open door with no sign. "This place." He took her by the hand and crossed the threshold.

From deep inside what looked like a tent came a booming female voice, with a French tinged English accent, "Doctor Jim, is that you? My Lord, it is. Come on in here."

Talia was a large woman with extremely dark, nearly blue skin and an electric smile. She ushered the couple through the boiling hot, darkened restaurant into the back patio. The patio was well lit with strung together naked light bulbs, tables made of large hunks of tree trunks sawed into thick disks with three smaller trunks protruding as legs. The whole patio was covered in a fine mosquito netting, nearly invisible unless one was looking for it. There were a few patrons drinking beer and eating with their hands. Talia shooed two old men from a table for two, making them take their beer with them. She wiped the table and offered the two chairs with one grand conductor's gesture.

"So is this the crazy wife, Doctor Jim?"

"Talia, you remembered. No, no. I'm afraid Madeline is no longer with us. This is my colleague, Dr. Sophie Miller."

"Nice to meet you, Doctor Miller. My mother was a doctor. I don't like the sight of blood so I became a cook." She chuckled.

"Well, I look forward to your cooking. Jim has told me so much about it."

Jim was impressed with the ease at which his colleague fit in. She was not an amateur. He was chuffed by his fellow intrepid traveler. "What happened to the old place, Talia?"

"She burnt to the ground, Doctor Jim. Nobody in there thanks God. So I put this place together. Business not so good as it was when you were here before. The rebels and soldiers ain't got a pot to piss in, but they still fightin' for who knows what."

"So sorry to hear that. So what are we going to have tonight?"

"Oh we got some daal, bamia and kudra. Tomatoes and peppers and kisra of course. There is a little mutton left, but I'd stick to the stuff from the ground if I were you."

"Sounds yummy. We'll pass on the mutton, but the rest sounds wonderful. And a couple of cold beers please, Talia."

"Coming right up."

Talia disappeared through the kitchen door, yelled something unintelligible and a young boy, no more than 10 or 11 years old, appeared immediately with a tray containing two cold beers and two towelettes.

Sophie opened both beers and towels, and handed one to Jim. Half joking, "So, I take it you've been here before?"

"The funny thing is, only once. We were on our way to Darfur and were forced to stop here because of severe weather. We stayed for three days and ate here every one of them. A bunch of white doctors tend to stick out in this part of the world." Jim changed the subject. "Speaking of which, where does the Miller come from? I know many French people, but never ran across any Millers."

"It's my husband's name. We met in MSF. He's American." She looked at her watch. "Oh shit, I have to call home and say goodnight to my kids. What time zone are we in again?"

"Well, let's see. It's East African Time, which is 3 hours past GMT. So, 7 p.m. in Paris."

"We live in Minneapolis."

Surprised, "Really? Well then, 1 p.m."

"Oh good. They are still in school. I will Skype with them before I go to bed."

"Why Minneapolis, if I may be so bold?"

"It's okay. He's a pediatric oncologist. He does research

at a hospital there. I can deliver babies anywhere. They just keep coming."

Jim laughed. "Ah, OB/GYN. I'm sort of an amateur one myself."

"That is a pretty old and tired joke for someone of your stature."

"No, I mean I actually do deliver babies. Since you already are one, you may not know that most MSF doctors do their specialty but also have to be equipped to deliver babies. As you say, they just keep coming."

"Oh, I see. I guess I forgot that. Sorry."

"That's okay. It was a bad joke too."

They both laughed and drank their beers. The food came on a large tray with a pancake like bottom layer and little piles of colorful minced, pureed and diced goodness on top. Jim went first, tearing a piece of the pancake and clasping a bite of one of the little mounds of food. He placed it in his mouth and licked his fingers. The towelette was making more sense to Sophie.

They devoured the spicy, tangy, sweet mélange of deliciousness in silence, except for the occasional giggle from Sophie at the thought of eating with her hands.

As they lapped up the last bits, Talia approached with a large plate of peeled and sliced giant mango.

Jim savored the first piece. "I have to warn you about the mango here."

Sophie, with a piece near her mouth, stopped suddenly. "What, does it have some parasite?"

"No, no, you just have to be careful not to eat too much."

"Is it because the skin is covered in DDT?"

"Oh heavens, no. Us rich westerners did away with DDT in the US and consequently here, setting these poor countries back many years in their fight against malaria. No, not

DDT."

"Is it an enzyme that we cannot digest?"

Jim laughed. "No, no, no. It's just if you eat too much of this amazingly delicious, sweetest most scrumptious juicy fruit...you will get sick of it. And what could be worse than losing your appetite for mango!"

Sophie slapped him on the arm for teasing her, and then changed the subject. "Can I ask you a personal question?"

"Of course. What happens in Africa stays in Africa."

"That is sort of the question. I was wondering, I mean I have heard, but not done of course. What I am trying to ask you about is the companionship?"

"Oh, I see. By "the companionship" I assume you mean, as the kids say, hooking up? This does occur in these far-flung territories on occasion. I, myself, abstain from such activities. I mean, there was a time in my earlier days ... Now I'm here for the food and the young boys."

Sophie was visibly astonished. She pulled back her head and shook it vigorously. "I beg your pardon?"

Jim chuckled loudly, "Ohhhhhh, no. I didn't mean that at all. No, no, to attend to the young boys medically. You know, mend their bones. No, no, no, I am quite straight."

"Oh, Jim, you scared me."

"Sorry. That was not meant as a bad joke, just a slip of the tongue. Why are you asking me this? Are you not happily married?"

"As you say, I think Bill likes the young boys. Well, young men, actually. I am not about to leave my children, but since I am so far away, and I am French..."

"I always thought that was just what silly Americans thought."

"No, it's true. We do understand the usage of a mistress, or...mister?"

"I'm sure one of the young doctors or nurses here would be more than happy to provide some discreet companionship. You are a beautiful young woman."

Sophie elegantly caressed his hand. "I'm happy that you think so."

Jim folded his hands together, "Sophie, as flattered as I am with the offer, I think you might want to find someone a little closer to your own age."

"I don't think that age has anything to do with it, but whatever you choose. The offer stands, if you change your mind. The French have a saying, one can tell from the first kiss."

"I believe in that too. Shall we get the check?"

Five a.m. came sooner than expected. The group waited on the tarmac for the first helicopter. Jim flew in the initial transfer and Sophie stayed behind and waited for the second flight. The South Sudan terrain below them was green, with the occasional mountain jutting out of the landscape. Jim thought that it looked a lot like Arizona in places and the Midwest in others. River marsh would give way to patches of desert and a checkerboard of city blocks would spring up out of nowhere. Thatched cottages were strung together to form small villages, separated by farmland with goats and sheep. The number of swimming pools was what Jim had forgotten from his previous visit. An impoverished country also needed relief from the heat with a little dip. He wondered if there were pool services like he had seen in the South of France or Los Angeles. How did they keep them clean and who worked on the filters?

Jim was also astonished at the number of sophisticated looking churches he spotted, something he definitely did not remember from his last trip. The pronounced schism between the haves and the have-nots was so much greater in poor African nations than anywhere in western civilization.

Because the terrain resembled many other places in the world, one was only truly reminded that one was in Africa when coming upon the Bandingilo National Park, a wildlife refuge over which they flew. It catered to rich westerners on photo safari and contained herds of giraffe, zebra, hyenas, antelope and Nile buffalo, most of which were visible from the helicopter. This Jim did remember and looked forward to as they approached.

Six weeks at the Awail Community Hospital flew by. There were a promised six or seven boys delivered to the ER everyday, presenting contusions and fractures. Rarely did Jim break a sweat. The boys were sweet and most spoke English. Jim thought that was because they spent so much time in the ER. They didn't complain about the brief, but severe pain that was inevitable when resetting broken bones.

Sophie and Jim managed to stay friends without benefits. She delivered many babies, a few breach, one or two stillbirths and an unexpected set of triplets, for which Jim scrubbed in and assisted.

The hospitality of the facility was barren. The living quarters for the visiting staff were a series of thatched roof boxes, with half walls dividing the sleeping quarters between the men and women. The showers were shared and only the toilets were private. Jim often wondered if Sophie achieved the companionship that she was looking for in such close quarters.

The communal meals were nutritious, if not a bit bland. The food was similar to the dinner Jim and Sophie enjoyed in Juba, but not nearly as delicate, spicy or enticing. Sophie didn't listen to Jim and was sick of mango by the time their rotation was finished.

As predicted, the director called a few of the doctors into his office and asked if anyone would volunteer to head north to Darfur. There were a few volunteers, but not Jim. The contract was always for a minimum of three months unless the rotation ended and there was nothing pressing. With a few volunteers to go to Darfur, and Jim being the senior doctor in the bunch, he would take a miss.

Sophie found Jim packing. "Hey. It was really nice meeting you. Thank you for being my friend."

"The pleasure was all mine. Thank God we had that meal. The food here was not great. Did you find the companionship?"

"It would be difficult here. Can I ask you a question?"

"Does it have to do with the first kiss?"

"No, something serious. I see that you are not going on to Darfur. I was thinking of volunteering. I still have six weeks left. I don't really have to go. I just wondered why you are not going. You have been, no?"

"I have been, yes. This might seem harsh, but you really can't help them. Sure, you can keep them alive, deliver their babies, fix their boo-boos. But, they have to help themselves. They've been in those camps for so long that they no longer know normal. Kids grow up and go off to fight for who knows what and most don't return. It's like a farm where the rebels grow soldiers. You can fix their bodies but their hearts will never heal. Until they end the conflict, nothing will ever change."

Jim wiped his eyes, hugged Sophie hard and ran for the helicopter.

11

Dinner service was in 45 minutes and, like a finely choreographed and well-rehearsed dance, everyone moved in sync to prepare the staff dinner. Brenda and Derek set the table for all the staff including Jim, even though he was still in Africa. It was Nancy's idea. She thought if they set a place for him, everyone would be reminded that they had a leader. Steve and Buddy carried trays of food down from the kitchen, and Nancy placed some soda and water around the table. She opened a bottle of the house red and white, but rarely did anyone pour a glass at "the family meal," but, by the end of the night, both were usually empty. As the evening wore on and boredom set in, one by one, the staff would sneak down and have a glass or three.

The table was positioned right in front of the downstairs entrance. When the door flew open and Jim, fresh from his world adventure stood there, they jumped in unison.

Everyone gathered around him, like children waiting for their presents when a parent returns from a long journey. "What happened? Where did you go? Are we going to cook anything special from there?"

Jim sat in his assigned spot and regaled the troops with stories of mangos and broken legs. He explained in great detail the herd of giraffes that he saw from a helicopter and how everyone took showers together, even the women. (He may have exaggerated that part a little.) As he described the amazingly thin and yummy pancake that is used as the food's conveyance, he aimlessly took a bite of the sandwich that appeared in front of him. It was a simple hamburger, but not just any hamburger. Jim bit into the best, most savory, juicy, spicy burger he had ever had, and he'd had some of the best in the world.

"What the hell is this?!" Jim exclaimed, somewhat inappropriately. "I'm sorry. I've been traveling for 32 hours. What I meant to say was, what is this burger? It is incredible, amazing, delicious, fabulous, fantastic, did I say amazing?"

Buddy, "It's a hamburger."

"No, this is not simply a hamburger, this is the best hamburger I have ever had in my life."

"Thank you. It is pretty good."

Jim jumped up and stood behind Buddy. "Wait. Why is this not on the menu? This is perfect. Any woman who wants to come, but couldn't drag her "I don't eat none of that fancy food" husband can now say, with impunity, "I hear they have a great burger" and because of this genius, we fucking do!" He grabbed Buddy's head and kissed it in a grand gesture. "I'm calling that television woman right now. Teach me how to make it in the morning, Buddy. Ten o'clock?"

Jim ran out the back door. Everyone looked at one another in disbelief. Did their fearless leader just return, praise the humble burger and leave?

Jim went straight home and slept for 14 hours before the telephone woke him. It was Bob Brewer's office saying that he had a meeting that afternoon. Jim showered quickly and drove to the restaurant.

Buddy was waiting in the kitchen when Jim arrived. He was an hour late and wore a suit and tie.

Buddy, "We have to hurry. I have to prep for lunch service in 20 minutes. Put an apron on."

Jim thought that Buddy had definitely grown into his managerial role.

Buddy, "And wash your hands."

"Yes, sir."

Buddy disappeared downstairs. He reappeared in a minute with a tray of various items from the walk-in, including a small tri-tip.

"So, the secret is the tri-tip. I usually only get it when it's on sale." Buddy dropped it in the meat grinder on the back counter. The counter was spotless and empty, other than the grinder. "When you go to the TV station we will ground some of this for you. Now, I also put some sirloin in there to get the fat content to about 25%." He placed all of the ground beef in a stainless bowl in front of him. "This is two pounds of ground beef. Now, by hand, mix in a tablespoon of salt, pepper, paprika, garlic powder, and a pinch of cayenne. Work that all in, but don't handle it too much. Then a dash of Worcestershire (he pronounced wor-chester-shire), a teaspoon of mustard. Add a half cup finely diced onion and a quarter cup Brooks Catsup. It has to be Brooks. That other stuff does not work. Mix this all together and let it sit in the fridge for 24 hours."

Jim, "That's it?"

"No, not quite. Here, I've got some I made yesterday. You get an iron skillet really hot, add a pat of butter and wait for it to turn brown. Make a ball of the burger, about the size of a golf ball, and flatten it out to about three-quarters thick. Cook it on one side in the butter for four minutes, turn it once and cover. Cook for three more minutes and remove to a plate and let sit for five minutes. That's it. Oh, and I like to use the cheapest buns I can find. They soak up all the juices. You don't really need anything on it, but a hunk of cheddar, not melted, is sometimes really good too."

"Wow, that is great, Buddy! But I'm not going on television and make this. We don't want anyone to have this recipe."

Jim walked down the stairs and opened his office. From the layer of dust, it looked as if the office hadn't been opened since he left. There wasn't any reason for anyone to go in the cluttered little room. The bills went directly to David's office where a bookkeeper paid them promptly; and the schedule was done longhand by Nancy on a calendar that hung in the kitchen. Jim only kept the office to have somewhere to hide when the restaurant was completely empty and the staff stood around staring at him, wondering what to do.

He looked through the old reservations to see if he could find the night of the accident. He found it, and found the driver's name, James Blue, table for 2. Setting aside the book, he thumbed through the morning paper until he got to the arts section. He dropped the paper, grabbed the book and ran up the stairs.

"Buddy, can I ask you to do an extra special favor for

me?"

"Sure, Doctor Jim. What do you need?"

"Well, first of all, could you make mini versions of those burgers?"

"Sure, if I could find some small buns. Wait, I saw some at the bakery the other day. Slider buns they called them. So, sure."

"How many can you make?"

"As many as you want?"

"How about on Saturday?"

"Why not? How many do you need?"

"How about four dozen. I'll get Nancy to come too. Saturday is the Ark Walk. I want to take them over there and hand them out. That should put a few butts on seats in this joint. What do you think?"

"Let's make six dozen. I can make about six at a time. That's three-dozen an hour. Nothing to it."

"Great. Order the ingredients. Let's meet here at ten on Saturday. I'll help you out." Jim headed to the door, then turned around and came back. "And we'll take the limo over there. That should attract the kind of attention we need!"

Bob Brewer was waiting by the elevator when Jim arrived at his office. "Hey, Jim, great to see you. I just came from the courthouse."

They shook hands and stepped into an empty elevator. "So where do we stand?"

"We have an initial hearing tomorrow. This would be a good time to make a settlement offer, if we were so inclined. The court costs start to go up once we get into discovery, choosing a jury, all that good stuff."

The elevator doors opened and they walked into Bob's office.

Jim, "So, what are you saying? You think we should settle?"

"I didn't say that. Did you bring the reservations book?"

"Yes." Jim tossed the book that he was carrying onto Bob's desk. "Did you find the girlfriend?"

"I found her. Her name is Trudy Winters and she lives just off of Linden Avenue, around the corner from the Black Dog Tavern. She's not talking. The plaintiff's lawyers must've already briefed her. But, I tell you what, we'll have some fun with her when we get her on the stand."

Jim gave him a look.

"Oh, sorry. Not fun. So, I paid a little visit to my pal Larry down at the Black Dog. Turns out our boy is a regular and so is little Miss Milkmaid."

"Who?"

"Trudy. Remember, she drank milk?"

"Oh, right. Go on."

"He's pretty sure they were in there the night of the accident."

"That's great. Was he drinking? Of course he was drinking. That should do it, right? Are we cleared?"

"Not so fast. We have to get her on the stand, which means we have to pick a jury, and her testimony alone may not be enough."

"So you're saying that we know that he was drinking at another establishment after he left my restaurant, but we still have to go through with this whole thing?"

"Worse than that. The only way to prove that he was drinking at the Black Dog is to get Larry to testify. And he won't do that."

"Why the hell not?"

"Because he wasn't named in the suit. If he admits that our boy was drinking at his establishment he will implicate himself."

"Shit. The plaintiff must know about the other bar. Why are they not named?"

"No money. They suspect you have some and know that all Larry has is a run down bar and child support payments. The girlfriend is our only hope. Did you talk to your server?"

"Yes, Nancy remembers serving them. They ordered a bottle of wine. She asked for the milk after. Maybe the Pho was too spicy for her."

"So a couple ordering a bottle of wine would not raise suspicions of a server. That's good. The Dram Shop laws are pretty specific."

"The what?"

"That's what these cases are called. The law says that the bar or restaurant needs to be negligent by knowingly over-serving a customer. I wouldn't say that Nancy knowingly over-served them, would you?"

"No, of course not. We're a fine-dining establishment. We aren't some honky-tonk or dive bar down on Linden Avenue."

"Jim, if we do end up in court, you have to be careful about that sort of talk. People around here, that is, people on the jury, do not like people getting all uppity."

Bob looked at his watch, "I gotta go. You don't need to come to this hearing. It's just the lawyers. We aren't making an offer, right?"

"No!"

The kitchen was empty when Jim returned. Buddy was sitting on the couch, drinking a pop. The restaurant was empty. Jim sat across from Buddy and was silent. Buddy broke the ice, "How did it go at the lawyers?"

Jim ignored the question. "I was thinking we should try some Somalian food this Saturday. I have some of the spices at home and the dishes are really easy to make. Let's see if we can reinvigorate International Night."

Buddy just stared at Jim as he absent-mindedly disappeared down the steps.

Saturday morning was rainy and sunny and rainy and sunny, exactly what Ohio weather was like in the spring and summer. The old saying "If you don't like the weather, wait five minutes" was definitely in full bloom that morning. Joey was the first to arrive in the lower parking lot. He wore his newly minted chauffer's hat–a present from Jim for passing the livery license test. Nancy and Jim showed up together, suspicious to Joey, but not to either Jim or Nancy. That party had run out of booze a while ago and nobody was looking for refills.

They all ascended the stairs to discover Buddy already hard at work on pans full of mini burgers. "Oh, great. Glad you're all here. Grab some of those buns and start traying these puppies up. I borrowed some pouches from my friend Steve over at the Pizza Palace. We can use them to keep the burgers warm. I have to get them back by five when they open, but I'm sure we'll be done passing them out by then."

Jim started preparing a tray with buns. "Good thinking, Buddy. The art fair is already open so I think Joey and I should head up there once we have a dozen or so burgers and get set up. I reserved a spot at the end of the bridge so we can drive right up with the limo and join the rows of artists and other tents. I figured we can open the back door of the limo and Nancy and I can pass burgers through the sunroof. I had a banner made that we can wrap around the car."

MAKE A PLAN FOR THE FIVE-YEAR PLAN

The Art Walk was surprisingly busy when the limo slowly lumbered through the crowd gathered at the end of the bridge. A band was setting up on a flatbed truck, opposite from the spot Jim had reserved. Nancy thought this was a bad idea, but Jim reassured her that music always attracts people, so they should be guaranteed an audience.

Joey managed to edge the Cadillac into the spot so the open back door displayed the plush interior in all of its glory and the newly minted vanity plate "5YearPln" could also be seen. Nancy draped the banner over the windshield while Jim removed a tall A-frame sign from the trunk. It read, THE FIVE-YEAR PLAN in large block letters on the top of both sides, and on the bottom, NOT JUST FANCY FOOD and in bold red letters was the biggest words, TRY OUR FREE BURGERS. Jim figured if free didn't attract customers he really was doomed to fail.

Jim engaged his audience in light banter and the burgers flew out the sunroof and into the mouths of passersby. The replenishments sent down by Buddy never lasted until the next batch arrived. Jim passed out sample menus and reassured all of the women that their husbands could always have a burger. The women smiled and nodded as their husbands–at least the ones that weren't on the golf course–devoured the free samples.

The Art Walk enticement took no time at all to kick in. That very night, "International Night" was full. The crowd was a wee bit rowdy, probably due to the free flowing draft beer at the Art Walk earlier that day. The rain had finally completely subsided, so the balcony was open and inviting. There was just enough chill in the air to have the outdoor fireplace blazing, warming the already festive evening.

Jim greeted his unexpected guests and sat them with pride and relief. Ruth held court next to the indoor fireplace (Now only burning candles for the summer), and Nancy made small talk with people that had never before seen the inside of the restaurant. Drinks were served and even a few "fancy" bottles of wine were uncorked, with the reassurance that the limo awaited anyone feeling the least bit tipsy.

The evening took a very early, and decisively abrupt turn when, upon the first several orders arriving at the kitchen, Buddy delivered the bad news that there were no burgers. He had used all that he had prepared for the Art Walk earlier that day. The only items on the menu were the roasted chicken, a Caesar salad, a rib eye steak (of which they only had six), and the Somali special—consisting of a large pancake that tasted similar to dirt, and four indistinguishable piles of spiced, smashed vegetables closely resembling homemade baby food, and some plain yogurt. Jim, the staff and all of the disgruntled patrons (and all of their friends that they wasted no time informing) did not soon forget the disastrous evening.

Sunday morning Jim spent on his screened-in porch, nursing a nasty hangover and glancing though piles of mail and newspapers saved up from his time in Africa. There was no good news among the basket of junk mail and bills. Fortunately, the local morning newspaper did not mention the prior evening's implosion at the restaurant; maybe he was exaggerating the degree of destruction done.

The Five-Year Plan

Bob Brewer knocked at the porch door. He figured that Jim would be, like most reasonable men on a Sunday morning, sitting on the porch reading the paper, drinking coffee and considering, if not already well into his first bloody mary. He seemed disappointed at the lack of the latter.

Jim looked up, startled but not frightened, and waved Bob in. "Hello, Robert. Coffee?"

"Sure. Love some."

Jim got up and stepped into the adjacent kitchen. He raised his voice in order to be heard from the next room, "Cream and sugar?"

"No thanks, just black, please."

Jim returned with a mug of steaming hot coffee. "I was thinking of making a bloody mary. Can I interest you in one?"

"I thought you'd never ask." Bob followed Jim into the kitchen and sat at the little café table while Jim concocted the morning cocktail.

"To what do I owe the honor of the counselor's presence this morning?"

"Oh, I was just in the neighborhood."

"It's Sunday morning, you live in Ridgewood and you haven't been down to church in a month of Sundays. I still wonder how you ended up being a lawyer. You were always crap at lying when we were kids. Remember when we snuck out and camped in the woods and you cut yourself with that hatchet. You told your parents you fell off of your bike."

"Hey, they bought it."

"Not for a second. They just rolled their eyes and took you to the ER."

Sheepishly, "I've gotten better at it. Really."

Jim changed the subject, "So what's up?"

"We got a court date."

"We what? I thought this was going to go away. We are now actually going to court? A jury and the whole thing?"

"Yes, I'm afraid so."

"What do you mean you're afraid? I thought this was going to be fun?"

"Without Larry, or somebody else from the Black Dog testifying about his drunken exploits, we're going to have an uphill battle."

Jim stared at him, incredulously. Bob took a few swigs of his bloody mary and excused himself. As he walked toward the front door, Jim, "When?"

"When what?"

"When do we go to court?"

"Two weeks from Monday."

"I thought you said these things take forever around here?"

"It's been forever, for around here."

The doors were open and the sign in the window said open, but there no customers walking through the door of The Five-Year Plan for the entire week. By Thursday, Nancy stayed home and said to call her if a customer did show up. Jim arrived without fail every day. Most days he sat in his office or on the riverbank, staring at the water, devoid of thoughts or brilliant new plans. He drank espresso from the $16,000 coffee machine he had shipped in from Seattle. It was a beautiful, retro looking sleek silver work of industrial art, with matching grinders and finely machined knobs for temperature, timing and grind grid. He calibrated it every morning based on the roast and freshness of the coffee that arrived twice a week from Portland, Oregon, via FedEx. It was the best coffee in Ohio–and nobody knew it.

The following week was slightly better. On Tuesday, they had one customer for lunch. He ordered the burger and a Bud Light. Even Friday night, often the one bright moment in otherwise dim and dreary weeks, was empty. The staff was beginning to slip too. They showed up late, left early. Buddy stopped most of his daily prep work and didn't bother carrying the day's supplies up from the walk in. Once a week he would clean out all of the spoilage and shake his head at the waste. He blamed himself for the great burger mishap, even though deep down, he knew this whole restaurant was a bad idea, and not his idea.

Another Sunday hangover on the screened in porch got Jim thinking that maybe he better lay off the booze for a while. He had never been a big drinker. He loved wine, and a cold beer on a hot day in Africa or Spain was like no other thirst quencher. He did even love the occasional cocktail, provided that the ingredients were well sourced, fresh, and the recipe was inventive and original. But drinking to drown his sorrows was uncharted territory for him and the lack of focus, both with his eyes and his mind, was wearing on him. Fuck it, he thought, I'm going to make a bloody mary.

The ingredients were lining the kitchen counter when Bob's familiar, playful voice rang out, "Who do I have to kill to get a drink in this joint?"

"Counselor."

"You making bloody marys?"

"Yes. I assume you want one."

"Love one, thanks. And I suspect I'll be able to finish this one. I've got some news."

Jim handed Bob his drink and gestured toward the porch.

"What might that be? Are we all set for tomorrow?"

"Let me start from the top. The problem with this case is that the girlfriend was bought and paid for by the plaintiff. But they overlooked one key component. She's got no dog in the hunt."

Jim looked at him with educated eyes. "English, please."

"There is nothing that incentivizes her to lie. I was thinking about this and realized that she probably isn't aware of all of the possibilities. So I paid her a visit and had a chat."

Jim interrupted, "You can't do that, right?"

"Officially, no, of course not. But it's still Zanesville. The judge is Jimmy D's cousin and I've known him since we were kids. Went to Philo. Besides, she doesn't know I can't talk to her. Or at least that's what I was counting on."

"And? Did she?"

"Nope. But it took a little doin'. I had to talk to her through the door until I told her that she could go to jail for lying in court. Well, that got her attention and she came out on the porch and listened, then let go of a few critical pieces of information."

"What information?"

"I told her that Larry had seen her with her boyfriend that night and that you were both drunk."

"Were they?"

"I have no idea. But it got her attention and she said, 'He wasn't drunk. He doesn't like wine so I drank it. He drove us down to the Black Dog then started drinking shots. I told him I didn't want none. I had milk at that restaurant because my ulcer was acting up and couldn't have no more to drink. He called me some names and kept drinking shots and beers. I finally got fed up with him and left.' I said, "Will you tell that to the judge?"

"What did she say?"

"I guess I have to. I just told you. Besides, Larry and all them were there. It's no secret is it?"

"So?"

"So what?"

"Is she going to?"

"Well, I called the plaintiff's attorney, relayed the information that I had heard had been expressed, not to me of course, and they must have confirmed this colorful narrative with their key witness."

"Why do you say that?"

"Because ... Jimbo ... They dropped the case!"

Jim jumped up and tried to hug him. Bob was not moving from his reclined position with his feet on the ottoman and drink resting on his belly. "You are a genius."

"Thought you said I was terrible at lying?"

"Clearly, you have developed a talent for it. I am forever in your debt. Come down to the restaurant tomorrow night and have whatever you desire. On the house, of course."

"I may pass on that. I'm not hearing great things."

With a renewed spring in his step, Jim walked into his restaurant Monday afternoon and was once again slapped with an empty house. Buddy was in the kitchen and Nancy was changing the candles in the fireplace.

"You might like to know that the lawsuit was dropped."

Buddy looked up from his food experiment, "That's great, Doctor Jim. Does that mean the restaurant will be busy again?"

"Sarcasm has no place here, Mr. Sanders."

Nancy popped her head out of the fireplace, "Sanders? I didn't know you had a last name."

"Very funny, Ms. Andrews. We need some new customers. Either of you have any ideas?"

The door opened and a familiar woman's voice said, "I might have a few ideas." In the doorway stood Rosemary Parsons, suitcase beside her and a colorful summer scarf draped around her shoulders.

Jim jumped to his feet, "Rosemary!" He rushed to her and they hugged.

Buddy and Nancy looked at Rosemary, then at each other.

Jim held her like a long lost lover, which was more than a little disconcerting to Rosemary, who pulled back and walked toward the kitchen. "Hi, I'm Rosemary Parsons, a former colleague of your ..." she looked at Jim, around the restaurant and then back toward them, "Your boss."

Nancy piped in, "Are you a doctor?"

"No, no, I was Doctor Langley's administrator."

Nancy and Buddy looked at one another, perplexed.

Rosemary tried to curtail their confusion, "Secretary."

Nancy, "Oh, nice to meet you. I'm Nancy, head of wait staff and this is Buddy, chief cook and bottle washer."

"Nice to meet both of you."

Jim, "What on earth brings you to Zanesville?"

"I promised not to tell, but I knew that was never going to work. Ruth called. Said you were having a hell of a time making this thing work." She looked around and was quite impressed. "Although I don't know why. This place looks amazing, and what a beautiful view of the river. Fireplaces in and out and this wall of glass. Wow, that is just incredible. You always did have good taste."

"Thank you. But why did she call you? I mean, no offense but..."

"She said that you needed some of Rosemary's finest organization. I knew what she meant and I am not surprised that you didn't. You always did think you could do it all on your own. But listen, Doctor Langley, you can't and I'm here to help." Rosemary realized that she might have overstepped her bounds. It had been more than a year since she was in the employ of the good doctor and she had grown much more independent. "Of course only if you want me to." She finished with a little less ebullience.

"Rosemary, as usual, you are a force of nature sent by God. Welcome to my nightmare."

"Could you please show me around, then I must go to the Holiday Inn and check in."

"Nonsense, you will stay with me. I have a wonderful little house with a perfectly appointed guest room, thanks to the furnishings from the Lexington house and the good taste of Madeline."

"I wouldn't think of it."

"Nonsense. Done. Now, for the restaurant. We call it The Five-Year Plan."

"What a terrible name for a restaurant."

"Thank you." Jim said without a shred of sarcasm. "Now, here is the kitchen. We have everything one needs to make the most delicious food. Fryers, high BTU burners and ovens, sous vide. The walk-ins and freezer are downstairs. We procure from a few great sources from Columbus and have a few things shipped in each week."

They headed downstairs. Jim showed the walk-ins, his office and the wine cellar. "My cellar, transposed. What was I going to do with all of that wine? Turns out, not too many folks in these parts enjoy old burgundies, so I guess I get to keep the good stuff for myself after all."

"I would hate to see you miss a day without wine." She wandered around the rest of the space and looked out onto the downstairs parking lot. "What's that and all of this?"

"That is the downstairs parking lot and the rest of the basement. We do family meal down here."

"This is a totally unfinished space. And the parking lot? There is a parking lot directly across the street from the front entrance. Does anyone use this space?"

"Well, we keep the limo down here, and I sometimes park here."

"The limo!?"

"Yes. I bought a limo. It's sort of a long story …"

"You have someone drive you around in a limo? You have lost your mind, Doctor Langley. What on earth are you thinking?"

"No, no, no. I don't ride around in it. Well I did once …" He decided not to relate that story. "We had a little drunk driving thing here …" He also decided not to go into that story, either. "We offer a service to our patrons who might enjoy a few glasses of wine the luxury of not having to drive to or from the restaurant. They call in advance and we pick them up and take them home. Or, if they are already here and have too much, we drop them home. The town is small enough that we can pretty quickly get everyone where they need to go with a few trips. Or at least we think we can."

"What do you mean, you think you can?"

"Well … Since we purchased the car we have had no patrons, except that one night and they all, well let's just say none were interested in that portion of our hospitality."

"So you have never actually driven anyone home in that hearse?"

"It's not a hearse. That is a 1975 Cadillac Fleetwood Limousine with a 500 cubic inch V8 and custom windows, stereo and privacy screen. It has 7200 original miles."

"What'd you pay for it?"

"Twelve, five."

"Twelve thousand? That's a pretty good deal if it's solid."

"Oh, it's solid alright."

"And what about the lot. Why is it sitting empty like that, right next to the river?" She stepped out into the lot. "Is that breeze fairly constant, even in the summer?" She looked up at the sun, "And this much sun. Full exposure?"

"Yeah, it's a pain in the ass for the balcony. We've got to keep the awnings up until around eight in the summer. Cuts off the view for some in the back of the restaurant."

"Those are the sorts of problems you are lucky to have." She walked back in and changed the subject. "Where's the computer?"

"My laptop is in the office."

"Where is the restaurant computer? With social media, POS master, QuickBooks? You know, the business?"

"We don't have one. I have a bookkeeper at my accountant's that pays the bills and my accountant does the taxes."

"And the rest? What about the till? And website, online reservations, advertising, social media, procurement?"

"We have good suppliers."

"Local? Organic? Seasonal?"

"We do try to be seasonal, but organic is tough …"

"We have got to get started. I'm going to the Holiday Inn now. I will take you up on your hospitality tomorrow, but I've already made a reservation for tonight. I'm going to need some banking information. Do you have a company credit card? I'll order a computer and the software. That parking lot's coming up tomorrow. Do you have a contractor? Email me his number. See you tomorrow."

With that she was gone, not unlike some of Jim's past exits. He just stood there, dumfounded and relieved.

The phone woke him up at 7:30 a.m. It was Nick on the phone. "Am I really supposed to come dig up the parking lot this morning? I booked the bobcat but I thought I better check with you first."

"Good morning, Nick. Yes, well, wait. What did she, Rosemary, say?"

"She said to get my butt down there and dig up the downstairs parking lot."

"Did she happen to say why?"

"Something about a garden and patio and sun and microclimate and why the hell didn't I do that when I did the other outside work?"

"Yes, she can be a little ... abrasive, but she means well."

"My mother-in-law is just like that. I totally understood and didn't argue. It's pointless and they are always right." He hesitated, "Damnit."

"Yes they are. See you soon."

By the time Jim arrived, big hunks of the parking lot were being loaded into a dump truck, one bobcat shovel at a time. It was nearly cleared and Rosemary stood by the doorway with a sketchpad in one hand and Nick's balls in the other. Jim stopped and reveled in another man succumbing to the powers that had always truly ruled his life. First there was Ruth, then Madeline, then Rosemary. He loved those powerful women, but knew that they were like dynamite. Alone they were perfectly safe, but with the first drop of testosterone they were fully charged and ready to go off at the flip of a switch.

He tiptoed through the rubble. "Good morning, crew. Looks like we have progress. What progress are we making exactly, Rosemary?"

"You have no local produce or herbs. I talked to Buddy last night. And you have this parking lot going to waste that is perfect for a garden and patio. Your patrons can bask in the glory of organic food while dining on it. Won't it be wonderful? And we've started just at the right time. If we can get this ground turned over and treated, we can have our first crop in by the end of the week."

"Are we going to have any parking down here? What about the limo?"

"Yes, here. Look." She dropped the sketchpad on the makeshift table and stabbed her finger at the plan. "There is a little section at the end with concrete tile. You know, that kind of driveway with the grass that grows in-between. It will be beautiful and just large enough for staff parking and the limo. There's also a path to the river. I think in phase two we should get the city involved and develop a walkway along the river. It seems like there was one at some point."

Jim walked into the office to find it reorganized, cleaned and well lit. Somehow, the straight back wooden chair from Rosemary's office at the medical center sat in the corner. He shouted, "Rosemary, how on earth did you …"

He turned around and she appeared.

"How did I what?"

"How did you already take over my office?"

"I called Nancy last night and had her and a few of the kids clear it out. I got here at 5:30 and finished. I should have the computer and the rest of the equipment in by 10. Do you like it?"

"Yes, but?"

"But what, Doctor Langley, but what? Do you not need this organization? Were you going to do it on your own? Do you not need a functioning office after I leave?"

"Wait, what? You're leaving?"

"Well, not right now. But, I am certainly not spending the rest of my life in Zanesville, Ohio. I don't recommend it for anyone, unless you choose to do so."

That was the most derision he had ever heard from her. He was both stunned and impressed by her curt, ruthless assessment and, he hated to admit, accurate portrayal. "Right. Okay, exactly how long do you plan to stay?"

"We have other things to discuss. I will stay until it's all sorted out."

Jim was about to sit at his desk when Rosemary gently glided him toward the stiff chair. "What other things?"

She took out a legal pad. Jim crooked his neck.

"Where did you find office supplies at 5:30 in the morning?"

"I figured I may need a few things, so I brought them from my home office. Recognize the chair?"

"Yes, I noticed that. And the lamp. Nice touch."

"I've see that you don't have the URL for the restaurant. I want you to get a credit card just for online use." She threw him a pad and pen, "Here, take some notes. So, go to the bank and get another card, make sure it's a debit card. Transfer five hundred in that account and instruct them to always keep it at that level and have them set up email notices in case of any suspicious activity. Got it?"

"Got it."

"Why is there no music in the restaurant? We need a system. I'll get Nick on that and you need to subscribe to an Internet Muzak service. Write that down. They are brilliant now. You can choose different levels of activity, types of music and all sorts of other variables. The restaurant will come to life"

"Sounds good."

"I read in the paper this morning that the old YWCA is going to be renovated. They're closing in a few weeks and the construction is going to take at least a year. I also noticed that the Rotary meets on Tuesdays at the YWCA. That means that they will be homeless soon."

"My dad used to belong to the Rotary."

"Yes, he did. That's how I was able to get you an invitation to be their guest tomorrow at lunch. Your friend David is also a member so you can sit with him. You don't need to do anything. Just go there, be nice, and when you will eventually be introduced to Alan Markman, hand him my card." Rosemary reached in the top desk drawer and removed a clutch of business cards. "Here, stick these in your wallet."

Jim stared at the embossed cards with Rosemary's name, email, cell phone number and a beautiful logo of the restaurant featuring the countdown clock. "How did you ...?"

"I did my homework. It's always been my job to anticipate your needs. Why should this project be any different? Now, back to the Rotary. Just get that Alan fellow to call and I'll close the deal."

"What deal?"

"The deal for the Rotary lunches. They'll need a place to hold their meetings and we have the solution right here." She waved her hand slowly toward the nearly empty basement area.

"Here?"

"This downstairs area has great potential and will take Nick and me no time to transform it into a beautiful function room, replete with garden view, dais and seating for..." She checked her notes, "Fifty-eight. Rotary ready in two weeks!"

"Fifty-eight? We don't have the staff to serve that many people lunch."

"Put it on your list. I also need a few other bits and bobs from you." Rosemary had spent part of her childhood in England. She didn't have a proper accent, but did retain some of the colloquialisms and charm.

"Sure. Like what?"

"I can't find the reservations book. Is there a customer database of some sort? Advertising budget? Artwork?"

"I will need to retrieve the reservations book."

"You will what? Never mind. Just get it for me, please. I read in the paper that there is a new mayor? Have you met him? And do you know the council members?"

"No."

"Let's set up a meet and greet, welcoming him to Zanesville. We'll need some other organization behind it. Can't come from us, but it can be here. Who do you know? Chamber of Commerce? Local AMA? Bar Association?"

"We can get all three. Doctors, lawyers and businessmen together in one room. Sounds dangerous to me, but what the hell."

Rosemary checked her list, "We need eggs."

"We have eggs."

"No. We need fresh, local eggs from a farm. Go find us eggs." She looked down and started to write, flip through her iPad and return to her note pad. She looked up at Jim as if to say, "Why are you still here?"

Jim stood up, notepad in hand, "I'm on it. See you soon."

By the end of the summer, the restaurant and garden were both in bloom. Rosemary had lived up to her name as well as her reputation and had planted herbs all along the balcony edges and around the new patio seating area. Raised beds constructed of railroad ties lined the patio. Tomatoes, peppers, half-runner green beans and cucumbers were in various stages of ripeness and were being harvested daily, inspiring Buddy and his new sous chef Ginger Hayes.

They also had a fulltime dishwasher, salad/prep cook and three rotating line cooks.

The downstairs was full of light from the glass doors leading to the patio. Rosemary and Nancy had devised clever, convertible tables that would expand into banquet tables for the twice-weekly lunches they now hosted. Rosemary had convinced the Rotary to commit to three years and used that leverage to sway the Kiwanis (not to be outdone by those Rotarians). After heated discussions with Jim about the wine cellar, which often ended in shouting and stomping off, she convinced him to replace the heavy wooden door with glass. This one improvement changed the ambience of the room completely. The phone booths remained, but got a fresh coat of paint and the fluorescent lights were replaced with more dramatic and pleasant looking halogen. When the banquet tables were collapsed, they became a row of round café tables lining the windows, looking onto the garden. Though rarely used for extra seating, they were nonetheless enticing.

Buddy's menu changes, inspired by the garden and the other local fare, were both inventive and delicious. The local paper ran a series of reviews. The reviewer came once and wrote a review, then came back the next day and the next, until she had sampled the whole menu. She continued to mention various dishes into the fall as the menu changed and her visits became part of her weekly routine.

The mechanisms for running a great restaurant were also in place. Rosemary had created a database and regular email blasts for returning customers. The website was as professional as any big city eatery, and had a reservations feature via Open Table, the first restaurant in Zanesville to do so. All of the social media were subscribed to and Rosemary even recruited a local high school student to keep them updated.

Rosemary packed her things and said her goodbyes as the garden was being turned over for the winter. All was in order. Her composter was installed and the kitchen and bus boys knew exactly what to do with it. Everything was organized. Everyone was happy. The restaurant sparkled and shined. Her work here was done. Champagne flowed as Jim, Ruth and the staff sent Rosemary back to Boston. There were hugs and tears of joy and thanks, and then she was gone.

And then nobody came. Not nobody, exactly. But the numbers began to dwindle as the first chill of autumn blew threw the garden. Other than the two groups for lunch each week—which consisted of a set price three-course lunch and required two extra servers and three extra kitchen help, and made little profit—there were only occasional lunchtime patrons. Dinner was a little better. Friday night was sometimes busy, but Saturday returned to a barren wasteland. In an act of desperation, Jim attempted International Night one last time, which bombed so badly that Nancy, feeling her reputation hanging in the balance, threatened to quit.

Christmas decorations made the downtown appear festive. Since nearly all commerce had abandoned the downtown area long ago, the streets were not exactly bustling, but the décor twinkled and Dasher pranced across the courthouse roof. People would drive down Main Street to see the lights and the giant snowflakes that hung from the light poles lining Main Street. The restaurant captured a few of the seasonal visitors looking for some holiday cheer. Hamburgers were back on the menu and one per table could be counted on when newcomers like the holiday folks came to visit.

The cold, the irregular customer count, and the boredom that was the reality of running a restaurant—no matter how successful—was making Jim restless. He sat in his office, attempting to not drink the whole bottle of Flowers Sonoma Coast Pinot Noir that had just arrived, and dreamed of being anywhere but there. "Italy would be nice." He said to no one in particular. His father used to always say to him, "Be careful what you wish for."

Jim's cell phone vibrated along the edge of his desk and fell off. He caught it just before it spattered on the concrete floor and read the text, "6.3 Earthquake, Foligno, Italy. 116 dead. 780 injured. Are you available?"

12

Forty-five minutes north of Rome, on the train to Spoleto (the closest station not damaged by the earthquake) Jim found the bar car. It was late afternoon, the sun was setting over vineyards and farm fields in the foothills of the Central Apennines and he was famished. The plane journey was fitful and the food unappetizing. He remembered the last time he was on a train in Italy; he ate the most amazing prosciutto sandwich on a baguette with nothing more than a thin layer of sweet mascarpone cheese and a little drizzle of young olive oil. He was in search of the same.

There was indeed a prosciutto sandwich, wrapped in cellophane, on a spongy white bun with a packet of non-re-frigerated mayonnaise—nothing approaching his dream sandwich. He ordered a half bottle of Chianti. As he approached the tables in the rear he noticed a young man who looked as out of place as he felt, dining on the same 14 euro sandwich and wine.

"Scusi?" Jim motioned toward the empty bench seat across from the man.

He was surprised to hear a Midwest accent, "Help yourself."

The Midwesterner held out his hand and offered a firm grip, which Jim heartily exchanged. "Steve Baxter."

"Well, a fellow American. I'm Jim Langley, from Ohio." Jim befuddled himself by offering up that awkward detail. He tried to link his thoughts. "Where are you from?"

"Des Moines, Iowa, but I live in DC now. Well, actually Maryland. I work at a hospital there."

"Really, which one? I've got several colleagues from down that way."

"Walter Reed. Are you a doctor?"

"Oh, sorry, yes. Ortho, from Boston General. Or I was. You?"

"Internist and administrator. I still practice, but they were really happy to rope me into the front office years ago and it sort of stuck. That's why I'm here."

"So MSF then?"

"That's right. You too?"

"Yep. Got the call yesterday. Didn't even get the brief, just an emailed plane ticket and the timetable for this train. Do you know what we're in for?"

"Oh, wow, you didn't hear? Yes. This town is about 50,000, has a nice, brand new, state of the art hospital. Unfortunately, it's still under construction. The old hospital was a makeshift, post-war, shoddy building and collapsed in the quake. Nearly all of the casualties were in the main building, including doctors, nurses and staff. Ironically, they only lost a few patients. The patients were in a single story wing that was spared."

"Holy shit."

"That's right. There are a whole bunch of us arriving in the next few days. Probably the reason you got no brief. Geneva was scrambling to get staffed up. I got the call because they need to permanently re-staff the hospital and have nobody qualified to administrate the new hires. Oh, and I also speak Italian. I'm sort of the trifecta."

"I guess you are. Well, anything I can do to help. I'm sure I'll set a few broken bones, but I'm glad to help in any other way. As a senior, I've had to run a few of these things, by default more than anything."

"Thanks, Jim. I really appreciate that. I'm sure it'll be all hands on deck."

They sat for a long while staring out the train window, taking in the Italian countryside and considering the disaster that they were about to face.

Foligno was a dichotomy of ancient beauty and post-war, sub-par replacements for buildings that were heavily bombed during World War II. Like so many European cities involved in the war, threads of a long history were all that remained. Not surprisingly, the buildings that sustained the most damage were built in the last 75 years, likely a combination of haste to rebuild after the war and a shoddy building industry. The older structures, mainly houses and shops in the center of town, looked untouched, while the newer three and four story apartments and office buildings slumped, split, and sagged, some missing facades and others looking perfect from one angle and crumpled from another. The outskirts of town sprouted more recent developments with little or no damage, including the beautiful new hospital—a post modern, low-slung series of jutting wings separated by architectural accents of angular walkways. It was going to be a gorgeous building, once the construction was complete. Above the winding, hilly roads loomed beautiful mountains to the east, inspiring and peaceful, yet easily a threat as weather systems crashed and collided, often turning a warm, sunny winter's day into a torrential downpour or even the occasional snow storm.

Jim and Steve, along with an uncharacteristically large group of MSF doctors and nurses, arrived at a Holiday Inn on the edge of town. It was late in the evening, but the organizers had arranged for the small bar and breakfast room to be left open and stocked with snacks, beer and wine; such a contrast to the welcoming parties of his past MSF missions. Usually they hit the ground running, quite literally. This situation was a little bit different. Early responders from all of the surrounding towns and cities got there quickly. This was not the middle of Africa or Asia, and, although in the mountains, it was easily accessible. Communications systems remained functional and power was only lost in small sections, places that had always been a bit spotty in the best of times. Other volunteer doctors had come from as far away as Rome and Florence and had already put in a long day, but joined the MSF arrivals that night. If it weren't for the tragedy of the old hospital, MSF would probably have not been involved.

The first days of the mission were not unlike any catastrophe for Jim, with many broken bones, contusions and follow up care. The big challenge wasn't the injuries, but making what was left of the old hospital into a functioning facility. Occupied beds needed to be re-evaluated. Patients that could not be moved were doubled up in existing rooms and those well enough to be transported were either moved to facilities hours away or sent home. Parallel to the emergency work, the new hospital—just weeks away from opening—needed to be staffed, filling the spots left vacant by those who perished in the devastation.

Steve sat at the Holiday Inn bar after finishing late one night. Jim poked his head in to see if anyone was still left at the bar.

"Hey, Steve. How's it going?"

"Jim. Have a seat. Can I buy you a drink?"

Jim got the bartender's attention. "Glass of the house red, please." Something Jim would never imagine saying in any other Holiday Inn bar in the world. "So, Steve, how goes casting the Italian version of General Hospital?"

"Ha. A lot like Central Casting, actually. I don't know if it's the Italian accent or the absurdity of the situation, but every single person I interview makes me laugh. It feels like I'm in some crazy movie where the American moves to Italy and tries to rebuild an old house. Except this is a new hospital and it's not a fucking movie."

Jim motioned to the bartender to bring another round for Steve. "Need some help?"

"Oh, boy, do I. I've only hired three people, and we need to fill forty-two spots in three weeks. I need nurses, I really need nurses."

"I've got an idea. Let me make a couple of calls in the morning."

"And have you seen the new hospital? It's beautiful and somehow sustained hardly any damage. Some plumbing issues, but nothing major."

"Plumbing?"

"Yeah, a water main broke and there's a whole bunch of flooding. It looked like the flooding was under control, but the guy trying to fix the water lines looked a lot like the guy from Super Mario Bros."

"I might have an idea about that too."

It didn't take long to track down Valerie Rousseau. Jim vividly recalled his last communication with her. He called her from London—just after leaving Marbella—to apologize for not being the playboy that she may have been looking for, but still could they please stay in touch. She said that she was thinking about returning to Florence and, if he were ever in the area, should look her up. She was in the book, along with 17 other Valerie Rousseaus. Jim got lucky on the second call.

"Yes, but of course I am still a nurse, Jim. I am so happy to have you call. When can we meet, darling?"

Jim blushed from a few hundred miles away. "I really need your help, Val. This place is mess and we need someone of your talent to… well, you know, do what you do. Make everything seem like it's meant to be."

"Jim, everything is meant to be. I need to find my driver then I will be there. I come this afternoon. Can I please stay in your rooms?"

"We will put you up and pay you." He said, a little too matter of factly.

"I will see you this afternoon, darling."

Jim hung up the phone and searched through his contacts. He said a silent prayer that Frank kept his US cell phone number, closed his eyes and pressed dial.

"Buongorno" said the Boston Irish accented man.

"Frank?" Jim said, hoping he had the correct number.

"I wondered if that was you. Nobody ever calls on this number. How the hell are you, Jim? Long time, no see."

"I'm in Italy. I just got here. Sorry for the short notice, but I didn't know I was coming until I got on the plane."

"Where are you?"

I'm actually not far from you. I'm in Foligno. Just up the road. You're still in Spoleto, aren't you?"

"Oh my God, the earthquake. Of course. We shook pretty good down here, but I heard it was really bad up there."

"Yep. It's done a ton of damage here. The biggest problem is that they are in the middle of building a new hospital, and the old one was destroyed and many staff died in the collapse of the building. We're dealing with the injured and helping to staff the new hospital—sort of a little out of our wheelhouse. The new place is nearly ready to open and it's beautiful. But we have one little problem."

"What's that?"

"We need your help, Frank. There seems to be a water main issue, or sewer or something, and the local fellows are perplexed. Any chance I can bribe you to come up and do a consult?"

"I'm on my way. Can I bunk in with you?"

"We'll work something out. Did I ever tell you about Valerie?"

"Who?"

"Never mind. See you soon."

By lunchtime Sunday, two great old friends surrounded Jim. He felt proud and helpful to be able to call on these experts that were not only willing to pitch in, but were geographically desirable. If an MSF staff member needed to call in an expert, it required approval, a great amount of travel and considerable expense. This day Jim got lucky.

Amid the chaos and demolition, Foligno was still Italian. All of the cafes on the piazza were open and busy. Jim, Valerie and Frank sat in one corner strategizing. Jim and Valerie planned the staffing of the hospital, and Frank planned the courtship of Valerie. Jim had predicted this possibility as he was hanging up with Frank and was happy to facilitate plumbing, nurses and romance all in one smooth arrangement.

Steve sauntered up to join them. The smile on his face when he spied Valerie should not have been surprising. Jim had forgotten the spell that she so nonchalantly cast on nearly every post-pubescent man. Jim had nearly fallen for her charm in Marbella. The thought of cheating on Madeline had crossed his mind many times, but the reality never did. Valerie would have been the one exception, but alas, it was not meant to be. One does not go back to a past denial, thought Jim, and easily shook off his own interest. He looked on with amusement as his male friends ogled the new-found Italian beauty, and he suspected any potential dalliance would end in tears.

Nobody worked on Sunday, even during a natural catastrophe. The piazza was full, even though it was winter and inclement weather was fast approaching. Lunch was served under heat lamps and heavy plastic sides were hastily attached to the awnings as the rainclouds burst open. They bundled up under horse blankets with Valerie wedged between her two new suitors. Jim was content with the romance of Italy. This was the first real meal that he had had since landing in Rome and he was going to savor every bite. The meal started with a refreshing Asti, a sparking Italian, much maligned by its exported counterpart in the States. Homemade pasta with white truffles was the first dish. Simple strozzapreti noodles with fresh butter, salty sweet Parmesan, startling black pepper and generous slivers of that most sublime of all delicacies: the white truffle. A simple drizzle of young olive oil rounded out every bite. Jim was in heaven. Anywhere else in the world this dish would be a seriously expensive splurge. Here, it was just the starter. Jim followed that with the wild boar, while the others enjoyed the pork with lemon sage cream sauce, into which Jim could not resist sticking his bread. The wine flowed more freely than during the workweek for obvious reasons, and for the first time Jim and Steve felt like they were in Italy.

Valerie laid out her plans for contacting the nursing schools closest to the region and also knew of a few experienced nurses in Rome with whom she had worked and who would probably love to relocate, at least until the roster was filled out. Steve was grateful for her connections, her experience, and her easy, seductive smile. Some men never get over the powers of Italian women.

Frank and Steve made plans to meet at the new hospital first thing the next day. The others said goodbye, while Jim and Frank sat sipping grappa and reminiscing, long after dark.

Jim, "So, been following the Bruins?"

Frank stared into his espresso, "This is not working out, Jim. I'm lonely, bored, nobody follows hockey or basketball, certainly not Boston basketball, and I miss working. I'm shit at this retirement thing."

"Yeah, I was thinking about you the other day. Sorry I haven't been more in touch. This move has been intense. I wrote you about the restaurant, but there is also the thing about being in my old hometown, the ghosts that are lurking around every corner, and the women. Oh, Jesus Frank, the women in Zanesville have been a trip."

"At least there are women in your life. I am bone dry

here. I speak the language pretty well now, but they have no interest. I'm not rich and, get this, I'm not married. Any good looking woman I meet either wants to be married to a rich guy, or a mistress to a rich guy. I swear to God, I would be much better off if I was married. Makes no sense."

"That reminds me, careful of my friend Valerie. She has a tendency to devour men and leave them in her wake. I think it's probably fun for a bit, but then poof, all gone."

"I suspected that. But, I'd be happy with a broken heart at this point. That young doctor isn't going to get anywhere. Married is good, but not to a woman in the States. I know enough to know she won't go there."

"You're right. And neither should he, but they're grown-ups. They'll figure it out."

"Great to see you, Jim. Thanks for calling."

"Ha. Well, I'm glad you said you missed working. You might need to get your hands dirty tomorrow."

"I can't wait."

13

March is actually the cruelest month. There is no sun, no warmth, and no signs of spring. Death hangs in the air. The post holiday lull created a social and sociological void in which nobody wanted to eat, drink and, least of which, be merry. This was the world in which Jim arrived, wreaking of the most delicious catastrophe of his MSF career. He felt guilty to bring such a positive vibe into what surely would be a dire Monday at the restaurant. So he decided to forego work and visit his mother.

Ruth sat in her usual position, on a stool in the middle of her kitchen, with brush in hand, staring at the sketch on her easel. Jim opened the kitchen door, and, as usual she didn't look up. "Doctor."

"Hi, Mom."

"Where ya been?"

"You know where I've been. Italy. It was fun."

"Fun? I thought you were saving people's lives in the middle of death and destruction."

"Yes, that too. It was a strange one, especially for MSF.

We were needed all right, but not for our usual blood and guts, life-saving gymnastics. We actually had to reconstruct a hospital. It really was a horrible situation; many doctors and nurses were killed in the quake. Our job was to help open a new hospital and find permanent or semi-permanent staff to open it."

"And how exactly was that fun?"

Jim looked in the refrigerator, an old habit. He knew there would be nothing with an expiration date in the current year. Ironically, "We ate well. And my old friends Frank and Valerie were there."

"Valerie? Isn't that the young Italian that you went to that island with and didn't want your wife to know?"

"How on earth do you know that?"

"Rosemary tells me everything. We talk all of the time. Always have. How on earth do you think she knew to come fix your restaurant?"

"Yes, Mother. I figured that much out. Valerie and I never did anything untoward."

"Oh, I know you didn't." Ruth smiled and made a long, jittery brushstroke and immediately rubbed it out with her fist. Loudly, to herself, "Damn shaky old broad."

Jim changed the subject. "Have you been down to the restaurant?"

"A few times. There were people in there. Everyone always seemed happy and on their toes. But without you there, it didn't really feel right. I must say, the one thing you did right was making that place feel like home."

"Wow. Thanks, Mom. That may be the nicest compliment I've ever received."

"Don't let it go to your head, sonny boy. I didn't say it was busy. You better get your butt down there and make it busy or it'll just be another one of your hair-brained schemes."

Jim shook his head, kissed his mom on the forehead and headed into the dull, freezing March air.

The next morning, Buddy was in the middle of lunch prep when Jim walked in the kitchen door and sidled up next to him. He slipped a shiny silver kitchen tool out of his breast pocket and slid it across the prep table in front of him. "I bought you a present."

"Hey, Doctor Jim! Great to see you. What is this? Of wait, I know what this is, but I don't have any ..."

Jim reached in the pocket of his tweed sport coat and produced a glass jar the same size as a baby food jar. "You don't have any truffles? Well, now you do! White, winter truffle to be exact. A little present from our friends in Umbria."

"Oh, my gosh! I've never even seen one before." He held the jar up into the light, carefully rolling three little balls around in their hermetically sealed container. He opened it, took a gentle whiff, quickly resealed the jar and smiled. "Smells like shit, but good shit. I heard about these musky little morsels in Paris, but we never got to touch them. We had some black ones at a fancy place on the Right Bank one night, when our teacher took some of us out for a special dinner. They were really, really expensive."

"Yep, usually are. These weren't, but we're still going to charge like they were."

"Do you think people in Zanesville will pay for a delicacy like this?"

"We won't charge New York prices, but just enough to educate. Not everyone will order them, and we don't have enough for lots of people to have them anyway."

"So how shall we have them? The one dish I had was with eggs. Amazing eggs, but just eggs."

"Oooh, I love them with eggs. But this is a white truffle, more delicate and subtle than its pungent black cousin. Simple pasta or risotto; the sliver of yumminess is the star."

"I can make a fresh egg pasta. What shape would be good?"

"I think tagliatelle works well, rolled out extra thin. We need to get some really good butter. That Parmesan we've been using will be great. It needs to be nutty and complex. None of that waxy, boring stuff."

"We're out."

"Oh, shit. I'll call Terek and see where he is. If he's coming through here soon he can bring us some from Baltimore. For some reason, it's not the same when they ship it."

"The Wilkes farm has butter. I've never tried it, but I bet it's probably delicious."

"Great. I'll pick some up along with their eggs."

"And they have a little mill. You can get some unbleached flour there."

"Wow! Perfect! I'll head out there tomorrow and get it all. We'll call this special, Wilkes Farm Pasta with Umbrian White Truffles."

Jim headed down to his office, but stopped mid-step and returned to the kitchen. "Buddy, I have a question for you?"

"What's that, boss?"

"What do you think of the name ... of the restaurant?"

"Ummm."

"Do you think it stinks?"

"Yep," he said without looking up from his work.

Jim paused for a second. Then, "Thanks."

Jim jumped right back into restaurant life, inspired by his Italian experience and the rediscovery of all the new improvements that Rosemary pumped into the place. He thumbed through the online reservation system to see what the coming weeks looked like, and it was bleak. He called Terek and arranged a special Parmesan delivery, bribing him with a bowl of the earthy delight. The Balkans were directly across the Aegean Sea from Italy and enjoyed many of the same dishes and culinary traditions. The delicacies were rare items found in the forests, or slaughtered with great irregularity, hence being delicacies. But they were always local, not flown in or purchased in a fancy store. Terek knew what he had to look forward to on his drive across Pennsylvania.

Nancy popped her head in the office to welcome Jim back. "Hi, Doc. How was your trip?"

"Actually, Nancy, it was wonderful. You know, as wonderful as earthquakes, death and destruction can be."

"Nice one. See ya later."

"Oh wait, Nancy. I have a question for you, and be honest."

"I'm always honest."

Jim knew that Nancy worked in the little white lie like other artists worked in clay, but he ignored her denial. "What do you think of our restaurant name, The Five-Year Plan?"

"It stinks."

"That's honest. I see what you mean ... about being honest. Thanks."

"Any time. Ciao!"

Ginger came into the office a few minutes later. "That name sucks!"

As the rest of the staff wondered in, one by one, the question was posed and the answer never improved: "Shitty!" "Are you kidding me?" "Worst name ever." "What were you thinking?" and "Better than butt face."

On the road to McConnelsville Jim made small talk with Carla. He couldn't believe that she actually agreed to go on his field trip. He had an ulterior motive and she suspected it. He only hoped that she didn't think it was of the romantic sort. Of course she did.

Carla, "I love the farm country down this way and these little villages are so cute."

Jim failed to see anything cute about town after town of little, non-descript houses adorned with either a pick up truck or a Harley, or both. There were a few tiny downtown areas, but most were just bedroom communities of Zanesville, albeit far from the city center. He slowed as they passed the free clinic in McConnelsville.

Carla, "Oh, I know the doc that runs that place. I've never been down here before. It looks cute."

Jim, getting to his motive, "Shall we stop and say hi on the way back?"

"Sure. I'll give him a call and see if he's in today. You'll like this guy. His name is Pete. He's a real straight shooter. Cute too."

They took a left just outside of town and headed over a few rolling hills towards the Wilkes farm. Jim, "So, I have a question for you."

Carla, hoping it was something personal, "Yeeees?"

"No, no, nothing like that. This is something sort of silly. What do you think of the name of the restaurant?"

"Which restaurant?"

My restaurant, goof ball! The Five-Year Plan."

"I think it's stupid. Nobody knows or cares what it means. Probably the reason nobody patronizes the establishment."

Dejected, "Thanks."

Wilkes farm was nestled in the cradle of three hills, with a cute white farmhouse and three matching out buildings. Down the road a hundred feet from the main buildings was an old red barn with a faded Mail Pouch painting on the side. There were a few fallow growing fields on plateaus up two of the hills in different directions and pastures in the distance. Chickens seemed to run wild everywhere, and a single goat nibbled on a green spot of lawn. Cows were mooing but not seen. They must have been in the milking barn directly behind the house. A lazy creek ran off to one side and disappeared, following the road around the bend. Currier and Ives could not have painted it any better.

Three barking dogs preceded Amos Wilkes as he appeared from between the house and the dairy, adjusting his winter overalls over his ragged wool sweater. "Howdy, Doc. And who is this? Is this the misses?"

Jim shot out his hand and offered a strong grip, anticipating his earlier experience with the quintessential old farmer. "Nah, this is an old friend. Carla Jenkins, I'd like you to meet the best damn farmer in all these parts, Mr. Amos Wilkes."

Carla held out her hand, which Amos immediately kissed and held onto a little too long. Embarrassed by the flirtation, "Nice to meet you."

Jim, "Where is Sarah?"

"Oh she's in ta town for somethin'. Damn cats are the only things 'round here that stays inside and don't eat what we grow. I'd set 'em out long side the road if it was up to me."

"Now, Amos, you know you love those old cats."

"Not hardly. What ya out for?"

"We need some extra eggs. Four dozen if you got them.

And I hear you've been churning up some butter. Any chance we could get some of that too?"

"Oh, Sarah cranks some of the sweetest butter. I have to warn you though; you will not ever be able to have that store-bought crap again after you taste this. You sure you want to go down that path?"

"I can handle it. I promise."

They all laughed and headed off to the dairy.

With the car full of eggs, milk, cream, butter, flour and an apple pie that Sarah baked when she heard Jim was coming, they headed back to McConnelsville. Doctor Peter (Pete) Wilson met them as they walked into the clinic waiting room. Carla and he embraced. He finally pulled away. "You must be Doctor Langley. I've grown up hearing all about you."

"You have? That sounds interesting and maybe a little boring. Nice to meet you, Doctor Wilson."

"Please, call me Pete."

"Call me Jim. How on earth did you hear about me when you were a kid?"

"We lived in Caldwell, but my dad knew your dad. He was an OB/GYN too. I think they may have taken call for each other from time to time. When you went off to Boston that was a big thing. I stopped hearing about you, well … Both of our dads died the same week. Isn't that weird? Zanesville had to scramble to find people to deliver babies."

"I'm sorry to hear that. You must have been young. I was a first year resident at Cook County."

"Yeah, I know. I was 16. Second year pre-med at Ohio State."

"Doogie Houser! You're probably sick of hearing that

one."

"Nah, it's okay. I finished in three years. I graduated med school on my 21st birthday. Kind of a freak, I guess. I actually went to Cook for my residency. When the option came up I remembered you trained there, and so I knew it was a good choice."

"Wow, Pete. I'm flattered and impressed."

Carla interrupted. "We going to stand around here all day doing the mutual admiration society thing, or we going to see this joint?"

"Oh, sorry. Let me show you around."

Pete showed them around the converted Mason's temple. Not really much of a temple; basically a store front with a balcony down one wall, now blocked off for storage. Several rooms lined the far wall with a central nurse's and doctor's station on the opposite side and a waiting room in the front. Clean and simple, but essential, serving three of the poorest counties in Ohio with at least 30% below the poverty line and a literacy rate not much higher. There are families in the hills south of the clinic that haven't had a real job for two generations. Poor is a way of life in these parts. Most live government check to government check and pick up whatever low paying jobs that come up. The women tend to work more than the men at regular jobs in grocery stores and gas stations. The men pull their weight by fixing cars and trucks, doing odd jobs, and a few manage to keep stills, but the demand and the ability to produce good moonshine have faded.

Carla felt duped. She thought there might be a rekindling going on, but Jim was just using her to get to Pete. "So this whole little field trip of yours was just so you could come here?" Carla snapped as they got back in the car.

"That, and I thought you might enjoy good ol' Amos and

his sheep."

"Goats."

"Whatever."

"How did you know I knew Pete?"

"Educated guess. I looked him up: Eligible doctor, about your age, single. I figured you at least took him for a test drive."

"I did not. We only went out once. He's a nice guy. A bit of a goodie two shoes, but a nice guy."

"That's what I figured. Thanks for coming down here and introducing us."

"What do you want with him, anyway?"

"I'm going to do a few shifts for him."

"In a free clinic in Hicksville?"

"It seemed perfectly adequate. And people need medical care, even in Hicksville. Want to join me?"

"Hell, no. I've got two brats and as many days as I can handle at our own disease fest up north." Carla crossed her arms in a huff and pouted.

As they drove through the countryside, after a respectful pause, Jim, "I'm doing early Monday and Tuesday, until 2 so I can get back up for dinner service."

Under her breath, "What does it pay?"

"For me, nothing. It's totally volunteer. I think Pete mentioned that they get a federal grant to pay for nurses and staff. Shall I tell Pete you're interested?"

"I can tell him myself. I don't work Monday and Tuesday right now and the boys are in school. But just for now! And don't get any ideas."

Jim knew that she meant the opposite but wasn't going to give her any ideas. He was glad to have someone to drive all the way to McConnelsville with twice a week. He hoped that once she saw him as a professional she would be less inclined to want to pull over along the river for a quickie. Time would tell.

Terek and a huge hunk of amazing Parmesan turned up a few days later. He pulled the truck alongside the restaurant and came in through the kitchen door. The lunch service was over and Buddy was at the prep station rolling out a test batch of pasta. He nodded towards the stairs. Terek descended into the basement and found Jim alone in the office. "Doctor Jim!"

"Terek! So good to see you."

Terek plopped the heavy hunk of cheese on his desk. It landed with a thud.

"And so good to see that cheese. How the hell are you? It's been too long this time."

"I'm well. Good thing it's cold out. I put the cheese in the back. Pretty sure it would have stunk up the cab. How's it going here?"

"I don't really know yet. I just got back from Italy a few days ago. Hungry?"

"Yes. Do you really have truffles?"

"Brought back a few white ones. A gift from my new friends in Umbria."

"Nice. I saw Buddy working away on something up there. It looked like he was rolling out pasta."

"Yep. Fresh tagliatelle made from farm fresh eggs. This should be really yummy. I haven't had it yet. Let's go see how he's doing, shall we?"

As they headed up the stairs, Jim, "Terek, can I ask you a silly question?"

"Sure, Doc. Shoot."

"The Five-Year Plan, what do you think of that as a name

for this restaurant?"

"Never made any sense to me, but you Americans have crazy names for everything."

"Thanks, Terek. I appreciate your honesty."

Buddy was mixing the fresh cooked pasta with melted butter in a large pan when Jim handed him the chunk of cheese."

"Oh man, that's a hunk of cheese." Buddy carefully cut a small section off of the wheel of Parmesan and quickly grated some into the pan with a micro planer. The snowy cheese covered the pasta as Buddy tossed it with tongs and continued grating. He ground a generous portion of black pepper and tossed again. He pulled three shallow bowls from under the warming lights and carefully twisted perfect portions of pasta with his tongs. He reached for the jar of truffles from below the shelf and produced his new shaver from his chef's coat shoulder pocket. After unsealing the jar and removing a precious truffle, he offered it and the shaver to Jim.

Jim, "No, Chef. You do the honors."

Buddy pushed up his sleeves and hovered over each bowl, carefully shaving very fine flakes of the pungent knob onto each dish. After applying a generous layer, he grasped a ceramic bottle, not of the usual olive oil but of a young, green, special oil reserved for a very few dishes. He held it and crooked his head toward Jim, seeking approval. Jim shook his head with a subtle declination, and Buddy returned the bottle to its perch, unused. He motioned toward the bowls and each took one and entered the empty restaurant. Buddy had set a single table near the window with a bottle of Chianti Reserva that Jim had suggested, already opened and decanted, water glasses, cloth napkins and forks. He included knives and spoons, but knew they would go untouched.

As they sat in silence, carefully rolling and forking each bite to include a well-considered portion of the truffle, the restaurant took on the essence of the delectable fungus. Jim knew then that if he could fill his restaurant with patrons, the strange, alluring aroma would cause a stir and propel the truffle pasta orders, regardless of the hefty price tag. As his old friend Terek and Buddy finished their delicious respite into the Italian countryside, he contemplated how to entice the well-heeled Zanesvillians out of their March stupor and into his restaurant.

Leftover snow from a storm while Jim was away piled along side most of the roads. It had long ceased to be picturesque, slowly melting and mixing with mud, salt and tire spray. March was just plain ugly. Ruth's house seemed to defy the realism of the rest of the town. Her front yard was a perfectly white sheet of snow, accented with evergreens and a black and white street lamp that she had imported from a trip to Amsterdam. The driveway was jet black and shoveled clean. The neighbor boy must be in need of a new video game. The picture was inviting, thought Jim as he approached, even though he knew the house contained his cantankerous mother. It didn't happen often, but he needed her advice.

"Mother, are you here?"

Ruth was in her other afternoon position—sound asleep on the living room couch, television blasting a game show, and a seven iron within reach. "Damnit, Jim, you startled me."

"Sorry, Mother. What are you doing?"

"What the hell does it look like I'm doing? I'm negotiating peace in the middle east!" She fumbled with the remote control and turned the television off.

"Can I talk to you?"

"What were you doing just now?"

Jim ignored her crabbiness and sat down. He knew that she was always like that when she woke up, especially if she was interrupted. "Nobody seems to like the name of the restaurant and I can't understand it."

"What the hell do you mean? It's a stupid name. What's so hard to understand?"

"I can't understand why every person that I ask is just completely honest with me. Nobody even tries to make up a story, or tell a white lie. It's strange."

"James my boy, you, of all people, should understand. This is what you do. You always have. When you don't know what to say, you tell the brutally honest truth. Do you not think that people notice? They're just giving you a little of your own medicine."

Jim sat stiff, stunned. He had no reply. At last, "What were you saying the other day about the restaurant? You said it was like someone's house or something?"

"Jesus, Jim. How on earth did you ever get through medical school? You don't listen. I said it felt like home!"

Still staring off, deep in thought, he didn't notice her insult. Long ago he had become inured to her jabs. "Home?" he said to no one.

Wednesday afternoon, before dinner service, Jim called a staff meeting. Everyone gathered in the basement, seated around a large banquet table left from the Kiwanis lunch meeting. The Rotary and Kiwanis were keeping the restaurant in the black through the cold, slow, winter months.

Jim entered through the garden door, accompanied by Nick Jennings carrying an aluminum extension ladder. Nick continued up the steps as Jim sat with his crew. "Thank you all for coming in early. I have a rather important announcement."

Everyone looked at one another. There had been much speculation that this "too good to be true" job would come to a premature end. There was no way that this nut could really keep a restaurant like this open without making any money, and everyone reckoned that there was no way that he was making any money. And they were right, but that was not what Jim was about to say.

"We're changing the name of the restaurant. I've purchased a new sign. Nick is upstairs changing it out as we speak. I've sent press releases to the paper and the television and radio stations. Saturday night will be our grand re-opening. Buddy, we'll be offering the truffle pasta. Nancy, we'll need all of the part-timers. If all goes well, we'll be packed."

Nancy looked perplexed, "Jim? What's the new name?"

Jim laughed, "Oh right, the new name. Home!"

"Home?"

Buddy chimed in, "I like it."

The rest of the staff, one after another, "Me, too … me, too … me, too!"

The press were obedient in their duties and Saturday had a slightly larger than usual turnout. Not packed, by any means, but enough that Home felt festive and alive. The fireplace was roaring and Ruth took her thrown. The truffles did not fly out of the kitchen, but there were a handful of intrepid takers, and the aroma did fill the restaurant. A few patrons complained about the smell and a few more were curious enough to increase the total take of truffle pasta to twelve bowls by the end of the evening, nearly finishing off the small jar.

Word traveled slowly but the uptick in customers was steady. Unlike in the past, every night had a handful, and most Fridays were packed. Saturday still presented a challenge, but it was no longer a challenge of having no customers and more about living up to the Friday night frenzy.

The personnel increased to six fulltime wait staff, two bus persons and five kitchen staff. Joey drove people to and from the restaurant in the limo three nights a week and sometimes more when requested.

By summer, Jim had to hire a maître d' because he became too busy with so many loose ends that previously didn't exist. He was constantly running errands, helping Buddy create new menu items and managing the staff and schedule. He was exhausted and happier than he could ever remember.

Mondays and Tuesdays were reserved for the clinic. Pete turned out to be a ray of hope for the people of Southeastern Ohio, and his optimism and dedication were inspiring. Jim was constantly reminded of his residency at Cook County, and how helping people was what made medicine rewarding. His MSF experiences were fulfilling, but this work was more immediate, albeit less exotic, nothing out of the ordinary. The more ordinary and routine the day, the more fulfilling it was for him. He had found a home in the clinic.

Rarely did Jim have patients in need of his specialty. He set an occasional simple break, but most complicated fractures required some sort of surgery and would be referred to the hospital in Zanesville or Athens. Truthfully, Jim had no desire to practice orthopedics any longer and was happy to diagnose run of the mill hypertension, strep throat and the all too common type two diabetes. Most of the patients Jim saw were suffering from malnutrition more than anything. It presented itself in many forms, but unfortunately, the cause was nearly always the same: poverty. Jim's dad used to say, "Poor people have poor ways," and he finally understood what his wise father meant.

August brought a big surprise. It was a very slow Thursday, just after the last few lunch patrons had gone. The front door swung open and the bellowing, distinctive accent rang through both floors of the restaurant, over the balcony and down into the garden where Jim sat, sipping on a glass of rose and discussing business with David Weinstein. "Buongiorno!"

Jim sat upright. "Excuse me, David. I believe we have a visitor." Jim took the steps two at a time and was face to face with Frank Monahan in an instant. "Frankie!"

"Jimbo!" They embraced, slapped one another on the back and hugged again.

"Wow, what a surprise. What brings you to Zanesville, Ohio? Oh wait, I have to show you around." Jim led Frank on a whirlwind tour, introducing him to whatever staff remained, ending up on the patio with a glass of rose in Frank's hand, all in about two minutes. David said goodbye and left the two old friends alone to catch up.

Frank took a breath. "I got homesick. I went to Boston. There wasn't really anyone there that I like, so I thought I'd come see you."

"Frank, I'm touched that you came all this way just to see me."

"You kidding me? I had to see this joint. I thought you were nuts when you first told me about it, and I still thought you were nuts when you went on and on about it in Italy. Now I know you're nuts. But a good nuts."

"What do you think of the name?"

"Great. It's about time. I had no idea why you thought anyone would want to come to a restaurant called The Five-Year Plan. Sounded more like a corporate proposal than a nice joint like this."

Jim was so tired of hearing about what a horrible name it was, and Frank detected it.

"Sorry, Jimbo. Just being honest."

"Yes. I understand. Everyone was honest. So, be honest some more. Do you think it feels like Home?"

"Not quite."

"What?" This threw Jim. He thought there was consensus on the new name.

"I love the name. It just doesn't feel like your home. It's missing something really important and, for the life of me, I don't know how you missed it."

Jim was perplexed. He was certain that he had thought of everything. "What on earth would that be, Frank?"

"No pizza oven!"

Jim's eyes widened, "Holy shit. Holy fucking shit, Frank! Oh my God! You're right." Jim leaped to his feet and ran up to the kitchen. He quickly scanned the geography and tore a piece of butcher's paper from the roll at the bus station. Nancy had suggested the less formal table covering for lunch. Jim added crayons to the place settings and it was a big success. Creativity was encouraged and spawned a lot of "art" and an uptick in afternoon wine sales. Several of the more distinctive pieces, some covered in wine or coffee stains, hung along the stairs leading to the basement, often causing traffic jams as patrons stopped on their way to or from the toilets or phone booths to admire the local talent on display.

Jim smoothed out the paper on the prep table and began to draw. In just a few minutes he had fashioned a pizza station to one side of the line, directly behind the fireplace. The fireplace would have to be partially rebuilt to add a second flew, deck and added insulation for the high heat required to achieve a true pizza di Napoli. He returned to Frank with drawing in hand. "You mean like this? Frank, you are a genius. We'll start construction on Sunday."

"How do you do anything that quick? What about permits?"

"We'll pull them tomorrow. We've saved some bricks from the original demo. This will be a piece of cake. I'll have to hire and train a pizza chef, but in the meantime I'll do it. Oh, baby. This is going to be great!"

Frank stayed for several weeks, living at Jim's and exploring the environs. Jim was happy to have his old pal around again. Frank was easy to live with and always knew when to disappear.

Nancy took it upon herself to act as tour guide and Frank didn't object. His recent history with female companionship had been bleak and Nancy was a breath of Marlboro Light drenched fresh air. The Monahan charm was on full display and, through the romanticized lens of Nancy, Zanesville was wooing Frank. He was falling in love, not with Nancy of course, but the town that much more closely resembled his desires than the fantasy of living in Italy. He liked the rivers and the countryside, so easily accessible. He loved the long row of bars along Linden Avenue with their regulars, pontificating about Harleys and politics, child rearing and the building trades. He also loved the little art and pottery scene, and the attempts at gentrifying the downtown area. He started to read about the history and even found a few 12-ounce historians at the Black Dog Tavern. People were not short on stories and loved a willing audience. Frank was in heaven.

Jim completed his pizza oven, but not without a few hiccups. The permits and inspection did not go well. The laws were much more strict about cooking with an open fire than they were about simply having fireplaces. The design had to be changed twice and required stamps by an architect and a structural engineer. Adding a single pizza oven cost nearly as much as the whole kitchen installation and took almost a month.

By the first Saturday in September, the oven was ready to be fired up. Frank was leaving the next day so a big pizza party seemed a fitting send off. Just that day Jim was digging around through some boxes at the house and stumbled across his old pizza peel from Boston. He thought it was lost in the move. What a good sign, he thought.

Buddy had set up the pizza station as instructed. He procured really high quality cheeses, prosciutto, arugula, pears, and pepperoni. He prepped roasted peppers, sautéed mushrooms and spicy sausage. The dough, made from imported Caputo flour from Italy, had been proofing in individual rounds for 48 hours, in the coolest, driest spot in the restaurant (Jim's office!). The stage was set. Buddy lit the fire at 3:00. Jim said that it would take at least one and a half hours to get the fire's temperature high enough for Neapolitan pizza.

Frank and Jim arrived at 4:30. Jim rushed to the thermostat. "Jesus, turn on the air conditioning!"

Buddy, "It is on."

"Then open the doors."

"We tried that too. This oven is hot as hell."

"That's the idea, but it's also well insulated."

Frank pipes in, "Must not be that well insulated. Did yours do this, Jim?"

Jim, "I never fired it up in the summertime. But I never had to have the heat on in the house when the pizza oven was burning. Shit!"

Frank walked out to the balcony. "Nice out here."

Jim walked back into the kitchen. "Man, it's hot in here too. Okay, where's your brother, Buddy?"

"Probably still at work. What do you need?"

"Frank, would you do me a huge favor? There's an industrial tool store in South Zanesville. They have large exhaust fans. Take the limo and buy a couple. Buddy, Nancy, open all of the doors. Let's strike anything from the menu that can't be cooked on a stovetop or in the pizza oven. Set up the basement with café seating and open all of those doors to the garden. That should do it. And this will be the last time we fire this baby up until the first frost."

The party was a big, sweaty, joyful bundle of fun for all in attendance. The pizzas were tremendous, especially the pear and prosciutto with arugula. Jim thought he might have lost a few pounds manning the oven—not the worst outcome from the evening. Frank was surrounded by all of his new friends, which had a curiously unintended effect of introducing a whole subset of Zanesvillians to Home. Jim couldn't speculate if they would ever return but, one after another, they took the time to find him and impart some sort of compliment.

Not all of the customers that night were Frank's party guests. The restaurant had been steadily growing in popularity since the name change and the Internet presence cultivated by Rosemary and her young team had started to make inroads into the online reservations. One guest that night was a random food blogger passing through town. The Open Table reservations for the area limited her choices to Home and a Mexican restaurant in South Zanesville. The story about the restaurant on the website intrigued her.

The blogger and her positive, creative and quirky review of Home did not have an immediate effect. Jim knew nothing about the chance review until weeks later when a customer called, saying that she read a blurb in New York Magazine. That reservation began an onslaught of calls, emails and online reservations. Nearly all of the reservations were from out of town, many out of state and a few from out of the country. The bookings were plentiful, but were spread over many months.

Jim found the New York Magazine blurb online. The source of the information in the magazine was unclear. It was in an 'Online Finds' column and had not attributed the original contributor. Jim had no idea who or what had posted the review. He Googled the restaurant and found nothing out of the ordinary. Not until he refined his criteria, adding Zanesville to the search, did he finally find the blog and blogger.

The blog was called Missysdinnerdate.com and was the brainchild of a young woman with pink and blue hair by the name of Missy Stansfield, who mainly resided in the Old Town section of Chicago, with pretty constant travel between her mother's house in Connecticut and her father's condo in Boca Raton, Florida. Jim was amazed to learn Missy's entire history by visiting her Twitter, Facebook and

Pinterest accounts. Her blog post regarding Home read:

"I stumbled into a party that was disguised as a restaurant called Home. To say the place was hot is an understatement. When I walked in the door I immediately broke into sweat. It was blazing hot and I had to get away from the kitchen, which was a slap in the face when I first walked in. I gravitated first to the balcony and spotted a beautiful garden below. The building from the outside looked like an old tire store, but the inside and garden were gorgeous. The property is located along the Muskingum River, just north of the locks. The view is pristine and the whole feel is, golly, it's just like home. HAHAHA! I loved it, and I still haven't gotten to the food. Oh BOY was it yum. The heat was from the pizza oven, and the pizzas were crazy good. I had a piece with pears and prosciutto and stinky cheese (that's what the guy called it) and my mind was officially blown. I finally sat down and ordered a few other little plates. They were all fresh, local and unimaginably well prepared. And I was in Zanesville, Ohio?!?!? Go figure!!! Wow...mind blown! Go now!! 5 thumbs up!!!"

Not exactly the New York Times, thought Jim, but somebody said something nice about the restaurant to a pretty big audience. How bad could that be? He did a little digging into something called analytics and found some astounding numbers. This young woman with the quirky writing technique and colorful hair had thousands of followers and had been picked up by, among others, The New York Magazine. He didn't know the first thing about how all of this worked, but her popularity was obvious. How was he going to turn that into more mouths to feed?

He called Rosemary who called Amber, the high school intern with a shrewd mind for marketing and deft control of the underbelly of social media. Amber showed up at

Jim's house at midnight, ready to work.

Jim opened the door, "May I help you?" not recognizing the young whiz kid.

"I'm Amber." She pressed herself and her backpack—full of laptop, vegan snacks and vape pipe—right past Jim and into the dining room. She set up in seconds, lit the pipe, which had a very faint aroma of something from Jim's youth, and looked him in the eye, "Let's get at this."

"What are we getting at, exactly?"

"Rosemary called. She gave me the 411 and the 911. Let's get to it. I've only got until 9. I have class, boring! But I gotta go or my dad won't pay for college. He said if he catches me skipping again, I'm cut off. So what's the chickie's website again?"

"Missysdinnerdate ..."

"Got it. Jeez, two mil uniques just last month. Tracking in Chicago, New York, Boston, Cleveland, oh wait, Columbus. She is wildfire. I love it. So, what do you wanna do? We can get this in every inbox of print and online, we can plant bombs and track them, go live from the restaurant to attract Google numbers. Strat the locals, buy pinpoints. What do you want? I mean, what's the end game here?"

"How old are you?"

"I'm 18. Why, you thinking of fucking me? Well, you're not going to fuck me. I haven't committed to that orientation yet, but it may be girls. I like them all right, but the male machismo is intriguing. I guess it's what you don't have that you always want. Anyway, no way, Jose. I don't want you, no offense. So let's get to work. Got any coffee?"

"Do you really think that's necessary?"

"Do you got it or not? I'll go to the Shell station. They're open."

"How do you take it?" Jim headed toward the kitchen,

resigned to this fresh new hell, courtesy of Rosemary.

"Black and strong."

Jim had many encounters with young interns and residents in his career, but he had never experienced this leap-frogging of technology, marketing, communication and social placement as he witnessed in Amber. He really didn't want to have sex with her and would never, but the energy and sheer voraciousness wreaked havoc with his fantasy world.

Amber understood how to market online, and the reservations poured in from all over. The blog was reposted, retweeted, picked up by print and online aggregators. Legitimate reviewers (in Jim's mind) came to the restaurant. A national magazine featured Home with pictures and recipes, all downloaded and made up, but Jim thought, what the hell, they got the address right.

For the rest of the year the restaurant was full. More staff had to be hired to keep up with the constant onslaught of guests. The limo seemed to continually shuttle out of town guests back and forth to the Holiday Inn on East I-70 or any of the other handful of hotels and motels in the area. Joey begged for another driver to handle the weeknight runs. The demand was affecting his duties for the cable company. Jim was exhausted and prayed for an MSF call. None was forthcoming. Ruth stopped coming to the restaurant because she didn't know a soul. It was no longer home.

14

New Year's Eve was packed. People showed up without reservations and waited in long lines outside in the freezing cold, being let in one or two at a time as tables came available. Fortunately, New Year's reservations were for a single seating. By the end of the evening there was still a small line that Jim had to send home, with apologies and pieces of pizza. Among them were many familiar faces.

The next week was much the same. Every day's reservation list was full, but people still showed up without reservations from all over, and were often turned away. On sunny days Nancy suggested opening the balcony and patio to make room for walk-ins. They didn't seem to care that it was freezing and they had to wear winter coats. The heat lamps were rolled out of the storeroom and Jim—tearing a page out of the Paris bistros that he had visited—bought horse blankets at Sampson's livery shop and offered them to the intrepid outdoor diners.

David Weinstein called and screamed at him for ten minutes before Jim had a chance to speak. "David, calm down. What are you talking about? You said something about your I.D. Did you lose your I.D.? Have you lost something else, like your mind? Why are you screaming at me? Please, just use your words and calmly tell me what's on your mind."

"I'll tell you what's on my mind. Your fucking restaurant is screwing the people that built it. You are leaving everyone literally out on the street."

"What did you mean I.D.?"

"WHAT?" David realized that he was a little out of control. "Sorry Jim, I meant that I had no idea that this thing was going to take off like this so soon."

"So Soon? What the fuck, David? We just finished our third year and are in the black for the first time. But, as my accountant, you know that. Right? Do I need to remind you that you originally said that there would be no customers in this restaurant? REMEMBER?"

"Now YOU'RE shouting."

"Damn right I'm shouting. Now what can I do for you? Why are you calling me? As you might imagine, I am busy as hell."

"Jim, nobody around here can eat in your restaurant. People are applying in record numbers to become members of the Rotary so they can have lunch there. You've got to do something."

"What am I supposed to do? Go online and ask people to stop coming?"

"You're a brilliant surgeon. Cut something out and make room for your town. You've converted these people into food lovers. You did that! Now you have to let them enjoy it. Figure it out!"

Jim called a meeting. By now the staff had grown to 48 people and just fit in the basement area. Still setup from Kiwanis, Jim stood on the dais, flanked by Buddy and Nancy.

Jim began, "Ladies and gentlemen, thank you for coming this morning. I know some of you don't work until this evening, and I really appreciate your commitment to Home and all that it means. We have done something unheard of in this part of the country. We have a world famous restaurant!"

The room burst into applause.

"Calm down, calm down. Yes, this is wonderful, but we have a serious problem and I need your help."

Nancy, brashly piped in, "Yeah, we're booked solid and busy as hell. What a problem!? Hey?"

Everyone laughed and applauded. Jim raised his hands to hold down their enthusiasm. "We are very blessed. The attention from across the state, the country, even the world ..."

More applause and a standing ovation before Jim gave them the look. There was immediate silence.

"Thank you. Answer me this. What is the name of our restaurant?"

A single, unison chant, "HOME!"

"I can't hear you?"

"HOME!"

"That's right, HOME. And what is missing from Home? We've now had guests from as far away as Beijing and Sydney. We have regulars from Pittsburgh and Cleveland. People think nothing of getting on a plane to come see us.

But we are missing the one thing that makes us great; that makes us Home! Our people. Our Family! How do we make it so our local people feel at home again? I need your help. Suggestions?"

Cindy, the new hostess spoke first, "The far away people don't always show up. I mean they do on Fridays and Saturdays, but the weekday reservations have a 5 to 1 no show, or that's what I figured the last time I calculated it."

Jim was impressed, "You calculate the no shows?"

"Yeah. I get bored just seating people. I like math."

"I like you, Cindy?"

"Cindy Greengrass."

"Well, Cindy Greengrass, do you have any suggestions?"

"No, but if you wanted to do something to get people in from the town I think we have some tables available from time to time. I think you could figure two two-tops at lunch and a two- top and a four-top at dinner at the very least."

"Thank you, Cindy. Anyone else?"

Nancy, "When I worked in New York we always kept a couple of tables for walk-ins. Why don't we do that?"

Jim, "Okay, great ideas. Cindy, when you take phone reservations you get a phone number, right?"

Cindy, "All of our reservations are booked online. I have to turn phone reservations down most of the time."

"We have a phone number left with the online reservation, correct?"

"Yeah, of course. What does that mean?"

"It means that we know where people are from based on their area code. Let's make the area code a preference in our booking. Do you think that would help? And let's do the extra table, walk-in thing. We can make this more like Home!"

Buddy stood up and showed a new leader's swagger.

"Why are we closed between lunch and dinner service? We really don't need to be. I can overlap kitchen staff. I'm here forever, and Nancy can stagger a few wait staff to cover it. Right, Nan?"

Nancy, "Sure. Don't know why not."

Jim jumped up, "Buddy, you are a genius. We just need to let the local folks know that we're open all day and only take walk-ins. We'll leave the reservations hours the same. Fingers crossed it works and we can welcome back our local patrons!"

The pane windows of the clinic were iced over. There was nothing living that wasn't bundled in down or multiple layers of wool. The world along the river was not for the faint of heart in the winter. Blue meant frozen and black meant dead. There was no pink or green. Grey was bearable and what most put up with. The sting of wind was like shards of glass to any exposed body part. The local news warned that five minutes of uncovered skin would result in frostbite. Most in Southeastern Ohio either ignored the warning or didn't own a TV set—what locals still called the 300-dollar flat screen HD displays that were available at every Walmart.

The waiting room was empty, except one young man, scruffy and stoic. Jim walked in and nodded to the boy sitting in the corner.

Lillian was the receptionist on duty. The rest of the clinic was quiet. Lillian looked up from her needlepoint and greeted him. "Good morning, Doctor Jim." She handed him the boy's chart. "We have one patient. He presents with nothing apparently wrong, complaining of a sore throat and being cold. Hell, we are all cold, so that ain't a symptom."

"Thank you, Lillian. We are all indeed cold, and I will be the judge of whether there is anything wrong. Ask him to please come back to room two."

"What's wrong with room one?"

Jim shot her that look.

Lillian stood and poked her head out the little sliding glass window. "Young man, please come through this here door and go back to room two."

Jim, "Thank you."

The young man did as he was told and sat by himself in the small, sterile exam room. There were no nurses yet at the clinic. The place felt cold and empty.

Jim looked at the chart and could not discern anything remarkable, other than a 17-year-old boy with the lack of parents. He took a deep breath and entered the room. "Jeffrey Wilkins? Is it Jeff?"

"Yeah, Jeff is good."

"Hi, I'm Doctor Jim. What seems to be the problem?"

"I have a sore throat. I know that ain't a big deal."

"No, no, it can be a big deal, but most of the time it's not. Let see what's up with you." Jim gently pressed on both sides of Jeff's throat with his fingertips. He removed a wooden stick from a glass dispenser on the counter and held down Jeff's tongue. "Say, ahh."

"Ahhhhh. Do you see anything bad, Doc?"

"Looks like you have a few little white spots. Probably Strep. I'll take a culture, but I'm sure that's what it is. A series of antibiotics should take care of it."

"Wait, I can't afford ..."

"Don't worry about that. We'll make sure you get what you need at no cost. Didn't you see the sign out front? Free Clinic. It's free!"

"Oh, okay. I just can't afford any of this stuff."

"May I ask you a personal question?"

"What kind of personal question?"

"I noticed that you don't list parents or an address. I can't ask you specifically about your parents, but I can ask where you are living."

"What does that have to do with my throat?"

"Everything and nothing. Look Jeff, we'll give you the drugs that'll make your throat better, but I want to make sure that the rest of you is better too. Do you have somewhere to stay?"

"I'm fine. I get along."

"What happened to your parents?"

"They died. Last year. My mom died of cancer and my father, I don't know. He couldn't live without my mom. He just didn't wake up one day. My aunt said he died of a broken heart."

"Where is your aunt?"

"Arizona. I was going to go out there but I don't have the money."

Where are you living, Jeff?"

"I live under the five-mile bridge."

"WHAT? It's fucking freezing out there."

"Chill out, Doc. Don't yell at me."

"Sorry, sorry. You're right. So, you're 17 so you can go into foster care, but you don't have to. Is there any shelter around here for teens? You're in-between aren't you? You're fucked."

"Yep. You got it."

"What about school?"

"I went through junior year. That's all I had to do. I took the GED test and passed. I'm done with those assholes."

"What do you want to do?"

"I want to get the hell out of here."

"Have you ever had a job?"

"Yeah, I worked in the Dairy Isle for two summers. I worked in the back. They didn't like we waiting on customers at the window so I chopped onions and crap like that. I sort of liked it when they weren't being mean to me. I washed the dishes, filled the ice cream machine. You know, simple stuff that needed to be done."

"You want a job?"

"Yeah, of course. You got one?"

"I think I might. Come back here in four hours and bring your things. You can stay with me until you get on your feet. Deal?" Jim shot out his hand, eager to please and wondering what the hell he had gotten himself into.

The first stop with his new roommate was Jim's house. A shower and clean clothes were in order. On the ride up from McConnelsville, the stench nearly killed them both. Jeff was a tall, lanky kid with a full head of brunette curls and a baby face. Although Jim probably outweighed him by nearly 100 pounds, some of his clothes would have to do until they had a chance to do laundry and make a trip to the mall.

Just before dinner prep they walked into Home's kitchen. Jeff looked even lankier in Jim's extra large, Brooks Brothers denim shirt and a pair of chef's pants Jim had accidently shrunk to just about the right size. Buddy was at his usual spot at the back prep table, flanked by his sous chef Ginger and a new hire that Jim had not yet met.

Buddy looked up, "Oh, hey, Jim. I want you to meet Bill O'Mara, our newest line cook. He comes from CIA and worked in Boston when he was in college."

"Nice to meet you, Bill. Where did you go to college?"

Bill, a slight red head with ironic facial hair and not a clue as to what that meant, could barely speak. "MIT, sir. I didn't quite finish. Went to CIA in my senior year. I worked in restaurants all through school. I kind of preferred cooking to rocket science."

"Wow! Okay. That's quite a change. Where did you work in Boston? I frequented a few of those haunts. Locke-Ober, by any chance, or Legal?"

"Actually I did work at Legal out in Chestnut Hill. But Barbara Lynch really changed my life. I worked at Number 9 for two years. It was way harder than rocket science."

"Bill, it's a pleasure to have you in our humble establishment. That's a fine culinary provenance. Welcome aboard."

Bill, although confused by the comment, recognized a complement. "Thank you, sir."

"Buddy, everyone, I want to introduce you to another new member of the staff. Everyone, this is Jeff Wilkins. Ginger, can you get him a jacket and put him to work. Jeff can fill you in on his kitchen experience and you can take it from there. Jeff, this is Ginger, Buddy and Bill."

Ginger gently guided Jeff by the front of his shirt with a playful finger. "Come with me, cutie, and we'll fill out some paperwork and get you dressed."

Amber showed up at midnight again. Jim was getting used to her late night visits, as long as she produced results. She set up and lit her pipe. "What are we slaying tonight?"

"Well, young lady, we are slaying ourselves."

Amber was confused. In the most curious of voices, "What the fuck?"

"Our mission is to inform the locals that we are open for business."

"Word on the street is that you're open but not for local business."

"Exactly, and exactly what we need to change."

"How the hell we supposed to do that?"

"That's what I was hoping you could help me figure out. We've made a few, shall we say, concessions to accommodate our residents. We have reserved a select number of walk-in tables per seating and we will now stay open between lunch service and dinner, but we don't take online reservations for those in-between times, so that should open up some more spots for the local clientele. What do you think?"

"I think it's a first world problem."

"You can say that again, but I'm getting pressure from my friends, and I know this phenomenon is likely a fad."

"Whatever, dude. Let's do it. So your online local scene is a little limited because, well because it's online. I do know of this one bulletin board—really old school—that a bunch of kids set up before they went off to college and kind of kept it going. They're sort of that anti-Facebook crowd. Most of them moved back here after college, with bunches of student loans and no money to live anywhere cool. You know that cliché about kids living in their parents' basements? That's what these kids do. They mainly telecommute to jobs in Pittsburgh, Cleveland and Columbus. I even heard about a girl that works for a company in California and goes out there once a month for meetings and sushi. Get this. They call themselves the Zanesville Underground. Get it? They live in their parents' basements! Creeps."

Jim studied his young genius. What does this have to do with our restaurant?

"They got tons of disposable."

"They have what?"

"Disposable income. They pay little or no rent, make buck and don't have any bad habits. They are a lot like you. They generally don't do drugs and like a nice meal and a bottle of wine. They are sort of the next generation Reagans. Go figure. That ain't me. They're weird but I think they might be your audience."

"Sold. How do we get to them?"

"I just did. I hacked into their bulletin board. They won't let me join. Say I'm too young. Asshats. Anyway, just posed as one and mentioned the secret hours. They like secrets. Pretentious Millennials."

"Will that work?"

"Hang on. Yep. Already working. They're now hip to your joint. Expect to start seeing them."

"They are hip?"

"Some jive talk just comes around again, Jim. Get a grip." She closed her laptop, loaded it into her backpack and headed to the door. "Toots!"

The restaurant's in-between seating took off right away. Tattoos, piercings and colorful hair filled the tables. The once sedate restaurant resembled an East Village coffee house. Laptops were on every table, despite the lack of Wi-Fi, and the liquid combinations of coffee, espresso, wine, booze and the occasional kambucha (smuggled in) were mind-boggling. Jim was grateful for the new locals—although not what he originally had in mind—and had to staff up accordingly. They didn't hesitate to order full meals, chef's specials and previously untouched vintage bottles from the cellar. The colorful locals began to infiltrate the out-of-towners, taking advantage of the area code preference and the new walk-in policy. It was the dead of winter and the place was hopping.

The April thaw brought bad news for the clinic. Pete called Jim and asked him to come down for a staff meeting, an activity Jim had previously been able to avoid.

Jim arrived to a full reception area. It seemed that there were far more employees and volunteers than Jim had imagined. The meeting was scheduled for 9 a.m. and Jim was ten minutes late, and the last to arrive.

Pete settled the masses and spoke, "Ladies and gentlemen, thank you for coming today. With a heavy heart, I am obliged to inform you that the clinic is being forced to close." Boos, moans and sighs interrupted him for a moment. "I know, I know. Settle down. I need to spell out for you all what has happened. There is a new state law that requires that we be a certain distance from an emergency room because we perform certain procedures here. Without those procedures, we lose the majority of our funding. The federal share alone is not enough to keep going, and they are now threatening to take that as well."

Shouts of "What can we do?" and "I'll work for free" rang through the reception area.

Unless you can write a big check, I'm afraid there's nothing that any of us can do. We will cease operations at the end of ..."

Jim interrupted by pulling Pete, rather forcefully, into the back. "This is very bad timing. I just got a call to go to Jordan, and I will have to be gone for three months. We cannot lose this clinic and I certainly cannot lose it. I keep my hours up by working here, and that's the only way I can continue with MSF. How much will it cost to stay open for the three months I'm gone?"

I don't know exactly. Probably about 40 grand. We get 250 a year and we are good for another month. Do you have any ideas?"

Jim produced his checkbook from his jacket pocket. "Here's 50 grand. I will see about raising some more and put my Rosemary on fixing this situation. There is more than one way to stay in business. Don't you worry. Promise me that you will still be here when I get back."

Dumbfounded, Pete, "I promise."

15

Ramtha Hospital was five kilometers from the southern border of Syria. Although the capital, Aleppo, was far to the north, there were still plenty of victims in need of help in the south. The violence was constant everywhere between the capital and the southern border. Every day and night truck bombs and suicide bombers wreaked havoc, and the devastating barrel bombs dropped from the sky, spraying shrapnel in a shattering radius, injuring and killing innocent Syrians. There was no discriminating in the acts of government sanctioned or rebel killing, maiming and uprooting of lives. Most who lived in Syria did not participate directly in the warfare. The lucky ones found a way to leave, refugees for the rest of the world to condemn. Many of the not-so-lucky ones were caught in the crossfire and ended up being transported across the border by MSF, Syrian and Jordanian ambulances, taxis and trucks.

Most of the wounds were to appendages. The more direct hits were deadly. The Ramtha Hospital was well equipped for the surviving patients. The new trauma center was a large, open room with pale blue walls and stark white curtain dividers. The walls were lined with state of the art diagnostic equipment. The local staff was a mixture of passionate Muslims and Christians, peppered with French, Spanish and English MSF staff. They all spoke multiple languages, were extremely well versed in triage, suturing and, most important of all, peace keeping among the various factions pouring over the border and into the facility.

Jim arrived early in the morning and wasted no time. His bags sat untouched in the men's locker room for the first two days. As soon as he read the brief on the plane he knew there was going to be very little sleep in his future. He slept on the plane. He slept in the airports in London and Frankfort, and he slept on the bus from Amman. He walked straight off of the bus to the locker room, showered, donned scrubs and washed in. For the next two days he did three eight-hour surgeries. He reconstructed two femurs, screwed and glued one knee and set various other simple fractures in the ER between surgeries. He didn't know any of the staff, but they knew him. Every nurse, assistant, anesthesiologist and orderly was provided with detailed CVs of all incoming doctors. Jim was provided the same courtesy. When chaos delivered truckloads of patients, there was no time for a getting to know you chat.

By day four Jim was shown to his living quarters; a single story tiled house a short walk from the hospital. Situated in a residential neighborhood, the house was clean, well-appointed and homey. The kitchen was large, with a substantial round wooden table that could seat eight. It was equipped with an American style refrigerator, modern appliances and a microwave oven. If it weren't for the occasional interruptions of distant shelling, the house could have been in any suburb in the Midwest.

Jim shared the house with a Spanish doctor, a French paramedic and two German nurses. French was the primary language spoken on all MSF projects, but Jim soon learned that everyone was happy to speak English. He spoke French passably but when he was tired his vocabulary shrunk drastically, and he often slipped into English without knowing it. This language fatigue issue was common among NGO veterans, and most were sympathetic to the malady and adapted. The result was a pastiche of shifting languages, depending on who was the most fatigued.

Andre Lopez, the Spanish doctor and housemate, was also an orthopedic surgeon. Rarely did similar disciplines cross paths. The organization tried to keep the orthos spread out, often not needing more than one specialty per project. This was a unique case. Since all of the patients were victims of this civil war, without fail, the injuries were bullet wounds and shrapnel, almost always involving bone. These two were valued talent.

Andre was diminutive, gentle and darkly handsome. He exuded confidence and a childlike curiosity, somehow not at odds. Maybe it was the bushy mustache and baby face, or the quick, efficient way that he moved. He was unique and likable, and Jim took to him immediately. They clicked. Within days they were finishing each other's sentences. Certainly it had to do with their similar professions, but they were also exactly the same age, born two weeks apart. They had both lost their spouses—Andre's to cervical cancer just the previous year. And they were foodies. Neither had been to Jordan and both were determined to find the best food in the region.

Another of the housemates, a German surgical nurse named Christian, enlisted in their culinary search. He had been in Jordan for months before them and had scouted the local cuisine with a similar passion. With German precision and the subservience and confidence of his surgical post, he was the perfect aide-de-camp in their taste explorations. Like many nurses in MSF, Christian was highly trained, single, dedicated and a little bonkers. His semi-chiseled features and mountain man build betrayed his gentle spirit. He loved food, fine wine and finely featured men.

This unholy triumvirate spent what little down time they had exploring, cooking and drinking in the local faire. They walked up and down the narrow passageways and streets, following their noses and talking to people on the street as best as they could. Whenever they would see a bustling restaurant full of locals they went in and gestured and pointed at food being served to others. They met a few local food lovers and managed to communicate through their common desires.

They often had surgeries together. And when tough cases presented, all three would brainstorm. They had a deep commitment to their patients. Nearly half of the injured refugees were children and young women, caught in the wrong place with no means to escape. The three men worked long, diligent hours, combining efforts and resources to make certain that these young people would one day have a chance to escape this horrible nightmare.

One of their first patients was Fatima, a bright-eyed 15 year-old who wore a hijab and a brilliant smile. She witnessed her mother and brother die when their living room was destroyed by a direct hit from a missile. She was in the adjacent room. Her pelvis was fractured and her left leg was mangled in several places. After the initial surgery to repair her leg, she suffered from debilitating pain. Infections plagued her leg and the pain from both her leg and her slow healing pelvis combined to make her suffering unbearable. Jim, Andre and Christian held constant vigil over her.

The pain management was barely working, so they studied her x-rays and charts, searched the Internet and Skyped a few colleagues around the world. The heart-wrenching conclusion was a partial amputation of the leg just below the knee, and a two-step surgery to repair different parts of the pelvis.

After the second surgery, Fatima's spirits were revived. Jim and Andre spent a lot of time at her bedside explaining their plans to make her better, listening to her stories and becoming friends. She spoke English very well. She would have bouts of sadness, but was generally buoyant. She managed to wash herself every day and would sit straight up in bed, refusing to be a victim.

Jim explained that the returning infection might continue to be a problem without further intervention. He carefully spelled out what was involved in the recovery from the amputation. She nodded and understood exactly what he was saying. Her only questions were pertinent, and pleasantly surprised Jim with her intelligence and level headedness.

Fatima, "Will there still be a sensation of my leg after you have taken it?"

Jim knew that she would only tolerate straight, precise answers. She was 15 going on 30. She had a positive outlook in the face of immense turmoil and smiled when others would be in tears. "Yes, Fatima, you will. It's called ghosting. At first you'll think that your leg is still there. It'll be a very real feeling. The sensation will subside after a while. How long is hard to tell. Every person's experience is different."

"What about the infections?"

"The primary reason for removing this part of your leg is to get rid of the damaged tissue and bone that is causing the infections. If all goes as planned you should be infection free and pain free."

"How soon before we do this?"

"We can do the removal as soon as there is space in the surgical schedule. A few weeks after that we should be able to do part two of the pelvic repair and you can get the heck out of here."

"So two more surgeries, and that's all?"

"Yep. You'll need some physical therapy to learn how to walk again. There's a camp up the road that has several people your age recovering from similar injuries. They're really great people, also run by our folks. You will be in good hands. I promise."

"Thank you, Doctor Jim. You're my hero."

"No Fatima, you're my hero. Hang in there. I promise this will all be over before you know it."

Jim wanted to sit and cry, but instead the doors of the ER burst open, a distant sound that he had come to hear as an alarm in his head. There would soon be an O.R. with patient after patient in need of his talent. It was good to be needed.

Jordanian food was made up of fairly standard Middle Eastern dishes: falafel, baba ganoush, shawarma and hummus. There were two dishes that the three intrepid eaters discovered that were different from the standard street food. Ara'yes were like grilled quesadillas, a pita stuffed with lamb, onion, parsley and herbs, and brushed with olive oil and cut into wedges. But the real stand out was life changing. Mansaf was said to bring people together and was more or less the national dish of Jordan. The dish consists of rice, lamb and jameed. Jameed is a hard, dried goat's milk yoghurt. It's re-hydrated and made into sort of a thick sauce. Jim, Andre and Christian found several restaurants that served variations of Mansaf, but only one that was truly amazing. Every quiet moment found them at one of the handful of tables at the restaurant Tawa. It happened to be the only restaurant in town with a bar—maybe the reason that they found it in the first place—and a few bottles of Jordanian wine, something largely undrinkable, with one notable exception. A local Tokai was dry, slightly fruit forward and a perfect pair with Mansaf. Near the end of the first month, Tawa ran out of Tokai and took a week before it managed to restock. Gloom set in over the house.

The days were unrelenting. Surgeries stacked up late into the night. On occasion a missile or barrel bomb would land just over the border and shake the hospital, temporarily dimming the lights and shaking the instruments on their trays. It was disconcerting and made the pulse race. Fortunately, there were never any slips of the scalpel or mishaps with other dangerous instruments. The possibilities sometimes kept Jim awake at night. It was a war zone and everything was unpredictable.

Fatima sailed through her remaining surgeries, with Jim and Andre sometimes staying late to complete. These sorts of follow up surgeries were considered a luxury at front line hospitals, and relegated to non-life threatening status. Jim thought that ironic since, strictly speaking, none of what he did saved lives directly and without the follow-ups, most of the lives would not be worth living. But such is the conundrum of bureaucracy in frontline medicine.

Christian found a source for Jameed and the three made several attempts to reproduce Tawa's version of Mansaf at home. It wasn't a particularly difficult dish to make, but the Jameed was finicky and took some doing to judge its strength and get the texture just right. Christian became the king of the Jameed sauce, but Jim paid close attention. Of course he was considering it for the restaurant.

Fatima was stable and ready to be transferred to the recovery camp for her long journey back to health and walking. For someone whose future was bleak, and whose possibilities were limited at best, she glowed with the drive of an Olympian. Jim, Andre and Christian saw her off. She smiled and waved and blew them kisses—a fifteen-year-old pillar of strength—while the three strong medical men wept like babies.

Nine weeks into Jim's Jordanian stay the hospital suddenly went quiet. The daily onslaught of patients flooding the ER, triage in every hallway and pandemonium in the large trauma hall, completely, without warning, stopped. Jordan had shut the border without notice or any logical reason. No more refugees, no more injured, no more patients. The sound of distant shelling, explosions and gunfire did not cease, but the unwitting victims of the violence no longer had a lifeline.

The recovering patients continued to be well cared for. Eventually they would all be released or sent to the rehab camp. But there were no new patients to take the beds. In just one week the hospital went from overflowing to ten percent capacity, and the operating rooms were silent.

The staff thinned considerably and Jim and Andre were both told that they could finish their three-month commitment early and go home. The emotional implosion echoed through every individual in the hospital. Going from the intensity of maniacal panic to the stillness of a single corpse was devastating. There were no words to describe the empty feeling; the helplessness of policy and agony, both out of reach. It rang through the empty hallways. The putrid smells of life on the verge dissipated and the sterile uselessness of an empty ward returned.

Jim and Andre hitched a ride with Christian out to the rehab camp to pay Fatima a visit. Christian had shifted most of his rotations to rehab since the surgery was no longer busy.

The camp was also quiet. Some long-term recovery patients were receiving physical and occupational therapy, but only one of the four wards was still in operation.

Fatima was being fitted with her new prosthetic leg the morning they arrived. She had already managed to walk across the ward without any assistance. She was all smiles, sitting comfortably in a straight-backed chair, sporting a brightly colored hijab. "Hello, my brilliant and handsome doctors."

Jim spoke first. "Hello yourself, you two legged, purple, walking machine," referring to her new scarf.

"Do you like it?"

"The hijab? Yes indeed. Very fetching."

Holding out her new prosthetic that—unbeknownst to her—Jim, Andre and Christian had paid for themselves, "No silly, my new leg!"

Andre, "Oh, I hadn't noticed. It looks quite nice. Might

we see it in action?"

Fatima jumped up, fell a little backwards and caught herself. She stared straight ahead, concentrating on looking casual. She took small, labored steps, careful not to put too much weight on her new appendage. She stopped at the far wall, turned around and returned, 20 steps in all.

The audience of three burst into wild applause, hoops and hollers. "Brava, brava," yelled Jim.

Shyly, "It's new still. I have to practice. I will run again. I know it." A tear formed in Fatima's eye. She loved to run, play soccer and race her brother. It was the first time that she had mentioned it in weeks.

Christian assured her, "You will run faster and jump higher than ever before you know it!"

"Thanks, Christian. I know I will. I will."

At that moment, a few other teenage refugees from different parts of Syria came into the room; one in a wheel chair, another on crutches and two with casts. They ran up to Fatima and made Arabic small talk, squealing like any girls their age, and making Fatima feel great about her new addition.

The three men nonchalantly moved to the side, watching as the real healing began. The great thing that the rehab camp could do that the doctors, with all of their experience and technology could not, was instill hope.

16

Pete Wilson sat with his head in his hands, alone in the clinic receptionist's area. Jim opened the door, but Pete didn't look up. Jim re-opened the door and slammed it shut, stunning Pete out of his despair. "Who's there?" he chirped before looking up and seeing Jim. "I'll be damned."

"Nice to see you too, Pete."

"I'm sorry, Doctor Jim."

"I take it things are not looking up around here?"

"We're days from closing the doors. There's a slim chance that we might get a check from the state if we agree to stop our women's services, or install a trauma center."

"Wait, what do you mean trauma center? Like a real trauma center with helicopters and all of that stuff? What exactly are the requirements?"

"Hang on." Pete dug into a file cabinet and found a folder. Reading from a letter, "Emergency services able to aid and assist in complicated birth, cesarean section, blood transfusion related to hemorrhaging and other birth related trauma need to be on premises or within a ten-mile radius of clinic performing such functions ..."

"So, this doesn't actually say that we have to perform these functions, just provide facilities required for such measures, and I assume have qualified personnel on hand. In other words, you and me."

"Yeah, I guess that's right."

"Okay. Next problem. How much is the check and is it reoccurring?"

"Yes, it's semi-annual and it's about 25 grand shy of what we used to get."

"So we need to raise at least 25 grand a year? Not bad. I think it's doable. Gotta run."

"Welcome back. Hey wait, what about the trauma unit?"

"I'll take care of that."

Jim drove directly from McConnellsville to the Zanesville television station, WHIZ. He hadn't slept since he left Jordan, but his mission was clear. The summer rain cascaded across his windshield, the windows steamed up so Jim rolled down the window to keep from being lulled to sleep. By the time Jim reached the parking lot of the broadcast center he was soaked. The rain had let up and, fortunately, his suitcase was in the trunk. He rummaged around for a clean shirt and settled for a dry one. Television didn't yet have smell-o-vision, and his on-air host would have to suffer the faded stench of the Jordanian heat.

Julie Michaelson, the host of "WHIZ In The Kitchen"—the occasional cooking segment—agreed to fit him in to her Saturday afternoon slot. Once a skeptic, Jim was now a fan of local television and its surprising reach. He was exhausted but there was no time to waste and this was, after all, for a good cause.

Jim smiled as Julie introduced him; he stood awkwardly and stared into the camera. "I want to thank you all for making our restaurant, Home, a great success."

Julie shot him a look. She had agreed to a Public Service Announcement, not a blatant plug. Jim held out his hand, indicating that he was soon to get to the heart of the message. The camera slowly pushed in as he continued, "I want to apologize for the difficulty in securing a reservation lately and we have taken steps to put our local patrons front and center and that's what I am here to talk to you about today. As some of you may know, we have a neighbor in need. The McConnellsville Free Clinic has lost their funding. This clinic provides vital medical services for people who otherwise might not make it to the hospital and who can't afford doctors and insurance. It's literally a lifeline to a community on the edge. I'm here today to ask for your help and to make you an offer. The restaurant will match any donation that you make to the clinic. Please call the number on the screen right now, or visit our website to donate. Not only will we match your donation, we will guarantee you a reservation for lunch or dinner at Home, your choice, in the next two months. All you have to do is pick up the phone and make a donation of 100 dollars or more. If you make a reoccurring donation for the next two years, dinner is on me."

The camera cut to a two-shot and Julie jumped in, "How about that, folks, a guaranteed reservation? Please call now, or go online. You won't regret it. Any new dishes that you want to tell the viewers about, Jim?"

"I am just returning from a fruitful trip to the Middle East so you never know. If I can find a decent curdled goat's milk yoghurt ..."

The fatigue of the trip set in quickly. Jim fell back into his chair, mid-sentence. Julie covered, "Sounds delicious. Please call in those pledges. I know I'm making the first donation to such a worthy cause. We'll be right back!"

Jim smiled sheepishly at Julie, "Sorry about that. I haven't slept in two days. I think I better go home."

"Are you going to be okay to drive? I can take you home."

"That's very kind, Julie. I think I can make it." Jim stood with a renewed, albeit faked, vigor. "That's better. Thank you, Julie. You are such a mensch. Come over next week and we'll have lunch."

Buddy and Nancy stood at the top of the stairs with their hands on their hips, waiting for him to appear. They heard the garden door open and knew it was Jim. There was no greeting or small talk. Buddy, "You did what?"

Nancy, "Where are we supposed to put these local donors, in the attic?"

Jim smiled, half expecting their reactions. He stood at the bottom of the stairs, "Nice to see you both. Come on down and let's discuss this like grown ups, shall we?"

They huffed their way down the stairs, still incredulous. Jim entered his office, switched on the light and looked around the room, sizing it up. Buddy sat in Rosemary's punishment chair and Nancy straddled the arm. Jim plopped into the executive chair behind the desk, the sole remnant of his Boston office. He leaned back with hands locked behind his head and casually put his feet up on the desk.

Buddy realized that they might have been a little harsh.

"How was your trip?"

"Extremely heart wrenching and disappointing. What people do to one another in the name of power and religion is disgusting and horrible. We are a barbaric bunch of apes. I am not very proud to be a human right now. But I'll get over it if we can save this clinic. So, I have a few ideas and I hope you both do as well."

Buddy and Nancy looked at each other. They knew when Jim went straight for the unadulterated truth that they were in trouble and would eventually have to do whatever he said. Nancy, "So what are your ideas and what can I do to help?"

"Ah, that's better. Okay, I've got two ideas. Fortunately, it's summer so fudging a few extras out on the patio is not so difficult. But here's another. How about this room? We get rid of all of this crap. I don't need an office. We could put some posters on the wall, maybe a wine rack. We can call it the private dining room. There's enough room in here for a six-top and a serving station. We'll change the door to one of those old opaque glass ones, like you see in detective movies. Maybe have something fun etched on it."

Jim always was manic when he returned from one of his trips. Nancy figured it was his way of dealing with the devastation that he had just been up to his elbows in. "That's a cool idea. We'll have to add a server just for the room. That will make it feel even more special, like a butler."

"Nice one, Nance. And what about the pizza oven? We've shut it down for the summer."

Buddy laughed, "We can't sit people in the oven. You couldn't even get a little kid in there."

They all laughed at the ridiculous image. Jim, "Not in the oven. Let's put two two-tops in front of the oven. We'll move the pizza prep table out. We'll call them the chef's tables. Everyone will want one. What do ya think?"

"That's great, Doc. Might be a little cramped, but it's on one end of the kitchen so there is no real flow issue, is there, Bud?"

"Nah, not really. I'm not sure about how the server gets between the tables, but we can work that out."

Nancy stood up and wandered out the door. She came back in, "What about the wine cellar? If we neatly stacked the boxes in the middle there's room for a long table in there. That would be cool."

Buddy, "Cold, you mean."

Jim sat straight, "No. I'm not having people in amongst my wine. Out of the question."

Buddy and Nancy stared at him, knowing he was acting like a petulant child. They had learned a long stare gave him time to recover. It worked about half the time, but was always worth a try.

"Alright, okay. But we put a camera in there. I don't want some joker walking off with a Haut-Brion under his coat. We limit it to three nights a week. More light exposure than that is not good for the wine."

Nancy got excited at all of these changes. "The extra server for the private room can do both, actually. We'll stagger the booking so courses don't overlap. This is exciting!"

When Jim returned from Jordan he didn't know what he was going to find. He left his house in the care of an orphaned teenager who he rescued from under a bridge, just days before he left. He couldn't care less about the house or its contents. There was nothing of much value other than a few bottles of wine, and he really didn't care about those.

He had ceased to care about all material objects. His need for things died with Madeline. He was still unsure what it was that he did need. The reassessment of his life took on many forms. Walking away from a prestigious profession, moving backwards to his hometown, opening a restaurant against all odds, volunteering in far-flung human devastation were all helping him to recognize the hole that could never previously be filled. Jeffrey Wilkins was another of God's clues to understanding the void.

Jeffrey never talked about his parents, but they must have been positive influences. The house was immaculate. The bookshelves were filled with the contents of the boxes no longer littering the living room and dining room floors. The last of the boxes that had arrived from Boston just before Jim left were unpacked and every little tchotchke was thoughtfully placed. There were candles on tables and paintings perfectly hung. The beds were made. The windows were washed. The kitchen was sparkling.

When Jim arrived, Jeffrey was in the kitchen making coffee. He was dressed in his chef's pants and tee shirt, showered and ready to go to work. He met Jim at the door, took his bags and ran them up the stairs. "There's coffee," he yelled down in a friendly voice.

"Jeffrey, what have you done?" Jim sat in the living room, stunned and shocked at the transformation.

Jeffrey bounded down the stairs. "Is everything alright? I just unpacked for you. I hope that was okay to do. You've been so generous to me without any real reason. It was the least I could do."

"No, no. Thank you. I would never have gotten to all of that stuff. It looks fantastic. Thank you."

"I gotta go. See you at the restaurant? Thank you again, Doctor Jim." Out the door he went, the screen door flopping behind him.

Jim sat and stared at a miracle. Did he just adopt the perfect son? He wandered around the house and marveled. The shower called, as did his bed. He slept solidly for 12 hours.

The summer was in full force. The local reservation and fund raising efforts were bringing in thousands of dollars and packing the restaurant. The wine cellar, private room and chef's tables were huge hits, and Cindy the hostess started waiting lists for all three. Although only reserved for locals, they were always full and people clamored for literally the hottest table in town.

The clinic was temporarily closed and had been for three weeks. Pete was panicking. After a long awaited call, Jim drove down to McConnelsville to re-assure him. He had a plan that he thought might cheer him up.

Timed perfectly, several volunteers were unloading a truck as Jim pulled up to the shuttered clinic. Pete stood out front, pacing, tears in his eyes.

Jim, "Oh good. About time this junk showed up."

Pete could barely speak. "This looks like an entire operating room. How did you, where did, what, how much ..."

Jim touched him on the shoulder. "Settle down, Pete. It is, in fact, an entire operating room. This is the fortunate result of the unfortunate failure of middle east governments to work and play well with one another." That was the last Jim ever said about the gift or its clandestine origin.

Pete shook his head in disbelief as the last of the equipment was rolled into the largest of the exam rooms.

Jim, "We'll set it up so the bureaucrats can wank themselves and tick off all of their boxes, but we'll never use it.

Shame really to lose an exam room."

Pete settled into the reception area. "The other good news is that we have 11 thousand in donations from your selfless efforts at the restaurant."

"First of all, this is not selfless. I need this clinic to stay open, so I don't actually have to go get a real job, and 11 grand is not enough. But I'll fix that."

Often, people thought of Jim as self-centered and arrogant, but in reality he was loyal and trustworthy. If he said he was going to do something, he did it. He never went back on his word. His father instilled this in him when he was a boy. "You're only as good as your word, boy." That echoed in his head every single day. He was about to betray himself, or at least threaten to, and he was uneasy about it, even if it were for the right reason.

Bob Brewer, his lawyer and old friend, had become president of the Rotary Club. The Rotary still enjoyed their weekly meetings at Home, and Bob knew that they were disrupting the "busiest restaurant in the state," according to Columbus City Magazine. He also knew that they had a contract. He didn't realize that it was about to expire (he didn't draft it) and that any extensions were at the discretion of the management.

Jim showed up on time for his appointment. Bob knew exactly the reason for his visit. Jim wasted no time, "I know I said that the Rotary would always have a home, but I need that space. I think we're done."

Bob was shocked at his old friend's bluntness. "You can't do that. Actually, you probably can. I'm sure you've read the contract."

"Three years is up in September, and the extensions are

my call."

"What do you want? Do you really want to do this?"

"Your organization's slogan is "Doing Good in The World," right?"

Bob knew where this was going. "Yes?"

"So how about you do some good right here at home. The Free Clinic fundraiser is still short. Twenty grand would be perfect. Can you raise it?"

"We will certainly try. We have a slate of …"

"Yeah, we all have a slate, Bob. Get your boys on it and you can stay."

"You're blackmailing me?"

"Yep. So sue me. I've got a really good lawyer." Jim smiled and waved as he crossed the threshold. "Oh, and I need you to do this every year. Put it on that calendar you all send out!"

Jim was in a blackmailing mood. The Kiwanis met on Wednesdays, and their contract was about to expire. As he arrived at the restaurant, their meeting was just breaking up. Perfect timing, he thought.

Dan Bradford was the head poobah or whatever they called their chairperson. He was standing at the dais alone, folding some papers into his briefcase as Jim entered the nearly empty room. "Dan, just the man I was looking for." Jim employed the same tactic as he did with Bob. There was no way that the Kiwanis would give up the space for ten grand. Jim knew that the Wednesday group was not generally as well healed as their Tuesday counterpart, but should be able to swing half as much. Unlike Bob, Dan—who was not a lawyer—didn't see it as blackmail at all, but as their collective civic duty.

Cindy came galloping down the stairs in search of Jim, who was standing at the back door seeing Dan off. "Doctor

Jim, I just got the weirdest call. I just got a reservation for New Year's Eve."

"Five months early. Hmmm, that is a little weird, but I suppose not that odd given how booked up we are. Don't we have rezzies for November and December?'

"Not this New Year's Eve! Next New Year's Eve, in a year and a half!"

"Well, well, well. I guess people have started to do the math."

"What do you mean do the math?"

"Cindy, darling, next New Year's Eve is our last day in business."

"Oh, shit. Oh, shit, shit, shit I forgot."

"Settle down. We still have plenty of time. Out of curiosity, who made the booking?"

"Somebody called Missy Stansfield. Do you know her?"

"Oh, shit. Oh, shit, shit, shit indeed. Brace yourself, Cindy. I have a feeling we're about to have several more of those calls."

Cindy started to get anxious. When Cindy got anxious she squealed. "What do you mean, Jim? Why?"

"If Ms Stansfield feels the need to be surrounded by her readers, and she will feel that need, she'll write about her reservation in her little blog and we'll be inundated. She's got enough loony foodies subscribers to fill this restaurant ten thousand times."

Jim looked around the lower level of the restaurant, picturing a party. He turned back to Cindy, gesticulating as he made his list. "Do me a favor, block out the wine cellar, the private room and twenty seats, no the whole downstairs for that night. I'll be damned if I'm going out without my friends and neighbors. The foodies can have the upstairs. We'll tent the balcony and the patio, but let's leave those seats off the chart for now. I have a feeling we're going to have a zoo here."

Alone in the kitchen, Jim dumped two white balls from a quart container of his new shipment in a stainless steel mixing bowl. The smell turned his head. He broke up the balls and added water.

Buddy walked into the pungent cloud of dried goat's yoghurt. "What the hell is THAT?"

"Good morning, Buddy. That is the strength, and delight of Jameed."

Buddy ran to the front of the kitchen to avoid the smell. "Christ, that's strong."

"I'm covering it now. It needs to sit for twenty-four hours."

"Where? That can't go in the walk-in."

"It'll be sealed. I promise."

Skeptical, "If I get a whiff of that in the refrigerator, I toss it in the composter."

A woman walked in the front door as Buddy was slamming an imaginary bowl of jameed into the composter. Embarrassed, he looked up and politely, "I'm sorry, Miss. We're not open until noon."

Jim walked toward them, carrying the covered jameed. He squinted at the vaguely familiar face. "Judy? Judy Archer?"

"Hi, Jim. It's Judy James now."

"Oh that's cute. Are all of your kids named John and Joe and Julie?"

"Still a smart ass."

They hugged and laughed like the two long lost friends that they were.

"Judy, I can't believe it. I heard you lived in Washington or California or somewhere. Mom said that you had a bunch of kids and married a genius." Jim showed her to a table on the balcony. "Buddy, would you do us a huge favor and make a couple of coffees? Latte for me. Judy?"

"Sounds good."

Buddy, incredulously, "Coming right up, boss."

"Oh, how rude of me. Judy, I'd like you to meet our executive chef, Buddy Sanders. Buddy, Judy ..."

"Yeah, I heard, Judy Archer James. Nice to meet you."

"Nice to meet you, Buddy. I've read great things about you. I can't wait to taste your cooking."

"You won't have to wait long. I'll bring you a little treat with your coffee."

"Can't wait."

"What brings you back here?"

"My mom died. Her funeral is Friday."

"Oh, I'm so sorry. I haven't been reading the paper since I got back."

"Got back from where?"

"It's a long story." Jim changed the subject. "Give my love to your brother and sister. No matter how old one's parents get, it's really hard to lose one. I'm still not over my dad, and it's been nearly forty years. Sorry, that probably doesn't help."

"It does. I really appreciate that, Jim. My dad died a few years ago. I'm still not over it."

Jim held her chair as they approached the end table on the balcony.

Judy stared out at the river. "Jim, this is beautiful. Who knew that this was even here?"

They both sat down. Jim, "So, what's he like?"

"Who?"

"Your California genius."

"Portland, actually. He was a college professor. Philosophy."

"Was?"

"He had a heart attack last year. He was kayaking the Columbia and had to be pulled out by his student."

"That sounds awful, but I suppose it's good that he was there with him."

"She. And it was good. I finally found out what I had long suspected."

"Wait. Are you divorced or widowed?"

"Widowed. The son of a bitch didn't have the balls to divorce me."

Jim tapped her hand gently, "I'm so sorry, Judy. That sounds awful."

"Yeah. Well, it wasn't that awful. We'd been leading separate lives for years. He traveled and spoke all around the world. Once the kids were grown—their names are Stephen and Heather by the way—I started working again. I manage a small law firm."

"That sounds … interesting."

"Not in the least, but it kept me busy and my mind off of the fact that, most likely, my husband was a cheating, slimy, asshole."

Buddy delivered two coffees and two slices of fluffy, bright orange hued frittata. "Not on the menu, but I sometimes make frittata for family meal. The local eggs make the most beautiful dishes. Look at that color! This is roasted red pepper, onion and chives. No meat, in case you are veg."

Judy smiled. "How did you know? I sure do miss bacon sometimes."

Buddy, "Just had a feeling. And yeah, life's too short not to eat bacon. Enjoy. Bon appétit."

Buddy left them alone and returned to the kitchen. They sat quietly and enjoyed the coffee and scrumptious treat.

Judy broke the silence, "What about you? How did this happen? I remember running into you in college in Boston. You were so cool and together and knew exactly what you were going to do. And then I heard that you married a woman that was also cool and together and knew exactly what she was going to do. I was so jealous."

"What on earth do you mean, jealous?"

"I know it sounds ridiculous but, I liked you. I could see myself married to you. But you wouldn't even ask me out."

"I was intimidated. You were older."

"One year!"

"And you were so incredible. I was such an idiot."

"You're still an idiot."

"What do you mean?"

"You know I'm single, I've been sitting here for at least five minutes and you still haven't asked me out."

Jim pushed his chair back and took her by the hand. "Judy Archer, sorry, James ..."

"Archer is fine. I may change it back."

"Judy Archer, would you be so kind as to accompany me this coming Saturday evening for dinner and dancing. I know a nice little place along the river."

"And dancing?"

"That will be a surprise. Interested?"

"Just for 37 years. I'm staying at my mom's house on East Highland."

"I can't wait."

"Me neither."

Buddy appeared down below in the garden, carrying the stainless steel mixing bowl. He looked up. "Hey, this shit is stinking up the cooler. It's got to go!" He walked to the back of the garden and deposited the contents in Rosemary's composter.

"Yeah, it really did stink. Sorry, Buddy. I think we'll leave those tastes in the Middle East where they belong."

Judy looked at him curiously, "The Middle East?"

"It's a long story."

The secluded driveway led to a colonial with a circular drive in front. Jim had fantasized about this date since he was old enough to drive. Judy was his only unrequited love. Their dates were left to his imagination, and imagine he did. Every turn and hill along Dresden Road, down Highland and into the winding driveway, even the confrontation with Doctor Archer, the town's leading cardiologist. He played this back in his head hundreds of times. So often that he could have done this blind folded.

As he parked and got out of his car, he noticed something odd. All of the lights were out and there were no cars in sight. There was a three-car garage off to the side, so the cars were probably in there. He stepped up to the door and rang the bell. He could hear the echo of the chimes throughout the downstairs, reflecting off of the highly polished hardwood floors. He imagined a uniformed maid would answer the door, but no one came. He rang again. Still nothing. He started to panic. She stood him up? There's no way she would have stood him up. He grabbed his phone off the front seat of the car. Shit, he didn't have her number. He got back in the car and sat. He panicked again, this time fearing that he might have, for some strange reason, been at the wrong house and the actual occupants might come home at any time. He started the car and drove to the end of the drive, turned onto Highland and pulled over.

Amazingly, he remembered her parents' phone number. He memorized it once, then chickened out and never called it.

"Jim? Where are you?"

"Where are you?"

"I'm at my mom's house, on East Highland. I thought you knew where it was."

"East Highland? Oh shit, I thought you lived on Highland."

"They haven't lived in that house since I was in high school. 2108 East Highland. It's the yellow house up on the hill."

"How embarrassing. I'll be right there."

The blush faded from Jim's face by the time he reached her house. Knocking on the door felt more like an adult rendezvous than an adolescent fantasy. He straightened his tie as the door opened.

Judy wore a royal blue short sleeve wrap dress with a provocative amount of cleavage. Jim's smile was involuntary, like a cat burglar stumbling upon the crown jewels. "Hi, Jim. You look handsome."

"So do you. I mean, you look beautiful."

"You sound surprised."

"No, no. I mean it. I mean, as always, you look ravishing."

"Let's go, Doctor Langley, before you dig your hole any deeper."

Jim opened the passenger door, "Shall we?"

"Thank you."

They drove through the north side toward downtown. Judy stared out of the window.

Jim felt the need to break the silence. "How was the service? I'm sorry I couldn't be there."

"It was really nice. Mom would have really appreciated it.

Thank you for coming to visiting hours. And it was great to see your mom again. She was my favorite teacher in grade school."

"Oh, I didn't know you had Mom. You know, I wasn't allowed to be in her class. The principal thought I'd get special treatment. Little did she know that she was doing me a huge favor. Can you imagine being in your mom's third grade class? Yuk!"

"You sound like a third grader."

"Thank you. My last date said I acted like a five year old. I'm moving up in the world." He smiled a toothy grin that disarmed her. She always liked his wit and charm. It set him apart from the dumb jocks that always asked her out and, she thought, it still did.

They pulled into his parking space behind the restaurant and entered through the busy garden seating. A few patrons greeted him, but for a quick handshake and a nod or two, he didn't give much of an audience. He led Judy through the downstairs and into the private dining room, which was all set for two, champagne chilling in the bucket beside the table, and the lights set to twinkling, yet not dark. It was summer and the early evening sun bounced through the glass door, the hubbub in the next room nothing more than a reflection of life outside. The room sparkled. Jim held her chair and Judy made herself comfortable, napkin in lap, her freshly manicured hands crossed on top of it. She looked as though she had just sat down at her own dining room table, with her long adoring husband. Her radiance captivated Jim. After all of these years a fantasy was coming true, and yet, unlike a fantasy, this felt as if it were meant to be.

She looked around the room, "This is fancy."

Jim opened the champagne on cue. He carefully lifted her glass and poured the bubbly slowly down the side, as to not overflow the flute. "Not really. This used to be my little office until we ran out of room. It's mainly for locals. We have an embarrassment of riches in our bookings. So much so that we were embarrassed not to be able to often accommodate our loyal local following. We made a few adjustments and this was one of them. I think it's kind of sweet. We get a lot of proposals and little anniversary celebrations in here."

Judy interrupted, "That's a little fast, don't you think?"

"I was ..."

Judy laughed knowingly, "I'm kidding, Jim. Yes, this is a sweet little room."

Nancy opened the door, breaking the awkward moment. "Good evening, Doctor Jim." She brushed invisible lint from his lapel and gingerly placed the napkin on his lap.

"Good evening, Nancy. May I introduce Judy ..." He looked at her for approval, "Archer?" and she nodded, "Archer."

"Very nice to meet you, Ms. Archer. I'm Nancy and I'll be taking care of you tonight. We understand that you're a vegetarian, so our chef has taken this opportunity to create some seasonal favorites from our garden and the surrounding farms in the area. Do you have any food allergies or preferences, other than nothing with eyeballs?"

Judy laughed right away, knowing that the last comment could be taken as offensive. She felt Nancy was both sincere and funny and she liked that. "That sounds wonderful, Nancy. Oh, and I do eat fish sometimes, and most of them have eyes."

Nancy laughed. "I'll let Chef know." She topped up their flutes and slipped out, unnoticed.

Judy, "She's a pistol. Where'd you find her?"

"Local talent. She's been great. Totally gets service, works really well keeping the other staff on their toes, but she's not pushy. They love her."

"I can see why. She seems to be enamored with you too."

"Oh heavens no. She tolerates me, thinks I'm pretentious, but I sign her checks and they don't bounce, so I'm of some limited use to her."

"I think she has a crush on you."

"No, trust me. We've been though all of that. Not my type and I'm certainly not her type." Jim planted his chin in his chest and looked her in the eyes. Playfully, "Jealous?"

Judy smiled a grown up smile. "I don't get jealous. I'm just observant. She likes you."

"She might like me but she doesn't LIKE me. We tried that briefly and I came to my senses very quickly, and I think she did too." Jim changed the subject, "So, tell me about you. What is your life like in Portland? Your kids? Your job?"

"My job is a dead end but I like the people. Stephen lives in Seattle. He's a vet."

"He was in the armed forces?"

"Not hardly. He wouldn't hurt a fly, or any of the other animals that he doctors as a vet-re-nar-ian."

Jim laughed. "Oh right. Vet! And your daughter?"

"Heather is a model in New York. She thinks she's just about done with modeling, so she's finishing her teaching degree at Columbia."

"Very nice. Sort of classic overachievers then?"

"Yep. They get that from their father."

"I doubt that. You were always the smartest kid in the class. You did everything at school: cheerleading, swimming, candy stripers. You made friends easily and made everyone feel special. I would say that qualifies as overachieving."

"You remember all that stuff about me? You would hardly give me the time of day."

"I was petrified of you. I really, really wanted to ask you out but just couldn't. I kicked myself, well, pretty much until right now." He held up his glass. "Here's to better late than never!"

"I'll drink to that." They clicked glasses.

Nancy entered as if the clink cued her, carrying a serving tray. "And for the first course, chilled pear soup. Chef has been playing with things that taste like something different from what they are. He wants to know if this reminds you of a flavor from your past." She thoughtfully served the soup in its bowl from the right, then offered a selection of breads from the left, a technique that Jim had learned from a captain friend in Paris and taught to his servers. 'Always offer from the left but serve from the right, contrary to the popular myth to serve from the left and remove from the right.'

"Bon appétit!" Nancy slipped out again, careful to gently ease the door shut.

"Oh my God, it's Bit-o-Honey. This tastes just like Bit-o-Honey!" She jumped up and ran upstairs. She waltzed into the kitchen as if it were her own. "Buddy, it tastes just like Bit-o-Honey. It's amazing."

Buddy looked up from the cook top. "Oh good, you got it. Some people don't know that taste. It's amazing, really. It shares no ingredients that you would think would be in that candy, including sugar."

"How did you do it?"

"Really well, don't you think?"

They both laughed. She turned to find Jim standing behind her. He looked entirely pleased that she felt so at home. That was a good sign. Not even one date and he was falling in love. He suspected that so was she. "Shall we return so Buddy can wow us with another surprise taste trick?" They walked back downstairs as a few restaurant patrons stared. There were enough people that knew Jim to know that this was a date, and the gossiping little town was intrigued.

The wine cellar was not occupied. Jim led Judy in for a tour and to select something for their next course. "I sort of combined my personal cellar with the procurement for the restaurant. We've ended up with quite an amazing cellar for such a small town restaurant. I've held a few of my favorites back and priced some others out of reach for most folks. Sometimes they surprise me. We sold an '84 Latour a few weeks ago for an ungodly sum." Jim scanned the Burgundies and picked out a '93 Cote de Beaune for the next course. He grabbed a corkscrew and led Judy back to their little dining room. Nancy had anticipated his next move and had placed two Burgundy glasses on the table as well as a decanter. Jim opened and decanted as he continued the conversation. "And what about Portland?"

Nancy next brought a Sushi roll with what seemed like finely diced orange sections in a soy sauce. It was served on a plate resembling a salmon. Either the suggestion or the food combination made the dish taste like something completely different. Judy's eyes popped out. "This is completely amazing. It tastes like caviar, exactly like caviar." She looked at both ends of the roll, smelled it and tasted it again. "I'll be damned. Caviar!"

Jim poured her a glass of wine. "This Cote de Beaune should go perfectly."

"Oh Jim, I'm not sure I can drink this much wine."

"Not to worry. I rarely drink the whole bottle. I leave it for the wait staff to taste so they educate their palettes. It's the only way they get a chance to taste such nice wine." He poured himself a glass. "Now, what about Portland?"

"Portland, so, Jim—that was also my husband's name— took a job at Reed when the kids were just going into high school. We settled there and agreed to stay at least until they graduated. We had bounced around before that: Colorado, Virginia, San Diego. We liked it, Jim got tenure and it sort of stuck. I hated the rain, but it is really beautiful."

"Why don't you leave?"

"I have friends there. It's my home."

Nancy appeared with two more dishes. "Chef says that these aren't necessarily different tastes than what they appear to be, but they are transformed familiar vegetables, which he thinks is," she makes air quotes, "neat."

"Oh, I love this one. Excuse me one minute." Jim stood and walked out, only to return less than a minute later with a Kistler chardonnay. "I know, you're not supposed to have a white after a red, but I think that's all nonsense. Besides, this is yummy wine and goes perfectly with this odd little dish. We'll just have a little." He grabs two white wine glasses from a shelf on the wall and pours two bountiful servings.

Nancy presented a pasta made from zucchini with mussels, and a spinach mousse that melted in your mouth. They sat in silence and enjoyed those delights. Judy made soothing sounds but didn't say a word. They finished their plates and nearly all of the Kistler. Nancy cleared the plates and Jim stared into Judy's eyes. "I am so happy you're here."

"What about you? Why did you come back here? I heard that you had it all, career, money, wife."

"I thought you knew."

"Knew what?"

"My wife? Madeline, she died. All of the sudden, she died.

It was a really nasty and pervasive infection. All of the best doctors at Boston General couldn't figure it out in time."

"I knew you were no longer married, but I didn't know she died. I'm so sorry to hear that, Jim. Is that why you came back here?"

"Sort of. I just realized that I was done. There wasn't anything that made me happy in Boston. My neighbor was quitting his job and moving to Italy. I thought that sounded good, so here I am."

Joey knocked on the door and popped his head in. "All set, Doc. Ready when you are."

"Thanks, Joey. See you in a few."

Nancy pushed her way past Joey with dessert. She presented a banana flambé with parting flair, pouring brandy into two small cast iron skillets and setting them on fire. "Voilà!" and she disappeared.

Judy's eyes got big. "I love cooked bananas."

"Then this if for you. I really love this dessert. Buddy blew me away with this one early on. The banana is one of the few things we import, very carefully I might add. These are organic and we pay a fortune to get them here from Hawaii. Not bragging or anything, I really think it makes a difference."

Judy took one bite, tilted her head back and closed her eyes. "This is like no banana I have ever tasted. It tastes just like vanilla ice cream, but there is no ice cream."

"That's right, and no sugar either. It's actually just banana and brandy. Most people don't know that there are thousands of varieties of bananas. This one is actually called the ice cream banana. Nothing to transform, it's already a food that tastes like another food. Neat, huh?"

"Incredible. Jim, this has been so special. Thank you for this evening. I would have just sat at home and cried."

"Oh, we're not done yet. Remember, I promised dancing?"

Nancy opened the door. "Doc, I just had the weirdest thing happen."

"What's that?" Jim pointed at the bottles of half finished wine. "Oh, Kistler and Cote de Beaune for the tasting table. Make sure you try the Beaune and Ginger tries the Kistler. She keeps going on about she doesn't get chardonnay. This one will blow her away. So what's weird?"

"I answered Cindy's phone and took a reservation for New Year's Eve, next New Year's Eve! That was a little weird, but have you looked at that page in the system lately? We are nearly full. A year and a half from now!"

Jim stood and moved toward the door as Nancy started to clear. "Yep, weird." He pulled Judy's chair out as she was still finishing her banana.

"I'm not done with my banana."

"Come back tomorrow and you can have another. Let's go. We're going to be late."

"Late for what?"

"You'll see." He held the door for her, waved a cute little wave to Nancy and got ahead of her to open the patio door.

Judy stepped back into the private room. "Thank you Nancy, and tell Buddy that I was blown away."

"Will do. Have fun with the doc."

Jim led her back through the garden and into the small parking lot where Joey was waiting with the back door of the limo open. He wore the hat and uniform that Jim bought him when they first got the Cadillac, no longer his standard dress. A sport coat or suit was fancy enough to tote foodies back and forth from the Holiday Inn.

Judy stopped short of the door. "What's this?"

"Our ride for the night. We had a bit to drink and I

thought it was safer this way. Besides, Joey likes driving the country roads in this beast. Isn't that right, Joey?"

"Yes, Doctor Jim. Ever since that first night out the River Road ..."

"Yes, well, we won't go into that right now." He smiled sheepishly and held the door for Judy. She climbed in the back and Jim followed. Joey secured the door and they were off. "It's not a long drive, but I think it will be fun. Comfortable?"

"This is very nice. Where on earth did you rent a limo?"

"It's not rented; it's the restaurant's. I bought it a few years ago as a service for our guests. Zanesville, as you know, is a pretty small town, but driving after drinking was enough to put off some of the good folks in town that can afford to eat out. I just gave them one less excuse not to come downtown for a nice meal. Now, since we've become inundated with out-of-towners, Joey schleps them back and forth to the local hotels. I actually had to reserve it for myself tonight. It's a treat for me too."

"Nice." Judy settled back, enjoying it more since it didn't somehow seem ridiculous, even though it was thoroughly ridiculous. The mind has an amazing capacity for rationalization, especially after champagne and a generous amount of fine food and wine. She was transported to another place, and in that place it was perfectly normal to be riding in the back of a 1975 Cadillac stretch limousine on the way to who knows where. "So, where were we? Let's see, your neighbor moved to Italy and that made you come back here?"

"Ha, not exactly. Frank, my neighbor, was a plumber married to a rich woman who bought the house next to us, and he and I became great friends. She left him for another woman and, even though I thought he was Irish, he was

Italian and decided to move to Umbria, where I saw him last year during the earthquake. So, I was going to move there too, then my mother ended up in the hospital. I came home and saw this building. My friends said I was nuts, and here we are."

"I think your friends may have been on to something."

"Sorry, it's such a long story and pretty boring, and sort of nuts too. I gave up a successful practice in Boston, something I had worked for my entire life. But I was missing something, my mom was not going to be around forever, and Frank showed me that there could be an alternative. I keep my hand in medicine, but this is my life now. Or at least for the next 16 months."

"16 months?"

"Oh boy, I did leave out a big chunk. Did you see that big sign in the main dining room that was counting down?"

"Yeah. It looked a little out of place, I thought."

"The restaurant wasn't always called Home. We just changed the name last year. The original name was The Five-Year Plan."

"That's kind of a weird name."

"That seemed to be the consensus. But there was a good reason. When I found the building and had the idea, everyone said I was crazy to open a fine dining restaurant here. So I asked my accountant friend, David, to calculate how long I could stay open, with a certain investment, if not one person walked through the door—a fully functioning, fully staffed restaurant with no customers."

"Wow, you really were crazy."

"Thanks. And so he said five years. Hence, The Five-Year Plan. And so, in 16 more months, on New Year's Eve, we will close our doors. That's probably why we already have reservations for that evening. Everyone wants to say that they were the last to eat at Home." The limo pulled along side the McConnelsville Grange. "Oh good, here we are."

"Where are we, exactly?"

"We're going dancing." The door opened and Jim helped her climb out. The Grange was all lit up and the parking lot full. There was a coat check in the front hallway leading to double doors that swung open as they approached. As Jim and Judy entered, the room broke into applause and the substantial crowd parted like the Red Sea. Judy stared at Jim in disbelief. They walked the length of the hall and off to a table next to the side of the stage. Jim held a chair for Judy, leaned over and whispered in her ear. "Sorry for all the hoopla. It'll be over in a sec. Excuse me." Jim leaped up the four steps to the stage. The bandleader handed him a mic. "Ladies and gentlemen, thank you so much for coming tonight. We are here for a special celebration. Thanks to the generosity of the community, the Zanesville Rotary Club and Kiwanis, the State of Ohio and, indirectly, the Jordanian government, I can proudly announce that the McConnelsville Free Clinic will re-open this Monday and stay open!" The crowd burst into applause and gave Jim a standing ovation. The hall was filled with local politicians, neighbors and many familiar patients' faces. Throughout the evening each would stop by his table and shower Jim with praise and thanks.

Pete came out of the wings and hugged him. He took the mic. "Ladies and gentleman, please thank our single biggest supporter, because of his generosity and resource-fulness," Pete winked at Jim, "our community and those most in need will once again have free health care." There was more thunderous applause that gave way to a bright two-step from the band. The leader took the mic and started his instructions.

"Everybody pair up two by two and form squares. Let's get this dance a goin'."

Jim returned to Judy who sat in disbelief. He took her hand and led her to the top of the nearest square. They do-se-doed, allemanded and promenaded the night away.

It may have been the champagne, the square dancing or the moonshine that Pete brought them well into the evening, but by the time the limo approached East Highland Drive, Judy was asleep in Jim's arms. Jim had never felt so warm and comfortable. She rubbed her eyes as the car slowed in front of her house. Without notice, she smiled and kissed Jim for the first time. It wasn't passionate or lustful. It was familiar and loving, and more intimate than Jim had ever felt. She smiled bashfully, touched his cheek and stepped out of the car. She turned and hung her head back inside the door. "This was the best first date of my life. I'm happy you finally asked me out. Thank you." She shut the door and Joey drove the long black car down the drive. She stood and waved until they turned out of view.

Sunday was always dark at the restaurant. Jim made very few exceptions to the Sunday closing. He had many offers since the restaurant became popular, but he never gave in. The only Sunday events were for the staff or a really, really good cause. The Clinic Donor Reception was one such cause. The affair was a simple cocktail party. The tables in the downstairs were set up in the sparse café setting, and only the perimeter two-tops were left on the patio. Most of the guests stood. The upstairs dining room was closed on purpose. Jim didn't want to encourage any drive by drop-ins. The party consisted of cocktails, tray passed small bites, and a martini bar that later was transformed into an ice cream sundae bar. Jim spent most of the evening looking out the window, waiting for Judy.

The guests had thinned considerably, the ice cream was gone and the solitary banana sat alone in the walk-in, prepped and ready for it's designated guest. She appeared in the doorway and Jim turned away mid-conversation from a couple of big donors. "Bananas Flambé, madam?" He showed her to an empty table in the outer corner of the garden. He caught Nancy's eye. She immediately turned to accomplish her pre-destined task. She re-appeared with the banana in the iron skillet and a bottle of brandy under her arm.

"Good evening, Judy." She lit the brandy, which made a spectacular shooting flame in the darkness of the garden. "Bon appétit."

Followed directly behind Nancy was Cindy with a bottle of champagne and two flutes. "Champagne?"

Jim sat across from her. "Thanks, Cindy." He held his glass and toasted, "Here's to old friends."

"Cheers. Thank you." She sipped her champagne. "I had a lovely time last night. I don't think I've ever felt so comfortable with someone before."

"It was a wonderful night. Shall we try to top it?"

"Jim, I have to go home tomorrow. I have an early flight so I can get back to work."

"Can't you stay for a few more days?"

"No. I have to get back to my life."

"Your life? Your husband is dead, your kids are grown and don't live near you. You said yourself you're in a dead end job…"

"It's still my life. I've got to go. It's an early flight." Judy got up, kissed Jim on the cheek and walked away from her champagne, her banana and his broken heart.

Autumn was beautiful in Southeastern Ohio. The leaves turned quickly, which usually meant an early winter. The crispness off of the river brought the heaters out, but not chilly enough to discourage outdoor dining. Ruth had not been to the restaurant in months, choosing her bridge club and painting over the hubbub. Jim took to holding court in her old seat next to the fire. Most of his time was spent composing emails to Judy, most of which were never sent. On the few occasions that he mustered enough courage to press send, he waited patiently for a reply. His in box remained bare. He studied the emails sent, searching in vein for some clue as to her lack of response. Did he say something wrong?

Christmas came with a whimper. Jim went through the motions. The business was booming and he couldn't have been less interested. His pizza chef called in sick on the first Saturday of December and they were packed. He dug his chef's jacket out of the closet and showed up for dinner service. He was exhausted by the end of the night; the intense heat of the wood fired oven coupled with being on his feet all night were reminiscent of his marathon surgeries. He was out of practice for both, so when the last of the pear-prosciutto pizzas was delivered to the balcony party, he collapsed into the couch.

Nancy thoughtfully delivered him a glass of pinot noir from the tasting table. "Thank you, darling. You are so good to me." His cell phone chimed. Jim dug deep into his chef's pants pocket. It was a text from Judy. "Coming to Z-ville at the beginning of the year. Bobby dropped the ball.

Coming to sell mom's house. See you then?" Jim stared at the phone. He read and re-read the text, searching for any hint of his stance in this relationship. See you then? Oh shit, he was supposed to answer. He typed, erased and typed again. Thirty minutes later he finally pressed send. "I look forward to it. See you soon."

17

January sucked. The first week of the last year of the plan was certainly not going as planned. Jim longed for his reunion with Judy and was grumpy. He took it out on everyone around him, and most of all on Jeffrey. He often jumped on Jeffrey for the most trivial infractions. A single dirty dish or a book out of place would spark a tirade that embarrassed Jim and cause him to apologize almost immediately, but did damage to their relationship nonetheless.

Jeffrey was not easily upset by Jim's treatment; he was grateful for the job and a place to live—kindness that he had never experienced before—but the constant brow beating slowly aggravated him enough that he packed up and walked out. He didn't say where he was going and didn't show up to work for a week.

The desertion was not limited to Jeffrey. Without any hint

of dissatisfaction or desire for change, Buddy announced that he had taken a chef de cuisine position in New York and was moving February first. The owner of Chez Blanc had visited Home in November and poached Buddy without any hesitation. The offer was too great for Buddy to pass up.

Another text from Judy announced a delay in her arrival until February. Jim felt betrayed. His trusted allies seemed to be nothing of the sort. He searched for solace. At least his colleagues at the clinic appreciated him. He decided to double his shifts and give Pete some time off; the least he could do was to lose himself in his work and help someone who so deserved a break.

February was looking up. The frozen ground, short days and lack of sunshine made little difference to Jim's disposition, but Jeffrey resurfaced, apologized for his disappearance and announced that he was moving in with Nancy. She had offered her spare room for a small amount of rent. It wasn't lost on her how neat and clean he was—a trait that had always been missing from her character. Jim was secretly delighted to have the lad back and rehired him on the condition that he give two weeks notice if he ever decided to quit again.

Fine cuisine chefs with experience and a culinary education were not prevalent in Southeastern Ohio and Jim was in denial about Buddy's sudden departure, so he spent little effort trying to replace him. Consequently, he was on the line, cooking both lunches and dinners from the first Monday of February. He loved cooking, knew the recipes and procedures as well as Buddy, maybe not with as much of his creativity and flair, but he could get the plates out without any fuss. At peak times he had always stepped in for last looks so the temperature and pace of the kitchen were not new to him. Ginger really stepped up to help carry the weight, secretly vying for the executive chef position. As Ginger stepped up Jim backed off to two or three lunches a week but continued dinners every night. Ginger was in charge when Jim stepped away or took the occasional night off. She was quick, efficient and the staff loved her. The restaurant could not function without two fulltime chefs though, so Jim was by no means off the hook. The work was long and hard, and he relished the occasional evening off. His first came directly after a late afternoon text.

It was surprising that she suggested one of Linden Avenue's favorite watering holes. Shaking off the snow and stomping his wet boots, at first Jim didn't see her in the corner. Once his eyes adjusted to the dark bar, he spotted her radiance. Never had he looked so forward to seeing a woman. He couldn't wait to look into her eyes again and feel her warm presence. As their eyes met she lit up. Oh, thank God, he thought. These months had been torture. Did she like me? Was I too pushy or rude? Did I say something embarrassing in my emails? Soon it was revealed that his torture was all self-generated.

She slid out of the booth and hugged him, kissed him deeply and stared into his eyes. They didn't speak. This was grown-up love, something not to be toyed with or ignored, not to be acted on rashly, but undeniable. She whispered in his ear, "I missed you."

"I missed you, Judy. I am so happy you've come back." They sat and Jim waved toward the barmaid, indicating two more of whatever Judy was drinking. He couldn't care less. It could be boiled onion juice. His appetite was for her.

"Jim, I have to apologize. I was not very nice to you after

our amazing date. I got scared. I really, really like you and I needed to think. I've uprooted my life before, and I just wasn't sure I was ready to do that again after one date."

"Sure. I understand."

"And your emails were so sweet and poetic."

"Why didn't you answer them?"

"I didn't know what to say. They made me smile and scared me too."

"You're here now. Let's start over, shall we?"

"That's what I wanted to tell you. I've moved back."

Jim's eyes widened.

"Don't get too excited yet. I'm not sure that it's permanent, but I'm here for now. I quit my job and rented my place. I have a bunch of work to do on my mom's house. Bobby let it go and didn't do anything about selling it. I certainly won't be able to list it until summer at the earliest. So, here I am."

"Well, Ms. Archer, would you consider accompanying me this Saturday night?"

"It would be my pleasure, Doctor Langley."

"Wait, I can't."

"What. You just asked me out and now you're already standing me up? Are you toying with my affections?"

"I'm really sorry. I forgot that I have to work."

"I thought you were the boss?"

"I am, but right now I'm also the chef. Buddy quit and moved to New York to take a fancy chef job at some French restaurant."

"That's wonderful."

"It is wonderful. I created a monster. I couldn't be prouder of him, actually. But Saturdays are not my own these days."

"How late do you work?"

"Usually last plates go out at about 10 on Saturday. I

don't do desserts or close, so I could probably get out by
10:30, but that's not exactly date time."

"Are you saying that you won't go out with me at 10:30?"

"Of course I would, but our choices are pretty limited."

"Are you usually hungry after you finish making all of
that fancy food?"

"Yeah, usually for a pizza or a plate of pasta."

"How about penne with asparagus and an arugula salad?"

"That sounds perfect. Where do we get that at 10:30 on a
Saturday night? Columbus is an hour away."

"East Highland Drive. When you get off come over and
I'll make us dinner. It's my turn. Except you bring the wine.
I'm afraid the only thing that Bobby did dispose of was
mom's booze."

"That sounds great. I think I can manage a bottle or two."

Half way through a busy Saturday night Jim's phone
rang. He usually leaves his phone off when he's cooking.
He didn't allow kitchen staff to use phones during service,
and he tried to set a good example. The back door was
opened to let some cool air in and he stepped out into it. He
thought that maybe Judy needed something, so he looked at
the display. It was his sister Jackie. "Hi, Jackie. I'm working. What's up?"

Jackie had panic in her voice. This didn't surprise Jim
much. Jackie often had panic in her voice. "Mom had
another stroke. I'm in the ambulance with her now. Can
you meet us at the hospital?"

"I'll see you there in 10." It was 8 p.m. and dinner service
was in full swing. He hated to leave Ginger with a full house
but he had no choice. She understood. They had both Jeffrey
and a new trainee in addition to the usual Saturday night

staff. The trainee was about to get a trial by fire. Literally, as his primary job would be to stoke the pizza oven and assist with prep.

Jim sped to the hospital. There was no traffic so he was there in 10 minutes. He met Jackie in the ER just as Ruth was being wheeled into a cubicle. He disregarded the orderly and walked back with the gurney. Ruth spoke to him right away. He knew that she hadn't had a severe stroke by the sound of her voice. He made eye contact with the paramedic and his suspicion was confirmed. But, she was 93, had already had a stroke, and was a prime candidate for another; so the tests were warranted. And a night under observation wouldn't hurt. If anything else happened while she was there, it could save her life. He was relieved but still concerned.

Jackie sat fretting in the waiting room. Jim stood over her. Jackie was whimpering. "Is she okay? Was it a stroke?"

Jim sat and put his arm around her. "She'll be fine. She may have had a little event, but it was clear by speaking to her that there was no damage. That doesn't mean that the tests shouldn't be run and she should stay for observation tonight. Can you stay?"

"I've got people at my house. She called and I ran over there and left them in the middle of dinner. Can you stay for a while until I come back?"

"I left about 100 people in the middle of dinner myself, but sure, I'll stay. I'll get her settled into her room. Can you come back later and relieve me?"

"Of course. I'll be back soon." Jackie, stood, put her coat and hat on and hurried out the automatic doors.

Jim sat back and fished in his chef's deep pockets for his phone. He searched both pant pockets, his jacket and his coat. He'd lost his phone. He started out the door to check the car when Ruth's doctor came through the ER doors.

"Hey, Jim. I just saw your mom. We're taking her up to a room now. Need to get a CAT scan pretty soon. I need one of my guys on it so it might take a while before we find him."

"Thanks, Jeff. What do you think? Didn't seem like it was much of an event."

"Probably not, but she is 93, strong as an ox, but still prone to strokes as we've already seen. Need to look at the CAT to find out for sure."

"Sure, sure. Thanks again, Jeff. You going to be around?"

"I'm headed out now but I'll get a text after the CAT scan. I'll see you then?"

"I'm here." Jim walked through the ER doors and met up with Ruth as she was being pushed through the corridor. They rode up in the elevator and Ruth was rolled into a private room. Jim sat down next to her and reached for the phone. Carla knocked as she opened the door.

"Good evening, Ruth, so nice to see you again. Hello, Doctor Jim."

Ruth's eyes were closed, but her wit was in tact. "Nurse Carla. You're a breath of fresh air. My children are useless."

Jim stood over her. "Mom, I'm right here."

"I know you are so why am I in this damn place again?"

Jim realized that maybe something did happen to her. She knew exactly why she was there five minutes ago. The same orderly came back in the room before Carla had a chance to transfer Ruth to her bed. "Radiology is ready for you, Mrs. Langley. Do you remember me, Mrs. Langley? I'm..."

"Keith Hendershot. Of course I remember you and your older brother Mark. Glad you have a decent job, Keith. How's Mark doing?"

"He's fine, Mrs. Langley, just fine. Works up in Columbus for the gas company." Keith rolled Ruth out and Jim followed.

The CAT scan took an hour and the radiologist, Jeff, and Jim took another hour reviewing the scans. There may or may not have been a couple more small lesions at the base of her skull. There didn't seem to be any residual change, but all agreed that a night or two in the hospital was still warranted. Jim delivered the news to a slightly sedated and grumpy Ruth. It was midnight by the time Jackie returned. He kissed Ruth, glared at Jackie and sprinted to the door.

His phone wasn't in the car. He must have left it in the kitchen after Jackie called. He raced to Judy's house, hoping against hope that she would understand.

The lights were off. He hesitated before ringing the bell, but it would be worse if he didn't explain. He rang the bell.

Judy came to the door in her robe. "I thought you said 10:30. I got worried."

"I am so sorry. I can explain. Can I come in?"

"I guess."

They sat in the living room. "My mom had a little stroke. Jackie called and I rushed to the hospital. I must have left my phone at the restaurant. Every time I tried to get to call you something happened. When I finally got out it was midnight and my phone wasn't in the car, so I thought I better just come up here and explain. I am so, so sorry. And I forgot the wine."

Judy got up, crossed the room and sat next to him. She put her arm around him and gently kissed his cheek. "Oh Jim, I'm the one who should be sorry. I thought you stood me up. I should have known better. I'm sorry. How's your mom?"

"I think she'll be fine. The CAT scan showed a couple of little spots, but we all thought it was nothing. She'll be in for a couple of days for observation." He turned toward her and wrapped his arms around her and they kissed, the first really passionate kiss of their relationship.

After a long embrace, "Are you hungry?"

"Not really. Just tired. I should go."

"How about breakfast?"

"I'm not really hungry right now."

Judy smiled and stood, taking Jim's hand. "Who said right now?"

March saw an early thaw. Maybe it was the warmth of his heart, Jim thought, as he inspected the garden, coffee in hand, and Judy on his mind. They scarcely spent a day apart since that night. They just fit. Everything about their relationship, from the sides of the bed they chose to how perfectly she fit into the crook in his arm when they lay on the couch in front of the fire.

His long lost love reunion was not without its trials though. He was neglecting the restaurant and Judy's progress on renovating her mom's house was glacial. Jim secretly endorsed that pace, as it kept her in Zanesville and close to him, but she was not pleased. She still had some semblance of a life in Portland and was currently at the Columbus airport on her way back to tend to some of those loose ends. This was their first separation since they slept together.

Jim kept telling himself that he was in the home stretch with Home but a recent, not so glowing review appeared in The Texas Monthly. Why on earth a reviewer from Texas was in Ohio and how on earth did he think his readers would care about Home? Perplexing as it may have been, it still stung. And he also knew that such a thing would not put a dent in the reservation book, completely full until August, with New Year's Eve totally sold out since last November. It may have been the home stretch, but he wanted to go out with a bang. So he racked his brain as he perused the dormant garden. He had done everything: farm to table; international nights; chef's tasting menu; charity events; hosted the Rotary and Kiwanis; made the best pizzas within 500 miles (including those disgustingly thick pies in Chicago that so many of his patrons raved about). What had he missed?

The question plagued him when he wasn't pining for his new love. Maybe he should continue the search for a new executive chef. He was considering promoting Ginger but thought better of it. If he was going to do something new in the last year it was going to have to be news worthy. Promoting a sous chef was certainly not that. He was stumped.

Ruth made another full and astonishing recovery. The hospital stay seemed to wake her up and energize her. She resumed her daily walks around the neighborhood and re-dedicated herself to painting. A phone call from Ruth was extremely rare, so when Jim saw her name on his phone screen he jumped. She wanted to see him was all she said and hung up.

Jim didn't hesitate and dropped lunch service in Ginger's lap. It took him 15 long minutes to get to Ruth's house. Construction on Dresden road caused him to have to take a long detour. Ruth sat on her usual perch, in the kitchen behind her easel. She turned to face him when he opened the back door, something Jim could never remember happening before. Now he really was worried. She was acting crazy. She smiled.

Ruth, "Well, that was quick. There's no need to have rushed." Ironic, coming from a 93 year old with a history of strokes, he thought. "There's something that I want to show you." Ruth hopped down off of her high stool and pranced through the hallway to the living room. "I have a surprise for you." The living room was long and narrow, with a high, beamed cathedral ceiling and a picture window with a magnificent view of the house across the street and the wooded area beyond. In front of the window stood another easel covered in a white sheet, a sight unfamiliar to Jim.

"What's this?"

"It's the surprise. Ready?!" She sounded like a kid on Christmas morning. Jim couldn't remember the last time he heard such joy in his mother's voice. With one swift pull, she revealed a large canvas with a colorful, pointillist impression of the restaurant, from the river point of view. It was summer, the garden was full of festivities and a warm, fictional neon sign glowed above the restaurant reading, Home.

Jim stood perfectly still, showing no emotion. A single tear developed and ran down his cheek.

"I wanted you to have something to always remember your restaurant. What you've done for this community and for yourself is truly remarkable. I've never been so proud of you and that's saying something. You've accomplished great things in your life, but nothing as great as this. I hope you like it."

"It's beautiful, Mother. I don't know what to say. I love it. It may be your best work, so far." They both laughed at the implication. "Thank you." He held his mother and kissed her head. "I know just the place for it, right above your spot next to the fireplace."

"That sounds nice. Now get the damn thing out of my living room." With that she turned on her heels and resumed her crusty façade.

Jim carefully loaded the painting in his car and returned to the kitchen, where Ruth was concentrating on the new canvas. "Thanks, Mom."

She waved him off and executed a long, flowing stroke, followed by a quick rub with the heal of her hand. "Shit!"

April ushered in the most glorious spring on record. The rains were perfectly timed, as if they were sprinklers on the lawns of Beverly Hills estates. Each morning it rained hard, subsided and revealed a rainbow over the river. By noon the patio and balcony were dry and set for lunch. The glass doors remained open all but two days of the month. The pizza oven was relegated to dinners, and then only when the temperature dropped below 50.

Jim had Ruth's painting framed and hung over the chair next to the fireplace. The spring flowers on the table in the entranceway burst forth with the colors and aromas of a new beginning. Every part of the restaurant bloomed with the hues of spring.

In the kitchen, asparagus blanched and spring onions chopped. Lamb roasted under new potatoes and a jalapeño mint jelly waited in a small dish to be cautiously applied. Jim enjoyed his new chef's role. He had found his stride in the kitchen choreography. Everyone functioned together like a machine, employing shorthand, sign language and well-honed kitchen skills. Jim was proud to be part of the dance.

Jim opened the oven to remove a leg of lamb and sat

the pan on top of the cook top. He crossed the kitchen to retrieve the mint and knocked over an empty paper bag, left on the prep table after an emergency run to the grocery. He reached down to pick up the empty bag and felt his shoulder move in an unfamiliar and immediately painful way. He stood up and squinted. He didn't yell, but he wanted to. Through his teeth he called out to Ginger. "Hey. I think I just did something stupid." He fell back against the wall, holding his shoulder. "Can you finish the lamb?"

Ginger dropped what she was doing and ran to him. "What did you do? What can I do to help?"

"Finish the lamb. I'm going to sit down and see if this goes away."

"Do you need some help?"

"It's my shoulder, darling. I can still walk." Jim crossed the kitchen toward the fireplace seating area, holding his shoulder. He was in pain and had a pretty good idea what it was. The bursa sack lined the shoulder joint and kept the bones from rubbing on one another. Jim could see the anatomical drawings in his mind's eye. The injury was likely not serious, but the process of recovery was long and painful. All of it flashed before him as he tried to work out a new schedule, writing himself off of the kitchen calendar for the next six weeks.

Doctor Miller met him at the imaging center next to the hospital. The single story building, built in the 70's, had seen better days. The walls were still that salmon pink made stylish by discos and leisure suits. The contrasting gray had faded into dirty white and the carpets were threadbare. Jim sat in the waiting room as Jeff checked him in. This may have been the first time that Jim had been on the other end of this process, and it was a rude awakening. He had no idea how much stress and hassle patients went through for such a simple procedure. It pissed him off.

Inside the MRI suite, Jim endured what he had put thousands of patients through before. The scan was louder and longer than he had ever imagined. If he only knew this when he called for these scans, he may not have ordered them so frequently.

The scans showed exactly what Jim had predicted. There was a small tear in the bursa sack, probably caused by an earlier incident and aggravated by an unorthodox move, such as picking up an empty paper bag. Jeff and the radiologist concurred. The only logical treatment was physical therapy. He could have a cortisone shot but he knew it was painful, temporary and only successful about half the time. He was just going to have to accept the inevitable and do the work, suffer the pain and, above all, stay out of the kitchen until he could lift his arm above his head, which could take weeks.

Judy made Jim comfortable. She brought him newspapers, cooked him meals and drove him to the psychical therapist three times a week. She also let him ignore the restaurant. Carefully, but passionately, they made love nearly every day. Her mother's house had become a construction zone so she spent nearly every night at Jim's. This could not have pleased him more. He had always fantasized about Judy being in his life and, as far as he was concerned, this was that fantasy realized. Judy may not have felt the same way, but she did love him and enjoyed taking care of him. The sex was also great.

The Sunday papers were about to get wet as the clouds

burst open. Still in her robe, Judy beat the rain by moments to retrieve them. Jim had gotten out of bed and was in the kitchen attempting to make coffee. With each movement he let out a little painful moan. Judy rushed to the kitchen, depositing the papers on the table next to the screened porch, and took over the coffee chores. "Here. I'll do that. Go sit on the porch. I brought the newspapers in."

"You are so good to me. What did I do to deserve you?"

"Nothing. You got lucky and don't you forget it, pal."

"Oh I don't ever." He held her by the waist and kissed her neck as she poured hot water into the Chemex.

"Careful. I've got a hot vessel in my hand."

"And so do I." He turned her toward him, slipped his hands inside her robe over her shoulders and dropped her robe to the kitchen floor.

"Doctor Langley, what are you doing?"

"Fondling the most beautiful woman in the world."

"Right here where we eat?" She touched him through his pajamas.

"Ms. Archer, what are you doing?"

"Reciprocating."

May flowers came in the form of Rosemary Parsons, Jim's able and trusting assistant that had already once saved his bacon. She showed up at Jim's house two days after the call from Ruth. Jim had stayed away from the restaurant, thinking that ignoring the problem would make it go away.

Rosemary stood on Jim's porch, a roller suitcase trailing behind, and her large, leather carryall draped over her shoulder. She rang the bell and waited. It took Jim a full minute before her familiar frame came into view. "Rosemary!? I take it Ruth called you?"

"Ruth calls me all of the time. But yes, she informed me of your condition and how poorly you were handling it." She pushed by him, toting her bags, admiring Jeffrey's handiwork around the house. "May I come in?"

"I believe you are already in."

"The place looks great. Much better than when I left."

"Jeffrey has done well." He stopped his explanation. "What exactly has my mother told you?"

"That you've hurt your shoulder—I imagine a bursa inflammation—and you're ignoring the restaurant because you are either too embarrassed or scared to hurt your poor shoulder that you have forgotten your responsibilities and all of the people that depend on you."

"Yep. That's about it."

"So, Buddy flew the coop? Is that young girl cooking on her own?"

"She's got the staff. Young Jeffrey is keen and there are …"

"So she's up to her eyeballs?"

"Yep."

"May I stay here for a few days? I'll get to the restaurant and have a word with Ginger and see if we can't work out a schedule that makes sense. How long have you been doing your PT?"

"Three weeks."

"Three weeks? You're kidding right? Doctor, heal thyself. I'll give you the rest of the week then you need to relieve her. What are you doing about replacing Buddy?"

"Umm. Haven't really …"

"I'll take out an ad in the trades, or should we see if we can find someone local first? What about promoting the girl? Are you really going to shut it down at the end of the year? Do you really need to bother hiring another chef, and who would take a job for seven months?"

"All good questions. No ad in the trades yet. I like the idea of local. Ginger isn't ready. Yes, five years as planned. If we don't hire someone, I have to cook and I think I should probably step back from the day to day."

Judy knocked on the door as she entered. "Yoo-hoo, anybody home?"

"Hi, darling."

Judy stopped suddenly as she noticed Rosemary. "Hello. I'm Judy."

"Oh jeez, I'm sorry. Rosemary Parsons, this is Judy Archer, Judy, I'd like you to meet the second most import-ant woman in my life."

Rosemary shook her hand. "And I take it this is THE most important woman in your life. Ruth told me about you. Very nice to finally meet you."

"Nice to meet you, too. Oh, right. Rosemary, the glue that held Jim's practice together." Judy bent over and kissed Jim. "How's the patient?"

Rosemary answered Judy's question. "Milking it. I'm giving him until Monday."

Judy smiled. What a relief, she thought. "I think you're right, Rosemary. It's about time he stopped babying himself."

"I am not babying myself. This is a painful injury that requires a PT regimen, and it's a slow recovery for a man my age."

"Oh bunk. How many of these did you see when you were practicing? You know exactly what they are. You'll be fine." Rosemary stood and headed to the door. "I'm headed to the restaurant. Nice to meet you, Judy. Ruth says you are the best thing that's ever happened to him."

Jim, "That's right, she is." He pulled her close with his right hand. "Ouch!"

"Oh, poor baby."

Rosemary excused herself and carried her bags upstairs.

Jim led Judy into the living room and sat her on the couch. He kneeled in front of her. "Judy, you are the best thing that's ever happened to me. You are my soul mate. I wanted to do this in a big, romantic way, but I can't wait another moment. Will you marry me?"

"Jim, I love you. I really do, but I need to shut one door before I open the next."

"Is that yes or no?"

"Neither. I love you. Please give me some more time." She kissed him on the head and stood. "Gotta meet the contractor at mom's house in 20 minutes. Love you."

By Monday, Jim was headed back to the kitchen. He wore a shoulder sling, mainly for effect. Rosemary was tending to the garden when he pulled up in the limo. He got out of the back, sporting the sling. She rolled her eyes. "Take that silly thing off."

"I will not. Everyone needs to be careful around me. If I get bumped it'll hurt."

"Oh, like Judy hasn't been bumping it on a regular basis." Evidently, the walls in his old house must not be as thick as he thought.

The staff was very happy and relieved to see him. Nancy ran up and hugged him, sending shooting pains down his arm. He smiled through gritted teeth. She squealed, "Oh, thank God you're back."

The spring weather lingered well into June. There were few boats on the river and those hearty enough to venture onto the water wore coats or windbreakers. The temperature on the Muskingum was always ten degrees colder than the restaurant, even though it was less than 100 feet away.

Ruth continued her second wind and re-took her spot under her painting. Never was she at a loss for words when engaged about the evocative work of art above her. Rosemary sat across from her, sipping a cocktail one night and did just that. "Ruth, this painting captures your son's vision so perfectly. When did you start painting?"

"As soon as I dropped that boy off at kindergarten. I drove directly to the Art Institute and enrolled in art class. I took that year off from teaching. Once I went back to school, I still dabbled. When Jim went off to college I retired and went at it full force. Jim's dad was slowing down. He'd reduced his patients and kept regular hours, so we decided to spend a little more time together. The result was me sitting in front of an easel and him in front of the TV. He never really slowed down. Then he dropped dead. I kept painting."

"So you must have hundreds of paintings just like this."

"Not like this. My main focus was on primitives, then decoupage and assemblage. I liked junk and used it to tell stories."

"What have you done with it?"

"For a while I sold them. I have a basement full. Jackie and Jim have a few pieces. There's a few in the permanent collection at the art museum. Somebody told me that they saw one on TV once. I doubt that, but it was flattering."

"You should have a show." Jim walked by. "Jim, don't you think that Ruth should have an art show? You could do it right here in the restaurant."

Jim crooked his head and thought for a minute. "I think that's a wonderful idea. Mother, is that something you would be interested in?"

Ruth grumbled, "Sounds like a lot of work."

Rosemary piped in, "I'll help sort through all of your stuff, and we can get a few of the kids from the restaurant to do the grunt work."

Jim interjected, "We could do it as a benefit for the clinic. What do ya think, Mom?"

Ruth knew he was serious. "Okay, but only if I don't have to show up for it."

Jim knew this was a total fabrication. "No, no, of course not. We'll do the whole thing and let you know how it came out. Just think of it as a way to clean out your basement."

Rosemary and Ruth spent nearly two weeks organizing, repairing and touching up various works from Ruth's basement. She had forgotten about some and occasionally sat fixated on a piece, transported back to the time of its creation. Ruth rarely reminisced. She had lots of memories but never dwelled in them. Life was still too rich to relive the past.

As predicted by Rosemary, Jim's shoulder was back to normal. Nancy and he started to plan for the art show. The opening would be on a Sunday evening, one of the few sorts of events that Jim would open for on a Sunday. Amber designed an online invitation and made a printed one for the older folks. Jim made a list of the most well-heeled, who might pay too much money for an unknown artist for a good cause.

Ruth came to the restaurant with Rosemary to deliver some of the more delicate pieces. "Can I see the list?"

Jim looked up from the little café table on the patio where he was finishing the guest list. "The guest list? I thought you weren't coming."

"I want to see who you think would buy my art."

Jim handed her the list. She took the pen from his hand and scratched several names off of it. "What are you doing?"

"Look Jim, I know far better than you who in this town will part with their ill gotten gains. So doctors yes, lawyers no, except Bob Brewer. He was one of my students."

"So then you will be here?"

"Yes, I'll be here. You clearly don't know what you're doing." She walked into the downstairs area where Rosemary was starting to plan the exhibition. "I don't really care how you hang most of the stuff, but you need to make sure that the black pieces are against a white wall and are well lit. They don't work in the dark."

Rosemary showed her the sketch of the layout. "I've hired a firm from Cleveland to come down and light the show. I figured it was worth a few of Jim's dollars to make it look as beautiful as possible."

Ruth, "I like the way you think, Rosemary."

The show was a big success. Many of the pieces sold for asking price, already a charitable mark up. What didn't sell would stay hanging for the rest of the summer to entice some of the foodie tourists with more money than sense. Jim lubricated some of the stingiest of the crowd—including his lawyer friend Bob—with some of his fancy wine. Somehow, when people were drinking expensive wine they were more willing to spend money. The art show would have been a psychologist's field day.

The biggest surprise of the evening was not the money raised or the wine poured. The biggest surprise was a mystery guest that only Rosemary and Nancy knew about.

His late arrival made it even more intimate and meaningful. Nancy came down the stairs. "Jim, could you come upstairs for a moment? There's something in the kitchen that I think you'll want to see."

Buddy stood leaning against a spotless prep table, nonchalant in his street clothes. He looked much older than when he left just five months ago.

Jim smiled. "Well, I'll be damned, Buddy Sanders as I live and breath. What brings you out to these parts?"

"I heard you were looking for a chef de cuisine. I could use the job."

"What happened to Chez Woga Woga?"

"I hated New York and those people at that restaurant did not want to be there. It was like they all had somewhere else better to be. And at the same time everybody wanted my job. The damn busboy wanted my job."

"You know we are only open for another six months. This is not a permanent position." Jim was toying with him on purpose. Buddy did not read sarcasm well.

"I know, Doctor Jim. I just need a job."

Jim put his arm around Buddy's shoulder. "Welcome back, Buddy. We're glad to have you Home." Rosemary, Nancy and the rest of the staff applauded from the staircase where they were spying on the reunion. "Ha. You guys knew about this didn't you? Of course you did. Let's go down and celebrate. Can I interest you in some art, Buddy?"

July brought the heat. Buddy was back and the restaurant showed no signs of slowing. The website announced that no more reservations would be taken for the rest of the year. Any cancelations would go to walk ins. Rosemary returned to Boston with the promise to come to New Year's Eve if they would have her.

Jim responded, "Of course we will have you. If you don't come I'll never speak to you again."

Rosemary laughed. Jim was all bluster and she loved him for it. "Good luck with you-know-who." Rosemary had continued to live with Jim and Judy and understood his relationship with her. There was no doubt that she was the one for him and all that was missing was her final commitment. Rosemary was convinced that it was to come soon. She had a sense about these things. Ruth concurred. The two together were rarely wrong.

Jim and Judy flew to Portland to escape the heat, and for Judy to take care of some business. They landed to the welcoming 100-degree heat wave that occurred about once a year in Portland. Sweaty and famished, Judy drove the rental car on a quick tour of Portland. She took Jim to her favorite spot for lunch—a little sidewalk café on 23rd offering quiche, sandwiches and an extensive list of wines by the glass. They sat in the window, the mid-day heat too oppressive for the sidewalk tables.

They downed a bottle of water and ordered two slices of quiche and glasses of a white Rhone blend. Judy had not shared with Jim the business that she had come so far to execute. She clasped her hands over his and looked him in the eye. "Jim, first of all, I love you. I have to tell you something that I didn't share with you before. There was another man. I broke up with him as soon as I came back last February but we owned a house together. I knew when we bought it that I was making a mistake, but I was on the rebound from a dead, cheating husband and I was a little lost. When we got together I knew what I really wanted, but it took me a very long time to accept it."

"Do you accept it now?"

She held one finger over his lips. "Please let me finish. I do accept you as the love of my life. We were always meant to be together. That's something that is very hard to admit. So, the reason that I've come to Portland is to sign the escrow papers. I've sold my share of the house to Perry. I need to get rid of a few things in the house and then I'm out of here."

"That's wonderful."

"There is one other thing."

Jim looked crestfallen.

"Oh no darling, it's nothing bad. I want to answer your question now. If the offer still stands, I would love to be Mrs. James Langley."

The rest of the month was filled with negotiations, pleading, planning and squabbling. The only time in their relationship that they fought was trying to come to an agreement on how, where and when they would be married. Judy moved out of Jim's house, she said, to put the finishing touches on her mother's house in order to sell it, but they did not speak for a week.

After work one night Jim drove to East Highland Drive. The house was now painted blue with fresh, yet wilting landscape—the lawn browning in the July heat. He rang the bell. She answered right away and fell into his arms. They sat in the living room, crying and apologizing to one another.

Judy, "I'm so sorry, my darling Jim. I'll do whatever it is you want."

Jim, "I'll do whatever you want. I love you."

"We are at an impasse again. I can't believe it."

"No, wait. Look. Let's make sense of this. You had a big

wedding right?"

"Yeah."

"Madeline and I had a huge and stupidly expensive wedding. We've both done that. Let's not do that again."

"Okay. Let's not. So Vegas?" she said, half joking.

"Justice of the peace?"

"Sure. We elope then. Agreed?"

"Agreed. When?"

"Sometime soon."

"Agreed."

On the first Sunday in August Jim called a full staff meeting. It was not optional. The long dais table used by the Rotary Club was erected in the front of the room and the garden was pre-set with glasses, champagne and wine, arranged by Jim and Judy. This was all for the loyal staff and not one of them had any idea what was about to happen.

Jim, Judy, and David Weinstein sat at the front table. The rest of the tables were full and several stood at the back of the room. The staff had grown to 68, including all of the gardeners, drivers, Internet online retail people and book-keeper. Jim stood and clinked his water glass. "Ladies and gentlemen, may I please have your attention? The first order of business this evening is this: Please consider this as all of your 6-month notices. You are officially fired!" The room burst into applause. An odd response to losing a job, but everything at Home had been odd. There was nothing typical about this restaurant. Jim raised his hands to calm the room. "But, I have a little surprise for you. First, I want to introduce an old friend, if you have never had the honor and privilege of meeting him before." He held a hand out to David at the end of the table. "This is David Weinstein, my life long friend, accountant, and in many ways the reason that you are all here. David thought I was crazy when I first came to him with this idea, but he supported my hair-brained scheme all throughout our five years. Thank you, David." More applause rang out. "And why Mr. Weinstein is here will become apparent in a few moments. When you all came to work here, you accepted a salary that was slightly higher than a usual restaurant because of our gratuity policy. What you were not aware of was that, after a three-month grace period, we opened IRAs in each of your names, matching your salaries and, yes they were retroactive. So, when we finish here, one by one come up and see David. He will give you your account information and your bonus account numbers. January first there will be a cash deposit made in that bonus account as a final thank you for all of your hard work and, hopefully, enough to help out while you find new jobs. Oh, and those bonuses are based on performance, so don't think you can just skate to the finish line. And Buddy ..." Everyone turned to look at Buddy, who was standing in the back of the room. "I sort of forgot to stop your deposits, so your account is intact. Thank you pal, for all that you've done." More applause. The room turned back toward Jim. "Any questions? There's champagne and wine on the patio. Thank you all for coming." The room once again broke into raucous applause that turned into a standing ovation.

18

By September Ginger and Buddy had the kitchen on cruise control. The harvest menu had all been finely tuned, but changed daily as fresh produce flowed from farm to Ginger's prep table. The steady stream of customers was always happy. Jim took advantage of the well-oiled machine.

September was the busiest month for the clinic. Jim took two more shifts per week. On Monday morning Pete was already with a patient and several sat in the waiting room. Lillian worked at the desktop computer. "Good morning, Doctor Langley. We've got a full house. Ready?"

"Just going to get a coffee, Lillian. How are you?"

"Peachy." Lillian worked in sarcasm as naturally as a mechanic changing oil.

Jim returned with a coffee cup in hand. "Okay, Lillian. Lay it on me."

"Cindy and her mom, Cynthia. I think she needs boosters.

But, quite honestly, her mom doesn't look so good."

"Show them in."

Lillian opened the door and peeked out. "Cynthia, Doctor Langley will see you in two." Lillian showed them to the exam room and dropped her chart in the little plastic holder outside the door and flipped the "Patient in Room" indicator above the door.

Jim entered right away. "Hello there. I'm Doctor Langley. I don't think we've met." He held out his hand to Cindy. The little girl smiled shyly at him and begrudgingly held her delicate little hand out. "Hi, Cindy. Nice to meet you." He finally looked at her mother. "And Cynthia, nice to see you too. How can I help?"

"Cindy needs her shots so she can go to school. They don't let 'em in now without gettin' 'em."

"Sure. No problem." Jim looked at her chart. "Looks like she needs her DTap." He lifted Cindy onto the exam table, felt her glands, looked in her eyes and ears and took her temperature. "Cindy, you are the picture of health." He turned and opened the door. Carla was standing there with the shot in hand.

"Doctor Jim, good morning. I believe you need one of these."

"Well, thank you, Nurse Carla." Jim shut the door and turned to Cindy, careful to hold the syringe at his side, just out of view. She began to cry. "Cindy, don't cry. This is no biggie. He picked her up and turned her over. "Look at that silly dog down there." As she searched the picture, hanging low on the wall for just this kind of distraction, Jim pulled one side of her pants down, and in one swift move wiped with a swab, injected and returned her pants before she could open her mouth. Years of experience with skittish poor kids in the jungle taught Jim that speed was his most reliable tool. He picked her up in his arms. "Done! That wasn't so bad, was it?"

Cindy stuck out her lower lip and shook her head no. She wanted to cry, but it was all over, so she just reached for her mommy.

Jim opened the door. "Carla, could you please take Cindy and help her pick out a lollipop?" He turned to the little girl. "Can you go with Carla? She's really nice. I want to talk to your mommy for a second. Okay?" Cynthia eased her to the floor as Cindy nodded her head and took Carla's hand. Jim shut the door and turned toward Cynthia. His tone changed drastically. "How long you been using?"

"What do you mean, Doc? I don't do nothin'."

"Really? So what happened to your teeth, and why are you so gaunt? Looks like meth to me. Do you want some help or do I have to report you? I don't have any choice. You probably know that. That's why you've waited this long to bring Cindy in for her shots. If we suspect any sort of abuse, it's our legal obligation to report it. I could go to jail if I let this go. So, what'll it be, treatment or social worker and child services? They'll take Cindy. You know they will."

"I don't have no problem."

Jim gave her a long, cold stare, not giving in.

"What do I have to do?"

"There's a treatment center in Athens. I write a referral, you check yourself in. It'll show in my records you came for addiction treatment, end of story as long as you get clean. The treatment center will call me if you don't check in by next Monday. I'll need to see you in three months for a follow up. Remember, you slip on any of these things and child services will take Cindy, period. Deal?"

"Okay, deal."

Jim handed her a piece of paper with the address of the treatment center and a card. "That is my cell phone number. Call me if you have any problems of second thoughts. You can do it, Cynthia. I know you can."

"I'm so sorry. Don't take my daughter, okay? I'll do it. I promise."

"I know you will. Good luck, Cynthia." He showed her out and said goodbye to Cindy.

The Monday morning call from the rehab center in Athens was unfortunately expected. Jim hung up with them and searched the database on the clinic computer for the child services number. He dialed all but the last digit and hung up. He looked up the address in Cynthia's chart. As he opened the back door he called to the receptionist, "Lillian, this might take a while. Call Pete and ask if he can come over and cover this morning."

Jim drove to the address on the card. The roads were narrow and winding—parts of the county where Jim had never travelled. The abject poverty was apparent in every face, yard and car. Trucks on blocks, tattered clothes flapping on clotheslines, children dirty, half-naked, staring into space from their rickety front porches. The scene was right out of a movie, impossible to believe. This was the sort of desperation he had only witnessed in India and the Sudan. It made him ill.

He pulled up to Cynthia's. The curtain fell back into place as he looked toward the house. She was home. He knocked on the door several times. Cindy must have been at school, but he knew Cynthia was there. He tried the door and it opened. "Cynthia, I know you're here. I just want to talk for a minute. I'm not here to hurt you or to take Cindy."

She peeked around the corner. "Ya sure?"

"Please, come in here. Can we sit down?"

"Okay. I guess. I couldn't go to that there place."

Jim sat on the edge of a tattered couch and Cynthia sat cross-legged on a folding chair. She seemed clean and sober. That gave Jim some hope of getting through. "Look, Cynthia, I'm not here to make you go to get help. I want you to, and you will eventually lose Cindy if you don't, but that's not why I'm here. I want to tell you a story."

"A story. What kind of story? You promise you ain't takin' me in?"

"No. I'm not taking you in. I'm going to tell you a story and then I'm going to leave. What you do after that will determine what happens to you and Cindy. Okay?"

"Okay."

"Is Cindy your only child?"

"Yeah."

"She's really sweet. I never had any kids. I really wanted them, but my wife and I couldn't have them and then we didn't want them, or she didn't want them, but it doesn't matter, we didn't have any." Jim took his time, pausing often. "I did have an older brother and sister. My sister's still around and is kind of a pain in the ass, but I still love her. But my brother, my brother went off one summer when I was pretty young. I didn't know exactly where he was going, but he was in the Army and was going far away. He promised me that when he came back he would buy me a bike. I really looked up to my brother. He was strong and smart and fair. He treated people really well, and he was really kind to me. I loved him. He told me that he would be home in six months. When that six months was up—I put it on my calendar—I waited every day, probably for about three weeks. Then school started and he still wasn't back. I remember coming home from school one day and my mom was sitting in the living room crying, and my dad was with her. My dad was never home during the day. I asked him why mom was crying and he told me that my brother was killed in the war and wasn't coming home. I ran to my room and buried my head in my pillow and cried all night. They let me stay home from school for the rest of the week. There were a lot of people that came and went and I had no idea what was going on, but I knew that my brother wasn't coming home and I had never hurt inside like that before. You know what, Cynthia? I still hurt inside. I still miss my brother. So, I've never had kids, but I would imagine if I was a parent and I lost one, it would probably feel a lot like that. I don't ever want anyone to feel like that." Jim stood.

"Is that all?"

"That's all. Bye, Cynthia."

October brought with it highly unexpected offers of purchase. Jim had never considered selling the restaurant. In one month two different New York hospitality groups visited; the owner of the Columbus soccer team breezed through, poking his nose in the kitchen, the wine cellar and the private dining room before exiting out the patio door without ever speaking a word; and Larry, the owner of the Black Dog Tavern—who must have recently come into some money—called for a meeting. Each made wildly different cash offers, oblivious to any other offers already proffered.

His first visitor with this ulterior motive was a famous chef who was known for wearing pink clogs. He arrived with a small entourage and sat in the wine cellar, a reservation that had been made months in advance. The week before their arrival Jim received an email from the famous chef himself asking if Jim would join them for dinner. He accepted the invitation. He liked meeting chefs, especially if they were paying customers offering him his own food and wine. The email was the only indication that the reservation was for the famous chef, so Jim decided to keep that little secret to himself, in order not to fluster Buddy and the staff. They were getting used to the occasional famous person sighting but, like Jim, a famous chef was much more intimidating.

They arrived on time (by private jet as Jim was later informed), with Mr. Pink Shoes entering through the downstairs door at Jim's suggestion. There were nine guests in all, and they ordered nearly everything on the menu. They passed everything around and tasted, as if judging Top Chef. Jim detected some sort of secretive conversation at the other end of the table and decided to check on the kitchen and let them have their little pow-wow in private. He suspected they were up to something, but had no idea what was to come.

After leaving them for more than twenty minutes, Jim returned with two bottles of a Super Tuscan that he had decanted earlier as his contribution to the little party. The famous chef was quite impressed, although only had a half of a glass before he and his partner asked if there was another private room where they might speak. Jim grabbed one of the decanters and led them into his former office, which by some rare chance was not occupied.

Mr. Pink Shoes sat silent as his business partner spoke. "Dr. Langley, we are quite impressed with what you have accomplished here. We understand that you are about to extricate yourself from the restaurant business, and we would like to make you an offer."

"What kind of an offer?" Jim honesty didn't know what they were talking about.

"We would like to bring Home into the Pink Shoes Empire."

That wasn't what they really said, but it was what Jim told Judy when relaying this story later. "I still don't understand. What do you mean bring into?"

Famous chef finally spoke. "We want to buy your restaurant. It's molto bene!"

The partner took over. "We are willing to offer one million, two hundred fifty thousand cash, plus five year employment contracts for you and your chef de cuisine and sous chef. We don't want to change a thing."

Jim poured himself a larger glass of wine than was couth. He took a long draw, sat the glass down and leaned back in his chair with hands clasped behind his head. "Gentlemen, you may have missed the concept of this restaurant when doing the due diligence that I'm sure, as experienced businessmen, you must have done. Or maybe you missed the clock on the wall upstairs that is ticking down to midnight this New Year's Eve. The restaurant closes, period. Home is not for sale. Would you like to see the dessert menu?"

After the first flattering offer, the next two didn't come as a total surprise. Different tactics were employed, including the absurd idea put forth by the Columbus entrepreneur that the clock could be reset and that the New Year's celebration should usher in another five years.

Larry from the Black Dog was the only offer that Jim seriously considered. He did like the idea of the restaurant remaining open if a local owned it, albeit with a name change. Jim detested chain restaurants of any sort, even if chefs that he admired owned them. Larry didn't come to the restaurant. Instead, invited Jim to the Black Dog for a beer. This impressed Jim. The Black Dog was definitely down scale, to say the least, but was the heart of Zanesville.

It was eight in the morning on a Monday, the time Larry set for the meeting. He was on his normal barstool at the far end of the bar. There was no bartender, although a few regulars sat toward the front. Jim noticed from time to time one or another of the patrons would round the opposite end of the bar and help themselves to beers from the cooler.

Larry, "Those fellas are here every morning. They're regulars from the nightshift over to the mill. Marylou don't come in until nine so the bar is more or less self serve 'till she gets here."

"What time do you open?"

"Six. Beer?"

"Oh, no thanks. It's a little too early for me."

"Coffee?"

"Sounds good. Thanks."

Larry reached up to his left and took a mug from a shelf above the coffee pot. He poured Jim a cup, then refilled his own. "Yeah, I have no idea how some of these guys do it. I've got regulars that come here every morning, have two or three then head off to work. I personally never have a drink before noon. Lived by that rule all my life."

"So, Larry. What's on your mind?"

"Jimbo, I really like what you've done down there at the old Nicholson place. People love it and I think they should be able to keep lovin' it. I know you had that gimmick to keep 'um coming, countin' down and all, but I think you can have a great restaurant without the gimmick. So, if you really are thinkin' of closin' it next year, I wanna buy it and keep it goin'."

"I am going to close it, Larry. I stick to my word."

"Well, I know you do. You're a good man. Your dad was

a good man and your mom was my third grade teacher. Did you know that?"

"I did not."

"So, what if you shut it down then I come in and open her back up under a new name and all."

"That would have to happen, no matter what."

"So you're interested?"

"I didn't say that."

"Well, let me tell you my offer before you say anything else."

"I'm listening."

"Two-seventy-five cash, I get to keep the little chef boy for three years and whoever else you think needs to stay. We shut down until spring, change the name, maybe make a few improvements. I wanna make that patio down there bigger. Maybe put in a bar downstairs. Whatda ya think?"

Jim turned his head and stared at the front of the bar. "Let me think about it, Larry. I will tell you that I've gotten higher offers."

"You've had other offers?" Larry was astonished.

"Yep."

"And you didn't take them?"

"Nope."

"Can I ask why not?"

"I wasn't interested in selling and they were all from out-of-towners."

"So you'll consider my offer? I can't go any higher. That's the money I inherited from my dad. It's all I got, plus another fifty to make a few changes. I shouldn't be telling you this, but I hear you appreciate the truth."

"I do, Larry, I do. I'll think about it. Thanks for the coffee."

The Five-Year Plan

An early dusting of snow welcomed in November. It didn't stick, but was a foreshadowing of the long, cold winter ahead. Jim spent his Sunday next to the fire in the living room. Judy brought the paper in, made the coffee, kissed Jim and headed off to Columbus for a day of shopping. Jim tried to talk her out of it, worried that the roads may be slick. Judy shrugged it off and slipped out the front door.

Carla knocked on the door. Jim saw her at the clinic a few times a week, but rarely saw her socially anymore. She took more shifts than Jim so they stopped riding together. Judy didn't like that they once dated and Carla knew it and usually avoided the confrontation. So this visit was certainly unexpected.

Jim opened the door. "Hello there, Carla."

Carla shook the snow off of her coat and pushed past him. "Do you mind if I come in. It's cold out here. Do you believe it's November?"

"Come in. Would you like a coffee?"

"No, thanks."

Jim led her into the living room and sat back down next to the fire and offered the seat across from him.

"I have some good news. I wanted you to be the first to know. Well, after my kids and my mom."

"What good news do you bring on this snowy Sunday morning?"

"I'm getting married, I mean, we are getting married. Pete and me are getting married! Isn't that great?"

"Pete? I didn't even think you liked him."

"I know. We've kind of kept it a secret until now. You know, small clinic, small town gossip, small-minded people. Aren't you going to congratulate me?"

Jim stood and hugged her. "Congratulations, Carla. That's wonderful. Pete's a lucky guy."

Judy came through the door as they were hugging. "Uhumm."

"Oh Judy, guess what? Carla and Pete are getting married!"

Judy sighed. "Oh, thank God, I thought for a second there that we weren't."

Carla, "You guys are getting married? That's fantastic!" She ran to Judy and gave her a big hug.

Over Carla's shoulder, Judy rolled her eyes at Jim. "Yes, but we don't know when yet."

"That's so great. Pete and I are getting married Thanksgiving weekend. All our families will be in town and we don't want to wait, so it's perfect timing don't you think?"

Jim smiled at Judy. "Yes, that is perfect timing. None of that dreadful planning and waiting a whole year."

"I've gotta go. I just wanted you to be the first to know. Put it on your calendar, Saturday after Thanksgiving at First Methodist. 2 p.m. with a reception after at my house."

The rest of the month was filled with calls and emails from friends and family trying to talk their way into the restaurant one last time. The only tables left were for walk-ins and they were constantly full. The only reservations still taken were for good friends for New Year's. Jim had blocked out the downstairs for that purpose. One day alone he got calls from Frank in Italy, Terek from somewhere on I-80 and Rosemary, all confirming their New Year's commitment. Jim was starting to get nostalgic. He was very excited about seeing all of his old friends.

After a few weeks of contemplation, he turned Larry

down. He didn't offer an explanation, but his gut told him that, if there was to be a restaurant after Home, Larry didn't seem like the best guardian of the property.

The Saturday after Thanksgiving, Jim and Judy found themselves sitting in a pew of the First Methodist Church. Remarkably, after all of the last minute planning, and Carla's volatile tendencies, the wedding was still on. Pete must really love her, Jim thought. As weddings tend to do, the thoughts of their own nuptials ran through both of their heads. Judy leaned over to Jim. "This is beautiful. Carla is a bit of a nut, but this is so romantic. And she looks amazing."

Jim held her hand. "Do you want to be next?"

"What, right here? Now? Sure."

Jim chuckled quietly. "I would too, but I fear Carla and Pete wouldn't appreciate being upstaged at their own wedding."

"Good point."

"I like the idea though. Maybe we could crash another wedding."

"Or bar mitzvah." They both laughed out loud, turning plenty of heads, including Pete. Together they mouthed, "Sorry."

December first, one month away from the last day of a dream, Jim sat in the waiting room while his mother saw Doctor Miller. She'd been having headaches and dizziness and Jim was concerned. She usually ignored him, but she was a little worried too and agreed to come. She liked Jeffrey. He was a nice boy.

Jeff came out and sat next to Jim in the empty waiting

room. "Her blood pressure was a little high. I've given her some Hydrochlorothiazide, 25 mil. Basically just a sniff. Nothing to make her sleepy. Sometimes the old stuff works the best."

"True. Just like Ruth herself." They both laughed. "See you New Year's?"

"I can't wait. Are you full?"

"Full. Ha. They'll be hanging from the rafters. Do you believe it? Five years."

"Congratulations, Jim. See you then."

The week before Christmas people from all over started showing up. Frank moved into Jim's, followed a day later by Rosemary. Terek checked into the Holiday Inn the day after Christmas because he could park his truck there.

Jim spent most of his time at the restaurant, planning the menu, overseeing the decorations and selecting the wines. There would be no charge for the downstairs, but the upstairs needed to be finely orchestrated. The paying customers were shelling out five hundred dollars a head for a fixed price menu, wine and champagne. The evening would be a single seating starting at 8 p.m. Nothing could go wrong and every move, morsel and Meursault needed to be planned in advance. Once December 31st came, Jim would relinquish the details of the upstairs to his finely tuned staff and enjoy his last night with his friends and family.

The downstairs opened at seven for any friends that wanted to beat the upstairs rush. Jim hired two extra drivers to escort people to and from the restaurant. Guests began arriving at 7 on the dot. Doctor Mark Fitzsimmons and his wife came down from Mansfield. Steve Baxter, the doctor Jim met in Italy, brought Valerie Rousseau. Jim imagined that he hadn't yet divorced, but that story was for another day. He was ecstatic to see them both. Larry from the Black Dog came with Marylou, the bartender and, as it turned out, his current wife. Pete and Carla returned from their honeymoon just before Christmas, tanned from the sun of Cancun. They still looked ravishing as they made their entrance.

Cindy came downstairs just after eight. She weaved and bobbed through the people to find Jim in the wine cellar with Frank and a few others. She pulled him aside. "There's someone upstairs that is asking to see you."

"Cindy, the deal is I am not doing any business upstairs this evening. Sorry."

"I really think you should come. It's not one of the regulars. I think it may be important."

"Oh, alright. Just for a minute."

He reached the top of the stairs and Nancy whispered to him. "She's at the kitchen door."

Jim shimmied through the crowded kitchen and cracked open the back door. Standing in the freezing cold was Cynthia, from the clinic. She wore a proper winter coat and toboggan cap with a little tassel. She held a single, pale pink Christmas rose—one of the few flowers that bloom in Ohio's dank winter. Jim slipped out into the frigid night. "Cynthia?"

"Hi, Doctor Jim. I'm sorry to bother you, but I heard that this was a special night for you and I wanted to wish you well. I also wanted to thank you. I've been clean for three months and it's all because of you." She handed him the flower. "Here, this is for you. Happy New Year." She stood on her tiptoes and kissed him on the cheek.

"Thank you, Cynthia. I told you that you could do it. Do you want to come in?"

"No. I've got to get back home. My mom's watching Cindy and she wants to go out. Thank you again." She turned to leave then stopped. She turned back to Jim. "And I think you would have been a great father." She started down the street. Over her shoulder, she, "Bye." She turned the corner toward the bridge and was gone.

As Jim came out of the kitchen, a flood of local friends arrived. Bob Brewer and his wife; David Weinstein and his wife; Carl Priestly, the junkman, who was so pleased to see his telephone booths in use; and Ruth, accompanied by a surprisingly awake and sober Dr. Hendrickson. Before he descended the stairs, Jim caught a glimpse of Missy Stansfield, sporting wild spikes of pink and purple hair, surrounded by her entourage, sipping champagne on the tented balcony and tapping furiously into her phone. Whatever she was posting, good or bad, no longer mattered.

The small bites were passed around and everyone wandered through to the tented patio for wine and cocktails. The last couple to arrive was Amos and Sarah Wilkes, Jim's favorite farmers. He was pleased to see them, even though he barely recognized Amos in a suit coat and tie.

The upstairs settled into their third course. Nancy stood on the stairs above the sea of people and rang a chime for everyone to take their seats. Remarkably, there were seats for all. Frank and Rosemary shared a table with Jim and Judy. Ruth and her date shared a table with Bob, David and their wives, and Jackie and her date for the evening, Father Brown.

Jim nodded to Nancy and she disappeared up the stairs. He clinked his glass and stood. Soon, the back of the restaurant was full of Buddy, Ginger, Cindy and a few other staff. Judy thought this was odd, but sat back, watched and listened. The room quieted down. Jim stood. There was some commotion on the patio, which Nancy hushed. Jim cleared his throat. "Good evening, everyone. Thank you for coming and Happy New Year."

The crowd responded, "Happy New Year!"

Jim continued, "As you all know, this is a stupendous occasion. This marks the end of our little restaurant experiment. At the stroke of midnight tonight, we will have been in business for exactly five years. I am a man of my word and the restaurant will close its doors permanently."

There were rumblings, boos and hisses throughout the downstairs.

Jim hushed them. "But, this is not to say that we should mourn our loss. We should instead look forward to new beginnings. In fact, as many of you know, Judy and I are engaged to be married."

Everyone applauded.

"That reminds me of a funny story." Judy looked at him quizzically. "When Judy and I had the privilege to witness Pete and Carla's nuptials last month, we joked that we could get married anywhere, as long as there were a group of friends gathered." Jim looked around the room. "Sort of like this gathering this evening." Judy began to blush. "I never thought about that. This would sort of be a great time, and I could even suggest to Judy that maybe we should get married right here and now."

The room burst into applause and chanted, "Do it, Do it, Do it."

"Hold on now. I'm not serious. We haven't planned anything. Plus, we would need someone to officiate, like a judge or a man of the cloth."

Father Brown cleared his throat loudly.

"Oh, I'll be damned. Sorry, father. I'll be darned, we do have someone of the cloth. But even with our friends gathered and someone to officiate, we're still missing a vital component. We would need rings. One cannot possibly have a wedding without wedding rings."

Frank stood up, made an exaggerated gesture and produced a blue velvet box from his pocket. "You mean like these?"

The crowd roared.

Jim got down on one knee in front of Judy. "Judy Archer, will you marry me. Right here and right now?"

Judy stood up, threw her napkin on the table and said, "Let's do it!"

The place erupted. By this time, as many of the staff that could fit lined the back walls. Jim and Judy hugged and kissed, then he led her out to a transformed patio with a makeshift alter, the product of the earlier commotion. Father Brown followed. He squeezed by them and took his place up front. Friends and family filled in behind and Frank, the best man, stood at Jim's side.

Judy whispered in Jim's ear. "You planned this whole thing? Nancy was in on it? Frank, Jackie!? You are something else, Jim Langley. I love you with all my heart."

"You're okay with it? I was taking a chance, but I figured you wouldn't say no."

"I already said yes and I never back down."

"No, indeed you do not." He kissed her lips. Father Brown cleared his throat again. "Oh, sorry, Father."

He spoke to the two of them. "Are we all set? Shall we proceed?"

They both nodded. He held his hands high above the couple. The room hushed.

Judy blurted out, "Wait!"

The room froze and Jim's eyes widened.

Looking around the room, she found Nancy and gestured to her. "Nancy, come up here." Nancy pushed her way though the crowd. "I need a maid of honor." Nancy hugged her and took her place at Judy's side.

Father Brown began. "Ladies and gentlemen, friends, family, distinguished guests from near and far, we have gathered together for a truly special evening. We are here to celebrate a long awaited ending and rejoice in a very special new beginning. It is through faith in God and being in the right place at the right time that, at this midway juncture in life, Jim and Judy have come together." The crowd laughed. "Love comes in many forms, sometimes when least expected, but when encountered, it is undeniable. The Book of Corinthians defines love thusly: Love is patient, love is kind. It does not envy, it does not boast, it is not proud. It does not dishonor others, it is not self-seeking, it is not easily angered, it keeps no record of wrongs. Love does not delight in evil but rejoices with the truth. It always protects, always trusts, always hopes, always perseveres. Love never fails." Father Brown paused, nodded first to Judy then to Jim. "Shall we do this?"

Jim, choked up, barely eked out the words, "Yes, please."

While the vows were being recited downstairs, the count-down clock upstairs had less than two hours left. Some of the wait staff had discreetly returned to fill wine glasses and clear plates. In anticipation of the wedding, the dessert service had been prepared in advance, needing only a Bic lighter to dazzle the tables. Buddy and Ginger were not going to miss the wedding, regardless of the daunting per plate cost.

The I Do's took only a few moments and everyone

returned to his or her seats for the main course. Nancy scurried up the stairs, followed by Buddy and Ginger. The kitchen came to life. Jim had requested simple fare for downstairs, but Buddy wanted at least one course to be special. They passed out pizza and canapés for small plates, but Buddy changed the main course without Jim's knowledge. He presented the surprise plate to Jim while Nancy simultaneously served Judy. Jim stared at the plate. On a bed of simple risotto were four seared scallops with hazelnuts and brown butter. "This is not ..."

Buddy held a hand up, cutting him off. In that hand was the real surprise. Buddy removed his special tool from the arm pocket of his chef's jacket and shaved a generous portion of white truffle over the risotto. Nancy did so in unison. Buddy, knowing that Jim would freak out about serving white truffles to this many people, leaned in to him and whispered, "A little gift from Frank."

From the end of table, Frank saluted and smiled. "Bon appétit."

Soon the downstairs was filled with the musty aroma of white truffles. A few of the upstairs guests followed their noses down to see what they were missing and were politely asked to rejoin the upstairs party.

As the guests finished their main course, some actually licking their plates, the first round of champagne was poured. Frank stood and clinked his glass. "It is my honor and privilege to make a toast to the newlyweds. I first have to apologize on behalf of our hosts. With these toasts, the restaurant crossing the five-year mark and, of course, ringing in the New Year, we are about to drink a lot of champagne. But I'm sure that you are like me and are willing to, just this once, make an exception and have more than one glass." Everyone laughed and applauded. "So, back to my duty here. Jim, we have laughed and cried together, we have mourned and celebrated, we have ate and drank and cooked. And that was just a Tuesday." The guests chuckled. "But seriously, I come from a big family with lots of friends. I have never known anyone as loyal, committed, generous, big hearted and honest as ..." He paused for comic effect. "Judy!" Everyone laughed. "You're a lucky man. Oh, and you ain't too bad either. To you guys!" Everyone laughed and cheered, raised their glasses and drank to the newly-weds.

The entire building was aglow with celebration. It was what Jim imagined when he first stood on the bank of the river and looked back at the brick shell of a dream. Laughter and raucous conversations rippled down the stairs and out into the garden. He admitted to himself that there was a very real chance that this could have been the day when he locked the door on an empty, failed experiment. But the stars aligned, or he got lucky, or maybe it was meant to be. All he could think was, this building full of joviality made it so and he was grateful.

Jim looked at his watch. There were ten minutes to go. He found his friend, "David, I screwed up. The countdown clock, it's upstairs and we're all down here."

David smiled and looked around the room. He caught Nick Jennings' eye and gave him a thumbs up. "We thought about that. Nick rigged a little something up."

"What?" Just then, three different projectors with the image of the upstairs countdown clock lit up around the room for everyone to see. The room cheered. "Oh my God, that is sensational! Thank you, Nick. You're a genius. Thank you, David."

Nancy passed and kissed him on the cheek. "Cool, huh?"

"Go get Buddy, bring six flutes and meet me in the cellar

in two minutes. And ask anyone in the cellar to vacate for the countdown."

"Will do."

Jim grabbed Judy and whispered to Frank to head to the cellar. "Judy, have you seen Ruth?"

"She said she was tired and had Joey drive her home."

"I hope she's alright."

"She seemed fine."

They made their way to the empty wine cellar and shut the door behind them. Jim rooted around in the corner, moving boxes and a few dusty bottles. Nancy came in with Buddy and the flutes.

Jim, "Oh, good. We're all here and we have just enough time." He produced a dusty, champagne magnum bottle with a stained label. "When I graduated from Med School I bought myself a present. I thought that I would put it away and someday have a special enough occasion to open it. I never had children and repairing a basketball player's knee just never seemed that special to me. But you people in this room, in this odd experiment of a restaurant, are what is special to me. It took me this long to understand that it wasn't a special occasion at all, but it was special people that I was waiting to celebrate." Jim held up the bottle and removed the foil. "This is a 1978 Dom Perignon, probably the best vintage of the best champagne of the century." He popped the cork and poured five glasses full of the golden nectar, barely effervescent, but exactly as it should be. He held his glass high, looked each in the eye and simply said, "To you."

"One Minute!" shouted someone from the crowd. Champagne in hand, the intimate group filed out of the cellar and found a vantage point from which to see the clock. Jim could actually see the corner of the real one at the top of the stairs. The staff poured champagne furiously as the clock approached thirty. Tears rolled down many cheeks. Jim held Judy by the shoulder, champagne flute held high. The crowd followed the clock, "FIVE, FOUR, THREE, TWO, ONE, HAPPY NEW YEAR!"

19

The house phone rang. Nobody ever called the house phone. Jim jumped out of bed, thinking that it might be about Ruth.

"Doctor Langley? This is Chief Hyland, Zanesville Fire department. I'm afraid there's been a fire."

"Is my mom alright?"

"It's not your mother's house, it's the restaurant. We've got four trucks on it now. You might want to get down here."

"Oh Jesus, I will right away."

"It doesn't appear that there was anyone in the building."

"Oh, thank God. I'll be right there."

Jim and Judy dressed quickly and hurried to the restaurant. There were barricades a block away where a few intrepid early birds stood and watched as the fire ripped through the roof and firefighters drenched the old brick building with water. Jim eventually found the chief who escorted them past the line. There was nothing to be done except move the limo to the upper lot to give more access for the ladder truck and to keep it far from the flames and cannons of water. They stood next to the warm limo covered in ashes and watched Home burn.

Jim laughed. "Well, I guess that's how it ends. Ashes to ashes, dust to dust." Judy held Jim tight and they both wept.

Four days later, Chief Hyland stood on Jim's porch. "Doctor Langley, our investigator had a chance to go through the rubble. He seems to think that the fire started in the attic by some faulty, old wiring. So, it wasn't arson; just an unfortunate accident that happens sometimes in these old buildings. I thought you'd want to know."

"Thanks, Chief, I really appreciate it." As the chief walked away, the house phone rang. Disgusted, Jim mumbled, "What now?"

"Jim, it's Jackie. You didn't answer your cell phone." She hesitated, "Mom died."

"What?" Jim screamed.

"I came over this morning to check on her. She was in her bed. She wasn't breathing. I called the squad. They said she probably died in the middle of the night. She went peacefully."

Jim stared at the phone, tears rolling down his cheeks. "Oh, Jackie."

Jim fell against the back door of Ruth's house. "I thought they'd never leave. God, I'm hungry. Hungry, Frank?"

Frank sat next to Ruth's easel. The hoards of people had just cleared out, leaving the kitchen littered with picked over food, homemade by Ruth's friends and neighbors. The tradition has never died. People bring food, good basic homemade food, in casseroles and pie tins, some with little sticky notes identifying the dish's owner. Jim secretly admired the thoughtful tradition.

"Not this again." Frank was on his way to the airport when he heard of Ruth's death.

Jim laughed. "I'm so happy that you came back, Frank. I miss you. We used to have so much fun, didn't we?"

"Yeah, we sure did." Frank's tone became more intentional. "Listen, Jim, this may not be a good time to discuss this."

"What, which wine do we have? Thank God that firefighter blanketed the cellar and saved the wine."

"No, not the wine. I'm sure we'll have some nice wine. We need to toast Ruth. I'm so happy I got to know her. She was a real gem."

"So, what's so serious?"

"I want to buy the restaurant."

"What restaurant?"

"Home. I'd like to rebuild it."

"You live in Italy." Jim slurred, quite drunk. "Besides, it's not for sale."

"I hate Italy. I can't speak the language worth shit, the women, well, you know that story. Plus I've always wanted to own a restaurant. I know exactly what to do. I'm in the trades for God's sake; I know how to rebuild her. I could work with your pal Nick!"

"You can't afford it."

"You won't make your friend a deal? It's probably not worth a whole lot right now anyway."

"The wine cellar is still intact, and the view." Jim grasped straws. "The garden is still there, and the limo."

"Two-fifty plus you retain ten percent."

"Larry from the Black Dog offered me two-seventy-five."

"Yeah, when there was still a kitchen and a roof. Wait, what? Two seventy-five. Final offer."

"And you have to keep Buddy and Nancy."

"Buddy wants to buy in with me and I've offered Nancy five percent. Seems to me like the best way to keep a manager honest is make her a partner."

"You're not so dumb for a plumber." They shook hands and embraced. "But you have to change the name."

"I figured." Frank contemplated. "How about," He made the big sign gesture. "My New Home. Whadya think?"

Jim gave that special look of derision that had long since been shorthand for "You've got to be kidding." He crooked his head and smiled that knowing smile. "How about Frank's?"

"Or Frank's, yeah Frank's. We'll call it Frank's. Sounds good."

Jim poured a glass of something handy and they toasted. "To Frank's!"

The smell of Bob Evans choked him as he crossed the bridge, a full three blocks away from the famed breakfast stop. Jim detested chain restaurants, but this venue was not his choice.

Dr. Lawrence Wilson sat in a corner booth. Jim had only met him once, but the distinctive grey goatee on a 65-year-old professorial face, along with the tweed jacket, gave him away. Dr. Wilson was originally from Zanesville, but had been a professor at Ohio University in Athens for most of his tenure. He had moved back to Zanesville three years ago to be the Dean of the Zanesville branch of that vaunted institution.

He stood as Jim approached. "Nice to see you, Doctor Langley. Thank you for meeting here. I'm sure it's not up to your usual standard."

Jim attempted to put his host at ease. "Don't think anything of it. I love their biscuits and gravy. They remind me of the ones I once had down in Mississippi during a flood."

The waitress approached. "What can I get you fellas?"

"Just coffee for me, thanks." Jim winked at Dr. Wilson. "Think I'll pass on the artery cloggers today."

Dr. Wilson nodded, "Coffee for me too. Black, please." He turned back to Jim, all business. "Jim, may I call you Jim?"

"Of course."

"Jim, let me get right to the point. I've admired you for quite some time. And since you no longer have the restaurant, I was wondering if you would consider coming to teach out at the Branch?"

"I was unaware that the Branch had a medical school. Is that a recent addition?" Jim said, somewhat sarcastically.

"I'm vaguely aware of your medical background and your sense of humor, neither of which do we offer. We want you to teach cooking."

Jim looked at him, puzzled. "Cooking?"

The waitress reappeared and slid two greasy cups in front of them along with the check.

"Thanks." He took a sip and continued. "You see, ever since your restaurant opened ..." Dr. Wilson corrected himself. "Ever since your restaurant became popular, we've received a steady stream of requests for what you were doing there. You have titillated the taste buds of our little community. We'd like you to call the course "Magic in the Kitchen," but that's really up to you. Or you could teach more than one course. Whatever you want. You design it and we'll offer it."

"That's very flattering, but do you really think people want that sort of thing?"

"Look, do you have any idea what you've given this community? You've awakened their palettes and their possibilities. There's a renewed sense of hope here. People talk about the world now; they want to travel; they want to cook like you do. Please don't let that hope rot on the vine."

"That's quite poetic, Doctor. I guess I might have a little spare time now."

"We're even thinking that you could lead tour groups, eating and cooking your way though Europe, Mexico, the Middle East. People change when they travel; they open their minds. They trust you. You're one of them, you go out into the world, but you come back. A lot of people really admire that."

Jim stared at him, speechless, for a very long time. "Can I think about it?"

"Of course. We could start in the summer. We always have a big run on continuing education in the summer. Maybe you could offer a summer tour group. Anyway, you think about it and be in touch." Dr. Wilson handed him a card and snatched the check from Jim's hands. "I'll get this one. I look forward to hearing from you."

Judy was coming down the stairs as Jim opened the front door.

Jim, "Oh good, we need to talk." Jim led her by the hand into the living room.

"But I need ..."

Jim interrupted, "Hang on one second. This is important.

You sold your mother's house, I am renting this house and my mother's house is just sitting up there. I think I want to fix it up and move in. What do you think?"

"Does this mean that you want to stay here?"

"For now, anyway. What do you think?"

"I think it's a great idea!"

"You do?"

"Yes. But I need to tell you something important."

"Okay, sorry. What is it?"

"Somebody called Mattias Berger left a message on the voicemail. He said that there had been an eruption in Azerbaijan, and then he left a long number. Then he said he booked 0769 and hoped that was okay. The last thing he said sounded like military time. He said seventeen hundred today. What does all of that mean, Jim?"

Jim looked at his watch. "Shit! Judy, do you remember all of those outdoor clothes I bought in Columbus a few months ago?"

"Yeah, I thought you were being a little extravagant for someone who never leaves the kitchen, but I didn't say anything." She smiled coyly. "We weren't married yet."

Jim became serious, nearly stern. "There are two green duffle bags, two blue duffle bags, two yellow ones and a red one in the attic. Now listen very carefully as I only have time to say this once. Go next door and ask Carla to get the mail and paper and watch the house and feed the damn cat, if she must. We'll be gone about a month. Change your clothes for a long flight, grab the two BLUE duffle bags—those are for cold weather—and grab the red one. Pick me up on Military right at the cemetery entrance in 30 minutes. Please, do not waste any time and DON'T be late."

"Where?"

Jim ran out the door, leaving her question unanswered.

He leaped off of the porch and flagged down a passing car. It was his neighbor Bob Greenberg. "Bob, could you do me a huge favor and take me out to Military Road? Now!?"

Jim walked around the cemetery for nearly 15 minutes, searching for the graves. Finally, he looked for a second time back where he had started and located them. He stood above the plot that had markers for his mother, his father and his brother. "Mom, Dad, I think I finally understand. It took me 66 years but I think I get it. Your lives were all about compassion, and you hoped that I would someday pick up on that. I'm truly sorry that it took me this long." Jim thought he heard a voice and turned. He was alone. "I know that you aren't here. I know that you're inside me, but I want to tell you something anyway. I'm staying in Zanesville. I now understand why you never moved. You didn't have to go anywhere else to be who you were. I did, but now I'm home. I love you both."

Judy was waiting in the car when Jim ran down the hill to the entrance gate. "Will you please tell me what the hell this is all about?"

Jim caught his breath. "That fellow Mattias is from an organization called MSF, or, as you might know them, Doctors Without Borders. He only calls when he really needs me. We'll go for a few weeks, a month at the most. My commitment is usually three months, but I texted him and said I could only do a month and he was good with that. I've been there before and know the drill."

Judy was confused about all the cryptic information. "Are we going to a volcano?"

Jim laughed. "No, the eruption is with rebel forces. Whenever they start fighting there's collateral damage and we have to put humpty back together again."

"What?"

"Sorry, sort of gallows humor. Whenever there's fighting there are injuries. Whenever that part of the world flares up, the hospital we run there gets busy and needs extra help. Don't worry, you'll be safe. Maybe we can go to Greece or Croatia before we come back home. Are you okay with this? I just kind of forgot to ask if you wanted to go on an adventure."

"I love you, Jim. You're the most unpredictable man in the world and I love you. Of course I'm in. I'll go anywhere with you."

"Can you please pull over?"

"What? Why?"

"Please, just pull over for one second."

Judy pulled the car over.

Jim grasped her hands and looked into her eyes. "Judy, I am not unpredictable. I was unpredictable. I was lost. But now I'm not lost. I have you, I have a job ..."

"What job?"

"I'll explain later. Where was I? Oh right. I have you, I have a job, we have a house, I have purpose in my life. Yes, I might occasionally go to far off places, but now I have a reason to come back. I have a home. And I think I'll stay."

THE END

THANKS TO THE FOLLOWING:

To Harrison Brooks for designing both the cover
and interior. Your talent and contribution are
immense and I could not have done this without you.

To Amy Jensen for editing a pile of commas and
turning them into readable text. You are the best.

My pre-readers: Greg Smith, Thomas Bähler, Kris
Tennant, Liz Gary, Stephen Schubert and especially
Candy Brooks for your endless encouragement.

My listeners: Joanie Diener, George Martin, Eric Blake,
David Mancini, Linda Mancini, Mark Yaeger, Bob
Skidmore, Beth Todd Wood, and Amy Jensen, who
pulled her car over and cried at the end.

My amazing children: Courtney, Harrison, Joshua, Noah,
and Elijah for all of your encouragement and patience.

And, as with everything I do, I owe it all to Jennifer
Rawlings Brooks, my partner in life, love and everything.

Christopher Scott Brooks is a novelist, playwright and author. His play, O'Donnell's Pub premiered in 2019 and his newest play Deadline is in the works. On the other side of his desk, Brooks is a music producer and editor, having contributed to over 300 feature films and television shows. Work with Rob Reiner, Francis Ford Coppola and Ben Stiller among many others led him to his life of story telling.

Born and raised in Zanesville, Ohio, his wife and he split their time between New York and Los Angeles. When he is not working on a play, writing his latest novel or finishing his book of short stories, he spends his time cooking and trying to keep up with their five children.

Made in the USA
Monee, IL
21 August 2020